ONE GREAT YEAR

To Kristine,
Enjoy the journey!

Live your Dreams!

ONE GREAT LOVE, ONE GREAT ADVENTURE . . .

ONE

TAMARA VEITCH

GREAT

RENE DEFAZIO

YEAR

GREENLEAF
BOOK GROUP PRESS

This book is a work of fiction. Names, characters, businesses, organizations, places, events, and incidents are either a product of the author's imagination or are used fictitiously. Any resemblance to actual persons, living or dead, events, or locales is entirely coincidental.

Published by Greenleaf Book Group Press
Austin, Texas
www.gbgpress.com

Distributed by Greenleaf Book Group LLC, except in Canada
Canadian Distribution by Red Tuque Books Inc. Unit #6, 477 Martin Street, Penticton, BC, Canada V2A 5L2

For ordering information or special discounts for bulk purchases, please contact Greenleaf Book Group LLC at PO Box 91869, Austin, TX 78709, 512.891.6100.

Design and composition by Greenleaf Book Group LLC
Cover design by Greenleaf Book Group LLC

Cataloging-in-Publication data
(Prepared by The Donohue Group, Inc.)
Veitch, Tamara, 1969-
One great year / Tamara Veitch, Rene DeFazio.--2nd ed.
p. ; cm.
Originally published: Surrey, B.C. : Intelligent Design Publishing, 2011.
Issued also as an ebook.
ISBN: 978-1-62634-023-7
1. Reincarnation–Fiction. 2. Memory–Fiction. 3. Soul mates–Fiction. 4. Good and evil–Fiction. 5. Fantasy fiction. I. DeFazio, Rene, 1963- II. Title.
PR9199.4.V458 O54 2013
813/.6 2013940339

Part of the Tree Neutral® program, which offsets the number of trees consumed in the production and printing of this book by taking proactive steps, such as planting trees in direct proportion to the number of trees used: www.treeneutral.com

Printed in Canada

13 14 15 16 17 18 10 9 8 7 6 5 4 3 2 1

Second Edition

For all of those who have loved us on our path.

ACKNOWLEDGMENTS

Our sincere thanks and appreciation to Shirley Anderson, Suzannah Denholm, Daryl Wakeham, and all of our friends and family who have aided and supported us on this journey. We offer our humble gratitude to the divine inspiration that has allowed this book to flow through us and to every reader who has chosen to spend his or her time in the world within these pages.

"There are only two ways to live your life. One is as though nothing is a miracle. The other is as though everything is."

—ATTRIBUTED TO ALBERT EINSTEIN BY GILBERT FOWLER WHITE[1]

CHAPTER 1

THE WEARY TRAVELER

Present day, Seattle, Washington

Maxwell Quinn had been reincarnated an exhausting number of times. How many lives had he lived? He could hardly count them. He knew that the evolution of human existence followed patterns that cycled roughly every twenty-six thousand years. Platc had called it the "Great Year"[2] and Quinn knew the ancient concept well. He had lived through the Gold, Silver, and Bronze Ages that had come before and had descended into this dark, brutal Iron Age. Quinn searched the night sky, knowing that the precession of the stars was truly a clock. He hoped that the most difficult time in his obligation was over, give or take a few hundred years.

Quinn rubbed his forehead with the back of his thumb, ruffling his messy black hair. He lit a joint and took a few puffs, brushing a flake of ash from his Lenny Kravitz T-shirt. It helped to slow the constantly spinning filmstrip of his mind. He opened the window a crack and exhaled into the cool Pacific Northwest evening.

Quinn rented a small apartment in the outer suburbs of Seattle. The forested hills and fields filled him with peace. He watched a bulbous black spider outside his window as it repaired its web. It had been there for weeks. He had watched it climb, trap, and mend, over and over, up and down the delicate grid. Quinn observed the microcosm of the greater world and felt at one with the creature.

Quinn had done it all—travel, exploration, rebellion—but now he was tired of trying so hard. He was an old soul, and he was weighed down by the memories of all his lives before. He pushed away the voice that reminded him that lessons remained yet to be learned. Human hibernation was not a viable option, even for him.

Quinn was a loner, an orphan since his fifteenth birthday, when his parents had been killed in an automobile accident. He had gone to live with a bachelor uncle, but the relative hadn't had or wanted children, and since the age of seventeen he had been on his own. He had only his buddy Nate and a few casual friends in his life. At forty-five, love had eluded him. Quinn got by repairing computers from home. He had chosen a job that required little human interaction but which fed his incredible intellect at least slightly. He didn't desire material possessions, and he warily avoided the spotlight and notoriety, ever on the lookout for his adversary, Helghul.

Quinn shifted his attention to the television behind him. After a moment he snapped it off in disgust. He tossed the remote onto the chaotic pile of newspapers and books that had buried his sofa. Television aggravated instead of relaxed him. It was pure hype, supply and demand. The fear-mongering talking heads smiled and reported, barely aware of the words that they read: immense tragedy, war, corruption, political unrest, another big-bottom bimbo or celebrity overdose. Gossip and propaganda were pasted like wallpaper over the truths that protruded and begged for attention underneath. Consumers ate it up and grew fat on it, demanding more. What about the others, the individuals doing good work and seeking to better the world? Quinn refused to watch while they were largely ignored and the dark souls absorbed the spotlight.

Quinn blogged as "The Emissary" and spent hours every day surfing the

Internet. The World Wide Web allowed ideas, hopes, and fears to be sent across the globe in a nanosecond. People shared and connected openly, and information was plentiful, though often erroneous. He searched for facts, for breaking scientific discoveries, and for signs that people were continuing to spiritually evolve. He followed changes in the world's weather patterns and kept an extensive spreadsheet on the natural disasters. Tragedy and devastation have a way of waking the soul, and Quinn was hopeful. He considered noteworthy people as they emerged and had boxes of haphazardly labeled information he had collected. He never opened them, relying instead on his comprehensive memory.

Quinn was not only looking for proof that the Dark Age was ending, but he was also tracking other Atitalans—Emissaries like himself from the ancient land who had been sent to guide mankind in its evolution. Many of the Emissaries were healers, musicians, scientists, artists, or teachers. They were the way-showers, laying clues for those who cared enough to seek spiritual growth. He could never identify fellow Emissaries for certain until he met them in person. Their special auras differentiated them like fingerprints but were rarely captured in photos and video, and if the karmic code did show up, the shot was usually discarded as overexposed. Seeing auras was no special skill. Quinn just knew what to look for. The human brain rejects ninety percent of what the eyes see,[3] but he knew how to see.

In Atitala, Quinn's name had been Marcus, and his Marcus-brain—a deep, ancient consciousness—was awake within him, constantly guiding, educating, and urging him to duty. Atitalan Emissaries had been sent to rebuild the world when the last Golden Age had ended. He assumed the others were active and contributing. He was confident that they were not sedentary, disgruntled, and stoned.

They don't know what I know, Quinn justified to himself, taking a hard final drag of his tiny roach. He flicked the dying ember and dropped the scrap in a soda can.

The red light on Quinn's telephone flashed to indicate a message, but he ignored it. It could wait until tomorrow. He refused to carry a cellphone, refused to be constantly accessible—there was a self-importance, an egotism, and a hollow neediness attached to those things. He was not a cardiologist; no one was dying on the table. He had no inflated sense of individual significance, though he could have and perhaps should have.

Quinn positioned himself in front of his keyboard, and The Emissary began his blog for the night. He had it all figured out—the meaning of life, what comes next—and he saw that the answers were all around him. For centuries people had been handed the clues, and yet they continued to ignore them. Maybe his inconsequential blog would reach someone who needed it. Hopefully he was contributing to the ever-evolving collective consciousness. His compulsion to expose humankind to the obvious truths surrounding them would not be denied.

For the first twenty years of his adulthood, Quinn had tried to ignore the obligation that weighed on him. He had traveled the world searching for an elusive spirit, one he had loved deeply beyond all others. Quinn's Marcus-brain urged him to seek out his soulmate, Theron, as he had for centuries. Despite his searching, Theron had not been found—not this time, not yet.

CHAPTER 2

MARCUS AND THERON

First Love

Theron lay limp in Marcus's arms, her eyes closed and her breathing ragged. "I thought you left me," she sputtered.

"I will never leave you," he promised.

Their wet skin was freckled with sticking sand. Marcus's chest heaved as he stroked her dripping hair. She was all length and limbs in his arms. He noticed the odd angle of her bloodied leg and protectively squeezed her against his muscular chest. He shuddered with the realization that he had almost lost her.

Above them, in the shadows on the edge of the excavation, stood a fair-haired young man unnoticed in the commotion. Helghul watched his fellow students with eager interest. He had heard Marcus call for assistance, yet he had remained still, fighting the impulse to aid the troubled pair. His conscience beseeched him to help but he had resisted, his mind in turmoil. His will had been torn as he had contemplated what it would mean to be rid of her.

The day had begun like many others. The sun rose on a gorgeous white sandy coastline. The place was called Atitala,[4] meaning "white island," and was one in a succession of great civilizations. Atitala was the seat of power to a vast empire, which was governed by eleven spiritual leaders called the Elders. The Elders ruled together, led by White Elder.

The Atitalans believed firmly in one creator or, more accurately, a single point of creation, which they called many names, including: God, the Great Spirit, the Eternal White Light, or the Source.

Atitala was stunning, built almost exclusively of white, black, and red stone. The rooftops and columns were embellished ornately with precious metals. There was a Great Hall atop the high plateau at the center, and on the outermost points of east and west were two impressive pyramids.

Marcus and Theron had soared to their destination, swooping through the canopy, steering the crystal glider easily as the leaves brushed past them.

Theron was an unusual beauty; her russet hair blew wildly as they rode. From a distance she looked like a torch, a fireball speeding through the forest. Her narrow green eyes squinted almost closed when she laughed, and days spent on the sunny coast had left her fair skin mottled with freckles. Theron's prominent nose marked her as oddly striking. There was something compelling about her, an allure not contained by her physical shell. She was almost always flush with emotion: passion, fury, competition. Her aura, or karmic code, shone violet, purple, and in rainbows of emotion around her. Despite her sarcastic wit and competitive nature, Theron was magnetic and charming.

In contrast to Theron's fair complexion Marcus's skin was a deep brown, and it looked as though he had been buttered and baked for a feast. His springy black curls were exactly the size of his thick fingers and fell across his forehead and dark brown eyes. Theron had wrapped her arms tightly around his narrow waist as they playfully dipped and weaved through the trees. The duo had channeled their energy into the small transport, and the crystal that had enabled them to fly had grown warm in the pouch at Marcus's hip.

Atlantium crystal was found only in Atitala and, because of its powerful properties, it was carefully protected. It was a power source that, when combined with a disciplined will, allowed the holder to control gravity and movement. It had allowed for miraculous advances in flight and was used in the building of all the great architectural feats of Atitala, including the perfectly designed pyramids. It was an essential tool in the Golden Age and had many other extraordinary capabilities.

Marcus and Theron had arrived at an inland lake at the base of a large quarry. The pool was surrounded by rocky cliffs to the north and dense jungle to the south. The young couple loved to spend time there and almost always had the remote water hole completely to themselves. They often held hands under the water and practiced the mind games and telepathy that all Atitalans learned as children. It was an intimate and familiar way of communicating used only between family members and friends. It was not an unspoken voice, it was not words, exactly; it was more like intentionally transmitted images, feelings, and meaning. Theron and Marcus would spend hours exchanging thoughts and ideas without a sound, immersed in one another's energy.

As they swam, Theron had been actively speaking in detailed mind pictures to Marcus. They had held their breath and glided just under the surface of the sparkling lake. Just as they had reached the steep cliffs adjacent to the atlantium quarry, an enormous boulder splashed dangerously close to them.

The pair had dived as two more large boulders rumbled toward them. The water rippled in anticipation, and the swimmers dove deeper to evade the heavy stones bearing down on them.

Suddenly, a stone broke through the water directly on top of Theron, submerging her and pinning her to the lake bottom. The panic-stricken young man had pursued her down but was unable to move the boulder that pinned her right leg. They had struggled frantically, pushing and tugging to no avail. Theron had watched in horror as Marcus left her and returned to the surface.

Marcus had known that he was almost out of time. The atlantium crystal in his pack was her only hope. The rockslide had opened a small gap where a steep cliff had once been, and the air was thick with dust. The determined man had scrambled up the shore, his feet slipping. His young body was being pushed to its limit as he foraged desperately through his rubble-covered bag for the crystal.

Through the new opening in the cliff, several of the quarry Nephilim[5]—the giant people who mined the sacred stone—had watched the frenzied man indifferently, uninterested in anything that did not offer material gain or gore. The workforce was welcomed on the island, as all beings were, though they were monitored closely to ensure that the harmony of Atitala was not compromised.

Atlantium crystal in hand, Marcus had returned to the pool, already summoning the inner energy he would need to activate it. Using his own life force, just as he had in flying the glider, Marcus had been able to touch the giant boulder and raise it off his motionless soulmate.

Marcus had pulled Theron from the water and immediately begun resuscitating her. Finally she had sputtered; there had been a freshwater flood and coughing, and the young woman had opened her eyes. She was alive, and Marcus was overwhelmed with gratitude.

"I thought you left me," she had choked, still gasping. She remembered the helplessness she had felt as she had watched him swim away.

"I will never leave you," he had promised, cradling her in his arms, his voice muffled and lost as he had placed his lips to her head. Theron's crushed leg was bloody and bent at an awkward angle, and Marcus held her still to reduce her pain.

From above, Helghul had watched with conflicting relief and disappointment as Marcus emerged with Theron. He had hoped she would drown. He had hoped she would live. He had been at odds as to what he had desired for her, though he had certainly wished that Marcus had died.

In their younger days Theron, Helghul, and Marcus had been friends. She was funny and clever and had created the most fantastic games and challenges. She was a great student and teacher, and she consistently outperformed everyone. Marcus didn't mind being outshone, but Helghul grew to resent Theron.

Though Theron consistently outdid Helghul, as they matured he concluded that she would be his ideal mate. She was intelligent, unusual, and so powerful in her telepathic and psychic ability that he couldn't help but admire her.

Theron was a phenomenon among her people. Astral travel was a skill that usually took centuries of the Atitalans' exceptionally long lives to develop, but Theron's parents had discovered when she was a child that she had a special talent for moving beyond the material dimension. Without training, she had shed her human vessel, connected only by an invisible umbilical cord, and her spirit had traveled the Astral Grid.

Theron's father had also been a gifted telepath and psychic, and at the time of his death he had been the Elder of the Sixth Chakra, also called the third eye. He had taught his daughter to control and respect her abilities. He had warned her of the dangers that lurked at the edges of the Grid and had urged Theron to stay within view of the Great Light, avoiding the dark Guardians that howled and thundered from the abyss of the outer realm.

Theron was the only student in Helghul's class that he believed to be his equal. He resisted the love that he felt for her, but he acknowledged that theirs would be a powerful alliance. In the early years it had not been clear that she and Marcus were anything more than friends, and it seemed absurd to Helghul that she could ever choose Marcus over him. Certainly she would choose brains and breeding over ease and brawn.

The defining moment came in their late adolescence when, working on a project, Helghul impulsively confessed his love for Theron. But Theron apologetically affirmed that she loved Marcus and hoped to someday become his mate. Helghul's vulnerability was plain, and he quickly looked away. His mind clouded with humiliation.

Theron was empathetic and kind, but no tact could have soothed Helghul's unrequited heart. Ever after he imagined Theron and Marcus were laughing at his vulnerability, and he bitterly retreated from them.

In the years following, Helghul avoided the couple whenever possible—his ego scabrous and infected where her rejection had wounded him. He watched her with begrudging admiration whenever she was near. His jealousy and wish to outdo her twisted into a torturous knot in his gut, filling his third chakra, fueling the fire in his belly and trapping him in the prison of his ego. Helghul's loathing for the irreverent slacker Marcus also consumed him, and he contemplated how the couple would be made to pay for their affront when he became White Elder.

Despite his apparent disdain for Theron and his open insults and bitterness, it was she who defended Helghul when others complained that he was a braggart. She maintained that he was misunderstood and good at heart. She believed that someday they would serve together in the senate as Elders, and she wished for harmony between them instead of discord.

Elders served for a lifetime, once chosen, but were not born to their posts. They were democratically and divinely chosen. Next to White Elder in importance were the Trinity, the three spiritual Elders known as Brown, Red, and Grey. They were named after colors because their divine titles were musical notes and could not be spoken any other way. Directly below them were the Elders of the seven chakras, who represented the material man and the seven energy centers of the body.

Only the most prestigious title of White Elder would please Helghul. He would have none above him.

Helghul decided that he preferred that Theron had died, rather than watch her be coupled with Marcus or replace her mother as White Elder above him. (Only White Elder knew that her daughter would never join the senate.) He was beset with jealousy as he watched Theron at the base of the quarry in Marcus's arms.

When Theron's sputtering and coughing finally subsided, Marcus wrapped her bloody leg with a strip of his clothing and placed her carefully in his lap for transport. He held the knot of atlantium crystal in his palm, and together they reactivated their swirling energies and summoned the crystal glider to return home.

Marcus had alerted the healers, who met them at the opulent home of White Elder. Theron was given relief from her pain, and Marcus was sent away so she could be treated. Despite his desire to remain with Theron, Marcus had no choice but to leave.

Throughout Atitala, people were preparing for the summer solstice festival that would take place the next day. On the morning of the celebration, the Sirius Star, which was the brightest in the sky, would re-emerge from behind the sun. After seventy days, it would once again become visible. The star was called the star of death and rebirth. It was believed to be directly linked to the spiritual evolution of mankind and had forewarned every shift in the pattern of human existence. The precession of the stars was truly an evolutionary clock.

Atitalan tradition dictated that the students would entertain the senate and the honorary visitors with demonstrations. The entire empire had painstakingly prepared for the festival, which would be attended by the Elders, visiting kings, dignitaries, and ordinary citizens.

Later that afternoon Theron woke. Her leg had been reconstructed from the knee down, and she contemplated her good fortune. Because there were few illnesses that had not been eradicated, it was normal for healthy Atitalans to live hundreds of years if they avoided accidents. Elders could live into their thousands. She marveled at how close she had come to dying in only her twenty-second year. White Elder stood beside her, concern deepening the many lines in her face. Theron smiled, her mind clear and rested.

How could Marcus let this happen? White Elder thought protectively, sending her question telepathically to her daughter.

I am fine, Mother, it was an accident. It wasn't his fault, Theron said without sound. The woman bent and took her daughter's hand.

I suppose swimming was your idea? her mother responded knowingly and, not waiting for an answer, added, *He is reckless, and he makes bad choices.*

You are too severe. He is just . . . adventurous.

Daughter, your injury comes at a most unfortunate time.

I can fulfill my duties for summer solstice, not to worry, Theron reassured.

There is much more afoot these days than solstice, daughter, White Elder's mind pictures spoke mysteriously. But as Theron stirred to question her, White Elder closed her mind.

"Heal well. I am glad you are safe. I must leave you now," the leader said aloud, kissing her daughter's head and exiting with a directive nod to the healer in the corner. Theron was intrigued but could not imagine the burden of knowledge her mother concealed.

As White Elder departed, Helghul paced his own chamber, reflecting on what had happened in the quarry. He worried that he may have been seen. He wondered what fault would have been his, what blame, if Theron had died. Would he have been responsible? Was failing to do right, doing nothing, the same as doing wrong? He wondered how he would be judged, and he shrank from the answers that his conscience gave him. Helghul knew that were he ever to become White Elder he would have to be chosen. He would have to atone for every action or inaction in his lifetime. His pale skin flushed with emotion as he justified to himself that he had merely been an innocent bystander.

Helghul had often gone to the quarry. He secretly studied the Nephilim as they processed the sacred rock. The energy released during the mining of atlantium crystal was too intense for humans to endure at close range. The Nephilim had always been the guardians of the method. The vibrations rattled his teeth and made him feel powerful and invincible. He watched the Nephilim as they worked, aware that atlantium in the wrong hands could be a great danger.

Though he had not gone to the mine with any ill intent, Helghul's conscience continued to rub. He felt shame and unease at the sinister feelings that had come over him so readily. He was aware that the dark emotions had begun to fill him more often, and, rather than concerned, he felt intrigued.

Atitala was changing. The Elders were troubled by the growing endarkenment of their citizens. There was a subtle transmutation occurring year by year. The Elders prayed and worked tirelessly to guide and teach their people. They surrounded the nation with positive energy but could not eliminate the growing undercurrent pushing back. It was a descending flow, and the Elders prepared for the inevitable.

Crime was a new phenomenon, a throwback to ages long ago. Citizens had begun to covet and to compete with one another. Envy was widespread, and an insipid restlessness and discontent percolated behind closed doors.

When the summer solstice festival began, a tired-looking Theron was at the right hand of Marcus, her injured leg hidden beneath her filmy robes. White Elder nodded, and the tranquil harp music abruptly ended and was replaced by a blast of horns heralding the commencement of the celebration.

White Elder watched from her central vantage point at the southern end of the room. Her uneasiness was apparent to no one but Theron, who felt it like an oyster feels a grain of sand against its soft underbelly. The other Elders sat next to White Elder in a semicircle. The Trinity Elders—Brown, Grey, and Red—were closest, and the seven Elders of the chakras were beside them. The visiting kings, queens, and nobles from distant lands took places of honor around the majestic Great Hall, shining in their multicolored robes, saris, and jewels.

The white-robed citizens of Atitala filled the remainder of the vast space, each of them highlighted by the rainbow auras that glowingly displayed their individual karmic codes. The gorgeous white, black, and red marble amphitheater held hundreds of thousands of people easily, with balconies and tunnels throughout to prevent congestion. The space was ingeniously designed for optimal viewing and auditory projection.

Huge gold pillars encircled the center court, supporting an intricate glass ceiling that was at least five hundred feet from end to end. The design allowed light from the dazzling sun, the moon, and the stars to warm and illuminate the chamber throughout the seasons. A stunning solid-gold statue of a chariot with winged horses large enough to seat a Nephilim dominated the northern point of the room and gave the impression that it might spring into flight at any moment.

As the burst of jubilant horns sounded, the citizens took their seats and became quiet in anticipation. The demonstrators and performers were seated in rows on the opposite side of the vast auditorium.

Across the hall, Helghul bitterly contemplated Theron's chosen future mate and mentally compared himself to the dullard. The rival was undeniably handsome and intelligent but lacked Helghul's ambition and drive. Marcus was patient and easygoing, while Helghul was intense and competitive. Marcus did not seek notoriety, nor had he set his sights on the senate despite his obvious popularity and ability. Helghul concluded that Marcus was lazy, but it did nothing to ease his envy.

The Elders were leading the congregation in sacred hymns and meditation. In keeping with tradition, the entire assembly joined in the celebration. Through the striking of deliberate octaves and conscious notes the room was electrified, and it buzzed with the building energy. The silver moonlight shone on them from its place in the center of the glass ceiling.

The Elders began to build the multicolored, sacred Unity Grid, beginning with the six-petal seed of life. Rapidly they advanced well beyond its simplicity and demonstrated a vast array of patterns and sacred geometric shapes, including the star tetrahedron. They called upon the congregation to join them. The building resonated with their chants and movement. The collective energy empowered and strengthened the people, unifying and filling them, while the vibrations caused by their voices lit the Grid around them and turned it like a kaleidoscope. One after another the beautiful designs were illuminated.

Marcus and Theron were filled with the vibration around them. They stood face to face, their hands tightly clasped with one another and their eyes locked in an intense connection.

Suddenly, something went wrong. As the group pushed to expand the scope of the Grid beyond the glass ceiling into the starry night sky, they faltered. The voices went off key, the image flickered, and large sections of the Unity

Grid faded. There were audible gasps, and a wave of fear—foreign to the Great Hall—blew through like an icy wind. All of the voices stopped their hum, and the lights and connection disappeared into silence. Then people erupted into frantic whispers.

The people of Atitala had never known a time when their will and voices were not purely united; the sacred unity ceremony had never faltered, at least not in Atitala. A sinister shiver had raised the hair on their arms and necks, and in shock they looked to White Elder for an explanation.

"Be calm . . . fill your hearts with love. Remind yourself of what you know to be true. Trust in our oneness and unity," White Elder instructed. "Fear is unnecessary. Join me now and clear your minds."

The people of Atitala joined White Elder in meditation, but many were unable to extinguish their concern. Some cleared their minds and filled themselves with love, but others could not, would not, and they were anxious to leave the Great Hall. They wanted to discuss the faltering of the sacred Unity Grid. The people of Atitala wondered if they had lost favor with the Great Spirit. The fear and uncertainty that they were feeling reflected new vibrations in their frequency. Something had to be done.

Amidst the chaos Helghul had felt empowered and, despite the confusion and concern around him, he had remained unperturbed. He had not been participating in the Unity Grid but had only pretended, going through the outward motions. He was happy that the unification had failed; it meant that he was not the only Atitalan feeling differently these days. He had been relieved to witness the weakness of others. It had been hinted that something like this might happen and that an opportunity could present itself. Helghul searched the crowd for his mentor and found him, his head and arms raised dutifully skyward.

After a soothing and reassuring meditation, White Elder blessed and dismissed the uneasy crowd. Marcus and Theron reluctantly separated as White Elder led her daughter to their nearby quarters, surrounded by the other Elders. Their calm was based on their surrender. Things were always as they were meant to be.

Marcus had returned to his chamber alone. He had no family with whom he could consult or speculate. His elderly parents had died years before, and he had been left in the care of the community. Marcus contemplated the breakdown of the sacred Unity Grid, but he also found himself thinking of Theron—her touch, her laugh—and he dreamed hopefully of their future together.

CHAPTER 3

THE DECLINE OF THE GOLDEN AGE

The changes in Atitala had become obvious. There were nights when the air and ground rumbled with thunder, though the sky was clear and cloud-free. The weather had begun to change—as if conjured, violent winds blew and sudden storms swept over the city without warning. Lightning strikes claimed property and lives, and again the thunder boomed.

The most distressing of the recent developments was the series of disappearances. It had begun with one missing child—an infant stolen from the cot next to his parents while they slept. There was no evidence, only a window they had confidently left open. Then another, a toddler, gone as her parents happily chased her through the marketplace. She had dashed lightheartedly ahead, mingling in a sea of legs, and then suddenly she had vanished. The frantic parents searched in confusion; the colorful fruit and vegetable carts hid no playful child. Her voice was gone, her mind pictures disappeared all at once, and her parents could not reach her in any manner. It was unheard of, unfathomable, yet children continued to disappear without explanation.

Nine young ones, all under five years of age, had inexplicably gone missing since summer solstice three months earlier. As a precaution, White Elder warned parents to supervise vigilantly until the mystery of the disappearances could be solved. The citizens were hopeful and prayed for the safe return of the lost little ones while growing understandably fearful and protective of their own children.

It was not only the children of Atitala who had alarmingly begun to disappear. The birds and insects had begun a mysterious migration also. At first it was undetectable, small flocks in formation above, but eventually there were enormous noisy clouds that cast shadows over the landscape and unnerved the people below. There was no apparent cause, yet winged creatures were fleeing and the jungle volume had rapidly decreased by half.

"It is a sign; the prophecies speak of this happening at the end of the Age," some insisted gravely, but most were too confused and frightened to openly speculate.

The citizens closed their doors and minds against the occurrences and looked to the Elders for guidance and protection. White Elder and her senate worked tirelessly to solve the mystery of the disappearances, but, despite their suspicions and intuition, they were unable to stem the flow.

The Elders grew rigid with their teachings, keeping their students unusually long hours. Theron and Marcus's schedules were grueling. Marcus begged Theron to skip classes with him, but she always refused, more serious in her studies than ever before. He grudgingly remained with her in lessons, spending every moment he could at her side.

Theron's leg had healed, and one day Marcus was admiring the faintly scarred curve of her ankle instead of concentrating on their lecture. Theron nudged him to attention as Red Elder informed the students of an important development. The sturdy instructor looked out at the four thousand faces that were casually regarding him from the stone amphitheater. The room spiraled like a nautilus shell to the high cathedral ceiling, and his voice carried effortlessly to every ear.

"I am sure you have all heard rumors," he said, walking out from behind his writing table, his white robes flowing gently. The tired students had been sitting a long time but were suddenly alert and interested. Red Elder stroked his short salt-and-pepper beard as he continued, "Our world has clearly entered an age of turmoil. Before your years, we were a nation of light and harmony. A shift has been occurring and the people are becoming fearful and suspicious . . . even dangerous at times. The descent from the Golden Age can no longer be ignored," Red Elder paused.

Marcus and many of his fellow students slumped, disappointed, in their seats. This information was nothing new; since summer solstice, it had been the topic in every household. Helghul picked at his nail cuticles absently. He was especially tired, still having been on secret assignment on top of all his other responsibilities, and he was bored with the rhetoric.

Red Elder continued, determined that his students understand the significance of what he was telling them.

"The Golden Age we have enjoyed for centuries falters, and we must prepare as the balance shifts toward darkness. The world we know will eventually be lost and will collapse into chaos, as has been the cycle since the beginning of time. There are those who desire power . . . power at any cost. They are calling upon the dark energies and are making the most of this shift in the stars," Red Elder explained, and the students stirred anxiously.

Marcus looked at Theron and knew immediately that this information was not new to her.

"But who? What kind of power?" a student asked anxiously.

"We don't know who or how many have already been corrupted. I do not share this information with you to add to your fear . . . fear is our enemy . . . I tell you because the time of the Emissary is upon us. White Elder has instructed us to prepare. As you know, the Great Cycle requires that someday the chosen of our people will be called to perform an important duty. Just as our ancestors did before us, our time has come."

Red Elder waited as the students buzzed with excitement and disbelief.

"As we speak, the Elders are preparing to choose from among *you*, the students of Atitala. Not all of you are destined to become Emissaries, but it is not for us to say. Those of you who cannot or choose not to take on this duty will be weeded out."

"How?" Marcus called out doubtfully. Theron cringed, and a few rows away Helghul sneered. Red Elder scanned the crowd for the source of the voice.

"By your ineptitude," Helghul interjected loudly, and a small chuckle erupted from some of their fellow classmates. Marcus smirked and placed his hand on top of Theron's. Helghul scowled, looking away, and did not see Theron throw off the mocking digits, annoyed to be a pawn in their competition.

"It will all be explained," Red Elder answered, glancing disapprovingly at Helghul. The students were frustrated with the professor's vague answer.

"Who will choose? What will the Emissaries do?" another student called out unbidden. Red Elder felt their doubt and concern and concentrated on projecting a comforting energy while responding as specifically as he could.

"My students, the Emissaries will be the keepers of the sacred knowledge. You will become the teachers, the healers, and the lights as the Age descends into darkness. Your frequencies will remain high and will help elevate the vibrations of those around you. Your greatest challenge will be to choose *your* path, to maintain *your* balance. The time will come when all of your questions shall be answered. I wish I had more to tell you. I must return to the senate. That will conclude our lesson for today."

Red Elder gathered up his belongings and exited. He was hesitant to say too much. The students gradually departed, chattering loudly to one another as they made their way to their next lecture or work station.

The Elders had been communing with the Great Light through meditation and prayer, but still they had no definitive instructions. They were waiting for a sign—one that would come sooner than they imagined.

As he walked to the senate chamber, Red Elder continued to feel the uncertainty of his students like a thick, humid fog clinging to his every cell. He was heavy with concern about them and their preparedness to become Emissaries.

Had he schooled them as best he could in philosophy, ethics, and higher thinking? Would they be prepared to sacrifice the needs of the individual and the self for the greater good? Should they? All of these questions plagued him, and, based on the strong negative energy that had been growing, he knew there wasn't much time.

As Red Elder opened the door to the senate chamber, his worries were forgotten. All of his senses were inundated. He heard a resounding hum of "Om"; there were whimsical visions of light and color. He smelled sweet jasmine and felt warm wind against his cheek. His skin prickled in response, and radiant warmth immediately enfolded him and drew him in like a favorite blanket. He joined the glowing circle that vibrated before him.

The Elders sat, heads bowed, chanting, meditating, sharing their energy, and wordlessly exchanging their thoughts and feelings. The swirling powerful force circled them, and though they were materially tiny in the vast room, they filled the space.

Red Elder gave thanks and opened himself up to the Universe. He called upon the collective consciousness of the group and sought knowledge and guidance. He centered on the chakras of his own body and released his energy to join the circle. He breathed the short, sharp breaths of fire and felt his own energy begin to cyclone around him.

At the end of this Golden Age, God was recognized within them, part of them. The Source energy flowed between the human conduits in thick bands of brilliant light and color as they flowed in and out of one another. They heard each whisper, thought, and question. They felt every joy and worry, not only of one another, but of every creature. The Elders saw overwhelming love and basked in the indigo glow of their shared hum.

The Greater Power identified the fear and doubt in the room—a lick of it, a tiny taste, hardly anything compared to the dark fear feeding on itself outside the senate doors in the private hearts and minds of the Atitalans. Soothing the darkness with love, like aloe to a burn, the Great Light cradled the Elders and the people of the city. It lived in them and through them. With every breath the loving energy flowed in and out—through their mouths, noses, eyes, ears, cells—and permitted them to exist as One, despite the illusion of separateness.

The Elders knew that they were One with creation and with one another, and they listened for the answers to the questions over which they had meditated. The balance was always there. Darkness was a part of everyone, some more than others, but one and all encompass both dark and light. The dark energy had grown stronger and was there in the room, gaining strength daily, but it was well masked. Despite the Elders' desperate pleas, the missing young ones were not found.

The ancient scriptures of Atitala explained that the Golden Age was the peak of a rotation. As the cycle continued, the Age would end; it always had to end. In that moment of shared meditation and enlightenment, the Elders were informed that the turn had come. The nearly twenty-six-thousand-year cycle would continue.

It was the end of the Golden Age, and the next thirteen thousand years would descend into darkness before the cycle would once again turn upward. The souls who had learned their lessons would ascend to a higher realm. Those souls who were blocked or dark would continue learning in their earthly incarnations. For a moment, darkness erupted from the perimeter of the light. The inky blackness sent overwhelming doubt and fear through the room and through the walls into the world afar. It projected an image of humankind without faith and light. Inside the chamber and everywhere beyond, people were momentarily stung and sickened by negative and foreboding images. They saw murder and selfishness—one was stealing bread from another. They saw a world corrupt with human sacrifice—a head bouncing and splattering blood as it tumbled down steep pyramid steps in faulty attempts to honor the gods. There were as many ominous, diverse visions manufactured by the energy as there were people.

For an instant the Great Source was rendered still by a hideous and powerful grief that rumbled through the chamber and through all of Atitala. Though fear tempted them also, the Elders continued their meditation and hum. The brightness re-emerged, bursting through and scattering the darkness. Once again the senate chamber was filled with glorious light.

It was then that the message came clearly to each of the Elders simultaneously: "The Emissaries must be chosen immediately. They will devise new tools of understanding to sustain the people. They will be beacons of hope in the coming dark days."

White Elder looked up from her place.

"The message has been given," she said, her voice replacing the hum of energy. "We must prepare. The reconciliation of man will come within days. The worthy and faithful Emissaries must be chosen, and they too must choose. As the prophecies have foretold, these Emissaries will be the way-showers and will carry forward the secret of Oneness. The knowledge must not be lost."

"What of us? Do we continue here?" Grey Elder asked.

The room remained quiet. Though Grey Elder was given no answer, a reply did come, instantly but silently, but only to White Elder. White Elder alone heard the Universe respond. *For those who remain, the wrath of the earth, water, wind, and fire will overtake all of the continents, heralding the end of this Golden Age. First will come water, that which sustains and takes life. Only the chosen Emissaries shall leave, accompanied by Red Elder and Grey Elder*, White Elder was told.

"Only the Emissaries will go," White Elder answered. "The rest of us are to remain here."

"How will they be chosen. What must we do?" the Elder of the Crown Chakra asked.

"Red Elder has begun the task already. The trials have been designed, and the students will be chosen and will choose. We begin tonight," White Elder said.

The Elders broke their circle, and their light and colors lingered around them. There was much to prepare, and the importance of the task ahead of them was daunting.

"Red Elder, one last thing," White Elder called, as she finished speaking privately to Grey and Brown, giving them each special tasks to complete before they departed.

"What is it?" Red Elder asked.

"Tell no one what I say now. As you know, a new beginning is upon us. For the next Great Year you have been given a task of prime importance: to accompany the Emissaries. It is a sacrifice; you could go on to the higher dimension and exist in bliss. Soon the Emerald Tablet will be removed from the Grand Pyramid so that, as the consciousness descends, the dark energy is not amplified. It will remain unused until the next Golden Age begins, when the energy is once again worthy. You will carry the message of the Emerald Tablet into the world. Do you accept this responsibility?"

"I am happy to accept. It is not a sacrifice, it is an honor. Will you join us?" Red Elder asked.

"No, my path and cycle are of a different nature," White Elder answered simply, and Red Elder understood that the journey is never done, no matter what level of enlightenment one has attained.

"Has this great Age truly ended, when there is still so much good in our world?"

"We have always been told to question everything, but the cycle continues as it must," White Elder explained.

"And the rock rolls downhill," Red Elder added. The Elders embraced warmly before departing.

Beyond the walls of the senate chamber, oblivious to the monumental events that had unfolded, Marcus and Theron sat shoulder to shoulder, thigh to thigh, and deep in conversation. The cenote that surrounded them glowed turquoise blue and white.

The cenote was a round stone chamber naturally eroded by an underground river with a number of tunnels branching off into darkness. The fresh water was dazzled by the sunlight springing through the overhead skylight, worn by nature's erosion. Their feet were soothed by the warm, still pool. Roots of living trees hung like chandeliers from the red soil ceiling, some reaching all the way to the water.

"I love it here," Theron said. "When we were young, Helghul and I found this place. We used to come here to practice mind games. One of us would use a rock to scrape an image or symbol into the soft walls over there, and the other would sit here with our feet in the water and try to guess what it was. He used to get so mad. I always won and he could never guess anything I drew." She smiled at the memory.

"So he's always been an ass," Marcus said, laughing and squeezing her tightly with one arm.

"He's not so bad, Marcus," she defended. "I don't know what the grudge is between you."

Marcus was barely listening now. He breathed in her natural clean smell, and as she had turned to speak her thigh pushed firmly against him, an instant distraction.

The sun peeking through the open ceiling was splintered by the dangling roots and dappled her in a golden glow. Her nose and her tiny eyes in isolation were nothing special, but somehow in her face they were perfect. All at once Marcus felt his breath sucked out of him.

"The last thing I want to do right now is talk about Helghul!" he said, placing his hand behind her neck and pulling her in for a deep kiss. She responded willingly, gently biting his bottom lip, and they wrapped their bodies together.

As their passion mounted she stopped him, as she always did. She pulled his forehead to meet hers, locking her hands behind his neck, and stayed there with her eyes closed, saying nothing. Marcus felt their connection deeply, and his frustration slipped away. After a moment he stood; unselfconsciously he slipped out of his loose trousers and pulled his tunic over his head, plunging into the welcome cool of the water. As he surfaced he swam to the edge and searched with his feet for the hollow nook on which to stand.

His caramel skin glistened in the speckled sunlight and his spongy curls almost touched his shoulders. Impulsively Theron stood up and, with one tug, dropped her airy white robe in a heap at her feet. There was only a brief moment before she slipped into the water next to Marcus, but that vision would be forever burned into his memory. It was the single most arousing moment of his life; to see her there, for the first time, free and naked. Her curves so perfectly long and lean, surrounded by the stunning blue and gold of the cenote. It was almost too much for him.

No amount of cool water could sate him. She came to him, her soft skin pressed against his, her mouth open before their lips met, and their hands explored one another. She felt his hardness against her and she floated into him. Instantly she felt the heat between her legs, the longing in her belly. Her second chakra burned and desire shot through her. Marcus's left hand slid tenderly from her hip up to her breast. Her nipple responded to his touch, swelling, and he brought his mouth to it. They held the edge of the pool for support and her free hand stroked his rippling shoulder. Soon they were kissing again, fevered and wet. Marcus was out of his mind with passion, overwhelmed with his love and longing for her.

"Now," she whispered in his ear, kissing and licking it seductively. He looked at her, searching her face. He needed to be clear that they were ready—it was their first time. Marcus placed his hands on her hips, lifting her as she wrapped her strong limbs around his waist. This was the perfect connection, the ideal moment.

"STOP!" A tortured yell tore through the cave, startling the couple and shattering their blissful state.

The moment gone, they watched in shock as Helghul approached the pool's edge, his eyes wild. "Get away from her!" he ordered. Marcus didn't move, but before he could say anything Theron shouted at her classmate irritably.

"What are you doing here? Have you lost your mind?" she snapped. Helghul ignored the question and angrily rounded on her.

"You bring *this* to our spot?" he hissed. "You spoil yourself with . . . with *this*?" he spat, pacing the edge of the water, glowering at her. His jealousy twisted his thin face, and Theron was stunned by his vehemence.

"You need to leave NOW," Marcus commanded. Theron placed her hand on his shoulder.

"Helghul please, just go," Theron said more kindly. Helghul stopped pacing and glared at her, his pale face blotched with rage.

"You are unclean! Don't speak to me," he hissed, spittle flying as he spoke. He was cut short as Marcus leapt out of the pool, his nakedness forgotten.

Despite Helghul's attempt to back away, Marcus's coiled knuckles crunched against the bone of his cheek. Helghul was thrown back by the blow, his counterpunch lost to the air as he stumbled.

"Stop!" Theron shouted. Marcus ignored her as she grabbed on to his bicep, both of them naked and dripping. "Marcus, let go! Let him go!" she shouted. Marcus backed the stumbling adversary to the water's edge and shoved him in.

"What is wrong with you?" Theron fumed, as she began to quickly pull her clothes back on.

"You're mad at *me*?" a disbelieving Marcus snapped in response.

Helghul began climbing out of the water, his sopping garments clinging to him. Theron's dress was awkwardly twisted and stuck to her as she instinctively reached out and offered Helghul her hand. As she bent toward him, he did the unthinkable. In a flash he backhanded her roughly across the face and sent her reeling on her haunches. Blood flowed from her nose as she skidded across the stone floor, landing on her tailbone. She was dumbfounded as blood and tears poured down her clinging dress. She had never been hit before. She had never been intentionally injured by anyone.

Before Theron could process what had happened, Marcus pounced on Helghul, who was now out of the water. They were wrestling on the stone floor, and Theron was shouting at them to stop, when Helghul unsheathed a small knife from the waist of his soaked clothing. He slashed at Marcus, opening a superficial gash in his right forearm. Marcus's eyes bulged at the realization of the weapon. He grappled with Helghul, ultimately sending the blade bouncing off the rock and into the deep water.

"ENOUGH!" A powerful voice boomed through the underground chamber, reverberating off the walls and simultaneously sending a debilitating telepathic screech that cut through their minds painfully. Marcus and Helghul let go of one another, bringing their hands to their ears in useless defense.

Grey Elder stared at the students angrily as they stumbled and pushed away from one another. The young men stood dirty and bleeding from miscellaneous scrapes and punches, and both avoided the intimidating gaze of the Elder. The older man was tall and extremely thin. He wore his silver hair shaved short, and his dark eyes showed little emotion. His face was red and his jaw was tightly clenched as he looked at the bloodied, miserable Theron and then back at the young men.

"Grey Elder . . ." Theron began.

"Say nothing, I have seen enough. I will bring this matter to the senate," he said. "We have no time. You need to go prepare, the students have been summoned. You are to report to the Great Hall within the hour," he said. Then, looking at Theron, he added, "Do not let your mother see you thus, Theron. It will distress her unduly."

Theron marched angrily out of the cavern, and Marcus bumped against Helghul roughly as he passed to catch up to her. The young men sneered openly at one another, and Grey Elder took Helghul by the arm and steered him away.

"There is no time for your nonsense!" he hissed at the student, and Helghul shook his arm free but stared dejectedly at the ground.

Grey Elder was annoyed and deeply troubled. There was so much to do and the offspring of White Elder only added to his worries. When he arrived back at the senate chamber, Grey Elder solemnly conveyed the story to the other Elders.

White Elder's face clouded with concern and she asked after Theron. "What of my daughter, is she badly injured?" At that moment she was less spiritual leader and more distressed mother.

"She is well, White Elder. She is in her room changing her robes," Grey Elder assured.

"This violence on the eve of the departure of the Emissaries . . . what does it mean? Can they be trusted on this odyssey?" Brown Elder questioned, folding her hands contemplatively.

"Perhaps they are not destined to become Emissaries?" the Elder of the Fourth Chakra proposed.

"Only the Great Spirit knows who will be chosen," Red Elder replied.

"We must trust, we have no choice," Grey Elder said.

"There is always choice," Brown, White, and Red Elder chimed in unison.

"We should meditate," another Elder suggested.

"We don't have time for this," Grey Elder complained. "The reckoning time has come!"

"So our unity and acts of faith are more important than ever," White Elder reasoned serenely. The Elders joined their hands and bowed their heads. Instantly a low hum and gentle glow surrounded them, and after a few minutes they broke apart.

"Gather the students but be mindful, my friends. We must take care not to panic our citizens. Fear is a powerful negative emotion and we have enough to deal with," White Elder said. The Elders filed quickly out of the chamber, splintering off to gather the potential Emissaries.

As the Elders dispersed, a dry, neatly dressed Marcus arrived at Theron's private chamber. She opened the door for him, but she was aloof and said nothing. She had quickly showered and washed the blood away. Her nose had a nasty bruise but was not broken.

"Are you angry with me?" Marcus asked.

"You struck another being," she said shortly, fatigue in her voice, but then added, "It's not your fault, it's mine. If we hadn't been there . . ."

"You can't mean that!" he said incredulously. "If Helghul hadn't been sneaking around none of this would have happened!" He was irritated by her inability to see Helghul in a realistic light.

"You didn't have to attack him. I wasn't badly hurt!" she chastised. "He's just jealous and misguided, can't you see that?"

"Poor Helghul? He hit you! With all of your intuition and still you can't see him for what he is!"

"And what is that? He's not a monster, Marcus! He loved me and I didn't know it. I walked around competing and throwing sarcasm at him, and I never realized until it was too late that I had led him on somehow."

"Led him on? That's ridiculous! Everyone loves you, Theron, do you lead them all on?"

"Be *compassionate,* Marcus! We should both have been more sensitive. You don't make it easier, holding my hand in class just to show off and torment him."

"And the knife, Theron? Is that our fault too?"

"Of course not!" she snapped.

Theron had always defended Helghul, but she had never seen him so brutal and hateful. She remembered the look in his eyes just before he hit her and she was devastated; she had felt all of his loathing and contempt as if it were her own. And there was more—when he had been unguarded, she had slipped into his mind and seen terrible thoughts. She prayed that she was mistaken.

"Let's not fight. We have to meet in the Great Hall soon," Marcus soothed, reaching to take her in his arms. Her rigid body stubbornly did not yield to him, and after a moment she moved away. Even in her aloofness the touch of her flesh against him made Marcus stir, and instantly he flashed back to the image of her naked and sliding into the water next to him.

"Have you thought about why they must have called this gathering?" she asked, but before Marcus could answer there was a loud knock on her door.

"The time has come," a page's voice rang out.

The couple looked at one another in anticipation, so unsure of what lay ahead and anxious to hear what the Elders would tell them. Theron turned to leave and, in her haste, did not notice Marcus reaching for her hand. He dropped his hands to his sides and double stepped to join her in the hallway. They walked in silence to the senate chamber, their curiosity growing with each step.

CHAPTER 4

THE EMISSARIES

The citizens of Atitala were unaware that the prophesied time of the Emissaries had come. The sky had grown red and stormy. An uncharacteristically cold wind bent the nearby palms and whipped at their clothing as the young students made their way to the meeting in a steady stream.

Marcus and Theron entered the Great Hall, relieved to be out of the wind, which chilled them through their flimsy tropical garments. They joined the group of nearly three thousand already assembled, greeting familiar friends and faces. Theron's nose was noticeably red and swollen, and Marcus had concealed his scabbing forearm with long sleeves. A number of people looked at them curiously, but the couple pretended not to notice. White Elder sat visible to all on a raised platform surrounded by the other Elders, rather than on her formal throne. She was relieved when she saw her daughter enter looking only slightly damaged after the still-unexplained encounter.

The room was alive with speculation and excitement but became silent when White Elder rose to speak.

"Good students, respected Elders, welcome. It is no secret that the decline into the dark days has begun. From among you there shall be chosen a brigade—Emissaries who will be called upon to be the keepers of the secrets and who will go forth into the world of man as beacons of hope and light. From among you the Emissaries will come. Only those who prove themselves worthy in the tasks ahead will be chosen. Only those who then accept this path will go. Each of you should go now and meditate on your role in this world. Ask for guidance and listen to your inner voice. Sleep well, for tomorrow it shall be clear who has been chosen."

"That's it?" Marcus grumbled. "They brought us all here to tell us they will decide tomorrow who will be chosen. What was the point?"

"Seriously Marcus, I am starting to wonder if you listen at all!" Theron said, shaking her head.

"What did I do now?"

"They told us to meditate. They told us that the answers and guidance in our path will come . . . sometimes you are like one of the children."

"There's nothing wrong with playing once in a while," Marcus said, moving closer like he would sweep her up. Theron jerked away and resisted the smile that threatened to escape her. He was a good balance for her. He reminded her that she needed to embrace adventure.

Marcus was relieved when Theron slipped her hand into his and aimed them toward her chamber. They walked, contemplating what possible tasks the Elders would have them perform to prove their worthiness as Emissaries.

"Definitely something with the mind games . . . telepathy . . . maybe demonstrating how far we've come in mastering our energy?" Marcus guessed.

"I am sure they will ask questions about the Emerald Tablet. Mother said we will be the keepers of the secret. It is the most sacred text, the understanding of the Source and the Universe; it must be a part of the choosing," Theron speculated.

"You'll be chosen for sure," Marcus said, suddenly stopping. *What if I'm not?* he asked, switching to the more intimate telepathic communication.

Oh Marcus, don't be ridiculous. You're underestimating yourself again, Theron broadcasted wordlessly, sending her irritation clearly with the response.

Would you stay with me? Marcus asked, still not moving as Theron continued to walk ahead. Theron did not turn to look at him because she could not give him the reassurance he sought. She couldn't promise or answer him honestly in that moment. He did not want to know. She hid her thoughts, hid her uncertainty, and spoke out loud.

"You will be chosen and so will I. Now stop this and walk me home," she said. Marcus said no more, and they continued on in silence.

Theron sent Marcus away with a brief kiss, distracted by her thoughts. He jogged the short distance to his chamber; there was no one else he needed to visit.

Marcus's room was cozy but small compared to the opulence of White Elder's family dwelling, but he liked that he was so close to Theron. Marcus was happy there. He didn't require much. He paced the tiny room, absentmindedly rubbing the tender, scabby wound on his arm and wondering about the tasks he would soon face. He continued to worry that Theron would be chosen and he would not.

Marcus took a seat on a fine woven carpet in the center of the room and lit a candle, preparing to meditate. He tried to clear his thoughts and still his breathing, but images of Theron naked as she had entered the cenote flashed mercilessly through his mind. The tortured young man became aroused beyond comfort at the memory of his love's body standing on the edge of the beautiful water. They had been so close. They had almost made love for the first time, something Marcus had imagined and fantasized about for years. Theron had always adamantly put him off. She had stopped him with an explanation about spiritual growth and being ready for their paths to converge. He was ready. He was so ready he was afraid he would internally combust.

It was many hours before Marcus was finally able to meditate. His mind was too full and his body was experiencing ripples of rage, violent feelings that he had never experienced. He had no frame of reference to understand them. He was torn between doing the right thing and wanting to avenge Theron's honor and her injury. When he finally let himself drift into his higher consciousness he felt relaxed and peaceful, but he finished after an hour without having received any clear message.

Across the compound at nearly the same time, Helghul had just awakened from a startlingly vivid dream. In the dream he had found himself on a precipice in the quarry looking down on Marcus and Theron as they swam. The dream was identical to the events of three months earlier—every sound, every bird's chirp, and the rumble of the stones. Helghul once again stood above a desperate, scrambling Marcus, but this time he acted. He did not stay motionless and watch. In his dream Helghul changed the outcome.

When the rock slide first began, Helghul felt the sensation that he had already been there, that he was in dream state, and he understood that he could control the flow of the rocks. In his unconscious he had the authority to make the rocks fall or be still. Helghul was intoxicated with his power, and when he saw Marcus and Theron swimming below, he knew exactly what he wanted to do. His conscience called to him and he disregarded the warning.

It's a dream, I cannot be held to account, he reasoned. Helghul released the avalanche and gloried in the destruction. When Marcus clambered onto the rocks, Helghul rewrote the script and released a second, more devastating landslide, crushing his reviled classmate in the rubble below. He stared down at the mayhem that he had unleashed, and he gloried in the supremacy of his will and mind.

Suddenly, he heard a deep male voice say, "Citizen!" and he woke with a jolt. The scene melted away, and Helghul felt panic and excuses bubbling out of him though there was no one near to listen.

"Citizen?" he repeated, unsure what the dream meant but afraid to wonder.

A bridge away, Theron was stretching and contemplating what she would do if either she or Marcus was not chosen. She leaned hard into her slender muscles as they burned and resisted. She remembered the darkness she had seen in Helghul's eyes and the shock she had felt when he had hit her.

Unable to relax, Theron played complex tunes on her harp-like instrument. She plucked the sensitive strings indelicately, and her music was unusually poor. Marcus had upset her with his self-doubt, and the call for the Emissaries coupled with the violence earlier in the cenote turned all thoughts into brushfire in her head.

Theron meditated as instructed and, despite the incredible energy vortex that she was able to summon, her messages were of a common nature. She saw the lights and colors that always soothed and warmed her. She felt the sensation of floating and swaying and even spinning as if in an eddy herself. She felt the euphoric acceptance and confirmation that she was on the right path, that she was working toward clarity and light. She saw the faces of her Elders, of spirits, perhaps of lifetimes before, but there was no message of a dire nature. There was no call to service or secret code. There was nothing that told her she would or would not be chosen as an Emissary. She reluctantly retired to bed, confused by the lack of communication.

Theron was not asleep long when she found herself aware in her unconscious and floating outside of her flesh-and-bone frame. An ethereal lifeline connected her to her sleeping human form, and it shimmered and swayed in the starry evening light like a silver fish-scaled string. Theron stared down at her shell for a moment, awed, as always, to see her body motionless and remarkable as she astral traveled. She willed herself up and out beyond the bounds of the city, and she soared into the heavens as other light beings darted past.

Theron had not been out long when she heard a familiar voice in her head. It was Marcus—he was speaking to her telepathically. She scanned the star filled sky in excitement; this had never happened before. In the distance she saw him and her heart leapt with joy. He had done it! Marcus had finally tapped into his deepest unconscious and he had joined her in astral travel. Their spirits rushed together like a gust of wind, and they circled one another in greeting and recognition. Their thoughts flew easily back and forth.

How did you do it? Theron marveled. Marcus noticed all of the other colorful spirits speckling the heavens around them, and he remarked in astonishment.

There are so many others! Is it like this all the time? he asked.

Theron confirmed it was. The feeling of being outside his body was thrilling. Marcus felt the temperatures—cold, warm, and hot—all at once. He felt like chili peppers had been rubbed on his skin, even though his physical self was far below him. Theron directed their spirits upward and together they shed the atmosphere of the Earth, still tethered by their glistening, infinite cords to their bodies back home.

When the Grid opened up before them Marcus gasped at the beauty. It was heaven—a paradise of lights, music, and awareness. The couple darted up and down the loops and circles like sparks in an electric current. The fractal[6] geometric shapes bloomed and receded in a kaleidoscopic display of mathematical perfection.

Marcus, I want to try something, something I have only heard about, Theron communicated excitedly. Marcus circled and dipped, waiting. With a thought and intention Theron crossed through Marcus and completely immersed her spirit in his. It was the ultimate spiritual union, not just the comingling of auras but the touching of souls. It was Oneness unimaginable in human form. Only material, Earthbound creatures had the illusion of solitary, loneliness, and separation. The ecstasy and beauty of their union was indescribable.

The loud and distinct clash of a gong reverberated with an "A" note through their bound spirits, interrupting them. Theron retreated and Marcus's soul cried out.

Come back. Forever come back, he begged.

We need to return, Marcus. The dawn is breaking and the choosing of the Emissaries is near, she said, looking toward the horizon.

Stay with me. This place is perfection. We have no reason to ever go back, Marcus contended.

We must go back Marcus, we are needed.

I won't go. I will wait here and meet you any time you come. That way it won't matter if I am chosen as an Emissary, you can come to me, Marcus reasoned.

I will be reborn and reincarnated; I may never have the skill to return here again.

All the more reason you should stay, Marcus said, still following her. As the sun rose higher in the distance Marcus followed Theron closer to home.

How will we ever lead others to this place if we keep it for ourselves? Theron answered, and she swiftly made her way to Earth and to her chamber, knowing that Marcus would certainly do the same.

"Marcus, citizen! Theron, Emissary!" a loud male voice boomed, and Theron woke in her bed with a jolt. Had it been a dream or had they astral traveled?

Citizen . . . Emissary—she had heard the verdict clearly. Theron trembled with the idea of it. She had to talk to Marcus immediately. He could confirm if they had traveled or if it had all been a dream; but then, she wondered if it mattered. Marcus, citizen. Theron, Emissary. It could only mean one thing.

Theron jumped up to dress, then rushed out into the glimmering pink sunrise. Marcus was not far away. She had to knock twice before he opened the door, disheveled and bleary-eyed from a night of little sleep.

"Did you astral travel last night?" Theron blurted out as Marcus led her inside.

"What? No, I don't think so," Marcus said, reaching to push her tangled hair from her face.

"Marcus, either you did or you didn't. You would know!" she snapped impatiently.

"Whoa, what is this? What happened?"

"I had a dream, I think it was a test, it was pass–fail. In the end, you were labeled citizen but I was labeled Emissary," Theron said desperately. Marcus looked stricken as he stared at her.

"I failed? Citizen? Why?" he asked.

"You begged me to stay . . . to stay in the Grid, and I said no," she said, crying as Marcus put his arms around her and led her to sit on his narrow bed.

"It was a dream, Theron. I wasn't there. I couldn't have failed if I wasn't there," Marcus reasoned.

"Did you . . . have a dream?" Theron asked hopefully; her green eyes glowed with tears.

"No, I didn't," he said. Theron rested her head on him, unsure what to think. Surely Marcus would not be judged for her dream . . . or would he? What did it mean?

A piercing trumpet suddenly pealed through the air, startling the distraught pair and preventing them from ruminating over her dream further. It was time. Theron ran to the door and threw it open. Things had begun to go horribly wrong. She shouted at Marcus to follow her.

Outside, the sky had grown dark and sinister, and sheets of rain battered the city. Buildings had begun to crumble and fall, and Theron knew intuitively that they must get to the wharf as soon as possible. Through the deafening wind and noise she shouted to him. The couple ran the two miles to the port, circling on the curved roads and passing over the canal bridge as it disintegrated behind them and fell into the now surging canal below. All around them people were running and yelling, and Theron sensed their fear but was unable to help.

When they arrived at the wharf White Elder was there, and she was ordering students in different directions—some onto the waiting boats and others back toward the Great Hall. A fork of lightning shattered the ominous sky, and the queue of students trembled as the thunder shook the Earth. The students were soaked through to the skin and shivered as they huddled in the bitter wind, waiting to be sorted.

"Theron, at last. Load on the boat, daughter. Hurry," White Elder directed. "Marcus, go back to the city, I will return there shortly."

"NO!" Theron screamed, her eyes wide and disbelieving. "No!"

"He has not been chosen, Theron," White Elder shouted over the din. The winds were increasing and she crouched slightly to steady herself.

"Stay with me, Theron!" Marcus shouted, as two surly men were summoned by a nod from White Elder and began to lead him forcibly away.

"Mother, please!" Theron cried, nearly hysterical as she watched Marcus being dragged farther and farther from her.

"You must choose if you are a keeper of the secrets. Will you become an Emissary? There is not much time!"

"Let him join me, please!"

"I cannot. It is not for me to say. You must choose!" White Elder commanded, as the tempest worsened.

Theron ran to Marcus. He was released by those holding him, and she flew into his arms. Marcus held her, crying into her hair without speaking. Theron held him but after a moment took a step back.

"I have to go!" she shouted through the chaos. Marcus looked as though she had hit him. Water ran in thick streams down their faces.

"You can't leave me," he cried, gripping her thin arms harder than he realized.

"I must!" she replied, twisting her body to free herself of his grasp.

"Emissary!" the deep baritone voice called, and Theron bolted upright in her bed, rescued, saved from the torture of her dream. She was soaked from head to toe with sweat, and her tangled hair clung in damp clumps to her skin. She had been put out of her misery at the first possible second—in the first moment that it was clear she had made a choice, Theron had been allowed to wake.

A dream within a dream, she marveled, shaking. She had been chosen as an Emissary. She was certain of that. Theron wondered if Marcus had dreamed, or astral traveled, or anything at all. It had all been dreams, and he was still safely asleep across the courtyard in his bed.

Theron looked out the window into the calm night. It was hours until dawn and Atitala slept peacefully, but she was unwilling to close her eyes and risk more dreams.

When Marcus finally slept, he had two powerfully vivid dreams. First he dreamed of astral travel, traveling the Grid and finding Theron there. Their souls united; he bathed in her light until the sound of a gong suddenly pulled him back into his body. He awakened from that dream with a start, excited and overwhelmed with his love for Theron, his skin vibrating with their energy. It took a while to fall back asleep, and then his second dream came like a tigress waiting to pounce.

He was back in the cenote. This time he was alone. The sun gleamed through the earthen ceiling above him, dancing in silver circles on the still blue water. Marcus was hot; so hot it was as though he were sitting in front of a roaring fire rather than in a cool underground cave. The water tempted him, but he felt as though he must not go in. Something inside warned him: a voice, an instinct. Marcus suddenly noticed that there was a water jug dripping with condensation across the beckoning pool.

He was dry with thirst and heat, and finally he stripped down, the muscles of his dark body glistening with sweat. Marcus jumped into the water and felt relief and coolness. As he reached for the jug and brought it to his parched lips, he felt the touch of a gentle hand on his shoulder. In his dream state he did not need to turn to know—he knew it was Theron, it was the beautiful girl he loved.

Marcus continued to drink, unquenchable, the jug ever full. Then he felt a hand on his other shoulder that did not quite make sense. He became confused as one can only in a dream and his unconscious struggled to sort it out, but he could not stop drinking the water to look. Finally he turned and there were three of them. Three beautiful women, each one more beautiful than the next. They were naked and smiling, and there was not a freckled nose or a crooked smile among them. The women were perfect.

Their breasts moved seductively as they surrounded him, laughing and smiling, and Marcus could hear music in the distance, his favorite song, and the heat and the thirst that had plagued him was all focused and centered now in his first and second chakras, and his groin felt as though it was on fire, and the women were caressing him and kissing him. Marcus ached with desire.

"Stop," he tried to say, but the words failed to come. He felt the softness of the tiny feminine hands on his body, and they teased him, touching his thighs, his buttocks, and his naval. Coming so close to his tortured organ but never taking hold.

"Do you want us?" one of the women whispered sweetly as she kissed his neck and rubbed her breasts against his arm. He felt them on all sides of him, and he felt their skin, their erect nipples, their bodies so soft and willing. He thought of Theron and his unconscious urged him on: *It's just a dream, she'll never know*, it said.

Marcus battled with himself and knew that he could have them, all of them, if he just stopped resisting, if he just reached out and stroked the soft warm place between her legs, any of them, the beautiful naked girls in the cenote would be his.

Marcus remembered his dream of astral travel and the soul connection he had experienced with Theron.

"I have chosen Theron," he said, but the women still clung to him.

"She'll never know," they purred.

"I'll know," Marcus replied.

The scene changed, suddenly and without reason as is the way in dreams. Marcus found himself once again walking into the cenote, but this time Theron stood in the distance, removing her filmy robe, her naked body resplendent in the glowing light as she lowered herself into the water. It was just as she had been only hours before and Marcus was anxious to join her.

Wait! Something was wrong. There was a deep voice, a husky laugh. She was in the arms of a man. A jealous rage welled up in him. Marcus saw Theron lifted up in the water; her legs and arms wrapped lovingly around . . . him? He saw himself holding her, his dark head shifted to the side as the couple kissed passionately. It didn't make sense; his emotions surged and burned within him uncontrollably. The dreamer was stunned, his mind scrambling to understand what he was seeing as he inched toward the water's edge. His stomach churned as fury swelled within him.

In the water he saw himself, no longer himself. He saw the pale face of Helghul looking back at him from his reflection. Confusion. He heard her voice, a faint whisper.

"Now," she said, and Marcus's mind exploded in outrage.

"STOP!" he shouted. Pain, excruciating betrayal was all he felt. There was no logic, no recollection or understanding that this world was a dream. Marcus was fully engulfed and choking on the bitter scene.

"What are you doing here? Have you lost your mind?" Theron said indifferently.

"You need to leave NOW!" the imitation Marcus shouted.

The dreamer's fury doubled as the imposter jumped out of the water and charged toward him. He felt the cold hard knuckles against his cheek and was sent reeling backward, his attempt to retaliate lost to the air.

Marcus felt the knife sheathed at his waist and before his adversary reached him he pulled it out. Every vessel in his body prepared for battle, and his muscles surged with adrenaline as he stared at the blade in his hand. In his dream conscious he had changed places with Helghul. He felt the sting of Theron's disregard. He felt the jealousy of her love for Marcus. The torment of her betrayal was fresh and devastating, fueling the dark passion that had always been latent within him but that had now grown and was eclipsing him.

In that moment of dark anger, Marcus contemplated his predicament. Had Helghul truly felt how he was feeling? Had he been so injured by seeing Theron in Marcus's arms? Marcus was filled with compassion, and he moved through the unconscious rage of his emotion and made a conscious decision. He threw the knife aside and instead prepared only to defend himself. Even in his darkest pain he would not attempt to take the life of another.

"Emissary," a voice boomed.

Marcus jerked awake as if he had dreamed of falling. He lay panting and unable to quiet his racing heart for some time. It had been so vivid, so terribly real. *Emissary*, he thought, understanding that he had passed the first test.

Marcus suddenly understood Helghul more fully than he had ever desired to. He reminded himself that there were more tasks to come, and he lay awake wondering what they might entail.

Throughout the city, potential Emissaries had meditated and then dreamed realistic and disturbing scenarios that challenged their greatest fears, alliances, and weaknesses. Some were designated citizen and others Emissary, but each had heard the deep judging tone.

The sunrise was pink and fresh, and Theron was knocking on Marcus's door. He opened on the second knock, squinting and bleary-eyed in the bright sun. Theron had the sick feeling of déjà vu as he pulled her inside.

"Did you dream?" she asked anxiously, her eyebrows bent with concern.

"I did. Obviously you did too," he said, trying to kiss her as she darted away impatiently.

"Well, what was it?" she asked, barely able to stand the suspense.

"Emissary . . . I passed, just like you said I would . . . I guess you weren't as sure of me as you thought," he remarked.

"My dream . . . it said you failed . . . I . . . didn't doubt you . . . it was so real, that's all," she stammered uncharacteristically.

"I passed, you can relax," he said, throwing himself down on his bed and making room for her to lie beside him.

"I am so relieved, Marcus. I am so happy we'll do this together," she said, a distracted smile relieving the stress in her face as she sat on the edge of his bed. "I dreamed we connected in the Grid," she added, taking his hand between both of hers.

"I did too. Our souls . . . touched," he said, happy that she had experienced it also.

"But you didn't want to come back," she said, confused.

"I had no choice, the gong sounded and I was jolted awake. But I could still feel you. It was incredible." Theron lay down next to Marcus and they rested silently, forehead to forehead.

After a few minutes, Theron stirred. "I'm going to talk to Mother and see what I can learn. I will see you in the senate chamber at the gathering," she said, kissing Marcus lovingly.

"You've got to leave now?" Marcus replied, but she was already half out the door. Theron turned back with a twinkle in her eye and flashed him a smile.

Marcus did not rush to dress; instead, he lay in his bed for a long time considering what task might lie ahead. The gathering was scheduled to begin in one hour; knowing that Theron was presently very distracted, he was in no hurry to join her and be ignored.

Just before the gathering began, Marcus sauntered casually into the senate chamber. Theron was hovering at her mother's elbow. Helghul and a group of his cronies were nearby, and Marcus noticed that he avoided looking in the direction of Theron and White Elder. His eye was purple and black where he had been punched, and Marcus rejected the shame that percolated inside him, determined to justify his violence.

"What did you find out?" Marcus whispered conspiratorially, pulling Theron aside.

"Where have you been?" she asked crossly. Without waiting for an answer, she continued. "Nothing. She completely blocked me. I expected she would. It is only fair."

Helghul glared openly, but Marcus no longer shared his animosity. His experience in the Grid with Theron and his cenote experience from Helghul's perspective had changed his smug condescension to begrudging compassion. It was strange that at the end of a Golden Age, Marcus's enlightenment had reached its peak.

Directly in front of the spectators was the white marble throne of White Elder. It was massive, and she was dwarfed by it. The chair back was straight and severe, reaching five yards into the air, capped on either side by a shimmering sphere of phosphorescent green atlantium crystal. The ornately carved arm rests and legs all had identical glowing globes at their ends. Throughout the entire chamber there were more strategically placed crystals, and the magic of the throne was fully realized when the sun was directly overhead. Through the impressive skylight, the sun sent beams to the atlantium crystal, which in turn reflected through the room to create a brilliant display of light and color. To the right of White Elder's throne were three smaller seats made of expertly molded solid silver. On its left there were seven more of copper.

The hour had arrived, and all of the potential students were in attendance. A trumpet sounded, heralding the start of the gathering, and the Trinity Elders—Red, Grey, and Brown—took their seats along with the seven Elders of the chakras. White Elder addressed them effectively with only the amplification of the well-designed room to help.

"Welcome. You are a worthy, courageous group and any one of you would make an honorable Emissary. What you must remember is that for each of you there is a plan. If it is not your path to become an Emissary, it is not a shame upon you or a fault. It is simply not your calling.

"What you may not realize is that the first of the trials is complete. Last night in your dreams you faced your fears, your weaknesses, or your desires. As I said, there are those of you who are destined to become Emissaries and those who are not. If you have been chosen, you clearly heard the decree of 'Emissary.' If you heard the verdict 'citizen' there is no dishonor; it is simply not your destiny to continue to the next trial. Many good people will stay here in Atitala."

Marcus and Theron began whispering, as students all around them reacted in a noisy assortment of emotions. Marcus searched the crowd for Helghul and saw him obviously flushed with anger. He filled with satisfaction, hopeful that the pest had been weeded out.

"Citizens, please return to your homes and families now, and pray for your compatriots as they journey forth," White Elder instructed. Scores of people embraced, cried, and offered encouragement, while many others skulked from the room, downcast and disappointed despite White Elder's assurances.

The crowd thinned less than Marcus had first anticipated; twenty-five hundred eighty-four of the original four thousand one hundred eighty-one students were still in the rows. Marcus was astonished to see that Helghul remained, though judging by his sour look he was not happy about it. White Elder spoke again as the last of the eliminated students exited.

"You have completed a significant task. There are two more stages in the selection process. We do not aim to trick you or to confuse you. Let me be clear, the first stage will be a simple test of your moral reasoning. The second is in your hands. We will explain the role and duties of the Emissaries. We will then ask you to exercise your free will to serve or to stay. Red Elder, let us proceed." White Elder was seated as Red Elder rose from his perch and began to speak.

"Good morning. It is a good day that brings us here to choose the heirs to the knowledge, those who will go on to serve mankind and protect the secrets of Oneness in the coming Age. First I will ask that you clear your minds. It is imperative that you do not communicate in mind pictures or speak with one another during this task. To do so will eliminate you automatically. I will give you a scenario and two choices. If you choose number one, I want you to stand on the east side of the room. If you choose number two, I want you to stand on the west side of the room.

"Now, imagine a land like this one . . . there is a great canal and it is bursting its banks, threatening to sweep a family of three into its rapids and to certain death. There is a mother in her mid-years, a toddler in his fourth year, and a newborn baby. The bank they are standing on is quickly eroding, and you have only room for three on your raft. Do you, one: take the mother and one child? Or, two: take the two children, leaving the mother, who might have some chance of survival on her own. Remember you have only room for yourself and two others."

Red Elder waited at the front of the room while people silently struggled with the dilemma. Before long, keen students began committing to positions and crossing the room dramatically. Like the choosing of teams in an informal sport, they made their way to either the east team or the west and greeted one another self-assuredly. Marcus did not contemplate at all. He didn't need to. He knew that he would go wherever Theron did, and he suspected that some others were doing the same. To Marcus's displeasure, Helghul had also stayed rooted to his bench in the center of the room.

Theron went nowhere. She stayed in her seat, her eyes closed, not wanting to know where others were going and wondering how many would miss the obvious.

When the room was divided Red Elder asked if everyone had decided. The group to the west, who had chosen to rescue both children, nodded confidently. The much smaller group to the east also nodded; they too were ready. Marcus was completely flabbergasted when the group of people sitting in the center of the room around him also nodded. They hadn't chosen! He didn't understand. He was sure that Theron would save the children; the mother might make it on her own but a young child certainly wouldn't.

"One last time, have you made a choice?" Red Elder asked, as one plain-looking young man ran from east to west in a last moment change of heart.

Marcus looked around him and wore the same look of confusion as those who had chosen east and west. Why hadn't the center group moved at all? What were they doing? Marcus cursed that he couldn't talk to Theron, but he had faith that she knew something he did not.

"Then you have all decided. Theron, why did you not choose, as instructed?" Red Elder asked. Marcus realized how fortunate it was that he had not been delivered the same question.

"There is a better choice," Theron said, opening her eyes and relieved to see such a healthy-sized faction next to her. The groups at the east and west sides both muttered unhappily. Theron had known that Marcus would stay, she had never doubted it for a moment, but she wondered if he knew *why* they had stayed.

"You said there were two choices, but there were three. Twice you said there was room for *three* on the raft, but at no time did you say that *I* had to be on it. So I would send the mother and her children, and I would take my chances on the disappearing bank and in the water."

The Elders, who had observed in silence up until then, rose to their feet and applauded the group at the center of the room, smiling and nodding approvingly. The students on the east and west flanks joined in the ovation hesitantly.

All around Marcus, students were smiling and nodding, and he was stunned at the simplicity and self-sacrifice of it. It hadn't occurred to him. The east and west groups were shamed by the realization that they had just killed a mother or a child when they should obviously have sacrificed themselves first—it had not occurred to them. But most said, if given the choice again, they would give up their place on the raft and sacrifice themselves.

After some discussion and commotion, the disappointed east and west groups exited the hall and shamelessly returned to their roles as citizens of Atitala. White Elder emerged once more to address the crowd, which was now just over sixteen hundred.

"It is time for you all to understand the role of the Emissary, and the difficulty and sacrifice that this choice will bring. A great calamity will come to all the Earth, as it has for many civilizations before ours. Divisiveness, doubt, and fear will cause chaos and seek to consume each spirit in the primitive world that will eventually emerge. We must bring balance. It is your purpose to spread enlightenment and to ensure that the symbols and knowledge of Oneness and the truth of the Great Source and creation are not lost to this darkness. We must ensure that the message of the Emerald Tablet, which was passed on to us from our ancestors, is not forgotten.

"Take the knowledge you have been given and weave it through the fabric of the new world—in its art, music, science, architecture, and mathematics. Let those who would ask find the clues and the way to consciousness.

"It is your destiny as the chosen ones to keep hope, truth, and virtue alive in the world. We are all a part of the Great Light, we are all One. There must be balance. Without goodness there is only darkness. Without the Great Darkness one cannot choose the Light.

The audience stirred and Marcus spied Helghul, who sat with arms crossed a few rows behind him. He did not understand how Helghul could be a chosen one. How could someone so flawed be an Emissary? Just as the question occurred to him, Marcus's inner voice reminded him that he too was flawed; that if not for Theron he would be already dismissed with the others who had not seen a third choice in the moral question.

"Have heart," White Elder continued. "Your power together as One will be greater by far than the darkness you face. I have faith in you, I believe in your goodness and light. Be honored in this task," she said. She took a seat as Brown Elder rose. The wide stocky woman walked to the forefront, not much taller standing than sitting. Her thick head sat directly on her shoulders with no sense of a neck at all, but her broad, flat face was kind despite her severe appearance.

"As you go forward, you will live among the people as equals. You will die and be reborn in their lifetimes. As it is here, you will feel everything they feel: pain, insecurity, grief . . . but you will always maintain your elevated frequency. You will always know your divine purpose. You will always be true to the purity of your nature. You have each been carefully chosen as Emissaries by the Greater

Power; it is your destiny, but only if you choose it. You are still free to remain here in Atitala."

"What will happen to Atitala in this time of chaos?" a voice rang out.

"The citizens of Atitala will follow their own paths," White Elder replied.

"If we go, can we return? Will we see our families again?" another student asked.

"It is a duty for the entire cycle of the next Great Year. It is not for us to know where we will be reborn. You will not return to Atitala, though your soul groups never leave you," Brown Elder answered simply.

"When do we go?"

"The vessels are prepared at the wharf. You will depart at noon tomorrow, and Red Elder will accompany you," White Elder replied.

The room erupted with conversation. Boats? So soon? And never to return! How could they decide something so serious so quickly? Theron was staggered by the realization that she would be leaving her mother.

"Why boats?" a student asked.

"Simplicity is best when future supplies and technology are uncertain. A boat's form lends itself easily to function and understanding in primitive times," Brown Elder explained.

"Will I know that I am an Emissary?" said another voice, female this time.

"No. In each incarnation you will be born fresh and clean, but you will understand what you need to know to serve, and that is enough," White Elder answered. The room was no longer silent as the potential Emissaries whispered and mumbled to one another.

"Will we know each other?" Marcus asked, cutting through the din. White Elder found his face in the crowd and searched his eyes knowingly.

"We are One with the Source of everything. Those of you who choose to fulfill this destiny and choose these lifetimes as the keepers of the knowledge shall not remember your ties to Atitala. As it is here, in each new life you will be free of past memory, free of memories that would cause feelings of loss, despair, and longing. You will be reincarnated to share your inner light and virtue with the world. Let this be clear to you all—once you die and are reborn in the world of man your only memory will be of your purpose, your sense of duty, and you will carry that with you always," the Elder clarified. The room again erupted with conversation.

I won't go! Marcus said to Theron telepathically.

Theron was shocked. Her eyebrows creased together in confusion.

Of course you will, she snapped back without sound, her mind occupied with the sadness of leaving her mother and her home the very next day. *It's our destiny.*

You are my destiny, he answered, his mind pictures vibrating with emotion. *I don't want to be apart from you! I don't want to forget you! I don't want to lose the knowledge of our people. If we stay here we are reborn here, we can find each other again as we have before!*

You can't mean this, Theron telegraphed.

Let's stay here, Theron, Marcus pleaded. *It's our choice. I choose you! Choose me. Most people never find what we have.* Marcus had a hold of her shoulders now, and she looked into his fearful brown eyes.

I love you, Marcus. We will still have this lifetime together, it is Atitala and my mother that I will leave behind, she said, softening, pulling him close. *I know my duty, and my life belongs to something greater than myself or us. I am meant to be an Emissary. I can feel it; I have always felt it.*

I don't feel it! Marcus communicated in anguish. *I only feel panic . . . panic that I could lose you forever!*

That is fear, Marcus. You know that we can never let fear rule us, she replied, placing her hand on his tightly clenched jaw. All around them the future Emissaries were in varied states of emotional uproar.

White Elder's voice called out. The fervor quieted but was not silenced. "The Emissaries will set out by ship from the wharf at noon tomorrow. Those of you who choose to stay behind should feel no shame, you have free will."

Marcus and Theron watched as all around them their fellow classmates talked and chatted in anticipation and turmoil. Theron saw Helghul at the edge of the room and tried to catch his eye. She wanted to make peace. She wanted him to know that she was glad that he had passed the trials and been called to be an Emissary. It confirmed for her the goodness she had known was within him. Helghul purposefully avoided Theron's gaze, and she felt a sad dryness in her throat.

Those who had chosen to stay in Atitala began to trickle out of the hall, leaving the Emissaries to their task. Some walked proudly through the golden doors, while others slipped embarrassed from the room. Twenty-four more had been weeded out and had chosen not to leave Atitala. The room now held fifteen hundred ninety-eight final candidates.

"Theron, let's stay behind!" Marcus pleaded once more. "Look, there are others who have been chosen who are not going. Let's make a life . . . a family of our own, *here*."

"If we do not fulfill our destiny, Marcus, there will be nothing worth living for," she replied. He knew there was no point arguing with her. She was resolute. It was he who wavered. Marcus knew that he could never tolerate life in Atitala without Theron, but he also knew that he never wanted to be parted or to love her one bit less than he did at that moment. He was overwhelmed by all of the unknowns ahead of them.

Marcus saw Helghul loitering at the edge of the crowd, alone and sullen. "I can't believe *he's* here," Marcus said to Theron, jerking his chin in Helghul's direction.

"He's as much a part of the unity as we are," Theron replied.

"It is time to choose your path. Those of you who will become Emissaries, please join us at the front of the hall for the commitment oath," White Elder announced.

The Elders stood spaced equally apart, and the students assembled in orderly lines in front of them. One by one the students took their places in front of the leaders. Placing their right hand to their heart while their left hand was embraced by the Elder in front of them at the wrist, they repeated the vows given to them.

"In the spirit of unity I choose to become an Emissary. I promise to share the truth of all creation and to lead others to the path of the Great Light and Oneness. I will seek to illuminate the Great Darkness where I find it. I will keep alive the knowledge that illuminates the pathway to enlightenment. May the Eternal Flame bless me in this task and help my fire burn strong and clear in service."

The Emissaries were then embraced and blessed and dismissed one by one. The vows were powerful and many were overcome with emotion, purified by the process.

From his place in line, Marcus searched the chamber for Helghul's flaxen head but could not find him. *Had he already pledged and left?* Marcus wondered curiously, still skeptical that his rival had been chosen at all. Marcus was scanning the room when Theron nudged him forward to face White Elder.

"Have you made a choice, Marcus?" White Elder asked, studying the young man's face carefully.

"I choose to accept my role as Emissary . . . with Theron," Marcus answered.

"Very well. It shall be as it is destined," White Elder said, taking hold of Marcus's left wrist and reciting the vow. Marcus repeated the words and felt the overwhelming joy of the cleansing, but at the same time he felt a weight—the weight of a task too large for him.

As he waited nearby for Theron to take her vow, Marcus wondered if he was up to the assignment ahead and grew apprehensive. Other classmates around him offered their congratulations, and he listened as they chattered excitedly.

"Theron, I am happy to see the choosing has been well done," White Elder said, kissing her on each cheek.

"Yes, Mother, but I am heartsick to leave you," she said, embracing her. White Elder asked her to place her right hand on her heart and took her left wrist. Theron marveled at the tender touch, her wonderful gentle hands. Theron knew them so well.

White Elder looked proudly into her daughter's emerald eyes as Theron recited her vows in a powerful, clear voice. She finished and they embraced again for a long time.

"I hope that you will join me for a walk . . . alone, before dinner," White Elder requested, eyeing Marcus casually. "I will fetch you from your chamber in two hours," she said. Theron looked from her mother to Marcus.

"Of course, Mother," Theron smiled.

"Let's go," Theron said, taking Marcus's hand. He joined step with her, grateful at the prospect of them being alone.

When they arrived at her quarters, a fire had been lit and a variety of delicious food had been laid out. The couple rested together on a wide settee, her head on his chest, alternately kissing, sipping wine, and discussing their future.

"We can still have our life and our own family wherever we end up," Marcus said. "We can do everything we planned, just in a new place."

"I hope so," Theron smiled. "But there is no rush. I sense that we are going to have a heavy load."

"I can't stop thinking about how we united in the Grid. It was so beyond this material world. I can still feel you in every cell of me," he breathed, as she nestled against his neck. She looked up into his eyes.

"There was so much more . . . awareness," she said. It was . . . like I *was* you. I had an entirely new perspective. I felt your feelings . . . but so far beyond our senses . . . like we traded souls."

"Not traded, connected. I felt all of you and me both, simultaneously," he corrected gently.

"We are spiritually bonded," she said, hugging him closely.

"Forever," he said lovingly.

"Forever," she replied.

He looked down at her, her eyelids heavy and full of passion, and pulled her up to him. He kissed her deeply and turned his body to meet hers directly on. She felt his excitement, and it increased as she pushed as closely to him as she could. They kissed and touched eagerly through their clothing, his hand rubbing and urging her on. She stroked his chest and ran her hand firmly down his body, stopping between his legs and holding him, so excited, so ready.

Marcus was nearly out of his mind when Theron released him and slowly moved away. She stood up, and he reached out to stop her. She tenderly moved his hands away and, instead of stepping back or taking a break as she would have done in the past, crossed her arms in front of her and took hold of her robe by either hip. She pulled the garment easily over her head, and the action lifted her thick, tawny hair and sent it cascading down her naked shoulders.

She stood smiling down at him, the firelight licking her freckled skin, just as he desired to do. He feverishly reached out to touch her. He sat on the edge of the settee now, his hands on her hips. She stood in front of him and he pressed his lips to the flat, soft skin of her belly. He moved down, kissing, licking, and pleasing her. She made small sounds, her breathing quickening, her hands stroking his hair and shoulders.

She whispered that she was ready. They had waited so long, so many years; their energy was undeniable and eternally connected. They shifted to the sofa, kissing lovingly and holding each other tightly so that their skin touched in every way possible. They moaned in pleasure as he entered her.

They found themselves exactly in the moment, not worried about the past or future. She opened her eyes and—whoosh!—there was a tug right at the core of her. He felt it too, and their spirits and energies mingled and twisted. He closed his eyes, trying to stay there forever, to make it last forever. *I don't have words for this*, she thought.

"I love you," he said. It was a total connection and an explosion of energy. They knew that they had always known each other. She wrapped herself around him and sent her soul deliberately deep into him. She felt his colors reaching back to her, sending her everything.

"I love you," she answered. They stayed close and touching long after the climax had come and gone.

As time passed, Marcus became more and more anxious. A feeling of impending doom plagued him, and though he tried to replace it with a soothing lightness and the memory of their lovemaking, he could not.

"This is so perfect. It's not too late to change our minds. Can't we just stay like this forever?" Marcus coaxed, stroking her hair.

Theron shook her head and sighed. She was tired and her mother would be ready for their walk. She took his hand and brought his inner wrist to her lips.

"This kiss holds all my love for you, my dreams for us. You're my soulmate.

We are connected to one another forever." She rested her petal-soft lips gently against him, and he cradled her closely with his other arm.

The lovers lay on the sofa together, their bodies entwined—feet, arms, legs. So happy to have their skin touching. Theron soon fell asleep against him, her soft breath against his neck. He lay still, not wanting to wake her, and watched the firelight dance across her angular face. A light knock at the door interrupted his reverie, and Theron stirred groggily and then jumped to attention.

"Oh Marcus! You let me sleep? Hurry, get dressed!" she scolded in a whisper, as she grabbed her discarded robe off the floor and pulled it over her head.

"Marcus, she'll see you!"

"She knows we are together, Theron," Marcus whispered, pulling on his pants.

White Elder knocked at her chamber door more loudly, and a disheveled Theron slipped out, leaving Marcus behind, half dressed.

It was now early afternoon, and with the mother and daughter off for a final stroll, Marcus was left alone. He waited for a while, but then grew bored and decided he would come back later when Theron returned. She was upset at the prospect of leaving her mother, and he wanted to be there to console her.

As Marcus walked through the courtyard around the Great Hall, he saw some of the other Emissaries literally vibrating with excitement. Marcus's apprehension continued to mount, and he couldn't help but think they were naïve, innocents being led to the slaughter, and yet they marched happily forward like ants to a feast. He saw the heavy burden they carried even if they did not.

As Marcus made his way to his own chamber, a satisfied grin firmly planted on his face, he caught sight of Helghul and noticed that he was heading in the direction opposite of his own home. *What's he up to now, always slinking about?* Marcus wondered. Suddenly, having no other interest to occupy him, he decided to follow.

Marcus was cautious, remembering the episode with the knife and uncertain how unpredictable Helghul might be. More than once Marcus was almost noticed: first walking across the central canal bridge when there was little to camouflage him, and then again while gliding behind his classmate over the jungle. Marcus had been forced to steer his glider dangerously low into the shadowed canopy to avoid detection as he followed Helghul out of the city and ultimately to the banks of the quarry.

Marcus assumed that Helghul was returning to the tunnels near the secret cenote, but he could not imagine why. The young man's body pulsated with curiosity and adrenaline as he passed over the location where Theron had almost drowned. Marcus loved a good mystery, and he was certain that Helghul was hiding something.

CHAPTER 5

CONJURING DARKNESS

The Exodus

His glider discarded, Marcus had to move quickly to keep Helghul in sight as he navigated expertly through the labyrinth of tunnels and caves in the mountainside. They had already passed the glowing cenote as they delved deeper into the Earth. Innumerable colonies of bats slept, squeaked, and flew through the caverns. Marcus flinched as a tough, bony wing brushed his cheek.

The smell of bat feces was overwhelming, and Marcus covered his mouth and nose in disgust. He tried to keep his steps as light as possible and was aware of the movement and life skittering around him in the darkness. Helghul's light source disappeared ahead many times, and Marcus had almost become lost in the overwhelming obscurity more than once. He listened for Helghul's footfalls and cursed his own unpreparedness.

As they wound deeper into the rocky maze, Marcus grew concerned. What if he got lost? What if Helghul had seen him and was leading him into a trap? How would he find his way out? Who knew what danger might lie ahead or what creature he could encounter? Marcus's skin prickled and burned as each hair and follicle bristled at attention. He was rushing to keep pace and held his arm bent over his head at eye level to warn of rock outcroppings, since the light was almost always only a flicker turning through the low, narrow passageway in the distance. He was almost bent in half and wondered if he should turn back from his reckless pursuit.

The tunnel narrowed further, and Marcus hurried as Helghul disappeared through a ridiculously small opening approximately two yards up the wall. Ignoring the sticky foulness of the bat feces and knowing that the rock face was rife with spiders and other creatures, Marcus pressed his body against the stone and found foot and hand holds. He then boosted himself up and cautiously emerged through the opening, which was only just large enough to allow his broad shoulders entry.

Marcus pulled himself up and was standing on a steep precipice. Below him was an open, circular pit that likely had an entrance from the other side of the mountain. It had obviously once been excavated, and he noticed the glimmer of residual atlantium crystal on the surrounding cliffs as the firelight danced in shadows. The hollowed cavern had no natural light but was illuminated by five large torches evenly spaced around the circumference.

Marcus heard the loud murmur of voices, and as his eyes traveled down the cave walls he was stunned to see the unusual and substantial congregation gathered below. Beneath each of the torches stood an enormous male Nephilim looking more harsh and menacing than ever. Each wore extravagant leather armor braided with silver and gold.

There were hundreds of humans, including Helghul. There were both women and men, and Marcus recognized most of them. They were all students, and he wondered which of them had been chosen as Emissaries, if any, and what business they could possibly have in this pit.

Helghul seemed to have a position of importance among the group. As he passed, each individual bowed to him in respect. On his order, the group began to chant, focusing on the chromatic notes. The inharmonious chant grated on

Marcus, and he rolled his head on his neck to shake out the tension that had gathered in his body. He gritted his teeth as the dark intonation continued and grew louder. He had never heard anything like the hum that vibrated through him, the air, and the earth, reaching the darkness just below.

Marcus's instincts were warning that he should flee, but his curiosity would not permit it. He was determined to see what Helghul was up to. It was a decision he would eventually regret many times.

Suddenly, the eavesdropper's attention was drawn by a burst of light to the opening through which he had just come. Marcus shifted as far as he could away from the hole and found a generous outcropping in the dark wall. Silently he cursed his white pants and tunic, aware that his dark brown skin would camouflage him much more effectively. He tucked himself out of sight as best he could, his belly flat against the ridge, knowing that it wouldn't hide his brawny frame if anyone shone a light directly at him. He saw a slender white hand reach up through the opening, and his heart hammered in his chest as he prepared to fight or flee, though luckily neither was necessary.

The figure passed within two yards of him and, as Marcus had hoped, the individual's attention and light source had been fixed on the spectacle and sound below. He was not discovered. Marcus released the air slowly from his lungs as the newcomer joined the others in the hollow.

The new arrival was obviously in charge and wore a heavy, dark cloak. Marcus regretted that he hadn't dared a look as the stranger had passed, desperate as he was to know who had convened a group of students in such an unlikely place. The ringleader's voice suddenly boomed through the eerie vibration of voices. It was familiar but quivered strangely, and Marcus could not place it. The glow of the torches flickered as a hot wind was conjured and twisted up from the center of the circle. Before he had time to think, a ceremony had begun below him.

"Shadows of the underworld, we call upon you. Empower your disciples. Your servants will go forward and be the Adversaries to the Emissaries of the Light. Give us strength. We come in service, to free you of your tethers, to open the door to your prison, and to bask in your power! The Golden Age has ended;

we share in your glory. We come willingly to suffer on your behalf, to sacrifice for your freedom!" the deep voice roared, as the chanting continued and grew louder.

Marcus was horrified by the words and he prayed silently, surrounding himself in white light. Again his intuition beseeched him to flee, but he would not. His curiosity, his need to know, could not be overcome by fear or common sense, and he stood mesmerized as a scene of horror and carnage unfolded at lightning speed below him.

"We bring the innocents at this time of decline, this time of change, and we give them to you freely, oh evil serpents of the world forsaken," the voice continued. The ring of students was circling, swaying, and jerking as if in a trance. The Nephilim, who had thus far stood silently observing beneath the five points of light around the room, disappeared to a corner of the cavern that Marcus could not see. Marcus could vaguely hear the squawk of creatures, perhaps birds, but the dark hymn was so loud that he could not be sure.

The fervor of the chanting group doubled, and their movements became frantic as the Nephilim returned to their posts beneath the torches. Marcus struggled to comprehend the scene. With horror, he realized that each of the giants held a flailing, squirming child. The indifferent Nephilim held the screaming babes like sacks in front of them and roughly passed them to members of the macabre circle.

I have to do something! What is this? Marcus thought in panic. Nothing in his life in Atitala had prepared him for this. In the brief second it took Marcus to compose a single coherent thought, it was too late to intervene, though it would have been useless at any rate. Without warning, or further ceremony, the central leader raised his hands into the air and shouted.

"Rise now, Darkness. Accept this sacrifice!" The toddlers were mercilessly swung against the cave walls as if they were mats to be beaten clean. Marcus dropped to his knees in shock, and a powerful howl inexorably escaped him and was swallowed easily by the noise below.

Too late Marcus turned his face away; what he had witnessed could not be unseen. He retched over and over, vomiting in the dirt as he sobbed uncontrollably.

The Nephilim had each taken up a wide drum, and they began to beat in rapid pulse, urging the humans on. Marcus rocked back and forth in horror, his eyes clamped tightly closed, unable to stop the retching that wracked his body.

The chanting continued, heightened by the carnage. Marcus dared not look. He did not want to see the gore; he could not fathom the violation of God's laws, the inhuman sacrifice of the innocent. He felt the evil grow exponentially around him, and he shivered and cried in horror. He wanted to disappear, to be anywhere other than where he was, and the burden of guilt was quick to envelop him. He should have done something! Anything! As the blood of the little ones stained the walls of the cave, so it indelibly stained Marcus's soul. He had witnessed humanity at its darkest.

Again the master began to speak and Marcus trembled, immobile and forever changed. He dared to look again just as Helghul moved to the center of the feverish, chanting circle. The student had removed his tunic and stood only in trousers; his lean torso trembled in anticipation and his pale skin glowed orange in the firelight. The females in the group churned and danced as if entranced; still chanting, they discarded their robes. Their varied shapes and movements, their exposed flesh, fed the perverse energy that was building in the room.

The Nephilim watched eagerly as the leader directed the many women to the torches on the wall. They ran their hands along the sticky, blood-soaked surfaces. They placed their soiled hands on Helghul's waiting body, smearing the gory mess across his naked chest, abdomen, thighs, and face. They kissed him and licked him, clutching and rubbing. There was no part of him unmolested, and the sexual energy of the rite raised the fervor of the group.

The cloaked master never joined, but directed the men in the outer circle to fall in upon the women in a base frenzy of sexual chaos: a reward for their allegiance. The Nephilim shouted and cheered in depraved appreciation. The remnants of bloodied white robes and tunics were torn away as the Adversaries' bodies became alive with the burning, compelling power of the lower chakra impulses, and they violently coupled, sodomized, and fornicated in every combination possible. Their unquenchable sexual desire was the hold over them. Lust was an age-old influence and power that had led many to the Darkness with its promise of pleasure. Their further wish for power, notoriety, and material reward had led each of them to the cavern.

The drumming continued, but the chanting had been replaced by guttural grunts and cries and moans and, more ominously, the sound of distant thunder. It was so far from the experience Marcus had shared with Theron only hours earlier. Helghul was at the center of the rite, shaking in twisted orgasm, when the leader shouted above the din.

"It is time for the initiate to become the host. The soul who will be offered to the dark entity stands willingly before us. Power will be yours!" the leader declared, and the group broke their chant and echoed him.

"Power will be ours!" they bellowed, robotically separating from one another and returning to their circle. When the drumming suddenly ended, Marcus could clearly hear the rumble of thunder, deep and ominous, and a distant roar like that of a lion.

Get out! Marcus's inner voice shouted in warning. He was overwhelmed by the feeling of impending doom that pressed his already overfilled senses. He was in shock, and there was no power in him to run away.

The leader began to speak in a strange language that Marcus did not recognize. The naked group continued to sway hypnotically as if drugged, as they began once again to chant, sweat and blood streaking their bodies. As he orated, the cloaked man circled Helghul with a large silver knife. The younger man stood fearlessly waiting with his arms outstretched.

Shadows stirred and moved through the cavern—shadows newly come, not cast by fire or form but with their own will and way. Helghul's bloodied face was turned boldly skyward, and he looked weirdly euphoric. Dark powers and ambitions not seen for many millennia were being called upon.

The sinister master brought the knife down, resting the glinting blade against the flesh of Helghul's forearm. Though Marcus's hatred for his adversary burned like never before, he did not wish to see his murder and he instinctively said a prayer for him. The master began to speak:

"Hear me now, Darkness of the night
Chained in the fetters of fire by Light
Reach now forth this sacred land
Misbegotten beast take now this offered hand
See me now, oh wicked eye
Seek this place from whence we die
Offer this, your sacred feast
Rise up now, all-powerful beast!"

On the final syllable the leader handed Helghul the blade, and the young man willingly slashed open his own extended forearm. His blood spurted across the dirt and a jagged crevice opened up in the ground, expanding deeper and wider where the crimson trail had fallen. There was a deviant howl and a loud crack as the rock bed beneath their feet split open.

Marcus prayed desperately, begging for divine intervention and sending light and positive energy into the cavern below. Marcus's single light was not enough, and the shadows and dark energy continued to spew forth. Repeatedly, the vast chamber filled and the Darkness moved easily through the walls, released into the world beyond.

Marcus trembled as a terrifying demonic presence emerged from the chasm like cruel afterbirth and filled the chamber. The ten-headed, dragon-like beast glowed in particles and waves. It was an ominous grey, purple, and blue like a bruise. The evil presence gnashed its jagged fangs, howling at the mesmerized group as they chanted and reveled in the dark vibration.

Helghul, formerly brave and defiant, inwardly shuddered at the sight of it. It was more horrible than he had imagined, more horrible than his worst nightmare, and his passionate fervor was replaced by cold dread. Denying his fear, he lifted his head proudly, drawing on the envy and admiration of the adoring assembly. He was the chosen one, and he offered up his bloody arm.

The roar was unbearable as the wraith entered Helghul like a drug through a syringe. It infiltrated his veins through his bloody, self-inflicted wound, and

Helghul screamed in agony as his body was lifted a yard off the ground. He jerked and jolted violently, defying gravity in the center of the circle and hovering over the endless crevice. The torches on all sides of the room grew brighter, highlighting Helghul's contorted face.

As the evil took hold, Helghul could not resist. He was no longer in charge of himself; he had been overtaken by his own choice. The new Helghul growled in twisted ecstasy. The room cleared of the last demonic shadows as they emptied through the walls into the vulnerable world outside. The transfer was complete. Helghul stood on his feet, a welcoming host to the Darkness. The King of the Adversaries had been ordained.

Fractures had opened around the globe as the membrane between worlds had been successfully breached and the underworld had been freed of its confines. The cloaked leader signaled an end to the chanting.

"We have succeeded. Through Helghul we have opened the gate to the Darkness, the cycle has shifted. Our strength will exponentially increase as the Age declines. The Emissaries must not succeed in bringing enlightenment to the new world. You, among others, will be the instruments of discord, and it is your calling to ensure that evil will out. Adversaries depart! Spread fear, isolation, and doubt, and by all means control the weak. Manage the unconscious and lead them as they grow in number. Keep their life forces bound and slumbering, and their frequencies will remain low and feeble."

The dark speaker was interrupted by the groan of shifting earth. "There is no time left. You must all get to the wharf! There is no time to lose!"

As if awakened from a deep hypnotic state, the students jerked upright, scrambling to dress.

"We have not been chosen as Emissaries. How will we board the boats?" one of the Adversaries asked.

"The passage of the Adversaries is assured. The Universal balance guarantees it. Like the Emissaries, you have chosen your path."

The Adversaries departed for the wharf. They were not the possessed, mechanistic assembly from moments before. They showed no remorse or shock, but rushed purposefully toward the waiting boats. The Nephilim were dismissed and filed out of the cave, their lust for blood fulfilled.

"What about the blood?" Marcus heard a woman ask, referring to her stained garments.

"In the chaos of tonight, it will never be noticed," the leader promised. "Take the east exit. Everyone hurry to the boats!"

Marcus heard the urgings of the dark leader, and though he knew that he too must hurry and get to Theron at the wharf, it was too dangerous to move. From below, the students swiftly mounted the stone steps and passed Marcus, hiding only yards away. Helghul was now alone with the grand master, and Marcus tried to see who was hidden beneath the dark cloak but his hood remained in place.

"Helghul, you have done well. You will go on to live many lives of great consequence."

"I feel the power within me—it's intoxicating—but strangely I still feel myself," Helghul answered.

"You are yourself, but more. You are immortal. As ever, your soul goes on, though your avatar material incarnation will be born and die. Your spirit is united with the Power but, though you may feel it, you are not invincible. Before you go there is one last thing . . . I have an elixir that will grant you life-memory. The potion will allow that when you reincarnate, one lifetime to another, you will have memory . . . an advantage the Emissaries will not have."

"Why would you not give it to all of us?" Helghul asked. Marcus had just been wondering the same thing and cringed that he had shared a thought with the monster.

"Because it gives one too much power. Power must be carefully protected . . . if it is shared, it ceases to exist."

"But why then, why did White Elder not give it to his Emissaries to empower them?"

"Her weakness and compassion—memory is a cruel burden she would not impart. She believes each lifetime must be a journey to enlightenment as intended, even for the chosen ones . . . even in the darkest times."

Marcus's hatred welled up in him, and he was enraged by the notion that Helghul would have the advantage of memory and he would not. *If there is a memory elixir, we should all have it. The Emissaries could do far more good, couldn't they? It would allow Theron and me to remember one another as well*, he thought. He must talk to White Elder and convince her.

The cloaked man handed a small bottle to Helghul, who dutifully took a sip and then tossed the container to the ground. The two men then quickly moved out of Marcus's sight. Would they come up where he was and find him? Had they taken another exit? Marcus waited, impatiently nauseated and distraught from everything he had witnessed. He was desperate to get to Theron and to inform White Elder of what he had seen and seek the memory potion, but he feared time was running out.

Once he was sure that the two men were gone, Marcus moved. Three of the five torches below were still burning, and though Marcus still trembled and loathed the idea of descending into the grotesque chamber below, he knew that he needed a light to get out of the cavern. He stealthily descended the stone steps and jumped the crevice with a shudder, remembering the Darkness he had seen and felt pouring from it. He approached the stained wall, intentionally keeping his eyes from the fragments at his feet. He knew he would be unable to function if he looked down or thought or remembered, and so he pushed the reality of the carnage he had witnessed from his mind and focused on speed and survival.

Marcus had to jump to dislodge a torch—it dropped on his third attempt, landing with a thud as he leapt sideways so he wouldn't get burned. He bent to retrieve the light and saw a silver flask discarded on the floor: the memory elixir. He retrieved the bottle and saw that it was not empty. There was a trace still in the bottom, perhaps enough for one.

Stop! his mind warned. Marcus felt a rumble below him, not just thunder, this time a tremor. All around him the ground shook, and he covered his head as dust and rubble fell from the ceiling. *Time, time!* There was no time. He knew he had to choose.

This elixir is a gift, he told himself. *Maybe this is why I am here. I can't forget what Helghul has become. I can't forget her*, he thought, as he put the vial to his lips and drained it. Marcus had chosen to become an Emissary with Theron, but now he had chosen to do it on his own terms.

The potion tasted of eucalyptus and mint and something bitter that he couldn't place. Marcus stared at his hands, expecting them to change visibly before his eyes. The potion bound itself to every molecule and fiber of his spirit, stripping the insulation and respite his spirit might have known and replacing it with knowledge. Like Helghul, Marcus had chosen a path of full memory, and he would struggle many lifetimes with the consequences of that choice.

Again the ground rumbled and quaked, and Marcus tossed the bottle and got out of the cavern as quickly as possible. When he finally emerged from the deep recesses of the mountain, nauseated and terrified, the weather had deteriorated. The sky was dark and foreboding, and a stinging rain pinched his exposed skin. Marcus flew his glider erratically, unable to focus, and rushed to Theron's home. Theron opened the door expectantly at his first knock.

"Did you have the vision too?" she asked nervously. She quickly picked up her heavy cloak and pulled it over her head.

"What? No, Theron. We have to find your mother!" Marcus said, barely able to keep from breaking down at the sight of her; his senses had been pushed too far. Marcus dripped puddles all over her floor, but neither of them noticed. He couldn't bear to tell her what he had witnessed. He didn't want to burden her, and he didn't want to break down. He must tell White Elder.

"I had a vision of floods and fires, Marcus! We need to go to the boats right away! My mother will find us!" she commanded. Theron was across the room putting on her sandals. "Come on!" she urged impatiently, and Marcus had no will but to follow.

The tempest howled outside, loud and ominous.

"We have to find White Elder!" Marcus insisted as they ran through the hallways. She looked at him in confusion.

"Do you think this is easy for me . . . leaving her?" she asked. "It was a premonition, Marcus, we have no more time . . . hurry!" she said, reaching back to him. He took her hand and they ran together. Strange winds whistled through the building, and when they opened the outer doors, Theron was shocked. A gale howled, rocking the vast island with its fury. Hard pellets of hail and rain pitched against them. The pair raised their arms to eye level to shield their faces. Marcus knew why darkness had come so quickly.

"Hurry!" Marcus urged, suddenly desperate to get himself and Theron safely on a boat. All around them the noise was deafening. Great trees were whipped like blades of grass, and they heard the loud crack and snap of breaking wood. Things were getting worse by the minute. Marcus and Theron were soaked to the skin now. As they neared the wharf, Marcus wondered if the structure could survive the anger and chop of the surf that was pounding it. He wondered how they could possibly get away safely. It was then that Marcus saw them: a steady stream speckled against the stormy darkness. All around him were drenched, determined Emissaries making their individual treks to the boats.

"A premonition," he heard over and over as they neared one another. Marcus briefly wondered that he had not shared the vision, but knew that he hadn't needed it. He had witnessed the hideous reality, not some directive hallucination.

Ahead he could see Brown Elder and Red Elder frantically loading the boats, and he wondered where the other Elders were at that critical moment. Marcus was determined to tell White Elder what he had witnessed in the cavern before he embarked. Hunched against the towering tidal spray and burning wind, the horde of students jumped as a blinding flash tore open the angry sky and a lightning strike met the earth with a violent blow. Fire erupted instantly in a perfect line, separating the city and buildings from the beach and wharf. The ground began to shake, first gently like a mother soothing her child, but quickly becoming a violent rocking force.

A deafening thunderclap rolled, and calm rapidly became chaos as the citizens of Atitala panicked. A wall of fire rose magically, shielding the fleeing Emissaries from the frightened throng of Atitalans surging to join them at the water's edge.

"There is no fear in death. Remember, you are eternal," a familiar female voice rang out. "This is a time of transition and transcendence. Join as One," she continued, somehow audible above the violent wind and thunder. Marcus searched the landscape to find the source of the ministry and there, on the wrong side of the wall of fire, he saw White Elder.

The good leader was calling the faithful people of Atitala to her, soothing them and leading them in prayer. Marcus knew that he would never have a chance to inform White Elder of what he had witnessed, but he knew it didn't matter as he saw the buildings beginning to buckle and sway in the distance. The Earth's floor shifted and moaned as if a beast alive, and Marcus knew that it was.

White Elder stood calmly, hands and face lifted to the pouring sky, surrounded by a jumbled mass of men, women, and children. All of them meditating and praying, a steady beat and hum, glowing in the light of the massive fire that was unquenched by the torrential rains. Above them the Grid became visible, beautiful against the punishing sky.

Not all of The Atitalans chose to unite; some embraced their fear. The departing Emissaries were horrified to see many of their fellow citizens running desperately into the vicious fire, burning, screaming, unable to make it through and dying a most horrible death. They pushed, scratched, and screamed trying to overcome the storm, the tremors, and the fire and to make it to the loading boats. The Emissaries were helpless and distraught but continued purposefully to board the waiting vessels.

Marcus and Theron were getting close to the wharf when another voice cut through the roaring night.

"Help me!" it called. "Someone please help me!" Marcus heard the shouting. He and Theron were only a hundred yards from one of the launch points. Most of the massive reed boats had already departed. The ground continued to bend and shift; wind and rain beat down on the Emissaries. The waves crashed, pounding and rocking the boats.

"Help me please!" the voice called again. Marcus looked back just as Grey Elder, limping, broke through the tall grass. There were only moments left; he had to decide. Theron drove forward through the storm, and it was certain that she would meet their destination. They were only ten yards from the gangplank.

"Please, Marcus, help me!" Grey Elder called, limping faster toward the wharf. Theron trudged on, nearly there, and Marcus made up his mind. He let go of Theron's hand.

"I'll be right back, go on!" he said. She understood and lowered her head against the weather. He turned and sprinted back the hundred yards across the shaking ground to help the older man. He wrapped his arm under Grey Elder's own, and they turned back toward the boats. Theron stood on the bow of the ship, beaten by the rain, wind, and spray. She turned just in time to see them lift the gangplank, struggling in the brutal conditions to pull it in.

"No!" she shouted, running to stop them. "You have to wait, he's coming!" Her voice was lost in the storm and the reed boat was pulling away. Theron heard a voice, a powerful reminder within her that told her to remember her purpose, but her connection to Marcus was too overpowering and she was determined to stay with him. She instinctively sprinted to jump the three-foot gap over the water back to the wharf. She knew there was another boat; she and Marcus would take the last boat. Just as she leapt, a strong arm swung out to stop her. She was held from behind by the waist while she struggled.

"Let me go! I have to go back!" she shouted, but the grip was relentless and the gap between the wharf and the boat grew—five, twenty, a hundred yards—and a wave lifted and carried them beyond chance.

Marcus watched from the shore, running and fully carrying Grey Elder. The boat had pulled away and he had seen his Theron, first waiting and then running to come back to him. He had watched as she had collapsed, the boat too far to reach. Helghul held her snugly, not loosening his grip as she fell helplessly to her knees. From behind her he smiled triumphantly as Marcus charged the dock, releasing Grey Elder. Helghul watched his rival, who stood on the shore shouting, railing, arms outstretched uselessly reaching to sea, but his pain and anger were lost in the night.

Marcus watched as Theron's ship was tossed and carried farther away. He howled in anguish, and his heart exploded to pieces in his chest.

"I am so sorry, my son," Grey Elder said. Marcus couldn't hear him, couldn't see, and couldn't fathom anything but his blinding pain.

She's gone! I've lost her, he thought, unable to stem the tide of his grief. Grey Elder realized he must act quickly.

"This is the last boat, Marcus; you can find Theron when we reach our destination. We have to get on the boat, Marcus!" He continued to say his name and reassure him. "If she is on a ship you can find her when we land! Marcus, this is your only hope!" he bellowed. Grey Elder needed Marcus.

Robotically Marcus let himself be commanded, and he carried the Elder across the unstable wharf to the last remaining boat. They boarded just in time, and Marcus rushed to the deck, desperately searching the angry black horizon for Theron's vessel. His stomach was churning, and it was growing harder to breathe. Suddenly they rose atop a ten-yard wave and crashed hard against the breaking wharf. He saw another ship like his own in the distance. There on the deck he saw Theron. Another wave lifted them, and just before they fell from sight, Marcus made out Helghul next to her. Even through the dark storm he imagined the smug, gleeful smile on the man's face.

Marcus was out of his mind with grief and concern, but by necessity his thoughts were turned to survival. The ship was rocked by giant waves and slammed as if it would break apart. The winds had grown to hurricane force, and the immense land mass trembled and quaked violently. The ship needed to get away from the land or they would be broken against the rocks, and then he would never be able to protect Theron from Helghul.

The Earth's crust shifted and broke. Fire consumed the great city, and only a few Atitalans still wailed and searched for a way to escape. The smell of sulfur and burned hair and skin was carried on the wind. There were visible dead everywhere—charred and defeated by their attempts to flee, they lay like driftwood in haphazard heaps at the edge of the fire. Even now, Marcus could see the luminescent rainbow glow of the Unity Grid hovering above the land. He silently sent them blessings through his tears. The rain was lit by sparkling orbs above their heads. He could see the ethereal spheres moving and beckoning and knew that they belonged to a higher consciousness, but he had no time to consider them now.

The entire world was in chaos. Atitala creaked and groaned as it was battered and beaten. The land receded away from the last boat. A deafening crack exploded from beneath—displaced by extreme pressure, the ground arched and lifted out of the water on the farthest southern shores. Molten rock glowed red and spewed miles into the air in an awesome show of natural power. Atitala lurched as the Earth's crust shattered under the strain and the northern coast was rocketed hundreds of yards into the punishing black sky. The descent began. Atitala slipped south, first slowly, then at a terrifying speed, displacing millions of gallons of seawater. The Emissaries watched, dumbfounded and devastated, as their homeland crested and submerged before their eyes. The boats would carry the messengers to their destined shores, and they embraced the task before them. It was the dawn of a new Age.

CHAPTER 6

LOVE LOST

After thirteen days Marcus's ship found land. The Emissaries had been cast like seeds to the wind and, like Marcus, each would land where they were meant to be sown.

After the first seventy-two hours of violent waves and storms, the seas had become friendlier. The conditions on the ship had been tolerable. The Emissaries had meditated, mourned, and discussed what might lie ahead. Marcus had isolated himself, alone with his worry of finding Theron.

The thrill of seeing land in the distance was replaced by horror as they drew closer to shore. In the shallows, the debris became thicker: reed boats, bits of shelters, trees, and bodies, so many bodies. They were huge and bloated, greeting them with hollow stares. The arriving Emissaries were deeply disturbed by the hideous scene.

A former ally of Atitala, Stone-at-Center had been a most sacred site, an example of beauty and function. But now the land was hard to comprehend. Everything was crushed and glistened with water and seaweed. Dead or dying fish, urchins, and all types of sea animals littered the ground. The homes were gone. The floods and earthquakes had wiped out millions of people, even some races and species entirely. Only a small number of people had survived. The only remaining structures were the enormous dock (built from precisely honed slabs, one as large as one hundred forty-four tons) and the walls (cut in intricately connected H-shaped blocks).

As the Emissaries of Atitala arrived, the cleanup and cremation of the decaying bodies and carcasses began. The Emissaries were in a state of constant prayer, and the ground and air around them vibrated with the healing energy.

Marcus frantically disembarked, ignoring the chaos, the sadness, and the stench. He searched the arriving boats and questioned everyone he met. No one had seen Theron.

"Marcus, I need you here," Grey Elder beckoned from a nearby heap of rubble that had likely once been a temple or school. There were injured and helpless survivors everywhere.

"I still can't find Theron, have you heard anything?" Marcus asked, visibly upset. She was gone, his love, his soulmate. Helghul was with her and she didn't know what he was. Marcus hadn't warned her, and now he had no idea where she was or how to find her.

"There is much to do in rebuilding this sacred land. We need to work together," Grey Elder reminded, taking a few faltering steps. As he limped, Marcus was reminded that it was the Elder who had unintentionally separated him from Theron by calling for help. The young man struggled silently with his resentment.

"I need to find Theron," Marcus said predictably. "I need to know she is safe."

"The Emissaries will all arrive safely if it is meant to be so. You must accept your role here and leave her to hers," Grey Elder said sympathetically.

"I need to find her. Helghul was with her. He is something less than a man, Grey Elder. I should have told you sooner . . . I just couldn't speak of it," Marcus said cryptically.

"What is it you should you have told me?"

"The night of the exodus, there was no time to tell anyone. I followed Helghul into the caverns . . . I saw a ceremony. Helghul was possessed by something powerfully evil that came up through the ground," Marcus explained desperately.

"Did you see anything else? Who else was there?" Grey Elder asked in horror.

"There were other students and a cloaked man . . . that's all I saw . . . no . . . there's more. They killed the babies, Elder, the missing babies. They smashed them like pottery against the walls," Marcus divulged hoarsely. He resisted the overwhelming urge to sob and leaned against the rock ledge behind him for support. Grey Elder reached out to comfort him, but Marcus moved away, certain that the slightest show of tenderness would undo him. Grey Elder understood and kept his distance.

"Did you tell Theron? Does she know what Helghul has done?" Grey Elder asked.

"No," he croaked miserably. "There was no time."

"It is better that we know. You shouldn't have been there, Marcus, but there must be a reason that you witnessed the ceremony . . . there must be a reason you chose to follow Helghul. We will have to wait and see how this all plays out," Grey Elder added.

"There was a memory potion that Helghul took," Marcus said, trailing off. "I took it too, but I don't know if there was enough; it was almost empty."

Grey Elder looked at Marcus in horror.

"This is a very bad thing, Marcus; it goes against the will of the Source to have memory in future lives," Grey Elder warned, closely re-evaluating the young Emissary.

"I am happy with my choice," Marcus responded defensively, regretting having witnessed the brutality and darkness he had seen but grateful for the memory potion.

"I wish you peace, my friend. You have chosen a very difficult path," Grey Elder said at last, and Marcus knew that it was true.

CHAPTER 7

THE SEARCH BEGINS

There were grueling days and months of work at Stone-at-Center—rebuilding wells, clearing debris, and tending to the bodies. Once the most pressing obligations were dispelled, Marcus became a traveler and spent days, weeks, and then years hunting for Theron. As he searched, he helped to reconstruct devastated villages in his path, but always he moved on at the first opportunity, determined to find his lost love.

Marcus never stayed in one place for long. He never failed to ask anyone he met if they had seen Theron. Had he known she was a continent away, across the great ocean in Khem (later called Egypt) with Helghul and Red Elder, he would surely have commandeered a boat.

His eyes grew poor and his knees gave him pain, and there were no proper healers to set him right, but still he walked and searched, sure that he would recognize her even in old age.

Marcus never found her. He always wondered if he might have just missed her—had she taken a left turn on a mountain pass when he had turned right?

Had he walked past a hut just as she lay down to rest? He never knew. Marcus found no peace and saw her around every corner, in every sinewy female figure and russet mop of hair. He heard her in every twinkling laugh. He would wake in the night, the feel of her hand in his, the smell of her skin, the image of her next to the blue cenote waters so clear and vivid in his mind, and then the lucid dreams would dissipate, like smoke to the heavens. He could only be with her in his dreams.

Marcus knew that when he died he would be reborn into another shell, a new body, another lifetime. He prayed that in his next life, he would meet his love again and recognize her by her distinct karmic code: her glowing aura.

Marcus died many years later at the age of ninety-one, young for an Atitalan. But that world was gone, and the days of great longevity were gone with it. Marcus was remembered and celebrated by the people he had served, who had grown to care for him, in a small village in the northern hemisphere. He had never coupled with another. He had traveled north from Stone-at-Center over two continents to find Theron, and he had died alone when his weak body would allow him to search no more.

CHAPTER 8

THE BURDEN OF MEMORY

Atitala was long gone, cracked from its seat of strength by violent earthquakes, floods, and fires. The tropical paradise had been submerged and now rested miles under the sea. The Earth, her terrain, and her people had been remade, and no continent had gone untouched.

The Emissaries had now reincarnated countless times. The wisdom and technological advancement of the Golden Age was lost and forgotten, as generations died and were reborn without memory and as consciousness further descended. The evidence of former glory was buried and drowned. Many of the people had been reduced to living in caves, but they had made advancements over thousands of years and were rebuilding more sophisticated civilizations.

Marcus had guided them as best he could, but he alone remembered the way it had been in Atitala. Though he shared his knowledge, without tools, proof, or understanding it was useless. It was like handing an infant a hammer. Even he did not now have the abilities he had once mastered. There was no telepathy, and he could not conjure a Unity Grid—the greater consciousness did not allow it. Only over time could people rebuild and ascend to the level of understanding and former glory they had once known.

In each lifetime Marcus's memories came back in pieces and, with them, feelings of loss. Childhood was a gift, free of past-life memory, but his adolescent years were complicated and painful. By adulthood he regained vague memories, not only of Atitala, but of every lifetime since. He recalled people, places, and grief, and he was haunted by the coming and going of Theron in his lives.

Marcus read the karmic codes of those around him and easily recognized the Emissaries, who radiated in broad purple and violet bands regardless of their current bodies. They never knew him, not as Marcus or a fellow Emissary, but they were drawn to him nonetheless.

In some lives, his memories—his true Marcus-brain—came back to him in tiny threads. As his consciousness grew, the tendrils wove a clear tapestry of who he was and all of the people he had been. However, in other incarnations, the memories would flood back like waves during times of stress, and the confusion and gravity of it all would make him question his own sanity.

Lifetime after lifetime Marcus endured death: losing the people he had come to love, remembering and missing them over and over again. Some he would see in future lives, a soul group with whom he had a significant connection, but he missed no one as he missed Theron. There were lifetimes in which he failed to find her, where their destinies did not converge or they perhaps missed one other by hours, minutes, or seconds.

When they did come together in a lifetime, it seemed to Marcus that they were like actors in the theater. They were playing different roles, but always there was something strong and undeniable that pulled them together. Though she never knew him, never knew her true self, she was always Theron deep down. He knew her colors—her karmic code, which was as distinct as DNA—and seeing and feeling her filled him to his core. She felt him too, and when they were apart neither was whole, though only he was tortured by it.

Try as he would, Marcus was at the mercy of fate. Who and when he would be born was beyond his control. He could only be, and seek to fulfill his role and learn his lessons in each lifetime. As Marcus continued as an Emissary, the loneliness and futility that he often felt wore him down. Still, Marcus's innate goodness and light, coupled with his memories of Theron, helped him to persevere. He had no other option. He sought Theron's energy, lifetime after lifetime, only to discover the many forms their love would take and how many more ways he would learn to love.

CHAPTER 9

MOTHER LOVE

823 BC, Stone-at-Center

Stone-at-Center was a most sacred site, a spiritual hub shrouded in ancient lore. Its energy was palpable, and the faithful from lands near and far made pilgrimages to its walls, its soil, and to pray in its temples. It was rumored that a visit there could cure the ill, soothe those in pain, and bring them closer to their gods. Because of its religious significance and central location, the city was a key market and trading route. The area boasted an ancient pyramid and a monumental interlocking wall of precisely cut and laid stones, thought to have always been there. Curiously there were many oceanic fossils unearthed, though the sea was many miles away. A stone boat, an example left to tell a story to future generations, lay mostly unnoticed. A greater power seemed to protect the sacred ground and preserve its ancient heritage.

The prosperity and importance of the community made it a target of ambitious neighbors. Many times the great walled city had been attacked, and many times it had been successfully defended. It was built on miles of lush green plains.

Traders and pilgrims approached from all sides, using the well-traveled, ancient roads to guide them. From the walls of the city visitors were easily observed, and well-trained sentries thwarted invading armies.

For a thousand years a noble family, believed by the populace to be chosen by the gods, ruled the sacred land, until one particularly cruel and cunning invader laid siege and fouled the succession.

Marcus looked out on the vista as a dark procession neared. This was another lifetime, and many had passed. He had been many people and had lived many places since the first time he and the other Emissaries had landed in Stone-at-Center. He had been born and died as male and female and understood that the shell housing his soul was irrelevant. The spirit was eternal.

Marcus was accustomed to his current woman's body. Looking down and seeing his hands so thin and delicate, so much like Theron's hands, they sparked him to remember.

His life as Sartaña, the high priestess of Stone-at-Center, had been rewarding. He was a spiritual leader and healer, and though he had not met Theron in this incarnation, he had experienced the miracle of carrying and birthing a child. He felt the love and concern of a mother for her offspring and was grateful for it.

Sartaña did not remember everything. Whether it was because Marcus had only sipped the remnants of a discarded memory potion, or because that was the nature of the elixir, she did not know. Her past lives were like hazy dream recollections, bits and pieces of pictures torn up and tossed to the wind, which she painstakingly tried to reassemble with the unpredictable assistance of her Marcus-brain.

The land she looked upon had changed considerably. The ocean that had, centuries before, carried Marcus to these same shores had subsided and was now miles away. The lush huarango treeline had receded as the population and consumption had increased, and the soil had become dry and dusty.

Sartaña prepared herself, waiting in dread, knowing that her warriors had been defeated. She watched from the higher ground of the palace as the people rushed between dwellings. The elderly left their outdoor perches for the safety of their huts. Fires were left to burn out. The women rushed about urging their children and animals indoors, concealed from the conquering army. There were no middle-aged men; only the very old and young remained. Everyone else had been called to the city's defense.

Word had come ten minutes earlier, by way of a frantic messenger, that the resistance had been crushed and a vicious conqueror was on his way. Sartaña could see the progression approaching from her window. She ignored her muddled Marcus-brain to concentrate on the task ahead. She must prepare her people, especially her son Amaru, for whatever would come.

Sartaña turned from her chamber window. She was dressed in traditional regal robes of finely woven cloth dyed deep pink. The hem of her long cape told the story of her people and had been stitched intricately with gold thread, symbols, and designs. Servants helped place a fine gold and feather headdress on her dark hair, which by its very weight and nature made her appear majestic and proud.

As she reached the door, her son was brought to her. Amaru was ten years old and small for his age. His dark eyes telegraphed his fear as he ran to his mother's waiting embrace. She bent to greet to him, eye to eye, skillfully keeping her heavy headdress in balance.

"My son, I know you have heard the news," she said, embracing him tightly. She felt his fear and confusion and drank in the smell of the dust in his hair and the fresh air on his skin.

"No one will tell me anything!" he complained. "What's happened? Is it Father?" Amaru asked anxiously. He absentmindedly traced the flower-shaped scar that was branded into Sartaña's upper arm, as he had often done as a toddler. Sartaña remembered how he used to run his tiny fingers over the raised white skin and ask her repeatedly if it hurt. He loved the story of her coming of age ceremony, when she had been honored with the symbol of the seed of life, which resembled a flower with six petals surrounded by a circle.

"I've had no word, but it cannot be good," she said, faltering as her son responded to the news, stifling his tearful outburst.

"Is he dead?"

"I fear it must be so, we are certainly conquered," Sartaña said seriously. "I need you to be strong. I must welcome our new leader and pray that there is no more bloodshed." The priestess lifted her son's tear-streaked face to her own, longing to ease the alarm and sorrow in his dark eyes. She used the edge of her precious robe and wiped his cheeks and nose dry.

"What will happen to us now?" the boy asked, conscious of behaving bravely and honorably.

"Amaru, this is a dangerous time. If we are to survive, we must submit to our conquerors. The citizens must accept this new order." Her face was lined with concern and desperation. She had no time to feel anguish for her loss. Her only concern was to save her son and protect her people.

"Will they kill us?" he asked intelligently, his stomach turning and contracting involuntarily.

"I do not know. We must be brave and cautious if we wish to survive. Our adversary must not see you as a threat. It is not safe to leave now, all the gates are breached, but I am going to send you away. You will live in a nearby village with the family of my servant, Malaya. You must not return here. You must not tell anyone who you are. They will protect you and say you are the son of a farmer, an orphan. She will take you now and hide you in the city until it is safe to leave. You understand?" Sartaña demanded, holding his shoulders and searching his face for comprehension.

Amaru understood completely. His father, the high priest and leader of these vast lands, had schooled him since the age of five. He had been taught the ways of his people—farming, politics, spirituality, and defense. Amaru knew that as an heir to the throne he would be eliminated by the conquering leader.

Sartaña's servant, Malaya, entered and gave the boy a bundle of worn clothing and sandals more suited to a peasant child. She handed the high priestess a small bowl. Sartaña dipped her fingers into the bowl and, while saying a prayer aloud, used the soil within to camouflage the cheeks and arms of her son. It served as both a blessing and a disguise. "You must change and go now, with

Malaya. I will see you again someday. Do not seek me out. I will come for you. I will send word when I can. Promise me, Amaru. Try to blend in. Do not bring trouble down upon these good people who help us."

"I promise, but when will I see you? How long?" he asked, his youth and vulnerability plain. Amaru realized that he was leaving all that he knew and that he might never see his mother again. He began to cry, and fresh tears streaked the dirt and grime meant to help him appear more common.

"I don't know. To know that you are safe is all I ask. Now go and do not be seen! We can no longer be sure who to trust," she warned Malaya as well as her son. "You must hurry, time is short. Know that I love you and carry you with me always," she said, touching her hand to her heart. Sartaña hid her own misery so that she would not upset him further. Amaru's tears fell in dark water stains onto her dress, despite his wish to be brave and suppress them.

Marcus ached to be saying goodbye. The love that he felt, this mother love, was like nothing he had ever experienced. The reality of having the most precious and vulnerable part of himself walking outside his body was overwhelming. It compared to the love he still felt for Theron but, in this lifetime, overshadowed it. The child was a miracle from Sartaña's own body, from her very flesh, and a child brings a helplessness and dependence that a lover does not. Theron was like fleeting smoke, but Amaru was present, real, and in jeopardy.

Marcus's losses were now so many. For each one in this lifetime there were a hundred more already survived, remembered, that were a burden casting their shadow on his heart. War was nothing new, and death and loss were a part of every life.

Amaru was courageously shuttled away by Malaya, and Sartaña left her chamber and moved out into the palace courtyard flanked by her personal servants and guards. She struggled to quiet the nervous tremors that shook her hands and legs, and she was glad that she had not eaten anything, certain that she would vomit if she had. She was conscious that she must appear calm and composed to reassure her people and to face whatever might come.

Sartaña walked directly to the two beautifully carved, massive stone thrones that rested in the center of the courtyard at the top of a stairway. Behind her an ancient arched gateway to the sun framed the scene and added to the spectacle of her beauty and courage. She took her seat and was painfully aware that the empty chair next to her would never again be rightly filled. Her grief assaulted her once again and mingled with the knowledge that she would very likely meet a cruel fate herself very soon. She continued to pray silently for Amaru, desperate that he should escape the wrath of the coming conqueror.

Sartaña waited. There was nothing else she could do. The sun moved overhead, warming her and causing beads of sweat to rise on her brow beneath the heavy diadem and prickle her spine. Finally a distant rumble grew to a roar as the conquering multitude passed the unprotected gates into the sacred city. Warrior after warrior marched, talked, laughed, and cheered as they followed their exultant leader to the central courtyard—a seemingly endless trail shrouded in a cloud of dust. The stench of sweat and blood filled the streets; the air was thick with their unfamiliar odor.

The citizens huddled in their huts, shaking with grief and fear. Some peeked curiously at the awful procession, instantly confused and terrified by the spectacle of spears and blood-soaked posts with the severed heads of their men stacked three and four high. Fathers, grandfathers, and friends all reduced to body parts and trophies and paraded ghoulishly through the familiar lanes.

The leader, Katari, climbed the stone steps unchecked, flanked by his personal guards. In his hand, dangling from his spear, he raised the severed head of their blessed high priest: conquered, staring in frozen shock, and still wet with fresh blood. Sartaña stared in horror at her mate's head swinging and bouncing with each step. His kind lips and laughing eyes were distorted and ruined. The grotesque object looked surreal, and her brain could hardly comprehend it. Katari ignored the dry blood on his skin; his thick flat forehead and wide nose were in direct contrast to the fine features of his victim.

The war was lost and the rewards were yet to be claimed by the victors. Sartaña, sitting erect and proud, concealed the fear bubbling up inside of her as she clutched the cold stone arms of her throne, her knuckles white and tense.

I have seen this before, she thought inwardly, staring at her captor. *I've seen him before!* An icy hatred filled her as the sinister Katari approached. His face became familiar somehow. Suddenly Sartaña was filled with overwhelming panic as her Marcus-brain recognized the karmic code through the grime, the paint, and the blood; saw the red, cruel energy emanating in all directions and leeching into the very ground at Katari's feet. His dark life force had been visible to her from a great distance but had been splintered in many directions. Now he was near enough and focused on her so that she recognized him completely. Her unconscious intuition screamed at her in alarm, and she acknowledged the pure hatred in his eyes.

Helghul, her mind bawled over and over. But she didn't know what it meant. She didn't have full recall. She searched her memories, panicking to understand. Her Marcus-brain was scorched by the sight and feel of him.

The conquering foreigner stopped in front of Sartaña, and he and the priestess met face to face for the first time. Not trusting her legs to hold her, she remained rooted to her seat as she wondered: *What will he do? Will he murder me here?* Endless gruesome scenarios played over in her head in the mere seconds it took for him to speak. He bent forward, his face only inches from hers. She felt the heat of his foul breath on her skin.

"You do not rise to greet your new king . . . Marcus?" Katari hissed in a low growl audible only to her. Sartaña was startled by the use of her spirit-name, and her mind was reeling. Her ancient Marcus-consciousness spoke to her then, more loudly than before.

Helghul, she heard again in her head. Katari's was the first face, the first eyes in which that karmic energy had been recognized, stronger and more evil than ever. Marcus surmised that Helghul had also learned a great deal since the days in Atitala.

"Helghul," Sartaña unwisely uttered, with far more strength and defiance than she felt. Her response unwittingly informed Katari that Sartaña also had memory. The warrior was startled by the unexpected recognition. He regrouped quickly and masked his concern with a scowl, displaying his jagged, filthy teeth.

He stepped back and reached his gruesome spear forward, dangling the monstrous head next to her face, taunting her. Sartaña closed her eyes and shuddered involuntarily.

Katari, laughing, turned to address his warriors and the villagers, who had begun meekly emerging to witness the inevitable transition of power. He raised his hands high in the air, still holding his spear, and effortlessly summoned silence. He walked to a nearby stone, only slightly shorter and wider than he. It had a thick, perfectly honed hole all the way through, into which he spoke. His voice was amplified to every corner.

"Hear me citizens . . . you see your master is my plaything, your warriors are no more. I, Katari, claim this land, these people, and all within its bounds. My warriors will garner the spoils of war and choose homes and wives among you. There need be no more bloodshed. Your daughters may stay and the elders, but your sons will fend for themselves. No warrior here will raise the boy of another man, only to have him slit his throat in his sleep some day. Women, do not think that you will take your children and run, it will not be permitted. Those who attempt to leave or to resist will die a cruel and painful death as others have before them. Any male child within the city walls by sundown will be executed," he commanded.

"Priestess, you may address your people. Choose your words wisely," Katari said, turning to her. She understood and proudly rose to speak to her people, most of whom had now come out of their dwellings and were in a state of extreme distress.

Sartaña moved in front of the speaking stone. "My people, good citizens, the battle is over and we have come to this wretched end. It is time now to save your children, to save our city, and to accept our fate. Our guardians have been defeated. Let the violence end today. Bundle your sons; put them in the care of the capable older boys. We will pray that the Great Spirit protect them and carry them to the bosom of a sympathetic neighbor," she called out, strong and steady in her urgings and seething silent hatred in her belly.

Suddenly a quick movement to her left drew her eye, and in an instant her calm dissolved. "Amaru, NO!" she cried, lunging too late.

In seconds the ten-year-old boy was cut down by an assault of spears from Katari's guard. The macabre head of his father, still in the murderer's grasp, jiggled and jerked in protest of the death of his would-be avenger and only son.

Sartaña screamed and ran to her child where he had fallen, three spears perpendicular to his crumpled body, cutting deep into his young flesh. Her headdress of yellow and purple feathers clattered noisily to the ground behind her, its fine gold bent and ruined. Thick, bloody strands of her hair were torn out by the weight of it and lay in the twisted mess.

"Amaru! NO!" she cried, crawling under his bleeding frame and pulling him into her lap as though she were cradling a newborn.

The boy was unable to speak or to focus, his eyes were wild with fear, and high-pitched squeals of agony escaped him. A small sword, not even a man-sized weapon, fell useless from his prepubescent hand to the dirt beside them. He writhed and twisted, pulling his right leg up to his belly; his left leg, obviously ignoring commands from his brain, remained limp and bent awkwardly in the dust. The wooden pillars protruding from his soft, young flesh swung and jerked as he moved, hitting against his mother as she frantically placed one hand to his cheek, trying to ease his suffering. Her other hand was pressed across his body to steady him against her and stop the flesh of his wounds being torn further by the protruding rods.

Moaning, tears poured from her. Her Marcus-brain was reeling and had no voice at all. In this dire moment there was no higher brain, no time for enlightened thinking; there was only survival and instinct. There was only the love of a mother and her child, a love-bond superior to and stronger than all others.

Suddenly his writhing and howls ceased. Amaru went limp in her arms, his young eyes staring, frozen in surprise, as his spirit was released. She fell, useless against her grief, and collapsed in anguish. In that moment she longed to die. Life was too cruel, too sad, and not worth living at all; first her mate and now her son. In the time it had taken the sun to cross the sky, her world had completely unraveled.

Sartaña prayed to join her son in death and was too overwhelmed to entertain the anger that tried to take hold of her. Her Marcus-voice broke through, reminding her that Amaru's soul was safe and well, and that her people needed her guidance, but she couldn't listen. The greatest part of her lay murdered in the dirt. Her pain was blinding and unbearable. Mercilessly, Katari bent behind her and whispered in her ear.

"The fool merely saved me the effort of the hunt."

Without a second thought, a howling Sartaña raked her fingernails across the stubbly cheek unwisely close to hers. Katari jumped back, clubbing Sartaña in the face with the blunt end of his spear. The blow jolted her and sent blinding white sparks to the pain center of her brain. She splayed on her side, unconscious beneath the corpse of her boy. At least for the time being there was peace and respite from her pain.

Katari ordered them removed, wiping his stinging, bloody cheek with the back of his hand, his Helghul-brain fuming at her impudence. His hatred for Marcus was further ignited and burned profoundly. At that moment he began formulating his plan for how to best use his fellow Atitalan to his utmost benefit.

Helghul wondered about this reunion. What cosmic intervention and meaning did it have for him? What purpose did it serve? He was pleased but not surprised to have discovered Marcus in that place of spiritual importance—it was certain to be inhabited by an Emissary. The men, however, had not crossed paths since the night of the exodus, though he had often hoped they would. His last memory of Marcus was gleefully watching him ashore, whipped by the violent storm, frantically running and calling to Theron. He could still feel the triumph he had experienced as she had struggled against him and was prevented from joining her unworthy lover.

Helghul had met many other Emissaries in past lives, and he had recognized and manipulated them easily. He worked ruthlessly toward his own purpose: to further the Darkness and add doubt and fear to the world of man. To create chaos, to rule, and to dominate, dividing the people from one another and crushing the hopeful, positive energy of his fellow Atitalans.

Marcus having memory and recognizing him had been a surprise. Who would have given Marcus the memory potion? Certainly not White Elder. It was an act of defiance unexpected of an Emissary. The new revelation changed things for Helghul and made Marcus a more formidable enemy than the other Atitalans. Marcus could be a danger to him with his past-life memory and understanding. He must be carefully dealt with.

Katari had contemplated murdering the priestess and eliminating Marcus. But understanding the reincarnation process as he did, and knowing that Marcus could be reborn only to face him again and possibly have the upper hand in the next scenario, he decided instead to keep his foe captive and under his control.

Stone-at-Center entered an age of tyranny and servitude such as it had never known. Katari immediately settled into the palace. The rotting, severed head of the high priest was still attached to the new leader's spear, which leaned carelessly disregarded in the corner of the very room where the deceased had once lived and loved in life. It was soon to be baked, smoked, and shrunken, eventually to be worn as a trophy on Katari's grisly belt.

Katari's brutal warriors had performed as commanded and now rested, rewarded with their new shelters and women. Murdering the high priest's heir publicly in such a ruthless manner had ensured the maximum co-operation of the citizens and eliminated Amaru as a future threat. Fear was a powerful tool and one that Katari encouraged and used readily, along with material reward of course.

The male children had been expelled to fend for themselves with little more than a water flask to sustain them. Even the very youngest infants were ordered out and were swaddled and tied to the backs of the older children. Terrified and confused, the parade of young boys, many crying and begging their mothers to allow them to stay, was marched away at the point of a spear. Toddlers wailed and screeched, dragged by the older boys, whose parents had warned them in no uncertain terms what would happen if they disobeyed.

"I'll be good, Mama."

"Please, Mama," so many little voices rang out. "Let me stay."

"Why can't you come?" the voices wailed, but on and on they moved, bewildered and lost before they were even outside the walls.

More than one young mother was unable to bear the parting and chose to take her own life and that of her children rather than sending them to the certain death outside the gates. Their huts were emptied and they were buried without ceremony, without prayer, and without respect.

Women continued to disappear in the weeks following the expulsion of the boys, unable to live with what they had done, searching for their lost children. Most of them were dragged back to the city in varying states of hopelessness, hysteria, and injury without their children in tow. They were punished publicly as an example to deter others.

A dark, heavy pall blanketed the region. The devastated citizens sadly accepted their new high priest and self-pronounced king and were as helplessly divided as the spoils of war.

Despite his disdain for Marcus, Katari was a wise and strategic leader who clearly understood Sartaña's influence. She was born of a highly revered family and was believed to have been ordained by the gods. The people were devout, and Katari intended to use her influence to control them. As he plotted, his plans for Sartaña reached beyond her role as the high priestess.

Two days after the death of her son, Katari sent an order for Sartaña to appear before him. He reclined nonchalantly, cracking a peanut and popping its meat into his mouth. The shell fell to the floor, adding to the heap already there. His breastplate and thin beard were littered with crumbs and casings, and he breathed loudly as he chewed. The ruler looked up from his food as Sartaña entered the large chamber, formerly her husband's private room. She still wore the blood-stained dress she had been wearing days before and was held on either side by a guard. Her hands were bound tightly in front of her, and a large bruise had swelled on her cheek where the butt of Katari's spear had struck her. Though her eyes were puffy from crying, there was no sign of tears as she stared hatefully at her captor.

As she entered, an unpleasant odor of rot mingled with body odor and smoke assaulted her immediately, and she wrinkled her nose in disgust. It was so unlike the scent of copal incense that used to draw her in. It was the first time she had been there since the invasion, and it pained her to see this pig of a man lounging so disrespectfully and familiarly in her mate's space. She noticed the head so casually overlooked: rotting, stinking. She forced herself to look away. She was determined not to cry in front of him, but for a moment a wave of nausea twisted her belly, constricting her throat, causing her mouth to water.

She turned her gaze toward the opposite side of the room where the bedroll lay, soft and inviting, a place where she had found so much pleasure and tenderness in times past.

Katari studied her as she adjusted to the scene. Even in her grief Sartaña was striking to look at. Her nose was prominent, and her mouth was full and sensuous. Her thick, luxurious hair hung to her narrow waist in loose dark curls, concealing the missing patches that the headdress had torn from her scalp. Katari let her wait while he dropped more discarded shells and chewed noisily.

Sartaña studied him, trying to reconcile the memories of Helghul that had been flashing back to her constantly over the past two days. Clearly there was something Marcus wanted to convey to her. Helghul's dark, prickly aura was obvious, and he revolted and offended her in every way—even without warning from her higher self. He had murdered her husband and her son and conquered her city; it was obvious he was a beast. Why had they been brought together?

Katari's energy raised the hairs on the back of her neck and arms, and she shuddered involuntarily. He felt her hatred and enjoyed it. He stood and walked around her, looking her up and down lasciviously. He stopped directly in front of her and finally spoke.

"Nice breasts, Marcus," he taunted, reaching out and roughly grabbing her through her blood-encrusted dress. Bits of nut flew out of his mouth as he spoke, and Sartaña stepped away from him, unable to use her hands. She had dreaded this.

Katari made eye contact with her for the first time, and a sharp pain shot through her skull to a bulging gland throbbing behind her eyes. The discomfort was hers alone and he smirked at her, seemingly unaffected. He grabbed the hair at the nape of her neck and wrenched her head back as he spoke menacingly into her ear. "I intend to take you as a wife. I want a child, a son to unite the people." Sartaña winced painfully at the word *son*.

"You disgust me! I will die before I let you touch me!" she snarled through clenched teeth, hoping to provoke him, hoping he would end her misery on the spot. Sartaña looked strong and defiant, her jaw jerked forward and her eyes on fire. But the truth of it was that she was tired, exhausted and beaten by the death of her mate and son and her inability to help her people. She had entirely lost the will to live.

"You are weak, as you always were! A cruel, unloved dark soul!" she goaded. Katari slapped her hard—once, twice, blow after blow. She was stunned, but she would not be silenced. She fell to the floor but her diatribe continued. "You are a pawn, used by darker souls like a fool," she continued, Marcus urging her on, sure if she continued that Helghul would murder her, releasing her tired soul to the Universe.

Sartaña begged for death with her venomous attack. Enraged by her relentless curses, Katari wanted to silence her but refused to strike a fatal blow. He was determined she would bear his child; he would own her, control her.

"You will die when I decide," Katari shouted. He nodded to the guards and they released her and took a step back. "I like to know exactly where your spirit resides, it eliminates any chance of surprises." Marcus understood that Helghul saw him as a threat. "It is my plan that you will bear me a son. He will be a king accepted by the people, and he will be wise and powerful, unlike your foolish first-born, who I happily destroyed."

Sartaña threw herself on him, her bound hands working together feebly to strike blows. Katari easily pushed her off and she slammed to the floor, unable to break her fall.

The guards hauled her up painfully, and she cried out against their grip and against Katari, spewing more hatred at him. He approached her now, the guards easily constricting her struggling frame.

"Oh, the hopelessness, the despair!" Katari gloated, holding her chin tightly in his coarse hand, his foul breath only inches from her nose. Then dropping his voice he added, "I feel your despair, Sartaña. You reek of it! I taste it and it arouses me. Have you considered it . . . killing yourself?"

"Never!" she said defiantly. Marcus knew that suicide was not an option. It brought disharmony in the afterlife, and he would never find Theron if he was stuck in limbo, his energy trapped and suffering in the world between.

"You'll wish for death," Katari warned, and in one motion he grabbed the collar of her dress and tore it clean down the front, exposing her breasts. The guards were fiendishly excited by the show and held her more cruelly, twisting her arms over her head. Katari directed the guards to turn her around, not wanting to look into her eyes. He lowered his trousers to his thighs and lifted the shredded garment still covering her. Excited by his power over her, he then entered her violently from behind, tearing her tender, fragile skin. Katari pushed her away when he was through, and she was taken back to her guarded room on the far side of the palace.

Sartaña had screamed and struggled that first time Katari had forced himself on her, but she quickly realized that the fight thrilled him. Regardless how much she resisted, he would injure but not kill her, though she wished he would. In the weeks and months that followed, Katari came to the small, plain chamber where she was imprisoned many times. She chose to lay limp and lifeless, though he struck her and goaded her mercilessly to try to elicit a response from her. He bombarded her with cruel comments about her dead son and husband, but she refused to rise to the bait. Her courage and self-control enraged him, and he was often unable to maintain an erection.

No matter what she did, he beat her, but through all of it Sartaña was comforted by her Marcus-brain. Her inner spirit offered some strength, aware that there must be a reason that she was still alive. There was a purpose and lesson to be learned in every lifetime, whether it was known or not.

Marcus spoke to her gently, soothing her, reminding her that Amaru's spirit was safe, and she could feel him still around her. She spent many hours alone praying, comforted by the soothing spirits that surrounded her in her meditations, dreams, and silence.

Sartaña's menses stopped by the second moon cycle of her captivity, and soon her belly became round. At first she was distraught, wondering if the child would be a demon like the father. Would she give birth to a dark soul sent only to cause pain in the world? Her concerns disappeared with the first movement of the fetus inside her. A baby was a miracle, and Sartaña filled with the wonder of the soul inside her. Marcus was awed once again to know a mother's heart and feel the overwhelming love and selflessness.

Unhappy to give Katari what he most desired, but grateful to end the cycle of rape and abuse, Sartaña announced her pregnancy to the wretched king. Katari was satisfied and halted his cruel visits to Sartaña. He was determined that she have a healthy child, so she was brought food and fruit and wine to comfort her as the baby grew. Her cold straw mat was replaced with a soft bedroll, and though she was always guarded and isolated, she rested comfortably in her humble room.

The flow of pilgrims and traders to Stone-at-Center had slowed since news of the violent takeover had spread. As a result, the prosperity of the city had waned significantly. Katari realized he must re-establish the confidence of the surrounding lands if he wished his kingdom to return to its former prosperity and stature. He began to parade Sartaña in public as the high priestess, but he never spoke to her except for the occasional harsh remark. Sartaña complied willingly, more concerned for the child in her belly than for herself.

The pregnancy was difficult; the fetus was never at rest and rolled, turned, and kicked relentlessly. Her labor started without warning, and in less than two hours, with the help of a midwife, a slick, healthy baby boy slid painfully into the world. The child was easily soothed at his mother's breast. Sartaña held his tiny hands and stared into his face as he sucked and slept. He briefly opened his squinting eyes to the newness of the world, and she wept uncontrollably for the love of her new son paired with grief for the one murdered before him.

Inti was a happy infant and made it easy for them to bond. Sartaña held him and sang to him for hours. Mother and child spent every day together, and their special relationship grew exponentially as time passed. Yet Sartaña lived in constant fear that at any moment her son would be taken from her.

The city and surrounding areas, desperate for good news, rejoiced at the announcement of the birth, and a carefully calculated celebration of one hundred days ensued. Determined to restore prosperity to the region, Katari hosted extravagant feasts and celebrations. The downtrodden citizens were easily manipulated, and they warmed to their new high priest when he joyfully presented his new son and heir. Katari insisted that Sartaña sit at his side, smiling and nodding regally to the people. She was determined to make no more trouble for Katari. She wanted only to protect and teach their son as much as possible.

Within months of Inti's birth, Sartaña found herself wondering at the spirit that had been born to her. This child was so familiar, touched her so deeply, that she ached at the briefest parting. Sartaña kept Inti with her always; he was typically slung across her body in a fold of finely painted fabric. The boy never cried except when parted from his mother. He radiated light and goodness to everyone he met. Sometimes in the quiet moments of the day she would see visions of him as someone else—a woman, vibrant and shimmering, but always so dear to her, so familiar and good. Finally, her Marcus-brain recognized the violet karmic code of Theron.

Sartaña knew it was inevitable that Helghul would also recognize Theron's aura. It was an energy completely opposite to the darkness of his own. Most likely Katari had already recognized Theron's spirit, though he continued to show little interest in Inti, other than at public events. The busy leader generally left the pair alone, consumed by his role as the high priest and plotting further conquests to the north and east.

As Inti grew, he spent many hours in Sartaña's humble chamber playing, singing, and telling stories. Early in life he proved himself an extraordinary child. He began walking very young and showed a remarkable ability for language and reason. Sartaña educated him in mathematics, healing arts, the science of the stars, and spirituality. She recited for him her imprecise memorization of the Emerald Tablet and taught him the nature of the Universe and Oneness. The universal truth was clear to Marcus, like it was for the other Emissaries, though loneliness and isolation remained a confusing aspect of the human condition.

Often, while Sartaña was weaving, Inti would climb into her lap and take her face in his pudgy toddler hands, bringing his forehead to hers. He would sit there, remaining still, unlike children of his age, and she would feel Theron's energy flowing through him.

Four years had passed since Inti's birth, and Sartaña had been permitted to resume her work as a spiritual guide and healer to her people. She had cultivated a garden of useful plants and herbs at the southern tip of the palace walls, and she and Inti spent hours there together telling stories, laughing, and learning from one another.

One day Sartaña sat against the shaded stone wall taking a break from the heat. Inti leaned against her and they shared a pear as he traced the scarred ridges of the seed of life on Sartaña's upper arm, just as Amaru used to do.

"Does it hurt?" Inti asked, not for the first time. He was always fascinated by the symbol.

"No," she said, smiling. "It's an honor to display the symbol of eternal life and unity. It is the mark of how we are all connected. We are all One," she explained. It was an exchange they had had many times, but this time his four-year-old mind posed a new, more challenging question.

"Was Papa chosen by God?" he asked. Sartaña paused, unsure how to answer. Was Katari chosen by God? Helghul? For every positive there is a negative, for every yin, a yang. Her Marcus-brain contemplated the question, and Sartaña considered her answer carefully.

"Yes, Inti, Papa was chosen by God," she finally answered, kissing his rumpled black hair and pulling him close.

Theron's energy grew stronger and more obvious every day. Though it filled Sartaña with a complete love and connection that she adored, she worried that Katari would take him away, that Helghul would tear them apart once again.

Near the end of his fifth year, as Sartaña had feared and expected, Inti's father began to take a greater interest in him. Katari had recognized Theron just as Sartaña had, but the resentment that Helghul had once exhibited toward his unrequited love was not evident in his relationship with his son. Inti spent more time learning at his father's side, severely limiting his time with his mother.

Katari was fonder of the clever boy than he would admit and enjoyed him as a companion and a student. Inti wished to please his father, but he felt frightened and intimidated by him, and he missed Sartaña.

Inti's fifth birthday was approaching, which, according to local customs, signaled a formal transfer from the care of his mother into his father's hands for instruction. Sartaña had explained to Inti that he would be seeing her progressively less in the days and months to come. Her intuition warned her that Katari would separate them more than was typical, and she was preparing him for that eventuality.

"But I don't want to go with him. He scares me. Why can't I just stay here with you?" Inti asked one afternoon in the back garden. Sartaña was crouched on her haunches, carefully choosing from her plants and herbs the ingredients needed to soothe the toothache of a citizen. She showed Inti the plants that she was harvesting and indicated to him how the leaves could be wadded up and chewed to numb the pain.

"A boy needs his father. You will grow to be a man under his tutelage. He will teach you things I cannot," Sartaña answered, trying to be positive but secretly dismayed by what lessons and morals Katari would seek to instill in their son.

How would a spirit like Theron's fare under such a dark, self-serving mentor? Could she be bent, twisted, altered to his will? As these questions passed through her mind for the thousandth time, Sartaña had a vision of Inti—knife in hand, claiming his first head as a leader and warrior, Katari standing over him, directing and demanding. It was a picture not of the future but an image of what the father would wish to see, how he would school his son.

Sartaña stopped working and drew the youngster into her lap.

"Follow your instincts, child. Always do what you know to be right and the heavens will smile on you. You are special, Inti. You come from a long line of healers and priests. If you listen, your intuition, your spirit voice, will never lead you astray. Stay open and loving and trust your inner voice, and you will be loved, a gift to our people."

Katari growled to himself only five yards away. He had come looking for them to have Inti join him on a survey of the outer boundaries, and now he stood listening, obscured by a row of bushes. His ire was raised as he listened to Sartaña's sickening, sweet sermon. She was now more a threat than a tool; the high priestess had served her purpose. The time had come to eliminate her influence.

Katari walked away without revealing himself. Soon enough he would enact the second stage of his scheme, and Inti would be his alone to mold. Together they would be the most feared and prolific conquerors of all time.

CHAPTER 10

DIM TRACES OF LIGHT

Without warning, Sartaña's door burst open and Katari entered in swift strides. She was startled and jumped at the movement behind her. The guard, who had become familiar over the years, flashed a concerned glance as he closed the door. The sentinel had always been kind and had benefitted from Sartaña's compassion and expertise when his own children had fallen ill. He was a good-hearted man, a husband and father, and he liked her and Inti and had witnessed what a loving mother she was.

Sensing the gravity of the unexpected incursion, Sartaña lowered herself from her seat and bowed her head, kneeling.

"I see you seek to ingratiate yourself," Katari laughed, devoid of mirth and seething with contempt. He paced her quarters, his square frame puffed up, appearing twice his size, as if ready to do battle. The shrunken heads, her first husband's included, jiggled sickeningly on his belt like charms. "There is nothing you can do to change the path we are on, Marcus," he continued. "I have planned for this day." Sartaña stayed silent, waiting for Katari to explain. "Your role as mother is fulfilled; I will be taking full charge of Inti from now on."

Sartaña looked up and was swiftly staggered by the leather of his foot against her face. She was lifted off the floor, and her head slammed against the stone wall behind her. She cradled her skull in her hands. Her cheek was red and bruised where she'd been kicked. She hung her head, unable to stop her tears, and she dared not look at Katari again.

"You have served your purpose. Inti has bridged the gap between our people. I have re-established Stone-at-Center as a profitable hub of trade, and I have gained even more through exploiting the weak-minded flock that seeks spiritual enlightenment and answers here. I couldn't have managed this without your help," he scoffed.

"But now you are done . . . a ghost . . . dead. As of tomorrow the city will be informed of your accidental death . . . a budding pregnancy gone horribly wrong. With no woman to help you, you tried bravely to tend to yourself and you bled to death in the process. They will mourn for you having died with your unborn child. They will pity me. I will hang my head in mock grief. No one would suspect me now. I have arranged for a wrapped body to be mourned in your absence."

"My absence?" she interrupted "You will not kill me?"

"Kill you? No, I like to know exactly where my enemies are, Marcus. If I release your soul back to the Universe, there is no controlling when you show up again . . . I don't want any surprises from you. I like the idea of keeping you, like a head on my belt, under my control," he said.

"Inti . . ." she began.

"My son is no concern of yours. To him, as to everyone else, you are dead."

"It doesn't have to be like this," Sartaña pleaded from her knees.

"No it doesn't, but this is how I want it," Katari answered. "There is more to be done, you see. It is important that no one here ever suspect that you remain alive. Inti must never know."

Katari approached Sartaña menacingly and she reacted like a cornered animal, no longer subservient or compliant. The fury in every cell of her body radiated hatred, and her Marcus-brain regretted that she had not tried to eliminate Katari before now. She could have poisoned his wine, put a knife to his throat as he slept. She might have died trying, but instead she had allowed Katari to unravel his evil plan. She had handed him control of her precious Inti, her dear Theron.

Sartaña shuddered at what Helghul would do to the spirit of her child. What kind of minion would he seek to create, and would he destroy the boy in the process?

Still on her knees, Sartaña lunged at the approaching Katari and tackled his legs, bowling him over. He crashed to the ground, but the diminutive woman was no match for him. The warrior was quickly back on his feet, more angry and vicious than ever. He struck a powerful blow to her jaw and Sartaña fell to the floor, cracking her forehead as she landed. She saw a blinding flash of light that disappeared to overwhelming black.

Katari knelt in front of her, triumphant, then concerned that he may have killed her in his rage. He found that she was still breathing, so he unsheathed the cradle-shaped stone blade from his side, swiftly bringing it to her face. Her small room was gory with blood by the time Katari finished his evil work, and he wrapped her in bloody sheets and carried her out past the worried guard.

Katari acted like a distressed husband and father as he moved through the palace, seemingly toward the sacred courtyard where all religious ceremonies and rites were performed.

Sartaña awoke alone, unable to move, in severe pain, on the floor of a cell in the deepest recesses of a prison. Her head felt like a swollen, pulpy mess, and she couldn't move or work her jaws at all. She had vague recollections of someone pouring water into her mouth and forcing her to drink even though it was excruciating. The rest of her world was agony coupled with blinding flashes of light. Only the total disconnection of unconsciousness gave her any reprieve.

On the third day, she woke for longer and was able to sit. Her head felt like she wore a crown of thorns, and she wobbled dizzily. Her body ached and burned for food. She was grateful when the guard opened the door to deliver her water. She recognized him as the guard from her former chamber.

Sartaña tried to speak but was unable. She had been horribly disfigured—there were deep lacerations healing on her face. She had a broken jaw as well. Someone had bandaged her head and chin. She had the strange sensation that her mouth was oddly hollow and cotton-filled at the same time.

She could only moan and make sounds from her throat, and she tried to use her tongue to assess the damage. She couldn't find it. Her mind reeled in confusion. She couldn't find her tongue! She willed it to move, and nothing; her mouth was empty and still. She couldn't feel her teeth, the roof of her mouth, there was no sensation at all. She frantically raised her hands, pushing against the bandages and, despite the blinding bolts of pain that reverberated through her head, she anxiously opened her slack, splintered jaw. Nothing: only a sickening stump where her tongue should have been. Katari had said he would silence her.

The jail was near the center of the city. When Sartaña was well enough to stand, she could almost touch all of the sandy rock walls of her cell at one time. She was grateful for a tiny square opening high on one wall and, though it did not allow her to look out, late in the afternoon it let in a single beam of daylight. The sunbeam was high above her, but if she stood on her toes her fully outstretched fingertips could just enter the opening, feel the sun's warmth and churn its shining particles as they rained down.

The tiny jail was almost empty. Katari did not believe in feeding and maintaining those who broke his laws or who opposed his views. His retribution was typically swift and final. Sartaña was confined alone. She was isolated and tended by just one guard.

Sartaña existed on a diet of water and a mealy broth with dry bread, and she languished, miserably tormented by the predicament of her child. Only the kindness of her guard sustained her. It was he who had filled her mouth with pain-relieving minced leaves and bandaged her injured jaw. His kindness later extended to communication. He provided the contact that she craved, and he kindly offered her updates about her child, though to do so put him in jeopardy.

Inti believed her dead. The pain he must be feeling, the anger, the mourning, and with only Katari to console him. Sartaña's Marcus-brain was tormented to once again be parted from Theron. The pain was made worse by the injustice of mother and child being purposely separated. It didn't matter what she thought, Katari was the father, the high priest. He had the power to do as he wished, and Sartaña knew that he had planned it all along. He had fooled her with indifference, convinced her to raise the boy and help win over the city. She had been duped into teaching him their ways, and he had planned to eliminate her all along. Her throat burned hoarse, dry, and thick with anguish, and she placed her desperate forehead on the filthy stone floor, praying for relief.

Understanding that there was great learning in suffering, she struggled to see the lesson, to embrace the strange path that she traveled. It was not for her to decide when or how her life would end. She prayed for the life and soul of her son, and she prayed for her vanquisher, hoping he could do better and therefore do right by Inti. Sartaña took solace in what remained of her limited voice. She had been reduced to the original primordial words of the Universe. From her gut, "aaa," from her throat, "uuu," and from her lips and nose, "mmm." Her Marcus-brain understood the impermanence of her predicament in the grand scheme of things; still, it was the vibration of Aum or Om[7] that brought her peace. It reminded her of the true nature of reality and helped her to feel connected in her isolation.

Inti had been inconsolable when Katari informed him of Sartaña's death. The child had not yet realized that he and his mother were separate people. He could not comprehend that she had gone somewhere that he could not go, and above all he could not understand why she had gone without saying goodbye. The child had begged to see her and was permitted to view the wrapped corpse laid out for the vast multitude of mourners who came from a great distance to pay their respects. He insisted that his mother was not in the wrappings, and he did not understand that dead meant forever. He asked the gods to bring her home every night. He promised to be a good son, and he was sure that he had somehow done something to cause it all.

Sartaña's funeral pyre had been the highest in the history of Stone-at-Center, and after her cremation the citizens had mourned for the prescribed twenty days, equal to one of their months. Katari had been thrilled with the economic benefit and gifts that the wailing pilgrims had brought, and he had ensured that the mourning did not interfere with the commerce.

With Sartaña gone, Inti spent every day at his father's side. He remained despondent and sullen, and Katari quickly lost patience with him, expecting him to behave as a much older child might. Helghul raged with jealousy and self-recrimination at the bond he had allowed to develop between Marcus and Theron, and he vowed to never be so generous again, despite how well it had worked in his favor as ruler.

While the rest of her kingdom believed her dead, Sartaña was healing. The trauma of losing a second son to Katari consumed her thoughts. She had vivid dreams of release and victory but would then wake to feel the true hopelessness of her existence.

She was alone, isolated and mute. Her Marcus-spirit tried to rouse her, urged her to believe that she still had a purpose. She was alive, therefore her journey was not finished. Only the occasional update about her son's well-being, relayed to her by her kind-hearted guard, slightly rekindled her faith in mankind and stoked her will to go on. Marcus knew that he and Sartaña could only understand the lessons of this lifetime when they returned to the Grid in the afterlife, in the life in between.

Years passed and Inti's recollections of his mother faded, though he tried desperately to catalogue and preserve each one of them. His father refused to speak of her at all, and the son no longer remembered the curve of her jaw, the shape of her eyes, or the feel of her hand in his. Despite the lost memories, he remained tied to her, constantly hearing her words in his head as if she was in the room with him. *Follow your instincts*, he heard. *You are special. You will be a great, compassionate leader to the people.*

Inti was only aware of his present life. His Theron-brain was completely unconscious, but his purpose as an Emissary overwhelmed him and flowed through every cell of his body. Sartaña called to him telepathically, and unconsciously Inti heard.

Initially, after Sartaña was mourned, the people had looked hopefully to Katari, anxious that he and Inti fill the spiritual void she had left behind. Katari, however, was unable and unwilling to put the needs of his people before his own. The oppression and poverty that the citizens endured, while Katari's personal fortune grew, led them to despise him. Trade once again slowed as surrounding areas grew protective and wary of the threat Katari posed.

People who had dared to speak out had been killed. Small groups of insurgents who had raided Katari's crops for food were captured and killed for sport in macabre competitions and games. Many of Katari's own warriors had become disgruntled. Now citizens and fathers themselves, they struggled to feed their families and were too often run ragged on brutal campaigns with little personal reward. Like the other citizens, they watched Katari's comfort grow while they toiled and starved.

Inti's innate goodness had caused problems and tension with his father. Though Katari had no tolerance for his son's so-called weakness, he was determined to methodically turn the Emissary. Helghul plotted carefully to win Theron's blind allegiance and to use Inti as a tool of his own will. When Inti questioned him in the face of simple commands, which no one else would have dared to do, the leader was deliberately patient, determined to undermine and reprogram his son's natural tendencies.

"Remember, you must always survey the danger," Katari instructed while they were on a hunting expedition in his son's tenth year. Inti was already an expert with his sling and could down a screaming monkey at twenty paces. He had learned to skin and cook the animal, which tasted good but looked alarmingly like a human on the roast.

"In peace and in war it is always better to let your underlings go before you," his father counseled.

"That seems like a cowardly thing to do. Shouldn't a leader lead?" Inti challenged innocently, still carefully scanning the horizon for prey.

"Bravery is for the simple-minded. It is the meal we feed our warriors to reinforce them and make them do what we want. A leader must be smart. Never sacrifice yourself for another. Never risk yourself when there are others to incur that risk. That is the power of being the king. That is how the clever lead and survive to maintain a kingdom. Our lives are more important," he said.

Inti had heard the advice many times, in many different ways. He had often seen it in practice. Katari secretly trusted no one and suspected everyone of selfishness, treason, and dishonor. Inti wondered if Katari would protect him; would he die for his son?

Katari constantly anticipated and countered the inner voices and urgings that he knew besieged his son's soul. He watched the Emissary carefully, always gauging how best to manipulate and control him. In lifetimes to come, Helghul would use every shred of knowledge he now gained.

"That voice you hear in your head, telling you to be merciful and sacrificial, is an evil demon sent to fool you! It will be your undoing as king. It will doom your people if you are weak and cannot do what you need to do despite the unpleasantness of the task. It is like the first time you had to skin a monkey. You cried like a baby," Katari said.

Inti's eyes flashed in embarrassment at the remembrance, and he scowled at his father.

"You will skin many monkeys in life. A ruler must endure much to do what needs to be done," Katari counseled.

Katari had continued to expand his lands, and he planned to take his son along on the next campaign to begin his lessons as a warrior. There was much to be done before Inti would be ready for the ruthlessness of a battlefield, and Katari was determined to thicken his skin and harden his heart. He would eliminate anything and anyone the boy cared for. Would he become bitter? Was an Emissary subject to the same responses as other people?

Katari had already taken Sartaña away. He had made sure there were no servants or guards who held any special meaning for the boy. Katari alone would be his mentor, confidant, and friend. No one else could get close.

When he turned ten years old, Inti was presented with a fabulous and unusual gift by Katari.

"What is it?" Inti said, as he rushed to the covered basket at his father's side. Throwing the top aside he uncovered a tiny black jaguar cub. The creature meowed and growled with hunger. Its sandpaper tongue licked, and his razor-sharp teeth searched for food.

"I named him Patha. It means 'the lesson.' Your ability to take care of this creature is practice for your time as king, when you will take care of an entire empire."

The boy fell instantly in love with his pet and held it in his lap, nursing it with llama milk fed through a leather skin.

CHAPTER 11

A CRUEL LESSON

Patha slept in a basket near Inti nightly for the next four weeks. The boy took his new pet with him everywhere, and in private he cuddled and held it affectionately. It was a blissful pleasure he had long been denied. Not since Sartaña's reported death had Inti enjoyed the closeness and affection of another living creature. The most he ever received from Katari was an approving hand on his shoulder. Theron's soul blossomed lovingly within Inti, a side effect that Katari had anticipated and planned to exploit. The name Patha, the Sanskrit word for "lesson," had not been chosen lightly.

Inti seemed oblivious to the animal's natural threat, though more than once he nursed a scratch or incidental bite. The cat was still small, playful, and manageable, and Inti loved it wholeheartedly.

Katari had known that the pet was impractical. He was aware that a full-grown jaguar would be impossible to manage. He had also known that it would never come to be. He had a plan.

"I cannot find Patha! I cannot find Patha!" Inti shouted down the corridors one morning. His heart raced when, after looking under every pile and object, his dear pet had not been found. He wondered if it had jumped out the high window into the courtyard below. Patha could be injured!

"Master?" a servant girl said, bowing as she approached.

"My jaguar, he's gone! Call everyone to help find him," Inti demanded. The animal was far too young to be a threat. Soon the entire staff of the grounds were calling and searching.

Katari had been up for hours. Early in the morning, he had quietly entered his sleeping son's room and removed the cat from beside him. He listened while the commotion in the hallways grew, and then there was a knock at his door.

"Enter."

"Father, it's Patha. He's gone!" Inti said. He hadn't cried in many years—his father had not allowed it—but tears now flowed freely down his cheeks as he scanned the room hopefully.

"Not much of a king if you lose your kingdom," Katari said knowingly.

"I didn't lose . . . I woke and he was gone," the boy sobbed.

"He cannot be far. Tears will not bring him back. Do not let the people see you so weak and childlike. A jaguar has long been a symbol of power and strength. Collect yourself and we will go find this animal together," Katari said patiently. Inti wiped his face.

Together they exited the palace, and one after another the servants shook their heads, skittering from Katari nervously.

"No sign yet."

"He's not here."

"I will take my group to search the fields," one guard answered sorrowfully, afraid to deliver bad news to the temperamental leader. No one wanted to bear the brunt of Katari's disappointment and suffer a beating, prison, or worse.

Inti and his father continued down the steep stone stairway into the city. They were surrounded by guards looking under bushes and peering through doorways. Inti continued to call out. Curious children scampered out of their way, and Inti commandeered them to help search. In awe of their young prince they happily obeyed, unaware they'd had no other choice.

Four hours later they returned empty-handed, tired and sticky with dust and heat. They were approached by one of Katari's most trusted warriors. He whispered to the leader, who grimaced exaggeratedly in response.

"What is it? What did he say?" Inti asked tensely, looking from his father to the glum messenger.

"They have found the thief, he's at the prison," Katari replied.

"Prison? A thief? Someone took Patha?" It had not occurred to Inti that someone might have taken his animal. He had assumed the pet had simply wandered away on its own.

"Prepare yourself, it's worse than we feared."

"Where is Patha?" Inti said in confusion.

"He is dead, mutilated for his heart," Katari said, feigning sympathy, his Helghul-brain watching carefully for signs of the effect the news would have.

"I don't understand," the boy said blankly, his mind racing to comprehend. He stumbled as they hurried toward the jail, and he was steadied by his father's quick hand.

"The beast tore the flesh from the helpless little creature to steal its strength for himself," Katari said brutally, needling his son.

"Are they sure? It might not be Patha. Patha is more likely hiding somewhere, exploring," Inti insisted.

"When they found the criminal he was covered in blood, and there were bits of the beast all around. They have a jaguar's head . . . you can see for yourself," Katari said.

Inti's stomach lurched at the prospect. "I'll know him. I'll know my Patha!" he said desperately.

From the beginning his father had been clear. Patha had been the boy's responsibility, his kingdom to manage and take care of. Inti was overwhelmed by his guilt and failure, though he continued to hope that Patha had been spared.

Inti ran the short and well-traveled path to the prison. Katari congratulated himself on his progress so far. The boy was responding just as he had intended. To what degree could Theron be bent to his will? What was an Emissary capable of if pushed?

The guards bristled at the arrival of the high priest, and they pressed their backs tight to the wall to get out of his way as he passed to the open chamber at the end of the longest corridor.

As always when Katari came, Sartaña could hear him from her cell and could feel his karmic energy flow in currents through the air. He would often walk the dim, putrid corridors and pound on her thick, wooden cell door barking warnings and threats. Sartaña always hovered near her door when she heard the high priest enter, hopeful that Inti was close by. When her son was near, Sartaña reached for Theron's buoyant energy.

Katari had ensured that Sartaña's cell was at the end of the hall, and he had made certain she could clearly hear the screams that echoed from the torture he delivered before new prisoners were taken to the central courtyard and publicly executed. There was a notch in the wood that made it possible for her to watch and often she did, but only to see her child.

Inti had been present many times as his father had tortured a prisoner. The first time was just after Sartaña's faked death, and he had closed his eyes and covered his ears from the cries of the victim. The scene had sickened the boy, but Katari had insisted he stay. The father was determined to harden his son; Helghul was determined to turn Theron to his will.

More than once since that first time, a weapon had been handed to the young boy. Inti had been forced to strike a prisoner while the king reminded him that as a leader, it was his duty to protect his people from the criminals. It was his duty to "skin the monkey."

It wasn't like hunting and survival, and Inti was sickened by the torture and abuse. He did not understand that he was as much a victim of his father as the captives were.

Sartaña was startled as she heard the commotion of Katari's entrance; he had been there earlier that morning, and it was unusual for him to come twice in one day. She peeked through the small sliver in her door, hoping for a view of her son and the beautiful halo of color that surrounded him.

The air vibrated with the cruel energy of Katari. The high priest pounded especially hard on Sartaña's door, desiring that she witness the scene he had orchestrated, which was about to be played out. She pressed her eye to the knot, watching Inti. His colors were strangely tumultuous, and his small hands were balled into fists at his sides.

Sartaña's soul reached out to him, and her heart and body ached to touch him—so close but kept apart by an inch of wood. She longed to see his face, to hold his hands in hers, to hear his voice. *Turn around*, she called wordlessly. *Look at me*, she begged, without a tongue and the ability to shout.

Despite his rage and upset Inti felt an itch, a gentle tug at his instincts telling him he was being watched. He turned his anxious gaze to her door and saw the eye pressed to the gap in the wood. It was so white that it seemed to glow and he paused, inexplicably drawn to the eye that seemed to smile at him and had strangely called to him.

The lump in Inti's throat bobbed and choked him as they grew closer. Katari felt his son lagging behind and losing his fury. He saw Sartaña's eye pressed to the door and became aware of their multicolored karmic energies intermingling in the corridor. He felt the weak telepathic strand forming between them and irritably corralled his son forward, whispering dark words in his ear and glaring threateningly at the space where the eye had been moments before.

Katari barked orders as a prisoner was led in to the chamber by two guards. The captive was heavy-set with dark, sun-worn skin, and his hair was alive with lice. His tunic and pants were covered in blood, and the stench of him forced his captors to suck in their breath in disgust. Katari ignored the bands of purple and indigo light that flowed beautifully in and out of the man, mingling with the similar karmic colors that flowed around Inti—the bands of an Emissary, which only Helghul and Marcus could see.

Sartaña gasped as her Marcus-brain recognized one of her own, and she watched in horror, dreading what would come. The prisoner had once been an

Atitalan. He was a vaguely familiar face in a crowd of students from long ago. He had had a strange name, Zarathushtra or Zoroaster . . . something like that. At present he was nothing more than a tool in Helghul's experiment, a test of his ability to turn an Emissary. Marcus struggled to remember him and began to pray.

"This man was found covered in blood and surrounded by the carcass of the jaguar cub. He's from a distant land. He speaks no language that we know," the captain of the guards explained.

Though he feigned outrage, Katari had invented the story himself. The foreigner had been an ideal pawn. A stranger to Inti and therefore unable to plead, explain, or beg mercy, he had come to Stone-at-Center as a pilgrim. Katari's Helghul-brain had identified the Emissary immediately, and he had detained him without explanation. The prisoner had languished, starving in the prison for many days before he was thrown the dead carcass of the small animal. In desperation he had fallen upon the creature for survival. Katari had watched merrily, his plan fully in motion.

Katari shoved the prisoner to his knees. Inti was shaking at his father's side, staring at the blood down the front of the filthy captive's clothing and on his chin.

"Where's my jaguar?" Inti demanded, clenching his jaw. The Emissary stared at him without understanding. Sartaña and Katari both wondered if Inti sensed the Emissary's energy. Would Theron recognize one of her own? There was no sign.

"He murdered your Patha. Bring the head, the paws, the skin! He ate his heart like it was a pear!" Katari said angrily, pacing threateningly around the Emissary on the floor.

Sartaña knew what Katari was doing. As always he was bent on twisting Inti to his will. Katari handed his son a heavy, flat stone that barely fit in the boy's hand and nudged him forward, close enough to touch the prisoner. Inti trembled with rage, and his legs felt as though they might buckle.

The boy gulped as the guard returned with the ghoulish head of the jaguar extended in his palm, too near his face. There could be no mistaking. All sympathy left him; there was only anger remaining. Inti had been exposed to violence his entire life. It was a part of life and of survival, and in that moment he was filled with murderous rage.

"Ripped apart while you slept . . . while you did not protect . . ." Katari goaded, determined to inflame him further. The young prince swung the rock and hit the prisoner with a sickening thud. A large gash opened up in the man's head directly above his left eye as he fell to the dust.

Katari glowed with satisfaction. It was as he thought! Even Theron, daughter of White Elder, could be used and turned under the correct circumstances! What great power this knowledge gave him!

The injured Emissary looked up from the dirt, and Inti felt a wave of compassion upon seeing the fear and confusion in his eyes. Suddenly, the stranger seemed familiar, as his karmic colors billowed and swirled through the room. Inti turned his face away from the victim, and Sartaña silently called to him, praying for him to stop, praying that Inti's Theron-soul would not succumb to Helghul's manipulation.

The boy stood shaking and remorseful, rock in hand, unwilling to strike a second blow and unable to rouse himself to the anger and brutality required to continue. Katari, sensing that Inti had lost his rage, pushed him forward. Inti snapped his shoulder back and glared angrily at his father.

"That anger you feel is for *him*, not for me! He attacked your kingdom! Will Patha's murder go unavenged?" Katari growled, but Inti remained frozen.

Angered by his son's mounting compassion, Katari took the rock from his son in disgust and pushed him aside. The boy turned his head away as his father slammed the weapon against the captive's yielding skull and sprayed them all with blood and grey oatmeal chunks of brain. Though Inti's eyes were closed, the sound of the stone as it connected reverberated sickeningly through him.

The colorful bands emanating from the murdered Emissary slipped upward like smoke through a chimney as his spirit was released to the place in between. He was once again a current, traveling the Grid until his next incarnation. Sartaña was overcome by the cruelty and waste she had witnessed. She mourned the loss of such a good spirit in the world, though she knew the Emissary's absence was temporary.

Inti would not look at the battered heap as a dark pool of blood spread slowly, covering the dirt and pebbles as it crept across the floor. Instead he stared at Sartaña's door. The eye was there. Even from a distance, Inti could sense it watching them. He wondered briefly to whom the eye belonged.

Despite her grief for her bludgeoned ally, Sartaña knew that her son could see her and she smiled. So rare was the occasion for her to smile that her scars pulled and stretched in complaint. Her lined skin creaked in protest but she continued, seeing that Inti's eyes were kind, as they had always been. Sartaña was flush with pride that Inti had been unwilling to do as Katari had intended.

Inti could not see the karmic colors that flowed down the hall and joined with his, but Sartaña felt her son's spirit reaching out to her. Theron's energy once again coupled with Marcus's like a key in a padlock. The chamber turned and opened them up, and both the child's and the mother's skin erupted in gooseflesh.

Katari regrouped as the brightness of the auras doubled in the dim hallway. He saw Marcus's familiar aura swirling around Inti, and angrily he hurled the blood-covered stone against Sartaña's door. The high priestess jumped back as it impacted with a thud, leaving a bloody imprint on the wood.

The tendrils of Sartaña's aura that had reached out now retreated. She had seen and felt the colors of Inti and the Emissary, felt the familiar warmth and goodness that radiated from them. It was stronger than human touch, so deep, not just barely-there tingles but complete and overwhelming connections, and it was more than she had felt in many years. She had been alone for so long, reconciling her Marcus-memories and cataloguing her previous lessons and lives. She had only seen her son from a distance through the sliver in her door, but this time they had connected.

Katari directed Inti toward the exit, leaving the guards to clean up the carnage left behind. Sartaña listened as her son was reprimanded by his father for being weak. She meditated and inexplicably felt a new strength, reminded that she was not alone.

CHAPTER 12

A NEW PURPOSE

Sartaña was grateful when she finally heard the rustle of her cell door, hungrier than she had felt in years. Her guard stumbled as he entered and, grunting, kicked the ground at his feet. He placed a wooden bowl of water and a small chunk of dried llama meat on the floor. Other than a thin reed mat for sleeping, the cell was empty. Opposite the door, under the tiny window, ran a narrow, fetid ditch the length of the entire building. The putrid trough was occasionally flushed with dirty water to wash away the human waste that had collected there, but the stench never waned.

Sartaña's guard retreated and, once again stumbling, he kicked aside the stone that was tripping him up. The door closed with a clunk. Sartaña crouched to eat and felt the stone beside her. In the dark she picked it up and felt the sticky blood and hair that clung to it. She remembered the crash of the rock against her door as Katari had thrown it hours before.

Sartaña dipped the corner of her tatty robe into her shallow water bowl, using almost all of her daily ration to soak the cloth. Respectfully, though she could not see in the darkness, the high priestess washed away the gore, all the while praying for the Emissary whose blood had been so cruelly shed. The rock was round and smooth, and once clean, Sartaña decided that it must become an object of reverence to remember the brave life it had taken.

The high priestess held the stone and meditated through the night. Her interaction with Inti earlier in the day had somehow lit a spark of hope within her. Sartaña's Marcus-brain was racing, and she prayed specifically for the knowledge of what she should do. What could she do?

When Sartaña woke, a narrow ray of light from her high window was spanning the length of her tiny cell and cascading beautiful silver light particles in its path. The beam illuminated the shimmering, hoary dust in smooth, straight rows that appeared to rain down and disappear where the light left off. Sartaña was grateful for the beauty. It reminded her that she was still a part of a miraculous world. As she watched, the beam in one small section began to swirl and change, and she was mesmerized as she realized a face had formed. It was the familiar curve and arc of Theron's cheek and jaw. The dust moved as Theron often had, tossing her hair from her eyes, and then it was gone. The sunbeam returned to its gravitational pull, returned to the silver rain, and Sartaña was left with the beautiful image in her mind.

Sartaña's Marcus-brain was at full attention and compelled her to take up the rock that she had so reverentially scrubbed the night before. Sartaña looked at the rock in the light for the first time and knew what she would do. She would carve into the stone. She had a clear picture in her mind of the design. She would draw a group of seven identical circles in a repeating pattern that would form a flower with six petals. It was the same pattern that graced her shoulder and that freed her soul.

Sartaña's role as an Emissary was begun anew with this random, seemingly insignificant undertaking. She searched at the edge of her cell in the dirt and pebbles and tried each small shard as a tool until she found one sharp and dense enough to make a scrape in the smooth river rock. She worked devotedly for hours, then days, and she was amazed by the divine design that flowed so easily from her untrained hands. Sartaña had never been an artist or craftswoman, yet she had produced an extraordinary, geometrically perfect carving in only a week, with an inadequate tool and no ability to measure. It was truly miraculous.

The evening of the seventh day, Sartaña's guard entered to deliver her rations. Sartaña did not have time to hide the stone in her hand. The curious man demanded to see what she held. Hesitantly she handed the stone to him, and he turned it over in his palm and stared at her dumbfounded.

"You carved this?" he asked, tracing the grooves in awe. She nodded tentatively. "Where is your blade?" he asked. Sartaña raised the small, worn-out scrap of stone up to him, and he shook his head in disbelief. "High Priestess, you did this without a proper tool? It's not possible! It's perfect!" he proclaimed. Sartaña glowed at his response to her work. Without another word the guard left, taking the stone with him. The woman feebly reached out to stop him, but the door closed with a clunk.

Sartaña was crestfallen; she had felt like her old self during the past week. She had felt a sense of purpose and distraction that had eluded her during her imprisonment. She lay down on her mat and wondered if the kind guard would take her handiwork to Katari. It had been worth the risk. Considering how compelled she had been to do the carving, she knew that whatever happened was meant to be.

Sartaña was not alone for long. There was a rustle at her door, and she snapped upright in alarm. She was relieved as her guard entered with a secretive smile on his face. In his hands he held a bulky goatskin sack. He dropped the bag with a weighty clunk and unloaded a small pile of river rocks in the corner of the cell. Sartaña stared at him in astonishment as he handed her a sharp, crescent-shaped stone with a worn wooden handle.

"This was my father's . . . he was a skilled artisan and carved his whole life. It is a strong blade and should make your work much easier," he said proudly. Sartaña held the tool like it was a precious gem, turning it over in her hands in disbelief. "Don't hurt yourself," he added pensively, glancing back and meeting her grateful eyes. She wished she could thank him. She knew that if Katari discovered what he had done, he would kill him. Her guard was a good, brave man.

Sartaña made her way to the heap of stones and chose one. She raised it to the heavens in blessing, and her mind flashed with visions from her many past lives. When finally she settled on one image, she began to scrape, scrape, scrape. She was a whirlwind, overcome with purpose and expertly carving with a skill she had never learned.

Day after day, week after week, month after month Sartaña churned out the spectacular etchings at an impossible pace. She engraved images from Marcus's past lifetimes, concepts that no one of her time or land had ever dreamed of.

There were days when Sartaña almost ceased to exist, fully transmuted to the higher part of herself. She carved stories, ideas, experiments, celestial maps, centuries of knowledge etched deep into the indigenous river rock. Her guard had begun leaving her cell door ajar, and the light and warmth from his fire comforted her and danced in patterns on her walls. He would sit next to the opening with his back pressed to the outer wall while she carved, and he'd tell her stories about Inti and the generosity and kindness of his spirit.

As the days passed, he shared humorous and interesting stories about his own children and family, as well as the daily events in the city. Sartaña loved the sound of his voice and worked in a new state of contentment. More than once he shared with her a hallucinogenic cactus drink, which helped her visions and creativity to bloom.

The guard continued to bring fresh stones and take the completed art away. Unsure what was happening to them, Sartaña found she didn't care. The stones would end up where they needed to be. Her job was to produce them, as prodigiously and prolifically as possible. What she did not know was that she was not alone in her task—other people nearby, Emissaries like her, were also busily carving without training or cause, but with burning determination and in complete awe of the results of their toil. They too were being guided by their unconscious higher selves, though they did not know it at all. The Emissaries were often confused and disturbed by the foreign images they produced, but they were compelled to continue.

The stones began to turn up in Stone-at-Center. Citizens found them and marveled at their intricacy and bizarre images. The community embraced them as signs from the gods riddled with messages too grand for them to understand, and they took them to their high priest to decode. Initially Katari dismissed the stones, intrigued but unconcerned by the images, assuming they were remnants from a time long past, a Golden Age that he had known well and did not fear.

Katari's interest in the stones changed as they grew quickly in number and the entire community could speak of nothing else. One afternoon Katari was handed a specimen that caused him considerable alarm. The image was of a young warrior, aiming a spear at the belly of an older man. In the sky above there were three stars, and at the feet of the older man there were oddly bent bodies that looked to be fatally injured infants and children. The boy was wearing the headdress of a high priest, and on his forehead was the eye of protection in the center of a triangle. Unlike the other stones that he had disregarded, Katari pulled this stone aside and kept it hidden in his chamber, disturbed by its imagery and its resemblance to both Inti and himself.

People continued to bring the perplexing stones to their leader, and his unease grew. He was given another specimen that depicted a young boy in a high priest headdress marked with the eye of protection, sitting on what was unmistakably a throne.

The next day, after a restless night plagued by nightmares, Katari decreed that all of the artisan stones were to be brought to him, and for each one he would pay a small sack of grain. The hungry people reaped the benefit of the high priest's interest.

Katari didn't know where the stones were coming from or who was producing them, but many of the images indicated the knowledge of Atitalans. He had murdered or imprisoned the few Emissaries that he had encountered in this life, but Helghul knew there must be more. The high priest outlawed the production of the stones, declaring that anyone caught carving them would be put to death.

Early one evening shortly after the decree, Katari was interrupted during his meal. He was especially irritable because the crops were doing poorly, and he had spent the day threatening the farmers and demanding they work longer hours to manage the grueling task of better irrigating their lands.

"Master, a load of stones has arrived," a servant announced.

"More of the same?" Katari snapped.

"There are too many to tell."

"Put them in the courtyard. I will see them after I eat," Katari ordered, through a mouthful of bread.

"Why do you care about a pile of rocks?" Inti asked sheepishly, too curious about his father's growing obsession to stay quiet as he usually would have.

"Any change is worth noting. The people care, they are mesmerized by them. A smart leader watches the crowd," he explained.

"The ones I saw were all children's tales: monsters and moons," Inti countered, his mouth, like his father's, spraying crumbs as he spoke.

"Have you heard them called the 'magic stones' or the 'sacred stones'?" Katari asked. Inti could only nod, his mouth bursting with half-chewed meat. "Doesn't that concern you? Have you learned nothing from me?" the father snapped at his son irritably.

Inti retreated back into silence while he ate. His hope was to endure his training with Katari and to eventually lead with compassion and humility. He continued to hear his mother's words these ten years later: *Trust your instincts. You will be a great and well-loved leader.* He missed her and wondered how alike they might have been. Would they have laughed together? Healed together? Would she be ashamed of him if she knew the things that he had done? He was ashamed of himself. As he aged, it pricked at his conscience, a constant reminder to do better in the future.

Katari was despised by his subjects. Selfish and cold-hearted, he had continued to claim the greatest part of his city's wealth and crops for himself. He ran the sacred sites and temples like a business. For thousands of years, Stone-at-Center had been open to all people. Katari had changed all that, limiting access and requiring "donations" of beans, grains, peanuts, and cloth. No one could enter without paying his toll, and many were turned away—the sick, the elderly—even after days and weeks of travel. The high priest had become powerful and rich, continually expanding his lands through commerce and force, but the people were left with barely enough to survive.

Inti was increasingly aware of the discontent in the kingdom but dared say nothing. He knew what his father would say, he had heard it many times: "A king must feather his own nest first."

After they finished eating, the duo stretched their thick frames, belched, and made their way out to the square. Inti was quiet as they walked, so similar in body but not in soul.

Upon exiting the low stone archway, they were stunned to see a pile of more than two hundred stones of varying sizes. The high priest and his son contemplated the stack.

Inti ran to the pile and crouched, laying the smaller stones in neat rows at his feet. He studied the images of maps and celestial charts, but he could not understand what they were. The knowledge was locked deep inside him. Inti wondered if the stones held prophecies or if they were from the Ancient Ones as rumors had claimed. Some were incredibly well done and detailed, but others were just scratches, no skill at all, undoubtedly by someone desperate for a sack of grain.

When Katari approached from behind, Inti was holding an intricately carved stone the size of a child's head. Through his fingers the eye of protection was easily visible. As he shifted his grip, Katari could see the familiar image of a boy high priest.

"Enough! Come now," Katari demanded. Inti responded immediately, placing the stone gingerly on the ground and jumping to attention.

As the weeks went on, countless more stones were delivered. As before there were many of noticeably poor quality, carved without purpose or skill to gain a sack of grain. It was the other stones, creative and fantastic, that continued to confound Katari. It couldn't be Marcus; Sartaña remained securely neutralized. Helghul knew the scenes and recognized Atitala and the ancient knowledge, but he could not understand the purpose of the stones, where they were coming from, or how the artisans were eluding his guards.

The image of the boy with the headdress and the eye of protection concerned him most. The number of stones grew and rubbed him like a blister, so the leader arranged for them to be secretly carted far from the city and placed deep in a stone cavern, well camouflaged by a waterfall. He kept only the stones depicting the young high priest, which now numbered thirteen.

Sartaña continued to work feverishly, inspired, and unaware that mounds of stones came and went. Her guard continued to smuggle out her finished work and supply her with fresh stones, and he spent hours talking to her.

Like the other citizens, the guard believed that the stones were special. He told Sartaña about the rocks turning up en masse, and she was bewildered. Her confusion quickly turned to happiness at the realization that she wasn't alone. It was the confirmation that her path, though it seemed insignificant, must have a purpose greater than she could understand. There were others like her, compelled to tell the stories in the stone. She was surprised to learn that Katari had proclaimed the rocks illegal, and she was worried for the safety of her guard. He never knew about her concern, but he put her at ease when he expressed his gratitude for the extra grain that the stones brought to his table. He also shared his pleasure at the apparent frustration the carvings were causing their oppressive leader.

One morning Inti and Katari headed out walking, with their typical entourage of personal guards and warriors, to survey the city and surrounding lands. Unable to contain himself, Inti interrupted the extended silence. "I have an idea . . . can I tell you?" he stammered meekly, not used to speaking to his father except to respond. Katari gave one sharp nod. "I have . . . an idea . . . for a watering system . . . to take the burden off the farmers. It's complicated . . . but I know it will work," Inti said. He was literally glowing with enthusiasm, and the violet and orange of his aura was particularly irritating to Katari when it intruded on him so. He encouraged Inti to elaborate, and after an enthusiastic explanation the boy waited for his father's response.

"I will consider the irrigation system, not because it eases the burden of the farmer but because, if it increases the harvest, my territory will grow richer," Katari said.

Inti was overjoyed. His idea had been accepted. "When will we begin?' he asked excitedly.

"You may return to the city now and tell your plan to my chief builder. He will be instrumental in its creation. I will join you this afternoon."

Katari let Inti leave, happy to be free of the overwhelming light that had been emanating from him. It was growing stronger every day, and the leader feared that Theron's energy might yet become too powerful to be subdued, despite his best efforts.

The space was widening between him and his son, and it might be a good thing to direct the boy's energy into a harmless project that could benefit the high priest at the same time.

Katari's Helghul-brain had begun sending him warning messages. Was Inti a threat? Not likely. He knew Theron's spirit well, and she had no memory. He was sure that he could control the boy and manipulate him as required. He would wait, but he was prepared to eliminate the Emissary if necessary.

Inti quickly made his way back toward the city. In his haste and distraction, he tripped on a stone and went over on his right ankle. Stumble, stumble, crash! He was unable to catch himself, and he sprawled awkwardly onto the gravel path. Wrist, elbow, and knee bleeding and scraped, he attempted to get up. A severe pain shot through his leg, and he turned over and sat, his eyes squeezed tightly shut so that he wouldn't cry. How would he walk now? He held his injured ankle gently in his hands. The tiniest movement sent pain through him. It was then he saw it, the stone that had tripped him. He picked it up and was shocked to see that it was intricately carved. It was one of the so-called sacred stones, just lying on the path.

It was unlike any of the others that he had seen before. It was the image of a flower, each of the six petals exactly the same size and surrounded by a perfect circle. There was not a gap, a chip, a single spot that was not precisely balanced.

Inti knew that he was going to have to walk, injured ankle or not. Using both hands, he carefully got to his feet. He was pleased that the pain in his ankle had diminished slightly, but he knew he must not turn it again. With care, he began to limp back toward the city, still holding the beautiful artifact.

Up ahead he was relieved to see a mule. He called out to the man beside it, who appeared to be struggling with a bulky pouch that was slung over the animal's back. The man jumped in alarm but immediately ran to help Inti. After a brief explanation, he brought the mule back to carry the boy home. The man nervously looked at the stone in Inti's hand. He bent to help him onto the animal's back. In that instant Inti recognized him as one of the guards from the prison. As Inti took his seat on the donkey, he saw that the bulky animal-skin pouches were full of the special stones.

"Where did these came from? Who's making them?" Inti asked inquisitively.

The guard looked at him in alarm, and he fully expected to be punished for having been caught in possession of the rocks. He did not respond.

After a brief moment of confusion, Inti wisely realized what was going on. "You need not fear me," he soothed, placing a reassuring hand on the man's shoulder. "I want to know where the rocks come from, I don't want to harm you. This will be between us," he promised.

The guard considered him carefully and answered, "I'll guide you."

They set off, Inti bursting with curiosity, his irrigation system momentarily forgotten. The pair didn't speak while they hustled the ass along the dusty trail to the city gates. Inti wondered if he was being careless, possibly putting himself in danger, but he intuitively trusted the man.

Before long, they stood outside the low sloping entrance of the prison. The guard realized the enormity of what he was doing. It was a gift, a kindness he was happy to pay Sartaña. He would reunite her with her son. Somehow, despite the danger to himself, he knew it was the right thing to do.

They made the short journey through the corridors looking official and determined despite Inti's limp. The other guards jumped to attention and assumed that the high priest was close behind. When his guide stopped, Inti recognized the door with the eye that had reached out to him so strangely months before, the day of Patha the jaguar's death.

Sartaña stopped working and put her knife and stone behind her at the sound of her door being unlocked. She waited tentatively to see who would enter at such an unexpected time. The familiar face of her guard came around the edge of the door.

The guard stepped aside and Inti, squinting in the dim light to make out the figure, came eye to eye with Sartaña. She was awful, an ugly old crone. Her filthy black hair was streaked with grey and the knobby, ridged scars that patterned her face made her distressing to look at. The guard backed himself out of the chamber and, clicking the door behind him, left them alone. Inti was slightly alarmed to be locked in, even briefly, and he did his best to ignore the overpowering smells that accompanied life in that awful place.

Sartaña gasped with astonishment. She did not move, and more than ever she was tormented by the loss of her tongue. Her inability to speak at that moment was exactly the reason the cruelty had been perpetrated.

"Did you do this?" Inti asked in awe. He held the sphere of the flower of life protectively in his hand.

Sartaña nodded emphatically, smiling her broken, damaged smile.

The room was alive around them. Inti couldn't see her karmic code, but their auras danced and mingled, elated to be reunited. He felt it, the energy, and he went to her. He crouched in front of her. "How?" he asked, his young throat closing with emotion as their eyes locked only paces apart.

She put her hand to her throat and shook her head, indicating to him her inability to speak. His pity for her compounded. She took her stone and blade out from behind her back and held them out to him. He looked at the tool and back at her.

"Who are you?" he asked finally, searching her face.

She took his young hand in hers. He allowed it and did not mind the dirty, cracked frailty of her grasp. Her mind screamed out to him. *My son! Theron!* She sent all of her energy desperately into his. *He doesn't know me!* Sartaña thought in anguish. *Theron doesn't know me!* her Marcus-brain acknowledged painfully. Sartaña maintained her composure and calm demeanor, afraid to scare him away.

"What is this?" he asked, again holding out the stone carved with the seed of life. She couldn't reply. He stared at her, searching her eyes for an answer.

Suddenly, Inti reached out with his free hand and pushed up her ragged sleeve to expose her shoulder. His recognition was immediate. He looked from the flower symbol on her skin to the rock and back at her disfigured face. "No!" he croaked, barely able to breathe. "It's you!" Inti's mind raced. *How is this possible? What does it mean?* The colors around them were frenzied as his conscious emotion joined his unconscious.

Sartaña nodded emphatically, bringing his hand to her lips. Her tears poured freely down her ruined cheeks. Her face was luminous and filled with love.

Inti embraced the frail ghost, and their souls danced and bubbled as their auras mingled, sending pleasant shock waves through them. She felt like a skeleton in his arms, and his concern and sadness for her condition welled up in him. "I thought you were dead. They told me you were dead!" he cried, his tears flowing down his face.

Sartaña just shook her head and held him until the most violent of his sobbing subsided.

"Why?" he asked angrily. "What happened? Why did he send you here?"

Sartaña's joy turned to heartache as she once again imagined her young son mourning her.

"I need answers!" he shouted toward the door. The guard re-entered, unsure that he had done the right thing. He was further alarmed by the vision of the young man before him, so distraught and wild-looking. "You! Guard!" he said, grabbing the man with his free hand, the other hand still tightly clasping the flower-carved stone. "Tell me everything you know!"

"The high priestess is of royal, sacred lineage. Your father claimed her and killed her husband and your half-brother when he conquered this city. You were born one year later. When you were five, your father took over your care and your mother was brought here."

"Who knows this? Who knows she lives?" Inti demanded through gritted teeth.

"Only the three of us and the high priest," the guard answered. "He disfigured her and cut out her tongue so that she could never speak against him. I nursed her the best I could, but you see what a mess he made."

"It is *your* tongue I should have cut out," interjected Katari's deep menacing voice from behind the guard. In a flash, the point of Katari's spear burst through the startled man's chest. Inti let out a shocked scream as the guard dropped to the floor with a heavy thud. Sartaña and Inti recoiled in horror. "Take him!" Katari demanded, brutally tearing his weapon from the wound. Two guards entered from the corridor obediently and dragged their murdered cohort from the tiny cell, a wide smear of blood following them.

Katari surveyed the Emissaries cowering before him. His power and insight had been compounding daily, and he felt stronger and more infallible than he ever had. His Helghul-brain whirred and catalogued information, always learning and plotting. He would not make the mistake of leaving witnesses in the future.

"I should have killed you when I had the chance!" Katari hissed at Sartaña, raising his bloody spear to strike again.

Inti let out a yelp as his rage exploded, eclipsing him. His reason and self-control disappeared in that moment, and he hurled the cool, hard stone still clenched between his rigid knuckles. In one swift motion the young man had propelled the object at his father, who was only steps away. The rock made a sickening impact with Katari's right temple.

Katari was stunned. He had never imagined that the boy was capable of this, that his son, the spirit of Theron, could surprise him so completely. Katari's inner Helghul-voice howled in reaction, but the injured man only grunted as he slumped first to his knees and then fell, face down in the dirt, dead. Katari's blood ran fast and warm across the floor, his hands empty. The spear had been launched. Sartaña's fingers were wrapped around the unyielding wooden post sticking out of her belly. She thought of Amaru, her first son, who had died the same painful death. Inti dropped to her side, desperate to save her.

I will never leave you, Sartaña thought, her Marcus-brain reaching out telepathically to Theron, but Inti could not hear.

"I didn't know about you . . . if only I would have known!" Inti said guiltily, as if he should have known what Katari had done. As if he could have made a difference somehow. Sartaña raised her weak hand to his lips, stopping his apologies. She didn't need them.

The guards returned to the cell as Sartaña's soul invisibly departed. Easily slipping away and upward, her karmic colors separated from Inti's.

Inti had not intended to kill his father, the high priest. He had not intended anything at all. He had merely acted. He had lost control and followed an impulse so overwhelming that he was powerless to stop himself.

Katari's words flooded back to him as the guards knelt above the slain leader. He was now only a shell, an empty sleeve. The spirit that had inhabited his body had disappeared like a shadow at dusk, creeping ever further, wider, thinner until it disappeared.

Inti heard his father's voice in his head: "You will skin many monkeys in life. A ruler must endure much to do what needs to be done," and he understood that he had done what needed to be done. He had done what was best for the people of Stone-at-Center, but he was filled with remorse.

"Remove him," Inti commanded, as the guards stared at the young boy holding his dead mother. Katari's lifeless body was dragged away.

The citizens did not grieve for Katari, only for Sartaña. They had learned the truth of the mother's incarceration and, happy to be free of their tyrant king, they had celebrated.

In a religious celebration, Inti was crowned rightful high priest and leader of Stone-at-Center and the surrounding lands. With assistance he led the people into an era of peace, prosperity, spirituality, and contentment. His wisdom was great, and civilization advanced at Stone-at-Center, despite a continued worldwide decent into a darker Age. Theron was a light in a narrow pocket.

The stone carvings had played their part. Even two thousand years later, by then called the Ica stones, they would incite conversation, speculation, and spiritual exploration for those who heard of them.

Marcus's spirit passed on, once more a spark in the Grid, to be judged, to be recycled, and to continue as an Emissary in the world of man.

CHAPTER 13

THE WORK CONTINUES

Present Day

Quinn's message light was flashing when he woke at noon. There was a customer coming to pick up a laptop in an hour and he was in his boxers, unshowered. The blog was taking up more time than he had expected, and he almost always wrote deep into the night, interacting with readers. He switched on his carelessly splattered coffee pot and dug his thumb into his aching neck. Damn computer fatigue. Quinn was muscular and slim and appeared closer to his midthirties than his midforties.

He walked around the apartment, opening the windows to the wind and birds while he brushed his teeth. He listened to the sounds, finding meaning in their simple rhythm and song. There was a list of chores he would likely put off for another day—the recycling was overtaking the kitchen, and it balanced precariously in cardboard and plastic mountains, monopolizing his limited counter space. He didn't have curbside service and he would not add the waste to the dumpster. *Karma*, he heard in his head, and he avoided the pile.

Quinn spit a mouthful of frothy toothpaste into the kitchen sink, sideswiping yesterday's fried egg skillet, and did a quick splash and rinse. He placed his toothbrush on the window sill next to a bamboo shoot thriving in its cloudy glass of water. He poured his coffee and returned to his computer. The screen was filled with the text of Plato's *Republic*. He found it invaluable: a work penned more than two thousand years earlier filled with insights that were still relevant today.

Quinn loved to make people think—in his blog he challenged others to soar beyond their lives to seek understanding and enlightenment, not just chase conspiracy theories and fantasy. The night before he had blogged about enlightenment.

> ***TheEmissary***: I have often been asked: What exactly is enlightenment and how do I find it?
>
> Enlightenment is a path, an eternal journey, one that never ends. One must first understand that between this consciousness and the unconscious, unlimited potential beyond mankind's current state of knowledge waits to be awakened.
>
> So we ask: How is our potential awakened? By becoming conscious. By living in a state of awareness and "in the moment" at all times, responsible for our every action and thought.
>
> The signs are all around us, but we cannot see them if our eyes and minds are closed to them. The Universe talks to us in three very simple ways: Synchronicity, Symbols, and Meditation.
>
> Carl Jung coined the term "synchronicity"[8] or "meaningful coincidence." It refers to the nudges to our unconscious in the right direction, seemingly totally unrelated events that are actually messages to us. If you expand your awareness and abate your doubt and skepticism, you will feel and see things 360 degrees with every cell, instead of in tunnel vision through limited and imperfect senses.
>
> Trust your intuition. Synchronicity is what might skeptically be

written off as mere coincidence. There are NO coincidences. It may come as a song on the radio with words that feel like they are just for you . . . a billboard saying "North Star" when you are wondering over and over in your head whether to turn south or north on the highway .... It is seemingly unconnected events that are connected for YOU.

Another way the Universe talks to us is through symbols. Large and small, symbols are the original language of humanity—the thousands of pyramids across the globe, the Sphinx, Stonehenge, the seed of life, the mandala, the yin-yang, vesica piscis, sacred geometry, etc. Symbols are found in art, science, architecture, and mathematics. The Ancients specifically intended to leave a legacy of understanding for future generations. Or, if we accept reincarnation, which I do, FOR THEMSELVES IN THE FUTURE. Every generation wants to pass on their wisdom and seeks to explain the meaning of life.

Meditation is the most important way we reach enlightenment. It has been said that prayer is talking to God and meditation is God talking back. Whether you believe in God, or some other manifestation of a higher power or universal being, Source, or nothing at all, it doesn't matter. Meditation is for everyone. When we quiet our minds, making them open and still, we create a home for consciousness to grow. Nothing can grow in a garden that is so choked with weeds that there is no soil or sunlight left to spare.

Sit quietly and empty your mind. Do it as many times as it takes. It is a skill and it takes practice to get good at it. Once you become proficient, meditation can become an adventure all its own. An adventure filled with images, sensations, lucid dreams, and answers. The answers to any questions you could ever ask are within you. Tap in and listen to your inner voice!

The ultimate road to enlightenment is through compassion, humility, introspection, and most importantly, love. It is by embracing these virtues and by seeking consciousness that one can find purpose, fulfillment, and spiritual enlightenment. As humans we are imperfect, though as the great philosopher Plato loved to say, "Perfection should be our goal."

Embrace and respect nature and seek to do right by others, and your path will be blessed. Karma counts! As the Dalai Lama says, "If you can't do good, then seek to do no harm."[9]

Materialism, money, ego, fear of change, and self-interest above the greater good are traps. They are the lead shoes that keep people from climbing up the pyramid out of the Darkness and into the Light.

Enlightenment is a process, a journey. I cannot carry you . . . you must travel your own path, and the path is lit as never before.

Yours humbly, The Emissary.

Quinn knew that his customer would be arriving soon; he got dressed quickly and returned to his desk nestled among the debris of his life as the reply postings started coming in.

Anchorage411: There is no empirical evidence that synchronicity exists. It is a totally unprovable concept, though many have tried.

Goodman567: I've always called it my Spidey-senses. Nice to know that there is actually a name for it and other people do it too. I'm not into the whimsical crap, but I know when something rings true, and for me, synchronicity absolutely does.

Anderson88: There's no empirical evidence it doesn't exist. There are plenty of peoples who believe in synchronicity and communing with the natural universe: The native people of North America, the Mongolians, the Hindus, the Chinese, and the Inuit, to name a few. I love the symbolism of the pyramids, the arrow to the cosmos:

both ascending and descending in equal balance. Did you know the blocks in the pyramid at Giza range in shape and size, despite its perfect proportions? That means that no two paths up, or down, are the same. Mirrors life, doesn't it?

hansonrocks: I've been reading that the Giza pyramid might have been a power plant. According to Chris Dunn's book[10] the pyramid is more than just a symbol.

savetibet911: I think Dunn's work misses the mark a bit, but there is some evidence that the pyramid had some purpose that can't be understood in our current understanding of things. To understand the ancients, you have to think like an ancient.

Musicman: There's evidence that the pyramids resonate energy and sound.

Msnd5687: If we are talking about enlightenment, how do we get together and find people like ourselves without getting trapped in the religion thing, or ending up with a bunch of nut jobs?

Anderson88: You are already coming to the right place. The World Wide Web is connective tissue. It is a grid by no mistake; it is a mirror image of the great energy matrix that links us all! Travel the Grid, your little zap of energy across the globe in a nanosecond! MIRACULOUS! And not by coincidence!! The answers are all at your fingertips. You are a part of something bigger than yourself just by reading and far more by writing.

Macdaddy1243: People are too quick to discount religion.

Quinn loved the banter. There were some regular readers offering intelligent opinions but, judging by the number of visitors to his blog, most of the faithful signed in and never sounded off. The perfunctory demands of life called. Quinn logged off.

Quinn sat at the kitchen table surrounded by laptops and towers plagued by worms and viruses. There was so much work to be done and he had put it off too long already. He was about to get down to it when he saw the corner of an old binder buried under a stack of books. He pulled it out, toppling the pile.

He flipped through a collection of photos—his memories from Greece and Turkey, the Acropolis, the Parthenon—and bits of ancient pottery and artwork. He thought of Socrates, Plato, and Aristotle. They felt like old friends, a comfortable sweater, and as he turned the pages Quinn was transported. His mind was miles away in another time, smiling, laughing, and living, his face lifted to the sun, the sound of seabirds calling in his ears.

CHAPTER 14

THE HONORABLE MENTOR

418 BC, Ancient Greece

Aristocles's father died when he was five years old. His mother, Perictione, according to custom, married her maternal uncle. Aristocles missed his beloved father but grew to love his stepfather. A child of wealth and privilege, he spent his sun-filled afternoons in lessons or at leisure.[11]

Aristocles's life changed forever when he was eleven. It was a sticky-hot day and he found himself unwisely wandering the docks of Athens, smelling the sour sea air. Commerce and hustle flowed all around him. Haggard fishermen lugged their heavy, rank loads by cart or over their stooped shoulders. It was a hard, dirty place that smelled of rotting fish and cat urine; he found it exhilarating. His fine leather sandals were little protection from the foulness of the place. Everywhere, servants haggled for their master's dinners and sellers scowled at being coerced down.

The boy noticed a quiet alcove cooled at least ten degrees by the shade of a nearby vessel. Tired and hot from walking, he ignored the filth and sat to rest. He opened his satchel and withdrew a scroll: the story of *Pyramus and Thisbe*.[12] In this tale, a beautiful girl and her true love are kept apart by their families. When the lad mistakenly believes that his love is eaten by a lion on the eve of their elopement, he kills himself. His intended bride, upon discovering him dead, kills herself.

Aristocles had carefully written out his favorite tale onto a parchment and had read it many times. He had only just begun rereading the story when the scroll was torn from his unsuspecting grasp. Startled, he looked up into the glare of the sun and made out the outline of three boys, slightly older but significantly larger than he, staring down at him with contempt.

"What here, little bull?" the tallest, thickest boy snarled as he waved the curling page in Aristocles' stunned face. He tried to get up but was pushed back to the ground, where he landed with a painful thump.

"Give it back!" Aristocles demanded futilely, still planted by a forceful palm to the hard earth beneath him.

"The pudgy *emperor* thinks we're his slaves," the leader crowed. "You don't rule here boy, this is our territory," he said, tossing Aristocles's document into the foul pool of seawater below. Aristocles was helpless to stop them and was now more concerned for his own safety than for his belongings. The boys laughed uproariously and squared off, legs bent, prepared to wrestle. Aristocles ignored the challenge and feebly covered his head with his arms in anticipation of their blows, helpless to stop them.

"Aih there!" a stern voice called out, intervening. Aristocles opened his eyes and looked past the three miscreants to see a wide, thick man swaggering toward them. "Bullies and bastards!" the man boomed, shaking a fist in the air as he approached. "To intimidate a boy and steal his belongings is play?" he barked, coming nose to nose with the nervous leader. In one swift motion, the rumpled man lifted the bully by the throat and dangled him like noodles over a pot, shocking all of them with his easy strength.

"How dare you laugh when your purpose is cruelty? In you go," he said, dropping the struggling boy into the filth below. By this time the troublemaker's two accomplices had run off. Aristocles watched gleefully as his would-be assailant splashed frantically toward the edge.

"Get that scroll and return it," the older man demanded, blocking the boy from climbing out. When the document was soggily ashore, the boy again tried to climb out. "Swim around to the pier and get out of my sight, or I'll let that putrid water bloat you like a discarded carp."

The breathless youngster began making his way to shore. Aristocles stood beside the unusual man, studying him, as they watched the swimmer struggle. He had the sense that the surly stranger would have jumped in for rescue at the first sign of the boy being in distress, but his theory went untested. The bully successfully pulled himself out of the water a few minutes later.

Aristocles guessed that the man was somewhere around his uncle's age of forty-five, but he had obviously lived a difficult life. His ugly face was a mess of scars and lines framed by sagebrush whiskers at his brow and chin. His eyelids had white polyps and bumps on them, and his nose was a twisted lump stranded just left of center. His hairline receded well behind his ears, and the strands that he did have were stringy and long. When the protector opened his mouth to speak, his teeth and tongue were purple from wine.

"Ha! A lesson taught is worth its time!" he said, clapping Aristocles on the back, unintentionally sending the young boy stumbling toward the water's edge. "Take care! My best effort to spare you will be wasted if you cannot hold your footing and you end up in that rancid soup."

"I owe you my great thanks. They would have left me in a heap," Aristocles said, holding his sopping parchment and grateful that his only injury was a dull ache where he had been thumped jubilantly on the back.

"What is it you are reading?" the older man asked. He looked carefully at the rotund boy. He was not an adolescent that one would typically see at the docks alone. Obviously a son of privilege, he was an oddity. He must be inquisitive, curious, and fearless, or possibly an imbecile.

"*Pyramus and Thisbe*," Aristocles answered condescendingly. He doubted that this unsightly commoner could read at all.

"They meet a tragic end," the man said simply, still sizing him up. Aristocles rudely rolled his eyes without realizing it. No longer in danger, his confidence and unwarranted sense of self-importance were restored.

"Yes, I am aware," he replied.

"It doesn't make for very enlightened reading," the man said critically.

"It says a great deal about the power of perception," Aristocles argued impressively.

"Well answered," the man said, pausing. "If you want to challenge your intellect, you should come find me at my school at the painted stoa," he said.

"The painted stoa? I have heard of you," the boy replied with the nonchalance of an adolescent too inexperienced to be properly impressed. "You must be Socrates. You were a teacher to my uncles."

"Aaaach! Never a teacher! A teacher seeks to impart only his limited knowledge . . . to pour from their own jug and fill the cups of others. I would rather learn what you know, and challenge each thought and its process . . . that is, if you are prepared to set aside your romantic drivel for more serious mental matters," Socrates said, amused and unperturbed by the boy's insolence. The older man preferred the genuineness of the interaction compared to the phony, fawning, backstabbing adults that he so often had to endure.

This boy was exactly the reason Socrates had opened his school; he was a white light and still a secret to himself. Socrates imagined an untapped well of thought and contemplation within Aristocles. Just the night before, Socrates had dreamed that such a student would come to him. He suspected that it was not chance that had placed them in one another's path that day. The squat, ugly man began striding away and Aristocles called after him cynically.

"What's your fee, old man?"

"The conversation is free, for the love of knowledge, but leave your condescension with your wet nurse," Socrates answered with a crooked grin and was gone.

Aristocles walked home distractedly, contemplating Socrates. He had never met such a fascinating character. He could not imagine his uncles dangling a fishing line, let alone a boy, over the filthy dockside. And this was the renowned philosopher and educator; how could it be so?

Within the week, curiosity and a desire to learn delivered him to the door of his new mentor, who expectantly greeted him by saying, "What took you so long?" His education began immediately.

Aristocles had been a playful, carefree child, but as early as eight years old he had grown contemplative, as though waiting for something. He had begun to feel ill at ease, and he was inexplicably in a constant state of "should be elsewhere." Aristocles had felt that he was different and that he was destined to do something great, but to others he seemed an oddity, an old man in children's clothing.

Aristocles discovered gradually, as he aged, that he had an internal voice, a daemonion,[13] that eventually became known to him as Marcus. Afraid of ridicule, the boy told no one about Marcus but grew to trust the voice implicitly. It was a part of him, a clever and ancient part of him that had many stories and much wisdom to share.

Upon meeting Socrates, Aristocles was compelled to join him, and his daemonion grew clearer and stronger as he matured. As the years passed under Socrates' tutelage, Aristocles's Marcus-voice fused with his every thought and they became symbiotic. As a youth, Aristocles had been relieved to learn that Socrates too claimed to have an internal voice.

Aristocles had not been in Socrates's school long before, without ceremony, in the teasing manner of adolescent boys, he was nicknamed Plato. It was an epithet given in reference to his stout girth meaning "broad or abundant."[14] The moniker was thoroughly embraced, and few people ever knew his proper name at all.

Aristocles became known to one and all as Plato, and he was a driven and focused student. Despite the close relationship that was forming with his schoolmaster, he was often forlorn and lonely. Late at night, when his studying was set aside, he would feel nostalgic for an ancient homeland he had never visited.

In his late teens, he was tortured by remembrances of Theron and craved the energy of her spirit. He searched for her colors in every new place and person. Marcus felt perpetually incomplete and saw her in flashes: at the sight of a beautiful sunrise, in the petals of a flower, in a tender moment between loved ones nearby. He knew that if she was near, it would quench his unbearable feelings of emptiness. Plato was unfairly burdened by the fatigue of lifetimes of longing and endured a constant ache. Marcus had become aloof to insulate himself from the emotional peaks and valleys of his lifetimes, and it affected his daily interactions.

Socrates educated by asking questions, not preaching answers, and he taught his students to question everything, including him. Plato demonstrated great aptitude, often challenging Socrates. As a result, he quickly became a favored student.

Plato's admiration and respect for Socrates grew and, despite warnings from his inner voice to be cautious, a deep connection formed. Marcus had lived and grieved many times, and the weight of his losses made him wary, but his friendship with Socrates came to be one of the greatest he would ever know. Plato often mused to himself that though Socrates was merely a man, he seemed to have all of the purpose and virtue of an Emissary.

In his bed at night, alone and able to consider his Marcus-memories, Plato was highly critical of himself and his nature. Had it been only in pursuit of Theron that he had left Atitala? If not for her would he have become an Emissary at all? Was he an Emissary by mistake? He was ashamed, and he was determined to prove himself worthy and to better the world if he could.

Plato matured and his pudgy frame grew solid and wide as he developed into a plain-looking man. He was a head taller than his gargoyle mentor but never matched him for swagger and confidence. The nickname Plato always suited him, and the name Aristocles was forever left behind.

When together in discussion, hours passed unnoticed, and the duo found no topic too trivial or too complex to divert them. Plato was unusually astute, and Socrates admired his ability to memorize and recall entire conversations and dialogues verbatim, even weeks later.

"It is a gift and a curse to have a parrot with such an indelible memory always at my shoulder! I rebuff him like a gadfly but still he natters on," Socrates would jibe affectionately. Plato did not mind the good-natured ribbing; he looked upon his teacher with awe. Socrates had come from nothing, a poor humble family, yet he was highly respected and was a wonder to listen to and learn from.

The men agreed that there was a higher world, a world of true knowledge, more real than the oft-misinterpreted subjective world of the senses. However, their analogous thinking and respect for one another did not prevent them disagreeing on many occasions. Marcus admired Socrates' unequivocal acceptance of the soul's existence. He understood the order of the Universe without past-life memory or instruction. He developed his own elaborate, brilliant theories, and his intuition and brainpower astounded his pupil.

Plato learned continually from his companion: how to question, how to orate, how to inspire others without becoming sanctimonious and self-important. At times he felt like an imposter, a cheat in Socrates's midst. The advantage of his Marcus-memories, his first-hand understanding, felt faintly deceitful. It was difficult to entertain ideas that countered what he knew to be true without growing frustrated and overbearing.

Socrates's influence in Athens continued to grow. He spoke publicly, encouraging people to question everything, for nothing was taboo, particularly religion, human nature, and politics. His unrestrained criticisms of the government and current democratic system made him an enemy to the regime and a target of their displeasure.

Plato grew desperately concerned for his friend and warned that he was drawing too much attention to himself, but Socrates was characteristically irreverent and would not be silenced or intimidated. The practical genius was undaunted and grew only more critical of the so-called democracy that he asserted defied its own definition and dragged the greater society into a pit of commonness and ignorance.

Socrates came under direct fire when government officials charged him with corrupting the youth of Athens, for encouraging them to question the social structure and the distribution of wealth in their society. Socrates railed against the establishment to his students.

"The educated aristoi of society need to stand out! Stand up and lead!

Democracy will be the ruin of mankind; wise men of wisdom and reason should govern our cities! You!" he said pointing at his students. "You! You! YOU! Men of thought and intellect need to be the decision makers and take care! Not the masses. The unphilosophical man is at the mercy of his senses, believing them real and mistakenly trusting them. The way a prisoner in a cave, his back to the entrance, might believe the shadows cast before him represent truth, so do the ignorant and easily led believe their eyes and ears. They look no further for enlightenment and a greater understanding of truth and reality!"

Charges were brought against the malcontent, and fortunately there was a law protecting freedom of speech that worked in Socrates's favor. The politicians, however, did not relent, and they continued their persecution. They exploited an obscure edict prohibiting the disbelief of the ancestral gods and charged Socrates with impiety[15] to silence him.

Socrates entrusted Plato with continuing his school during the trial. Though Plato wanted to attend court, Socrates was adamant. "It is more important that debate go on, especially now. This trial is a ruse, a stratagem by Meletus and the other politicians to silence me," he said. "I'll not be thwarted, and these phonies will bear the humiliation of their ridiculous mendacity. It is their intent that I am intimidated and stifled, but I will not be controlled. There is no strength in words without action! Worry not, Plato," he assured. "The law is on my side and justice will be the victor."

"I have less confidence in the law than in you. I have many times been witness to the darkness in men, and those shadows burgeon in the courts as they currently exist. I have no faith that justice will prevail," Plato answered. "Laws are fashioned and perverted by those in power for selfish gain."

"And that, my friend, is why we speak out. Why we orate and question and challenge. It is the very reason I will not act contrite in the face of these self-serving reprobates."

Socrates clapped his gnarly hands together and, patting his stout belly, suggested they eat. He was famished and longing for a strong cup of ale to lull the commotion in his ever-active mind. Together the men adjourned to a long wooden table in the back courtyard. Bread, meat, olives, and a strong beer were brought, and the fellows spoke of greater things than the trial.

They philosophized about the role of man in the world, the role of God in creation, the role of mathematics in everything. They discussed mankind's connection to the cosmos and to one another. Plato was inspired as always. The men lit a fire within one another and never grew tired of their conversation or of each other's company. They did not always agree, and those times were the best, the most heated, the most challenging, and brought the greatest epiphanies and revelations. The bliss that they knew as they delved deep into the workings of the world and the Universe fed their friendship and bonded them in heart and mind.

The trial continued, and as it progressed Plato was finally able to attend. He worried for Socrates and urged him to take the charges more seriously.

"It will be as it should. What lessons there are to be learned by this process will come despite my smirk. I will show this jury the audacity of their allegations. I will continue to emphasize the ludicrous nature of these claims indicting a poor man of words," Socrates answered.

The unperturbed accused spoke at great length on his own behalf, and, to the annoyance of the jury, he surmised that he must be the most knowledgeable of all the men in Athens "for I alone know that I know nothing."[16]

Constantly surveying the displeasure of the jurors, Plato continued to caution him. "Socrates, it is clear to all who observe that your irreverence and lack of concern serve only to enrage Meletus and the other jurors. They are determined to silence you and to punish your apathy and disregard for them. I can feel their energy; a bad turn is coming."

"I am but a seed to their dirt. By my unwillingness to be silenced, others will be encouraged and will take root," he replied. Socrates appreciated Plato's concern but altered nothing in his behavior.

The gifted philosopher delivered a brilliant oratory to the court, easily debunking the weak charges against him. It was with sincere shock and disbelief that he heard the guilty verdict. The jury of five hundred and one had only narrowly found him guilty, and the expected penalty was a fine.

"Perhaps I should dine at the table of the winning Olympians?" Socrates suggested, further aggravating and insulting the jurors by mocking what his consequence might be.

Despite his popularity and fame, Socrates, his wife, and his three sons lived in relative poverty. He offered a paltry one hundred drachma to the court and it was rejected. Plato had appealed to Socrates' students and raised three thousand drachma to appease the court. But to their mortification, as requested by his accuser Meletus, the jury ruled that Socrates be put to death for his crimes.

"Arrangements have been made to get you out of Athens tonight. The three thousand drachma are yours. You can be gone in a few hours," Plato informed him.

"I shall not flee," Socrates answered calmly. "I am old; I will not scurry like a rat in a deluge. I have never run from debate, confrontation, or challenge. I will not now become less than the man I have always been. I have earned the esteem of many and intend to maintain my self-respect at the end of my life. I will be steadfast and fearless as the consequences are brought."

"The consequences are unjust! A travesty and a symptom of the illness that plagues this foul city! This jury, these men, exact a most heinous wrong upon you in seeking to silence your galling voice. You are a light to this time and these people. You cannot slip silently into death. I have been told that they will not pursue you. I have been given a promise. They want you out of Athens, and you can live out your days peacefully in the country somewhere."

"Cowardice! Would you wish to remember me as such a man, Plato? Should I leave this world a eunuch, a flower stripped of every leaf and petal and trampled underfoot?" he fumed. "Would you choose to end this life a spark instead of a flame? I would not! I will leave this world happily, willingly, into the extraordinary life that awaits me on the other side, finally privy to all of the answers that we so desperately seek. Only at my death will I leave Athens. She is my blood, my bones. I am nothing without her walls, her people. I will go out a flame, my friend, a light intense and glaring upon the wrongs I have tried to expose."

"Athens does not deserve you. They will not remember you in two generations.

We are all as insignificant as a skin shed by a snake," Plato replied miserably. His heart burned in his chest as if he had just run an Olympic sprint.

"I do not seek to be remembered. I desire only that the philosophy and knowledge are not lost. Continue to teach the students to question everything; they will pass on the wisdom. Record what we have learned for future generations."

The realization that he was about to lose his beloved companion and mentor in such an unjust and preposterous circumstance devoured Plato's patience and regard for mankind. Time after time they extinguished the brightest lights. Fear, doubt, and the quest for individual interests above the greater good consistently desecrated and destroyed the most perfect selfless beings. Plato's Marcus-brain was flush with overwhelming anger and sadness and then . . . nothing. Numbness spread through him like a poison—like the hemlock that Socrates would be forced to drink in one day's time.

Socrates did not fear death. He was more concerned about the burden of grief that he was leaving behind for his loved ones. On the eve of his demise, Socrates was surrounded by distraught friends; only Plato was not present. The condemned sought to console those in attendance but grew impatient with their emotional outbursts. He optimistically anticipated great clarity and knowledge after death and spoke with eagerness about his journey into the next realm.

Plato was too heartbroken, too angry, too tired of it all, and he wondered what sort of grand lesson he was supposed to be learning. How did this cycle of continual life, death, joy, and grief evolve? How was he supposed to make a difference in this ruined world, where men execute the likes of Socrates and raise up the idiotic, cruel, and self-serving? He had first-hand knowledge of the afterlife, heaven, hell, and the waiting place that he later called the "Meadow" when he wrote about it in the *Republic*, but none of his awareness soothed his disappointment at the waste and brutality of mankind.

Plato had watched helplessly the dissembling of his beloved professor and friend. How was he to be an Emissary, a guide to people who would not hear or see what was plainly put before them? What could his role be? Feelings of uselessness engulfed him and he grew angry in response. He found himself wandering at the docks, remembering the day that he so fortuitously met Socrates. He almost smiled at the idea that it was chance that had brought him there, for he knew that it had most certainly been destiny.

What now? What now that the foul, foul deed was done? The murder of a genius, a light to all mankind, had occurred without ceremony, like closing a door, snuffing a candle, without even a trumpet blast or shaking ground! Death by corruption, fear, and ignorance and yet the world went on, unaffected and uncaring.

Marcus's armor, honed from many lifetimes of loss, registered a hearty dent. Mankind was unworthy. Time after time, they ignored the messages placed so obviously before them and embraced waste, chaos, evil, and pain.

Where was the unity? Could they not feel their connection to God, to each other? Could he? Marcus felt hopeless and alone, bringing all of his centuries of angst to his current life as Plato. The lifetimes of fighting, teaching, and searching for Theron had exhausted him.

Plato drifted through the port until sunrise, and as the sky lit with gorgeous arrays of red, gold, and orange he was struck again by how life went on eternal. In that moment, and not for the first time, Marcus regretted taking the potion. He regretted his past-life memory. One lifetime of winning, losing, birth, death, beauty, and horror is enough to remember. It was too much. He longed for Theron's company as deeply as he ever had.

Marcus looked at the image carved carefully in the filigree on the hull of the boat beside him: the seed of life. The significance of that symbol finding him in that moment did not escape him. Each petal signified lifetimes of lessons learned and that lives were a cycle, a process. Even as an Emissary, he had come to understand that he too must complete his cycles, and being the thinker that he was, it set him up for deep contemplation.

Plato looked to the heavens for guidance, and after a few moments of silent introspection, he decided he would leave Athens. His Marcus-brain urged him to continue the search. Finding Theron would make him whole again. He had to escape Athens and the inhumanity of Socrates' wrongful death.

CHAPTER 15

PLATO IN EGYPT

The Oracle

Plato departed Athens soon after Socrates's death and spent the next twelve years searching for Theron, tormented by his inability to find her. Socrates had been a fine companion and a distraction from Marcus's loneliness, and Plato continued to miss him bitterly. He couldn't identify the grand purpose he supposed he should feel as an Emissary and his path unfolded day by day.

Plato began plotting the cycle of the Great Year. Plato hadn't coined the phrase or come to the realization alone. It was ancient knowledge, and Marcus had learned it in Atitala, though he wished now he had paid better attention. He studied the constellations in the night sky, knowing that from his place on Earth, they shifted bit by bit and appeared to move over the ages. The nearly twenty-six thousand years it took for the entire zodiac to cycle in the sky from one exact position back to that same position was one "Perfect Year" or "Great Year."

Plato made certain that, should his writing survive, this fundamental concept was recorded for future generations. It mattered where the constellations were in the Earth's heavens: Taurus, Leo, Aquarius, and the rest. They each had their own significance. The energy that came to living Earth through the cosmos made a difference. The Ages were set: Gold, Silver, Bronze, and Iron. With each Age came a level of knowledge and enlightenment that the Emissaries had been sent to safeguard.

Plato identified exactly where he was in the cosmic circle of evolution—after all, knowledge was power . . . and sometimes torment. How far from the Golden Age of Atitala had Marcus come? By his best estimation he was in the middle of a Bronze Age. It was disheartening; he was only a third of the way through, and as ugly and ignorant as the citizens of Athens had proven themselves to be, things would get much worse before they got better.

The world was descending into a time when the Darkness had the upper hand. How would Marcus cope with having such great knowledge and memory through times that were increasingly cruel and backward? Where was his Theron? He could bear it, if only she were at his side. Once again he wished for the bliss of ignorance, the serenity of a clean memory.

Plato searched for Theron's energy as he traveled, and he kept himself busy passionately writing. He remained aloof, isolating himself from other people and determined to avoid the pain of attachment and loss that had affected him so deeply. He spent some time in Italy and was befriended by a philosophically minded man named Dion. Dion looked up to Plato and the two men enjoyed great philosophical debate, but after a brief time Plato moved on. Plato did not know then the role Dion would later play in his life.

Plato ended up in Egypt. The ancient land of Khem felt like a comfortable second skin. He had been there in more than one previous lifetime. His memories came back to him in lucid dreams, as real and vivid as daily life.

As the Great Pyramid of Giza had risen up before him, owning the vast landscape, Plato had been reminded of Atitala. The pyramids were a gift from another Age and were the ultimate symbol of spiritual connection, ascending and descending, pointing to heaven but anchored in the Earth. Plato smirked when he heard that the Egyptians were claiming the pyramids as their own creations.

The memory of the Sun Gods—Emissaries who had engineered the structures—had been lost or relegated to myth over time.

The School of Mysteries was Plato's ultimate destination in Egypt. It was a legendary and secret society founded by Hermes who, unbeknownst to Marcus, had once been Red Elder. The hidden schools were modeled after those in Atitala and Lumeria and were in place around the globe to enlighten and educate the worthy. Marcus had been there before in other lives, though he had never crossed paths with Red Elder in those times.

While still at the Academy in Athens, Plato had listened gladly to stories about the Egyptian Mystery School. It was said that the ancient mathematician Pythagoras had spent many years there, and Plato was sure he must have been an Emissary. He wished he had shared a lifetime with the genius; they could have discussed the mathematics and geometry that Plato found so enthralling.

Unlike the civilizations of the Golden Age when the schools had operated openly for everyone, the current corruption and darkness of humanity made secrecy a necessity. Only the honorable and trustworthy seeker could be given the knowledge. Only the solid and unwavering could study in the sacred halls. Marcus had more to learn . . . and perhaps Theron would be there.

Plato was happy to be returning to the Mystery School; the difficulty was that he had to find it. Like water, the mystery schools were constantly moving. Plato had made his way to Heliopolis but, though he felt that he was very close, he had been unable to find the enigmatic location on his own.

The marketplace in Heliopolis bustled and squawked, hot and pungent in the noonday sun. Plato inhaled the scents of spices, humans, and beasts as they rose and fell around him. Despite having adopted the robes of the locals, Plato was recognizable as a foreigner.

"Mister, you need?" a young boy called to him in several broken languages, trying each in turn. Plato was struck by the boy's tenacity and language skills, and he turned. There was a familiarity. He did not see the indigo karmic code of an Emissary, but he did recognize the aura of this soul. They had met before. Marcus knew it was the same soul who had once shown him mercy as Sartaña's guard in

Stone-at-Center, and he filled with gratitude at the memory. It was remarkable to find him once again. It must have meaning.

"Yes, I need," Plato answered. "I need . . . School of Mysteries?" he said in broken Egyptian. The boy's eyes opened wide, and in one swift motion he ducked past the shoulder of a fig seller and ran away. Plato called after him in disappointment.

Deep in thought, Plato continued his walk through the noisy bazaar and purchased his daily bread. Plato munched the hard, dry loaf and sipped tea before he made his way to the largest of the nearby temples. Sweat ran in itchy streams down his back. The high columns and ornate structure of the temple were borrowed from another time, and they had begun to crumble and falter in disrepair. Plato entered into a vast stone courtyard.

"I wish to see the high priest," he requested of a nearby boy wearing temple robes. The boy hurried away and returned moments later demanding an exorbitant fee, a donation of gold from the foreigner. Plato was appalled and refused the boy's request, sending him back to his master empty-handed. The Greek was leaving when, from a nearby corner, a boy emerged. Plato recognized him instantly. It was the boy from the marketplace who had run away.

"The high priest is bad man. I take you to Mystery School," the boy said in choppy Greek, stepping back into the shadows and beckoning Plato to follow. The beautiful green and blue glow of the young man's aura pleased Plato as it mingled with his own, and he felt sorry for the masses, blind to the glowing energy hovering around every person.

"How did you find me?" Plato asked when they were outside.

"Everyone who seek Mystery School go here, so . . . high priest rich and fat, but he don't know where is school. He torture me if he think I know. I still not tell. He not worthy."

"How do you know I'm worthy?" Plato asked.

"You not pay," the boy answered, smiling openly. Plato admired his logic, though he himself would have required more evidence.

The young boy's name was Amnut, and he was older than he had first appeared—about thirteen years. Plato soon learned that he and his uncle had led many deserving, and some not so deserving, seekers to the site of the secret institute. Apparently Amnut's uncle was not quite as discerning as he.

Plato followed his guide adeptly, scurrying through the maze of alleys and carts. The smells of cooking and urine assaulted Plato's nostrils. Laundry hung overhead in colorful strips, and bells and metal clanged and chimed around them chaotically.

Amnut came to an abrupt halt. There was no grand portico, no signs. There was a steep stairway leading into a cellar beneath a two-story, grey stone building that had been built and rebuilt in the same spot many times. A cart almost blocked the access completely, and without his guide Plato would surely have missed it.

A mother hollered from above them, and he heard the sound of children running while a baby cried for food or sleep. At the base of the stairway there was a thick wooden door, above which Plato looked for the carving of the right eye of Horus inside a gold circle. Marcus knew the symbol well and had seen it in other times and cultures, always referring to the great third eye or "eye of protection." It was the sign of the Mystery School within.

Plato overpaid Amnut and sadly bade the grateful boy farewell. Marcus guessed that the young man's sole purpose in this lifetime was to lead travelers to the School of Mystery. Amnut had never entered the rooms himself.

Arriving at the Mystery School was exciting. Plato's Marcus-brain revved with anticipation. There had been no secrecy in Atitala—there had been no need—but now there was a password. Plato knew the sacred statement that would identify him as a friend and would open the school to him. It was catalogued with every other significant and insignificant detail in his Marcus-brain.

As expected the door was locked. Plato knocked on the thick barrier. Nothing. After a few moments he knocked again. This time the door opened a crack and a middle-aged man in a colorful robe peered out.

"Anima mundi," Plato whispered quietly, though it was unnecessary. The village was so loud around him he could have shouted. The words meant "world soul," the energy that unites everything.

"Anima mundi," the man repeated, stepping back so that Plato could slip inside. The door swiftly closed and locked behind them.

Plato immediately searched the faces of the men and women, girls and boys all looking at him curiously. The room glowed with the indigo hue of the Emissaries, but none of them was Theron. Marcus was disappointed and retreated deeper into Plato's consciousness, despite the abundant warmth and friendship of the place.

The small space was lit and sweetened by beeswax candles that were placed on each of six rough-hewn tables. The seats were simple wooden benches, grooved and polished from centuries of use. The floor was dirt and sand that was often swept and neatly raked. There were twenty people huddled in cozy study groups in the quaint front room. The stone walls were unadorned and were dark and grey. Small sporadic holes up high near the ceiling allowed for airflow but let no light in.

The cleric who had opened the door welcomed Plato and listened intently as the newcomer accounted for his arrival. Plato was led further into the school to meet the high priest. He entered through a low doorway and came soul to soul with the familiar and powerful karmic energy of Red Elder. He was elated.

"Good high priest, I am known as Plato. I come to you a humble student," Plato said, lowering his head. His Marcus-brain was at full attention, sending him waves and zaps of information through past-life memories and images.

"Marcus," the high priest said cautiously. "I am happy to greet a familiar soul from ages old."

"Red Elder? I cannot help but wonder how *you* know *me*," Plato replied suspiciously, his mind reeling. Red Elder had memory. Could Red Elder have been the cloaked director in the caverns with Helghul on the night of the exodus from Atitala? Was it possible?

"And I cannot help but wonder . . . why . . . unlike your fellow Emissaries . . .

you know me? Your memory was immediate. How can it be?" Red Elder asked. "I feel your mistrust but worry not, I am with the Light."

"But you have memory?"

"Yes," the high priest confirmed, wanting to alleviate the Emissary's alarm. "It is my role to educate and to be the Keeper of Records. It is essential that I have unlimited memory. It is a blessing and a burden in *equal* measure, as I am sure you have learned."

"It makes sense. What good is it to have no memory? What good can an Emissary be without memory?" Plato inquired. "I see them faltering, their auras bright and bountiful but their heads foggy and unaware."

"You are mistaken, friend. The knowledge of the Universe is woven through their souls. It does not leave them. Once learned, the wisdom stays with them and grows stronger as they learn, deep and eternal. It is like the foundation of a great building, forever remembered in every cell and vessel. It is *your* predicament to remember what you need not, Marcus. How does it haunt you?"

"Theron. Have you seen Theron? I search for her still."

"I have known her many times and she has made a difference—she is the brightest of an impressive group. You will be tested, Marcus. Your choice to have memory brings much heartache and pain with it."

Plato nodded, but pressed the priest further. "I have no doubt that you are correct. I hope that by coming here I can move further on my path, but is she here now? Do you know where I can find her?"

"No, she is not here. You must know that to look for her is futile. The soul of Theron is well at work somewhere on this plane or another. Only when it is destined . . . only then will your paths cross again."

"I understand," Plato said miserably.

"How is it that you remember? How is it so? Leave nothing out, I am not your judge."

"The day of the reckoning I followed Helghul, do you remember him?"

"Go on," Red Elder said, nodding.

"It is still not totally clear to me, though I know that the images of that day have plagued my dreams and sent me nightmares in many lifetimes . . . I remember a high cavern and I hid from view and watched . . . I can still feel my fear, my overwhelming horror . . . they murdered the children . . . smashing them . . . but I did nothing."

"They killed the innocent to strengthen the Dark Energy . . . the Darkness feeds on murder and sacrifice," Red Elder explained.

"Helghul was there with others, chanting . . . and there was a person in charge . . . someone leading them, though I couldn't tell who it was. Helghul was sacrificed."

"Helghul? They killed him?" the high priest asked, his eyes wide with surprise.

"No, not dead . . . he was cut or injured, but something *took* him . . . from the inside out. He was consumed and a darkness entered him. I looked away . . . I cannot speak as a scholar about what I saw, it is too inconceivable . . . and even now my mind runs from it," Plato said.

"What happened next?"

"Helghul drank from a vial. I heard it said that the liquid would enable him to remember in future lifetimes. I hid until all were gone and . . . before I left . . . as I was leaving I saw it . . . I retrieved the discarded bottle."

"You risked dark magic? Were you not afraid or hesitant?"

"I was afraid to forget. I chose to remember," Plato said defiantly.

"Is it possible that you endure this choice for the love of Theron?"

"Yes, for the love of one," Plato replied.

"No . . . for the love of Theron. The love of One is something altogether different," the high priest corrected.

"You remind me of my mentor Socrates, with your challenging and reorganizing of my words," Plato said, smiling. His initial distrust had been eliminated and he was calmed by the soothing karmic energy of Red Elder. The men spoke for a while longer, and then Plato was taken to a group with which his needs for learning would be met.

Plato remained at the school for many months. The students were advanced in thinking and understanding and were led almost exclusively by Red Elder personally. Plato read and studied the ancient wisdom of the Emerald Tablet, first expanded into texts centuries before by Red Elder when he was Hermes. The scriptures were always a new lesson, in every word and phrase a myriad of meaning and direction. Each carefully chosen syllable was a beacon on the path to the purest form, to the ultimate Oneness with God, and each time he read the documents Plato gleaned new meaning and understanding.

Plato never saw the actual Emerald Tablet; it was carefully hidden and well guarded. When Plato inquired about the need for such precautions, the high priest explained that the tablet was the key to universal power and balance.

"How?" Plato had asked, intrigued.

"That is not for me to tell. Each soul must journey on its own path to find that answer," Red Elder had replied.

Plato heightened his spiritual awareness and understanding alongside his fellow seekers. As his Marcus-brain grew clearer in voice, he found himself thinking more often of Theron. Plato remained uncertain about what he should do next in the world. He meditated, wrote, and prayed, but Marcus doubted himself and blocked the growth that he was not yet ready to receive.

Plato wished that Socrates could have visited such a miraculous place and could have met Red Elder. They would have had brilliant conversations, and he would have loved to listen to them. Plato often had questions for the high priest, and Red Elder was always willing.

After a few months of intense practice and study, Plato became restless and sought out the leader of the Emissaries.

"Why are we hiding? Why do we not parade the universal truth through the streets?" Plato asked.

"It is our role to make them think, not to feed them what they have no stomach to digest. Each person must begin a search of their own. Mankind is not ready . . . is not spiritually developed in this Bronze Age. Those who are meant to study will end up here or at one of the other schools around the world. When the light among men is bright enough, we will open the records and share the wisdom. There are Ages . . . prophets and development that have yet to occur. We cannot yet reveal the great knowledge and trust that it will not be misused or misunderstood. The magic science could be used for evil, to gain power. As we, the keepers of the Light, are striving, so are the conjurers of the Darkness. If the knowledge was freely given now, it would deepen the shadows into which we are currently descending. We are on the eve of a Dark Age of man."

"How will I know when the time is right? When will my work be done?"

"For every soul there is a theme, a path that must be followed, and lessons that must be learned. It is for the Emissaries as for all others in the Grid of creation. Even when in service for the greater good, you must honor your own destiny and complete your own cycle of learning. I know you feel weary, but you are early in this journey. The journey *is* the reason. The experience and growth *are* your purpose. Milk each moment for the lesson and experience it offers. Do not spend your days searching for what is not there. See the lesson and wonder in every moment."

"How can I find my theme or . . . my personal lesson?"

"It will find you, but you must be open, you must meditate and contemplate and live a mindful life. Your time here in Egypt is finished, Plato. You must move on."

"I feel it also, but to where? Back to Athens? There is nothing for me there."

"It is your choice. If you seek answers, you may choose to journey to the Oracle of Amun in Siwa and ask your questions, but it is certainly time for you to move forward."

Plato contemplated the advice for a moment. The Oracle was renowned, and Plato had previously wondered if it might be a worthwhile journey. It may help him find Theron.

"In future lives, how will I find you?" Plato asked.

"When our paths are meant to cross again, they will. If it is wisdom and comfort you seek, you need only be introspective as you have practiced, and you can join the Universal Web of Energy. You are never alone, Marcus. We are all

One," Red Elder reminded. Though Plato knew it was true, he did feel alone, and Marcus was no less determined to find Theron.

Within days Plato sent word to the young guide, Amnut. Siwa was three days away across difficult desert terrain, and Plato needed experienced guides. Amnut, with the help of his uncle, was efficient and well prepared with camels and provisions, for a price. Amnut's uncle's colors were dull and gloomy compared to the luster of his nephew's, and his surly disposition was obvious.

The journey to Siwa was smelly and uncomfortable. Plato ached from the relentless jostling, but he loved the efficiency of the camel's physiology. He watched in wonder as the animal's toes spread and gripped on each sandy step.

Amnut was a joker, and Plato found himself laughing aloud as he had not done since losing Socrates. He would truly have felt light and happy in his adventure if he could only have lived in the moment, if he could only have been a man with one lifetime and no longing for Theron tugging at the corner of his contentment. Marcus was sad to be alone in his past-life memory and wished it were Theron speaking jovially from the camel beside him.

They rode for three scorching days across the vast golden desert. The sameness of the landscape and the slowness of the mounts gave the illusion that they were standing still. It was a different world, and it was hard to imagine that this place existed on the same planet as Athens. On the cold nights they slept under the expansive starry sky, and the moon and stars were bright and close. Plato was happy to converse with the curious Amnut.

"So you say, everything has . . . soul and moves in patterns? The planets, sun, and moon?" Amnut clarified in choppy Greek.

"Yes, and they are all spheres. They are like a ball, not flat like papyrus. And, yes, they have an ethereal soul and are alive, just like you."

"How do you know? Why do I believe you?"

"You shouldn't. You should seek knowledge for yourself, not let your head be filled by others. Your questions are well thought and indicate a strong mind. Have you been to school?"

"My father say . . . school is for weak and wealthy . . . and I am none . . ."

"Your mind is like clay. If you shape it and mold it constantly, adding new wetness and knowledge, it will stay malleable and changeable. If you let others form it, never seeking knowledge of your own, it will harden and grow brittle and weak," Plato replied.

Amnut's uncle snorted his disapproval from across the fire.

"You disagree? Please share with us your thoughts. I am a man who believes my knowledge can always be improved upon," said Plato.

"You would have him believe the lessons of his father are worthless," the uncle said clearly.

Plato was surprised by his mastery of the Greek language. He had not heard more than a few words from the older man thus far. "No disrespect was intended. It is only that I see in this boy a great mind, and I hope that he will continue to question the world around him and learn what he can to improve himself."

"Who are you to say that he needs improving?" the old uncle groused, and he slumped his body away from the fire, not wanting to offend a paying customer who had yet to pay.

"Oh, Uncle, only this morning you shout loud for everyone to hear, the many ways I could be improved!" Amnut laughed, and his offended uncle smiled despite himself.

The temple of Amun was a lush oasis, rewarding the weary travelers. The sanctuary and its community rested on the bank of a large lake surrounded by thick vegetation and groves of shady palm trees.

The village was bustling and there were many dressed in the robes of priest and monk. The locals regarded the party curiously—always welcoming but cautiously aware of visitors. Amnut accompanied Plato to the base of the main temple.

"This is . . . best I can do. We wait outside?" Amnut asked.

"No. This is where we part, young friend," Plato said, climbing down from his camel after Amnut directed it to kneel. "You are free to return to Heliopolis when you wish. I do not know where and when I will go from here." Plato paid the balance of coins owing for his transit, fleetingly grateful for the continued patronage of his wealthy uncle.

"I sad you not come back. You good man with smiling heart and much ideas. I learn much by you."

"And I you. I have no doubt we will meet again, if not in this life, in another," Plato said, embracing the young man warmly and kissing him on each cheek. The uncle snorted again—a nonbeliever, a skeptic.

The holy temple of Amun was built on a hill of indigenous rock that overlooked the village. Steep stairs led to the main gate, through which there was an open courtyard. In the center of the compound, near the entrance, a circular stone altar housed a sacred flame. The fire had been blessed by the Oracle and had been faithfully kept burning by the devoted sect of priests who maintained the building and its unusual treasure. People from all around came daily to pray and to light their torches. Many also came to seek an audience with the famed Oracle, and many were turned away. The Oracle granted audience to very few. Plato was hopeful that he would be successful in his quest.

Once Plato disappeared from sight, Amnut finally agreed to leave. Plato passed the congested fire pit toward the entrance. It was a narrow marble archway ornately carved with symbols of gods, animals, and oracles. The eye of Horus was carved at the pinnacle of the archway. Priests and others not recognizable by their clothes stood in groups, talking in hushed tones. As Plato grew closer, the groups clustered casually in front of the door, blocking his progression.

"I have come to see the Oracle. Anima mundi," Plato said to those who were passively blocking his path to the door.

"Many come. Move on traveler, seek your fortune elsewhere," a robed priest answered protectively. Plato's Marcus-brain urged him on. He wondered how he could demonstrate himself worthy. The Oracle might tell him his theme and his path, and surely it would lead him to Theron.

"I am sent by Red Elder. I come with the knowledge of many past lives," Plato said boldly.

There was a gasp and the group stirred excitedly. Red Elder was known to them. A path to the door opened up.

Plato walked in silence, led by a priest. They passed through the main sanctuary and, instead of turning toward a hallway that led to the secondary chapel, they proceeded through the building. The ceilings were high and arched, vaulted by enormous rows of stone pillars. Torches and candles burned throughout, and Plato breathed in the sweet, fragrant incense as he walked. He felt the positive energy of his surroundings. He felt the history and the universal connectivity. He knew that this place, like the Great Pyramid of Giza and the earth of Stone-at-Center, was sacred and holy.

The priest guided Plato through a heavily carved wooden door. The walls were hung with woven, colorful tapestries, and the image of the seed of life and other sacred symbols welcomed him. In the center of the round room there was a massive copper scale the size of a large elephant. On the right stood an ancient-looking priest in red and orange robes. Plato felt an overwhelming enigmatic force in the chamber and bowed his head respectfully, consciously filling himself with white light and humility as best he could.

"I come seeking the grace and wisdom of the Oracle," Plato said. After a moment the wrinkled priest nodded.

"Follow me," he said, and Plato was ushered through a stone panel that was indistinguishable from the wall around it. The wall shifted easily under the slightest pressure. Plato had been granted audience with the Oracle, and his Marcus-brain was relieved and excited.

Plato entered another chamber, much smaller, barely large enough for him and the tiny woman who sat cross-legged on a small platform draped in a finely woven blanket. The Oracle of Amun wore the skull and horns of a ram on her head, though she looked hardly strong enough to lift the expansive headdress. Her dark ebony skin was mapped with wrinkles and shone with fragrant oils. She was rocking forward and back in a slow rhythm, and she spoke as he took a seat on a well-worn silk pillow directly in front of her.

"Good Emissary, why do you censure yourself so?" the Oracle asked in a strangely deep and masculine voice. She did not look at him directly. Her eyes were rolled up in their sockets with almost none of the pupil and iris visible. He could see only whites that had turned pale yellow and were lined with veins of deep red. Her eyelids fluttered but did not blink, and Plato was unnerved by the demonstration.

"Is it not a wise man who knows his own failing?" Plato answered in the typical Socratic response of a question for a question.

"You have the ancient memory, which I have rarely seen in a seeker. I wonder why you come to me, when you know that the answer is within you?" the low voice rasped.

"Where is Theron?" Plato asked in a rush, the urgency of countless lifetimes plain in his voice. "Will I meet her in this life?"

"Is your question not of your purpose?" the Oracle asked.

"It is—I am lost and feel drowned by my own uselessness, despite my best attempts to live better. If I just know, if I can be sure she will come or will not, I can rest and shed this constant state of vigil."

"You are one of three in this destiny. Your fates are woven together like the strands of a whip. Your wisdom will be summoned by another and will be instrumental in the initiation of a great boy king."

"Is it Theron? How? When?" Plato asked.

"Patience," the Oracle reprimanded sharply. "It is only time . . . you will find her soon enough. You must return to the place you have loved the most in this lifetime. You must honor a promise forgotten. All will unfold as it should. Situate yourself where you can be found . . . where you are in service and tutelage of others."

"I need more. I don't understand," Plato said.

"You will find your way. You have said that 'perfection should be life's goal'."

Plato nodded.

"Do not expect it of yourself. Strive for it but do not berate yourself so. God is within you. Your memories and experiences allow you to grow. Do not look darkly upon them."

"How can I do more? I am failing."

"You ask too much," the Oracle answered abruptly. She stopped her rocking and her eyes stood still. In the whispered, high-pitched croak of an old woman, she sent him away.

Plato was upset with himself, disappointed that he had somehow offended the Oracle and had squandered his final questions. What the Oracle had actually meant was that Plato was asking too much of himself; after all, he was only human.

In the days following, Plato repeatedly contemplated the message from the Oracle. He never doubted the mystic. The perfect parrot-memory that Socrates had lovingly teased him about once again aided him as he replayed the Oracle's responses. He was convinced that he would meet Theron again, and he was determined to do so as soon as possible. He must find the boy king and all would be as it should be. But first he must return to Athens and continue Socrates' legacy.

CHAPTER 16

SQUARING THE CIRCLE

After his audience with the Oracle, Plato returned to Greece. He carefully recorded the lessons he had learned at the Mystery School while he waited for signs of the boy king. His desire to carry on Socrates' legacy was revived, and in 385 BC he opened a school in the country outside of Athens. The Academy was begun, and Plato took his place as headmaster. He enjoyed leading his students around the grounds in deep discussion, just as Socrates had done.

Despite having successfully moved forward with the Academy, Plato continued to feel that his purpose was incomplete. He asked the Universe for guidance, but the years passed without change or message. The acclaimed Academy flourished and grew. Plato had done as directed by the Oracle. He had returned to the place where he had known love in this lifetime, he had honored his promise to Socrates, and he had placed himself in the service of others. Marcus yearned to be found by Theron.

Plato continued to orate and write, painstakingly recording the philosophical contemplations of his day. He further developed his theories on geometry and contemplated the teachings of the Mystery School.

Many years passed, and Theron's karmic colors did not emerge. Plato progressed through his forties and into his fifties, never marrying. At last, eighteen long years after returning from Egypt, a message finally came. Plato received a letter from his friend Dion of Syracuse in Sicily. The men had met while Plato traveled Italy, prior to going to Egypt. Dion had opened his home to Plato and they had shared wine, conversation, and more than one hearty laugh. Dion was a progressive, spiritual thinker, but it had been his attempts to master the phorminx—a seven-stringed instrument—and his determination to sing along, despite being tone deaf, that most amused Plato and endeared Dion to him.

Dion was the brother-in-law of the Tyrant of Syracuse, and he was soliciting Plato's assistance. He explained that his impressionable young nephew, Dionysius, was poised to assume leadership upon the death of his father. Dion proposed that, with Plato's guidance, Syracuse could someday model the archetype of the ideal state and leadership that Plato had often spoken of. With the proper tutoring and direction, Dionysius could be molded and shaped to become the model philosopher king.

Plato read and reread Dion's letter joyfully. The words of the Oracle, worn out in his head from constant repetition, were new once again. He, Dion, and the boy were three—their destinies could be tied together. The coincidence was too great! The boy might be Theron or could somehow lead him to Theron! It fit . . . Plato's Marcus-brain was determined to make it fit. Full of hope, Plato left the Academy in capable hands and traveled to Sicily.

Upon arriving in Syracuse, Marcus was downcast to discover that Dionysius was not Theron. Her karmic energy and light continued to elude him, but, determined that the prophecy finally be fulfilled, he ignored his initial disappointment. He would make the scenario fit if he could.

Plato would spend the next ten months schooling the boy. It was during this time that he also further developed his theory of the Platonic solids—the five fundamental, universal elements that he believed made up everything: earth, water, air, fire, and ether. He stated that each one, reduced to its most minute form, would be a single sacred geometric shape.

Dionysius was a quick study and showed great promise in mathematics. Plato taught Dionysius the overwhelming importance of geometry in the order of the world, especially the golden ratio, which he explained was an aesthetically perfect proportion governing everything in the Universe. He showed the boy that the distance from his fingertip to his wrist and his wrist to his elbow was almost exactly the same ratio as the spirals in a nautilus shell are to one another. Plato believed that geometry developed the individual's ability to think abstractly and to go beyond the world of the deceptive and inaccurate senses.

Before long, Dionysius proved to be an overindulged brat who lacked self-control. The student's temper often flared uncontrollably when Plato corrected or challenged him, and he threw papers, pounded his fists, and turned red in the face like a toddler in a rage.

One day, upon having been scolded for an especially destructive outburst during which he tipped over a chair and scattered maps all over the floor, Dionysius verbally attacked Plato.

"Remember who I *am*, tutor. You are *nothing* but a servant here," Dionysius hissed, his eyes burning with contempt. Plato was startled by the malice in the boy's voice. He understood the spirit of adolescent boys and respected their need to assert themselves, but Dionysius had never addressed him with such disrespect.

"You will never be a wise philosopher king if your theories and rationales have gaping holes in them," Plato said calmly, his own emotions well-ordered. "Set aside your pride and conceit, and earn the respect you crave."

"Do not speak to me of *respect*. What respect do *you* deserve? Great men *do* the things they speak of; weak men talk about action in endless dialogues and lectures," Dionysius snarled. "You are a coward, too afraid to lead after the death of your teacher. You talk to me about his great theories, the great truths, but all of it is talk, talk, talk! You hold yourself up above others with your massive intellect and knowledge, but you *do* nothing! You do not seek office, you do not engage the people, you sit here in my father's court and eat his food and listen to his mania . . . and you *do* nothing."

Plato was cut to his core by the remarks, which exposed Marcus's most vulnerable and secret insecurities. Though he had done more in his life as Plato than in any other, he still wondered if he was doing enough.

Plato had seen the malice in Dionysius's deep brown eyes and had recognized the hollow, self-serving cruelty within him. Marcus had seen the same look in Helghul's eyes many years before. As the world continued to descend into the Iron Age, he knew that he would encounter the horrendous Darkness more frequently.

It seemed a simple decision at this point for Plato to return to Athens. However, it was not. On the very night that Plato informed Dionysius's father of his intention to resign, the leader was poisoned. Shockingly, Plato was imprisoned and accused by the son and heir of committing the murder. Plato had been a convenient pawn in the patricide, and he seethed at being so used.

From within his cell, Marcus burned with self-recrimination. How could his judgment have been so flawed? He had time to reflect. The philosopher's initial theory had been proved incorrect. Despite the appearance that his call to Syracuse had been his destiny as described by the Oracle, he now knew it certainly was not. As a result, the venture had been plagued by misfortune and failure, as misguided ambitions always were.

Theron had not been in Sicily, the boy king had been a miserable disappointment, and even though Plato had spent an entire year trying to make an inadequate square fit inside a perfect circle, the boy had never had the potential of becoming a wise philosopher king. Marcus wondered if having past-life memory and his constant searching for Theron had steered him off his path.

Would he do better if he was guided solely by intuition, like the other Emissaries? Did having memory make it possible for Marcus to expedite his path . . . could it be done? Was anything inevitable besides death? Did his intentions, choices, and consciousness create his world, or was the future set no matter what he did? Plato pondered these questions and more while he waited to be liberated.

With the assistance of his allies in the town, Plato managed to manipulate young Dionysius by spreading rumors and finally arranged his release from prison. Though weary and disillusioned, he boarded a merchant ship, relieved to be returning to Athens.

Plato's sixtieth birthday had come and gone, and his dreams of Theron and the boy king had been dashed. Decades earlier, Red Elder had assured him that he could not force destiny and that the greater plan of the Universe was not his to manipulate or understand. Marcus accepted that advice now. At least for this lifetime, he was prepared to stop searching.

He would continue recording the philosophies, theories, and complex systems that he had spent so many years discussing, debating, and dissecting. What else could he do? He was resigned to letting events unfold as they would. He was tired of wandering blindly. He wondered if the other Emissaries faltered so uncertainly in their lives, feeling such doubt and confusion about what they should be doing, or if it was an agonizing result of having taken the memory potion. Would the works he was laboring over ever matter?

CHAPTER 17

PLATO AND ARISTOTLE

Plato was glad to be returning to his sanctuary. The impressive white stone building stood out from the landscape. It was early in the day, and the morning sun cast beautiful gentle hues over the portico and gardens. His spirits rose, buoyed by the view of it. The steep, wide stairway leading up the hill to the entrance was purposefully designed as an assembly point. He smiled to witness the sea of white togas gathered there, as an enthralled group of students congregated around a central speaker. Above them in the white marble fascia of the building was inscribed "Let no one ignorant of geometry enter."[17]

Plato slowly climbed the stone steps. His age was wearing at his joints, and he cursed his younger self for designing such a steep incline. Only the view had interested him back then.

The sun illuminated the assembly in front of him, casting an angelic glow as he approached. The light was too white and he raised his arm against it, squinting, and realized with a happy surge that there was a purple karmic glow from within the group. *Perhaps an Emissary or two has found their way to the Academy*, he thought. As he got closer he stopped abruptly, his heart pounding, his ears and scalp tingling.

"A true friend is one soul in two bodies,"[18] a soft, fluid voice intoned. Plato craned his neck to find the owner of the words. The sun's beams were blinding and only when he grew nearer did the glaring mass of faces become discernible. Plato's eyes skipped over the folds of the fabrics, the arch of each forehead, and the bridge of each nose. He stood at the edge of the group, now anxiously scanning each face and straining to hear.

"Friendship is essentially a partnership," Aristotle said from the center, answering his professor while turning to face Plato directly on.

Plato was overcome. His energy exploded in every direction, and for a moment he disappeared completely, reduced to a seismic commotion of matter, thought, and emotion. Violet and indigo light rippled through him, and his Marcus-brain soared. The karmic colors were flying, intertwining, meeting, mingling, and touching his soul in every way. Intense beauty, love, and joy recognized and enveloped him. He caught his breath. The familiarity and lightness of Theron's being radiated from Aristotle.

Plato saw with his soul—Marcus was calling to Theron, and immediately her energy had rushed to his. Tears, overwhelming relief, and pure happiness surged through him. Aristotle looked kindly at the much older man, who appeared overwhelmed and ill, and interrupted the dialogue to call out to him.

"Are you well? Do you need assistance?" he said. Plato's body was again electrified by the voice, the underlying timbre and rhythm so familiar, so loved. Plato collected himself, every hair and whisker still at full attention. An electric current ran through him as his soul boiled to meet the creature before him. A whisper echoed through the group as Plato was recognized by his former students.

"I am Plato. I beg to know to whom I speak," he said unsteadily. The professor, Eudoxus, approached him enthusiastically, but Plato irritably waved him away, beckoning to the young man who had affected him so strongly.

"I am Aristotle, good professor. It is a great honor to meet you," Aristotle said, moving past the other students and standing before the founder. Plato looked up at the face so full of hope and optimism, already inches above him, and wept inwardly with joy. At long last, after so many lifetimes and so much disappointment, he had found her. The current between them flowed freely: eros and philia, every kind of love, intertwining, swirling, and humming. Plato's head was singing in symphony and churning with the fragrant odors of jasmine and sunshine. Marcus was grateful for the magic of the potion that allowed him to know her, and he cursed the will of the Universe that kept his Theron sleeping and unaware of him.

Plato found it difficult to speak, not wanting the assault on his senses to lessen even slightly. The spectators wrongly assumed that the older man was fatigued by the walk up the stairs in the warm morning sun. Aristotle steadied him and assisted him up the final steps and inside the building. Plato let himself be led. Aristotle's hands on him were like hot stones in his bed on a cool night. Butterfly wings fluttered manically in his chest. Once seated, Plato was handed a silver goblet of water, which he drank in one gulp, settling his churning chemistry.

It was always like this. Overwhelming, exhilarating, sometimes slightly nauseating. In each lifetime he had searched, and in too many he had not found her, or he had been kept from her by circumstances beyond his control and forced to agonizingly love her from afar. Not this time. This time she was his student, waiting at the Academy for his return. How long had Aristotle been here? How much time had Plato wasted in Syracuse? Marcus grieved for every lost moment.

Plato looked from his cup to the radiant smooth face of Aristotle. The younger man, not yet twenty, looked at him with clear admiration in his pale blue eyes.

Eudoxus broke their gaze by exclaiming, "If you would lead the oratory today, it would be a pleasure the likes these men have never known."

"You flatter me, though you know I abhor it, Eudoxus. Today I have more to learn than to share. A wise man knows when to speak and when to listen," Plato answered, smiling. "Return to your dialogue, I would like to absorb for a while," he said, standing, once again strong and steady. Together Plato and Aristotle—Marcus and Theron—returned to the group on the steps in the warm sunlight.

For the next two hours, Plato listened in rapture to the dialogue and discussion, every molecule and cell of his body vibrating in ecstasy. Aristotle felt it—something magical and energized. He assumed it was Plato's charisma and his own nervous excitement at meeting the legend. He did not understand that every ounce of him remembered this soul and magnetically reached out to him and was embraced.

Plato took a small humble room in the Academy wings, and he was barely able to restrain his happiness. Aristotle, still barely a man, looked upon his mentor with awe. The young student was the most promising and impressive of the pack and, not surprisingly, Plato took him under his wing. He taught him to question and to challenge every thought and assertion no matter how small, just as Socrates had encouraged him.

Plato reclaimed his life at the Academy with unprecedented vigor and optimism. The founder and his favorite student spent endless hours in study and discussion. It was not long before Plato realized that, unlike himself and Socrates, Aristotle had a very different way of thinking about the world and its makeup. He challenged almost every point that his mentor asserted, testing and frustrating Plato. Plato's ancient understanding of Atitala and of God, the Great Year, reincarnation, and the time in between, as well as his complete understanding that all matter is created from identical building blocks, made it difficult for him to tolerate Aristotle's views that opposed his certain wisdom. Marcus wished that Theron had taken the memory serum with him, so that her understanding of the Universe would not have been fouled.

Plato struggled to comprehend how her lack of awareness could possibly be helpful in her role as an Emissary. It seemed to Plato that his greater comprehension and recollection were his gift to the world of man and the reason why he recorded everything so carefully. It was all there—he wrote everything down that would free mankind from its doubt and ignorance. One had only to seek the knowledge. He assured those who would listen or read that each person has a soul and that justice is the function of the soul. To be happy one need only be just and do right. Plato believed that those worthy of the information would seek and find it; those ready for the messages would embrace them and understand the universal connection and be free of the doubt that paralyzed so many.

Finally he had no choice but to accept that Theron's path was fundamentally different than his own and it was not his place to question. He wondered what her role would be. He could only guess. Marcus was still searching to understand his own path and life cycle. For the time being, with his most beloved soulmate at his side, Marcus was absolutely content.

Walking in the garden one day, Aristotle questioned Plato about his time in Sicily.

"Was it eromenos? Was it for love that you went?" Aristotle asked pointedly.

"My love has only ever been here . . . I placed my faith in an errant vessel. A prophecy, given to me by an oracle in Siwa many years ago, led me to search. I came home a greater mathematician but no closer to finding the boy philosopher king that I sought," Plato answered, enjoying the physical nearness of Aristotle as they strolled.

"The prophecy was of a boy king?" Aristotle asked, indulgently, though both men knew that the student believed no more in oracles than in centaurs.

"Yes. I am rife with frustration and bitterness when I remember my time in Syracuse. I could have been here."

"Do you still believe that you will find a boy king and that an oracle can predict future events?" Aristotle asked skeptically.

"The Oracle said that I was one of three in the destiny and that my wisdom would be summoned in the initiation of a great boy king. I have found my destiny here and do not wish to leave again," Plato chuckled.

"I do not believe in mysticism and oracles. Nor do I embrace the notion of fate. I have observed that each man is his own visionary. There is no foregone conclusion, no predetermined future. Yet the prediction by one who is trusted may very well affect the behavior of the hearer, who then, by his actions, causes the foretold to occur."

"Perhaps we are born with our knowledge and it is revealed to us as required . . . or as we can bear it. It is possible that there are many choices and paths that lead to the same result. Could our free will be an illusion? Perhaps we merely choose *how* we will arrive at the ultimate predetermined outcome," Plato asserted.

"The soul does not exist without the body, without material cause of life. No one can know if I will spontaneously reach for a mango as the asp slithers past, or lean too far from my window and fall to my death. Our choices and paths are just that, there is no ultimate goal or result," Aristotle replied.

"You cannot prove, therefore you cannot be certain, that death is the end. Nor can you be sure that oracles cannot predict. You certainly have no evidence that the soul does not go on outside the body," Plato retorted.

"The evidence is the absence of life. There is no evidence that anything goes on. The soul is the final cause of the body; the body dies when the soul dies," Aristotle debated.

The men continued to consider, to counter, and to connect. Aristotle was inspired by Plato and sought his counsel and company. Their friendship quickly grew. Having lost his parents at a young age, Aristotle was grateful for the bond he and Plato had easily formed.

Marcus felt Theron in every moment and rejoiced in their time together, but at times he was lonely even with her spirit nearby. Their closeness was not close enough. He wished so fervently that she would wake to him, that her kindred soul would be conscious again and know him as he knew her. As he sat or walked at Aristotle's side, he would concentrate and send streams of color, light, and energy into him. His student would respond warmly, sometimes in a way that implied a glimmer of recognition, but then, as quickly, it was gone. Plato was left desperately alone in his awareness.

One afternoon Plato wrote tirelessly while Aristotle worked nearby.

"Why do you write your dialogues without your voice and name to the philosophies on the page?" Aristotle interrupted.

"My name is irrelevant. My philosophies and personal beliefs are likely to change and grow with my understanding and experience, and I do not wish to be tied, forever fixed to one way of thinking. I do not seek to record one true answer, only the myriad of necessary questions. A conversation is so much more entertaining than a lecture," Plato replied.

"But you have an opinion. You are bursting with opinions, will you not claim them?" Aristotle asked.

"I would rather show an argument and let the reader deduce reasonably how he would think," Plato said, and Aristotle shook his head skeptically.

"There is obvious leading in your words. You claim to present an argument but you are not unbiased, you seek to sway the reader."

"I cannot create balance. I cannot create an equality of ideas where they are unequal," Plato laughed.

"Your neutrality is false, Plato. You seek to sway others, but will not admit it."

"There is no falseness, I seek only to shed light on contemplation and ideas and the importance of reflection. What is it that irritates you so?"

"By writing in dialogue, by speaking through characters, you distance yourself from your statements. I think you should claim your beliefs and give them the power of your status."

"My status is fleeting and false. It is a pretense and a flaw of our society born from the desire in the belly of men who seek notoriety. Humility is a virtue, Aristotle. The ideas are what matter, and they were here before I came and will be here after I am gone. We are not creators, Aristotle. We are blind explorers plundering dark caves that have been discovered many times before with barely a flame to cast a glow."

"What if we are here only once? Here and gone, nothing before or after. Your words will guide those who come after you. Do you not wish to claim them?"

"It is not a question for me whether I have lived before and will die and be born again. I know it to be so. I would shed this corporeal body today and rejoin the incorporeal world if I knew you would be there with me, surrounded by the proof of the ideal forms," Plato answered.

"You beg others to question all, yet in unguarded moments you speak definitively about the world after death. Where does this certainty come from? How does it fit the paradigm of questioning all?" Aristotle challenged.

"I cannot pretend not to know what I know. You now understand why I write in dialogue, not as Plato, not as myself seeking to become famous and convince others of my beliefs. It matters not what Plato thinks, it matters only that I lead others to question and think for themselves."

"You ask impossible questions that are of a nature not even you can answer."

"And what is an answer but a supposition not yet disproved? Yet where there is a question, there must be an answer! Should we not wonder or ask because we do not already know the answer? Should we not walk the road beyond because we know not where it leads? If there is a road, there must be a destination. If there is a question, there must be an answer. To seek the answers in the purpose of life," Plato said, leaning back comfortably in his chair.

"I believe in proof . . . in the value of my senses to understand reality," Aristotle explained.

"Yea, and are your perceptions truth? And what is truth? You cannot separate what you see from what you interpret, and they are likely not the same. Show two men the same image and they will each report differently."

"But if both men question and puzzle over the same image . . . if they discuss and study its form . . . they must find agreement," Aristotle reasoned.

"Yet experience has taught me that they do not. Truth is subjective. Answers are often conclusions not yet disproved."

"Truth can be found through solid deductive reasoning where proof is evident," Aristotle argued.

"And again we disagree," Plato said, smiling.

The years passed and Plato and Aristotle remained together at the Academy. Marcus was overjoyed to be near Theron, and their relationship flourished despite the fundamental differences in their beliefs.

Occasionally, Plato would get the sense that Aristotle was growing more in tune with Atitala. Plato had a plan to try to spark Aristotle's past-life memory. For the first time in all of his lifetimes Plato openly revealed the story of Atitala, in the *Critias* and *Timaeus* dialogues. He wrote of his homeland's beauty, perfection, and downfall. And though the name Atitala would be lost and mistranslated to Atlantis in years to come, many of the details would be immortalized. He described the layout of the city, its politics, its esthetic beauty. He explained the higher thinking, emotion, harmony, energy, and Oneness with God and each other that the citizens had gloried in.

Plato was not only interested in inspiring Aristotle's memory, he also hoped to present Atitala as an example of what mankind should aspire to and emulate. Plato remained true to his memories of the fair land and also warned of the darkness and deceit that had emerged and were threats to all societies. There was always balance, the dark to the light.

Aristotle read the dialogues and debated their contents, and still Theron slept unconscious in him. She was awake only in Aristotle's goodness, purpose, and desire to contribute.

Plato was passionate and, at times, melancholic while he wrote of Atitala. His soul longed for his home as he remembered the beauty and closeness of Theron in their final days. With the beauty came the ugliness, and he was haunted by the dark scene he had witnessed in the caverns.

Aristotle listened, studied, and questioned. His nature was to be optimistic, to embrace art, and to trust science. He wanted proof, not metaphysical assertions. Plato argued that science was nothing but perception, and they spent endless hours debating, even arguing, and helping fine-tune one another's beliefs.

Aristotle graduated from student to teacher, taking his place as a mentor at the Academy. While his reputation grew, Plato withdrew, concentrating instead on his writing. His Marcus-brain pushed him forward with his writing, certain that it was important. He loved the hours of respite that the work offered him.

As Plato aged, his eyesight and hearing grew poor. He would often miss bits and pieces of conversations, and he became increasingly moody and cantankerous. The students at the school began to avoid him, and only Aristotle, now in his late thirties, sought him out daily. Plato, nearing his eighty-second year, was frustrated and betrayed by the breakdown of his human shell. His mind was still sharp, spry, and young, and his days had become increasingly focused on his time with Aristotle. They chatted often but argued and debated less.

Plato's life was nearing its end, and he hadn't thought about the Oracle prophecy in many years. Once he had found Theron, he had lost interest in the prediction. The Oracle's prophecy had amounted to nothing. The boy who was destined to change the world had not materialized. The Oracle had foretold that Plato was one of three: fates woven together like the strands of a whip. She said that Plato's knowledge would be summoned in the young regent's initiation, but it had not happened. Not yet.

CHAPTER 18

PLATONIC LOVE

343 BC

Aristotle stood on the luminous, white Academy steps surrounded by students. The sun was bright and the gardens around the school were at their most lovely. A young servant ran into the fold of scholars and beckoned timidly to the professor. He had a message from Plato.

Aristotle rushed to the bedside of his ailing friend. The headmaster's humble chamber was cool and dark as he entered. The old man lay in his bed, small and frail. What remained of Plato's hair was white and coarse, his eyes were heavily lined from years in the sun and years of broad grins, and his lids sagged loosely, ready to close forever. He smiled as he felt the familiar aura snug against his own like a snail in its shell, and he reached his feeble hand to him. Aristotle moved to his side, taking the arthritic fingers in his own.

"You have given me the most valued friendship of my life," Plato croaked dryly.

"My dear friend . . . drink," Aristotle said, reaching for the water beside him and placing it to Plato's lips. The patient refused with a subtle shake of his head.

"Death, which people fear to be the greatest of evils, may indeed be the greatest good. But for me to be parted from you, to be so betrayed by this weak bag of skin and bones, is a tragedy," Plato whispered. Aristotle's eyes filled with tears, and his dying friend attempted to soothe him. "My dear Aristotle . . . must not all things at the last be swallowed up in death? No evil can happen to a good man, either in life or after death."[19]

Though Plato sought to ease Aristotle's grief, his Marcus-brain was in turmoil, bitterly resisting the inevitable outcome. He would die and once again be separated from Theron. He lay there, steeped in her vigor. She was everywhere, but she remained oblivious to him. Light, sound, and energy resonated between them at the most basic molecular level. The love of Aristotle had been earned and enjoyed and his friend stood grieving before him, and Marcus was suffocated by the reality that he was losing her once again.

"Philo se, I love you," Plato said. Marcus wondered how many years, how many lonely, difficult lifetimes, he would have to endure before he found her again. He breathed in her violet aura and basked in her light. As he began to slip away he wondered, had he done enough as an Emissary in this lifetime as Plato?

It happened quickly. Plato's soul passed through the room and through Aristotle, mingling with Theron's soul like dust particles in a sunbeam. Unseen, he was reclaimed by the Source. There was not a rush of wind or a whispered goodby.

Marcus was once again flowing through the Grid, destined for the place in between, the "Meadow," as Plato had called it. He was at complete peace, in harmony with the divine Source and all creation, and he suffered no conscious separate thought. He existed in complete bliss, lightness, and color.

Marcus, like all of the world's souls and Emissaries, was born and reborn in the generations to come. Each lifetime had its own lessons, difficulties, highs, and lows. His childhoods continued to be unfettered by past recall. But eventually in each life, his memories came to him as lightning or in whispers. They always came, piled upon one another like a wardrobe from countless centuries, layer by layer.

Without fail, in adulthood Marcus searched for Theron's spirit in everyone he met and was wary and alert for Helghul. Entire lives passed without finding her. He was tortured, knowing too much yet not knowing enough to certainly lead him to his love.

CHAPTER 19

UNDERSTANDING THE PAST

Present day

Quinn studied history intently. He was thankful for the gaps the scholars filled and the clues as to what had occurred in the lifetimes flowing in and out of his own.

Marcus had awakened in Quinn, stronger and louder than in any other lifetime, perhaps because of the turn of the Great Year to an ascending Age.

Where was Theron? What had happened to her? He was obsessed as he looked for threads of her. Aristotle—how grateful he was that she had been someone important and that her words, or almost her words, were contemplated even now. So much had been lost. Aristotle's most brilliant works had vanished, most likely in the fire at Alexandria. The great library had been torched during the darkness of the Iron Age, and thousands of years of carefully collected ancient knowledge had been destroyed. What a terrible waste.

Alexandria and the importance of Egypt could not be overstated. Quinn felt it deep in his bones. News articles, documentaries, movies, travel advertisements,

Ashton Kutcher on Jimmy Fallon in front of the Giza pyramids with an iPhone. Images of the ancient, sacred land inundated him and with them came a rush of familiarity.

Quinn had returned to Egypt in this lifetime. He had wandered the same dusty terrain he had walked thousands of years before as Plato. He had returned to the Great Pyramid of Giza, the oasis of Siwa and its temple. Quinn had heard that a new ruin had been discovered, and it was believed to be a calendar of the Great Year. He went to Nabta Playa to see it for himself. Unfortunately the stones had been dismantled before he got there, under the guise of protecting them from vandals.

He had again felt the heat and mystery of Heliopolis, though the symbol of Horus was now found on T-shirts and tattooed arms rather than over a secret doorway. It had seemed a good a place to look for her, but Theron had not been found.

Quinn had done his homework. He found that after Plato's death, Aristotle had gone to Macedonia to teach a young prince, a future king who became known as Alexander the Great. The boy king had indeed been great, but he had been terrible as well. "Three destinies tied together," the Oracle had said to Plato. Marcus remembered the prophecy with a shiver, and Quinn pulled closed his sloppy black velour robe.

Alexander the Great was rumored to have visited the Oracle of Amun in Siwa and to have found the Emerald Tablet in the tomb of the rebel, Pharaoh Akhenaten. Akhenaten was the father of King Tut and had recorded, for the first time in history, the concept that there was only one God. He seemed likely to have been Red Elder, the protector of the Emerald Tablet's secrets, but Quinn could only guess.

Aristotle had probably helped Alexander to accomplish this feat. Perhaps the knowledge of the Mystery School that Plato had shared with Aristotle had been instrumental.

Quinn thought of Amnut, the guide who had helped Plato find the Mystery

School so long ago. Had he helped Alexander as well? He wished he could ask, and just as he thought it, his computer pinged with an incoming message.

"U up?" it said. Quinn smiled at the coincidence—the uncanny connection they all had and the synchronicity of the Universe.

"It's noon," he replied.

"Ur point?" the faceless person typed.

"Come on over," Quinn answered, without thinking, as if he had been born with keys connected to his fingertips.

"15," the screen announced.

Quinn had his theories about Alexander the Great. So close to Theron, so important in history, second only to Genghis Khan as the greatest conqueror the world had ever known. Quinn suspected that Alexander had been Helghul, just as Alexander had supposed, thousands of years before, that Plato had been Marcus. They had both been correct. They had missed one another by a generation, but Theron had linked them once again.

Alexander was said to have found and displayed the Emerald Tablet. Quinn wondered where it had gone next, certain that Helghul would have hidden it for himself to find in a future life.

Quinn read and reread, looking for new information, new blogs, new links, and evidence of other Emissaries. Theron might be out there somewhere.

There was a quick rap and the door opened.

"Dude . . . you should lock your door," Nate—a metrosexual artist in his late twenties—said as he let himself in. He wore skinny jeans, a long sloppy sweater, and a toque that covered his mop of dark hair, except for the pieces that were arranged in deliberate poky bits across his forehead.

"If I had, you'd still be standing in the rain," Quinn pointed out, readjusting his robe.

"How goes the computer biz? You look like you got some work," Nate said, eying the pile of hard drives and laptops on the kitchen table as he helped himself to a cup of coffee.

"Yeah, some. How's it going with you?" Quinn said, pushing back from the computer and rolling closer to the overstuffed chair behind him. Nate moved a small pile of newspapers and a dog-eared copy of *The Secret History of the Mongols*[20] and sat sideways. His long legs dangled over the worn arm as he drank.

"Not doing well, actually. My car's not driving for shit these days and I hate the thought of taking the bus at my age. I really thought I was done with that, you know? Anyway, Sarah's been nagging like, insane, about the whole marriage and kid thing, and I was thinking, like seriously, if she's going to nag and bitch like this do I really want to get tossed into some crazy, formal, man-made cage with her? Voluntarily? Fuck no, so we had another huge fight. Hey, whatever happened with that woman who gave you her number at the art gallery?" he said, finally taking a breath. Quinn passed him a joint and blew out a lungful of smoke.

"Man, when someone says how's it going . . . seriously . . . do you have to go into the unedited, Bible-length version?" Quinn asked, shaking his head.

"Yeah . . . explain *that* why don't you? Why do people ask if they don't wanna know?"

"I wanna know, relax," Quinn said, amused by his friend's rant.

Nate was so easy to rile, but it was only because he cared so much. When Nate asked someone, "How's it going?" he meant it. He wanted to know. Right down to the smallest, most insignificant hangnail. If it mattered to you, Nate wanted to know. Quinn loved that about his pal. He had loved that same energy when he had known Nate as Amnut in Egypt centuries earlier, and before that as his merciful guard in Stone-at-Center. He was a good soul, and Quinn wondered what they were meant to accomplish together. There must be some reason that they were a part of the same soul group and that Nate had come into his life once again.

Three years earlier, Nate and Quinn had met on a small plane between Lake Arenal and Montezuma beach in Costa Rica. They were the only two passengers on the tiny, turbulent flight, and they had been delighted to learn that they lived a mere ten miles apart back home in Washington State. It was no coincidence.

Though Nate did not have past-life memory, nor was he an Emissary, his aura was distinct, a fingerprint belonging only to him, and Quinn had recognized his spirit when they met.

"You didn't answer about that woman, the blonde. Did you call her?" Nate asked hopefully.

"Naw, I don't need the complications."

"You're already practically a monk, dude . . . don't have to marry her," Nate teased, picking up the Mongolian text next to him and shaking his head at Quinn's strange preferences.

"Yeah, look who's talking," Quinn said snorting.

Life was always complicated enough. Relationships, especially romantic ones, never worked out for Marcus. There was only one Theron, and no matter who or where he was, no one else could reach that place within him. It was unfair to put other loving souls at such a disadvantage, so Quinn stayed casual and aloof, ever vigilant.

CHAPTER 20

CHILGER AND BORTE

AD 1171

Borte ran unchecked through the marketplace; sheep, wheels, grain—all obstacles to be avoided. The tips of her plaited hair, dark and glistening, blew free of her fur cap. Her black eyes sparkled with the chase, her cheeks permanently ruddy and burnt by the constant winds that cut across the plains of her homeland. The crowd was loud and moved deliberately, ignoring the children as they darted and played joyfully. Borte and Chilger, laughing and running, stopped breathless behind a shelter, unnoticed by the adults nearby. Chilger opened his hand and produced a date, easily snatched in passing. He held it out to Borte and she took it happily, biting it in half and returning the other portion to him. He popped it in his mouth, flashing a broad white smile, and suddenly, without a word, they were off again. She looked back, her heart racing. How close was he? Bam! She slammed to an abrupt stop. The tribal leader, her father, solid as a stone wall, loomed unyielding over her. She bounced off like a pebble, and he easily caught her before she hit the ground.

"Ay, ay!" he grumbled. Her smile already wiped clean, she was contrite and lowered her head respectfully as her father steadied her and used the moment to subtly scold her under his breath. He hurried her along and his swiftness unnerved her. It was unlike him to move quickly or say much, so she thought that he must be quite upset with her to act so. He was a quiet, contemplative man, typically cautious to smile but unlikely to anger, very good qualities in a chief.

Chilger watched from a distance, sorry that he had caused his friend to suffer her father's disapproval. Borte's father eyed the boy cautiously and waved his arm in the air toward him once, as if swatting a fly. Chilger sadly watched her go; they were from different clans and he looked forward to their chance meetings at the market, as they always had great fun together. There was something unusual about her, and since the first time he saw her, he had been compelled to seek her out.

The daughter was loaded onto the family cart, and they made the long journey home in customary silence. They crossed the endless grassy landscape, empty to the untrained eye, aware of every rabbit, fox, and magpie for miles. Even under the bright sun the temperatures cut hard and cruel as they rode; the wind from all directions stirred the dust and grass in alternate sweeps.

It was the early months of autumn. The days of snow would come soon to make life difficult, but the people of northern Asia would endure heartily. In tune with the elements, the heavens, and the Earth, they survived the bitter cold by hard work and planning—the furs must be plenty and the food stocks full. The angry cold and blizzards could hold them captive for weeks at a time, isolated and dependent on their herds, which needed grazing land to survive.

The nomads positioned themselves the best they could to accommodate their need to be self-sufficient, often going months without the option of trade in a shared marketplace. Common sense and preparation were second only to pleasing the gods in their beliefs. There was no chance; events unfolded as they were meant to at the pleasure or displeasure of the countless deities which abounded in the living, breathing land around them. Borte smelled the snow that had not fallen yet; the sweet flowery scent of summer had gone and been replaced by the frigid crispness that warned them to make haste.

Borte and her father arrived at their nomadic tent, which was one of a group of fifteen gers spread out along that section of the remote steppe. Their fellow tribespeople were busy with their work and did not stir as they arrived with the dust billowing around them. Their sheep herd, back from the pastures for the night, milled around them, and Borte's father forgot her, busy with his work. She climbed out to help unload, casually looking at the distant horizon. She saw something there, a cloud, an unusually large smudge of movement approaching their camp. She pointed. Her father turned, his square silhouette momentarily obscuring her view of the evening sunset.

"Go daughter, there is much to do, they come quickly," he instructed, nudging her toward the shelter. Her brothers had already joined their father in attending the cart, and he directed them with few words to position the sheep for the night.

Borte was unsettled at being sent inside. Her father was acting strangely—her ten-year-old mind reflected back to the marketplace and Chilger, and she assumed that she was to blame. She knew that she was getting too old to behave in such a carefree, childish way, and she felt shame that she had disappointed him.

In actual fact, she was responsible for his preoccupation, but not for the reasons she supposed. Though she remained unaware, it was a monumental day in her life. Borte was being introduced to her prospective husband that night, and if the meeting went well, an alliance would be made and a contract agreed upon. The fathers were both tribal leaders, and they had met months before to discuss the possible alliance of their like-aged children. It was a time of discord and uncertainty between tribes, and wars were not uncommon; an ally would be welcome.

"Daughter, you may meet your husband tonight. You see they approach. Come quickly and be washed and dressed," her mother said as she entered. Instantly she noticed that the ger smelled deliciously of roasting lamb tail and fragrant tea, and she was grateful for the warmth of the healthy fire in the center of the room. She saw that the traditional circular dwelling had been neatly arranged to receive guests at the north side near the altar, respecting Father Sky, Mother Earth, and the ancestors. It was laid invitingly with their best furs, skins, and carpets. Borte walked clockwise the short distance east to the women's side of the quarters. She stood compliantly while her hair was tightly rewoven and her over-clothes were replaced with fresh ones that she had only ever seen folded carefully in her mother's personal belongings. Her mother and grandmother rubbed and dressed and cleaned her, the whole time clucking around her like hens.

"This is a special day, Borte," they explained briefly in their spare but happy sing-song way. "You will always remember the first time you see your husband."

Borte's mother stepped away from her, attending to the food preparation and arranging tea and spirits, while her grandmother continued to fuss over the wide-eyed girl. Borte noticed that both of the women had also taken special care with their dress and had scrubbed themselves and retied their hair. They were beautiful; their wide, round faces were perfectly symmetrical and kind. Even the elder woman, almost in her forty-third year, had an unusual sparkle in her almond eyes.

"Will they take me away?" Borte asked bravely. Her respected grandmother's face creased into cheerful lines and, smiling widely, she displayed the gap where she had lost a side tooth. She held the girl tightly by the shoulders.

"Good girl to be so strong," she said, nodding. "You won't go now, not until your thirteenth year at least. This is just a time to make sure that the choice will stick and that your temperaments are in balance. If it is heaven's will, he will join us here to serve your father until the year of the marriage ritual," she said, while at the same time rubbing her thumb superstitiously across the girl's forehead in a protective sign.

"But who is he?" Borte begged to know, her excitement and curiosity building.

The dust cloud grew closer, ox and cart and more men on thick, wide, heavy horses. Father rushed around the outside of the ger, still preparing, then pounded the dust from his layers of clothing. The sun was barely a sliver on the scarlet horizon and the cold of evening was settling upon them. Each breath and word hung like smoke in the air. A blazing outdoor fire had been built to welcome and comfort the visitors, and the sheep, their long winter coats growing in, had been gathered nearby to rest for the night, where they could be heard bleating occasionally.

Tribal members from the other gers just beyond the chief's began to gather a few hundred paces away, anxious for a first-hand view of the visitors.

Nine-year-old Temujin approached, accompanied by his father, Yesugei Khan, his uncle, and numerous attendants. The group had traveled on horseback for three long days, but they were a traveling people and were unfazed by the journey.

The men arrived looking rested and well. They were an impressive sight, and it was obvious that their clan was large and prosperous. They brought gifts of spice, grains, and textiles for their hosts. Borte's father led the honored guests through the southern tent flap into the traditionally appointed ger, warm with fire and food. Her brothers stayed outside with the remaining entourage and gathered at the fire, where they enjoyed a simple meal and exchanged stories and shared good humor.

"I hope you find your horses fat and your sons strong," Yesugei Khan began, demonstrating his friendly intentions to his hosts as they entered. His uncommon ginger hair and beard were bright against his fur cap, and his weathered face was nearly the same shade.

"You are generous and wise. I hope that your yak has the muscle of many," Borte's father answered graciously.

As was mandated by custom, the men walked clockwise around the ger to the northern side and took their comfortable, warm places among the furs. The night had become harshly cold compared to the heat of the day, and they were glad to nestle in. A wind gust whistled through the ger, sending chills through Borte's body at the mere sound. She thought compassionately of her brothers outside, though they were well accustomed to adapting to the rapidly changing environment.

"We bring well wishes and good luck from our tribe to yours. My wife

Hoelun was born of your tribe. The Olkut'hun are hearty, powerful people. It is with satisfaction and humble pride that I introduce my son, the future chief of the Borijin, Temujin."

The young man had been silent up until then, but he bowed his head respectfully and expressed his gratitude at being honored in their home. Borte listened intently, drinking in the voice and enjoying the sound of him as he spoke. He was not silly or arrogant as she had feared he might be; he used very few words but they were well chosen, and she decided to like him.

The prospective bride had not yet been introduced, and she sat excited and silent at her grandmother's side. Her head was lowered, and she peeked curiously through wisps of hair that had once again broken free of their leather ties.

Temujin stole sidelong glances whenever he thought he would not be seen, but nothing went unnoticed as the adults watched the pair with amusement. He was anxious to see the girl's face; he cared not if she was beautiful, but rather if she was proud. He did not want the headache of a proud wife; his father's experience had taught him that.

The meal was offered first to the gods, and then it was shared and properly appreciated and acknowledged. Finally the youngsters were brought together so they could interact. Borte was small and thin for her age, unlike the thick, hearty-looking body type more common to her people. She stood especially erect, pushing out her chest to puff up and compensate for her scrawny frame. She kept her eyes on her warmly wrapped feet, her naturally rosy, round cheeks flushing deep crimson.

"T-t-t," her grandmother scolded, nudging her chin upward with a lumpy root of a finger. Borte's innocent brown eyes met those of her future husband. Even though he was a full year younger and only nine, he already looked like an adult to her.

Temujin felt a jolt at his core and electricity shot, burning, searing throughout him. Light and dark sparred and danced, vibrating up and down his spine and radiating out from every chakra. Each hair on his body stood at attention. He watched incredulously as a beautiful rainbow of color sprang from her, streaming and filling the ger with beauty and light. He felt like he couldn't breathe, and he stood confused and overwhelmed. Could anyone else see this and feel this? He looked at them all watching, unchanged, unmoved. What was happening, and how had he not noticed it from the beginning? Helghul, awakened, stirred sleepily inside his head, still barely known to him in this lifetime but budding within to eventually overtake him like a parasitic weed. Temujin struggled to understand what was happening to him.

Helghul's energy was shaken by Theron's underlying luminosity, still only a faint glow in Borte. He somehow understood that her power and energy would grow exponentially as she aged, and for the first time he had a brief glimpse of his own potential and power. He decided he must certainly have her, and he stood speechless and staring.

Borte watched him, unsure what to think. He was behaving very strangely, and she wished that he would ask her a question or at least pay her a perfunctory compliment. Finally he spoke, and then behaved admirably, despite his inner turmoil. In keeping with custom, he wished her the blessings from the gods, and then remarked on her home and her dress garments, and again praised the food.

Temujin struggled valiantly to appear at ease and comfortable, convinced he must win Borte over and have her as his wife. The humble gathering continued, and no one noticed the difference in him. Outwardly he was unchanged, but as he spoke calmly of livestock and family members, his mind shared cloudy past lifetimes filled with blurry pictures, impossible places, faces, memory after memory playing like a dream sequence in his head.

Borte decided that she liked Temujin, more by her instinct and feelings than because of anything he had done or said. He had in actuality been a bit odd and wooden, unlike her brothers and the other boys that she had grown up with, but she decided it was most likely just his nerves, and he would eventually relax and become . . . loveable.

Temujin's father's party departed the next day, anxious to return to their camp before the season's first snow. Temujin was left behind in the care of Borte's father. He would remain with them for the three years until he was twelve, at which time they would marry and return to his tribe together. Yesugei Khan said good-bye to his son and started out across the expansive plains toward the distant mountains. The skies were clear, cool, and endlessly blue in every shade and hue.

Temujin was stoic; if he was sad to be left behind, he hid his feelings well and said nothing. The youth was still reeling, contemplating the voice and pictures in his head. Was he going crazy? Were they real? He was not afraid, in fact he felt more powerful and manly than ever in his life. Were they spirits sent to drive him mad or to guide his way? He decided it was the latter, and he chose to embrace a new awareness of his divine function in the world. His belief in Tengri and Eje—Father Sky and Mother Earth—became absolute overnight. He decided that he was a tool of the gods, sent to the plains with a divine mission yet to be understood.

Clearly Borte was a big part of the equation; she had been a catalyst for him. Just meeting her gaze had instantaneously catapulted him to a whole new level of understanding and enlightenment. Her light and virtue, so foreign to him, were familiar at the same time. The process of recall, at least this time, was like a fine cashmere vest that had just begun to be woven—there was a great deal of painstaking work yet to be completed before it took shape. Temujin would have to bide his time and do the work, but he was sure that the information would come. He would be patient. He would develop his relationship with Borte and follow the path that opened before him. He had no doubt it would be worth it in the end.

Temujin had intended to spend the next few days sorting out the shadowy images bombarding him, but before nightfall he was informed that his father had been assassinated. A passing tribe of Tatars had customarily offered the chief an exchange of food and had poisoned him. The murderers were long gone before anyone realized what had happened.

The boy was overcome with emotion and anger. He left immediately to rejoin his clan, vowing that someday he would exact vengeance on the Tatars. Borte watched in confusion as her betrothed mounted his broad steed and bolted away on the horizon.

Temujin and his uncle and the other tribe members returned to their kin three days later, wrapped warmly in thick skins. Their fur caps obscured their faces, making them recognizable to one another only by wardrobe, mannerism, and voice. The season's first snow covered them, sticking to their hats and beards as they announced the news of the dead khan. It was unlucky to speak of the dead, and the shaman attended with his drum and mirrors, beating and flashing to confuse and ward off evil spirits. Within hours, the nine-year-old Temujin, with his uncle's support, addressed the elders and the men of the village. He proposed that he should inherit the title and position left unfilled by his father's murder. The men refused outright and mocked the boy.

"In his ninth year and hardly able to hold his own cock!"

"His only hair is on his head!" they jeered.

Temujin was irate but powerless, and he was sent away from the gathering, humiliated and denied.

Temujin's mother, Hoelun, now a widow, was left to care for five young sons and a daughter. She did not cry, she did not mourn. There was work to be done. She canvassed the village for a sponsor. Any man—old, young, married, single—she cared not. She knew that she needed a protector to exist in the tribe but, atypically, no one came forth. No one accepted her. Beautiful, but notoriously proud and outspoken, she was left to fend for herself and her children.

True to her acerbic nature, Hoelun projected her anger outwardly and accused the tribesmen openly of being too weak and insignificant to be worthy of her. She called the women stupid, ugly, and jealous, and the few who had held any pity for her turned away in disgust. Hoelun, with her pride and arrogance, had doomed her family, and they were soon abandoned by their nomadic tribe.

It was a brutal, deadly winter but, accustomed to the hardship of life on the plains, Hoelun and her children beat the odds and survived. They were a part of no tribe and had to fend for themselves. They had no herd to sustain them; their possessions had been ransacked and appropriated by the new chief when they had been abandoned. Their remaining shelter was a barely adequate ger of wood and poor-quality skins, but somehow they had the fortitude as a family to get through the next nine months of frigid battery.

They ate wild currants and blueberries that Hoelun and her daughter had collected and dried for winter, and they hunted small game. They had fire and they prayed many times a day to the fire god, grateful for the life that it gave. The days were short and the nights were long, and Hoelun regaled her children with stories of better days: tales of ancestors, strength, and triumph.

Hoelun anticipated their return to clan life someday and prepared her brood for that eventuality. She taught them the ritualistic offerings and assured them that they were favored and, as little as they had to eat and drink, they always shared first with the gods. They learned to be wary and cynical and, as a former khan's wife, she explained the ins and outs of the region's politics and her thoughts on how to gain advantage over others.

Hoelun and her small family remained independent and alone for many years. Temujin continued to grow and thrive and was at least a head taller than all of his brothers, including the eldest, who had been born to Hoelun from a previous marriage. He looked remarkably like his father—his red hair thick and wiry, his dark eyes hard and cold.

Temujin had changed drastically since his meeting with Borte and the death of the khan. His focus was on survival and on devising a plan to return his family to a place of sustenance, power, and honor. His twelfth birthday had come and gone unnoticed; the marriage agreement, impossible to fulfill, was unceremoniously ignored. He had become sullen and suspicious, and he manipulated his family, constantly challenging his older half-brother's authority in their small camp.

It was a beautiful warm spring day. Thirteen-year-old Temujin and his brothers were stalking the plains, a sea of multicolored, fragrant flowers laid out for miles around them. The gorgeous weather was a welcome reward for bearing a brutal nine months of harsh cold, but it had been an unlucky week. As the boys hunted, they were acutely aware of their hunger and the oncoming short-tempered desperation that the too familiar pangs brought with them.

In a flash of movement, the band leapt at a noise—Temujin had speared a marmot, and it lay squealing and struggling in the field ahead of them. Temujin ran to the animal and gently laid his hands on it, honoring its sacrifice and respectfully thanking the marmot spirit for fulfilling his need. His brothers crowded around and silently knelt, also happily honoring the spirit of the animal. It wasn't until the methodic, ritualistic butchering and division of the spoils that the merriment was quelled by an argument that erupted between Temujin and his elder half-brother.

"The heart is mine," said the older boy, as Temujin deftly removed the coveted organs according to tradition.

Temujin had said the prayers and done his thanks, and he was in no mood to step aside. "The marmot is mine. You eat only by my skill," Temujin retorted, covered in blood and still cutting deep into the animal to expose its prized bits.

The half-brother came closer, his hunting knife drawn, to retrieve the animal's heart. Temujin went against custom and denied his older brother, refusing to unhand the carcass.

"You will have to take it . . . you know I am the stronger hand," Temujin warned as his brother got within striking distance.

The older boy sprang and the fight was on. The two square-brick young men, heavy with their layers of clothing, wrestled on the grass, tangling themselves up in the blood and guts of the beast.

"Off the meat!"

"Watch out!" the other brothers shouted, excited by the battle but conscious of the disrespect being shown. Surely the spirit of the marmot would be angered by such disregard. They were used to wrestling and scuffles among them, it was a way of life. Temujin grunted hard and managed to flip his attacker onto his back, and now he sat wild-eyed on his chest staring down at him.

It should have ended there, as it had many times before, but Temujin, panting, realized how close he had come to losing this time. Perhaps one of these days his older half-brother would overpower and submit him. With that thought in mind, Temujin deliberately and unexpectedly raised his hunting knife, still gory with the blood of their dinner, and sank it deep into the throat of his half-brother. The victim's hand had come up in self-defense and was pinned to his flooding neck.

Gasps and yelps rang out as the brothers howled in disbelief. Blood poured unchecked from the fatal wound. No one dared come near. The siblings ran back to their camp, forgetting their food, forgetting their hunger, and terrified by what they had seen.

Temujin felt no shock or sorrow. He climbed off his half-brother and cleaned his knife on the corpse, power surging through him. He felt invincible. The marmot heart was his, and he was now the undisputed head of the family. Blood-soaked and victorious, he threw his dinner over his shoulder and headed home.

CHAPTER 21

THE TRIALS OF THE SHAMAN

Chilger had not seen Borte since years before in the market, though he had casually searched for her at every opportunity. They had first met when they were very young. She was the only girl that he had ever noticed, and her energy had resonated with him. For as long as he could remember, she had looked like an angel to him. Just as a child can fail to notice a difference in hair or skin color, Chilger had been oblivious to the warm violet glow that surrounded her like a thick second skin, visible only to him, if he had cared to take notice. As they matured his Marcus-brain had begun to stir—not a thunderbolt this time, but in whispers and confusing, comforting flashes. He was older now and their childish play should be long forgotten, yet the memory of her continued to haunt him.

Chilger had become a strong horseman and hunter, and by twelve years of age he had proven himself an asset to his Merkit clan. Always profoundly spiritual and in tune with the natural world, he had a way of communing with animals and birds that was unusual, even among his holistic peoples. His parents had approached the shaman for direction and advice for their son on many occasions, and always the spiritual leader was impressed by the youngster's insight and depth of contemplation and understanding.

When he was halfway through his twelfth year, his destiny was laid out. It was late spring, and the cloudy expanse of blue sky overhead was at its kindest and most brilliant. The eagles soared and swooped, floating effortlessly in the warm sun. The sweet chirping of many birds rose from the flowering, fragrant plains, and as Chilger and his horse passed through, they continued their song in harmony with one another.

Chilger felt the strange energy of the day even before anything unusual had happened. He had felt a tingling in his hands, his feet, and the Tengri-god center at the top of his head since he had awakened that morning. This vibration was usually accompanied by strange visions, yet today none had come. He had never told anyone of the strange pictures that he saw in his mind, the stories and images that unfolded. Only the shaman had ever spoken of visions and premonitions, and Chilger's father, a hunter and herder, was far from understanding such mysterious concepts, and lived life simply. He prayed and gave offerings as he was taught, without questioning or seeking deeper meaning and enlightenment. Chilger learned early that too much conversation and too many questions were met with a stern glance or a firm hand. He kept his visions and metaphysical contemplations to himself. He lived like the other boys his age—hunting, wrestling, and herding, always preparing for the coming grueling winter months—but he was different somehow.

Chilger, alone as usual, was on horseback when he entered the woods in distant view of his clan's camp. He saw the beams of sunlight breaking through the leaf canopy, lighting strips of the forest floor, and it filled him up. His spirit drank in the beauty and godliness of the vision before him.

Just then a large black bear meandered carelessly into the sunny clearing, positioning itself in front of a particularly abundant berry bush. She dropped her heavy rump with a thud to the earth, and a dry cloud rose up around her. The dust glowed in the sunbeams like sparkling silver rain, and Mother Earth and Father Sky touched one another and danced before him.

The forest was alive with the spirits, and Chilger breathed them in and traveled inside the particles that mingled in front of him, drinking in their energy, sharing his own—at one with the Earth. He marveled at the muscles rippling in the bear's broad shoulders, the sun lighting her coat with a golden glow. She would have made a fabulous kill, and her fur and meat would have been celebrated by the clan. Yet, though he held his bow in his hands, it never occurred to him to kill her. Moments later, the bushes near her rustled and snapped as three growing cubs playfully joined in the feast. A twig under his pony's hoof snapped, and the mother bear protectively swiveled her heavy head toward him to assess the danger. They watched one another curiously, unafraid, both one with nature.

He would have been safe had he been on foot, but his horse was spooked once the zigzagging winds carried the scent of the large bear to her nostrils. She whinnied in alarm and bolted, catching her youthful rider by surprise. When the horse jerked, he and his loosely held bow were thrown to the ground. As he went down he saw the bear, no longer a lounging restful creature, bounding toward him. His flailing image had been seen as a threat. Chilger hit the ground hard, and the back of his head slammed violently against a rock as he landed. The last thing he saw was his horse sprinting away and the enormity of the black fur mass as it reached him, threatening and snorting. She sent tremors through the tranquil forest. Unseen birds and small prey scattered as her energy surged and warned all creatures away.

When Chilger's horse arrived back at the camp without him, a search party was immediately sent out. It was dusk when he was recovered, and he was unconscious and near death when they found him. The ground beneath him was soaked with blood, and the enormous paw prints that surrounded his body told the story that he could not. The bear had swiped him only once and left a gash across his right cheek, throat, and chest. He had been unconscious by the time she reached him and, though she had obviously moved him around a bit based on the patterns in the dirt, she had not harmed him otherwise. Most of the blood had come from the gash to the back of his head caused by his fall, but the bear had shifted him off the offending stone and onto the mossy ground inches away, which had ultimately saved his life by padding the wound. The bear had likely continued to feed nearby for some time afterward, inadvertently warding off any predators that might have enjoyed a half-dead meal.

Chilger did not wake for many days. A fever set in, and in his delirium his visions were particularly powerful and terrifying. He called out, sharing the disturbing images in his native tongue, but also in languages unknown to his family. Soaked with sweat, the boy yelled and writhed, and the wrinkled, stooped shaman attended him hour after hour, his gravelly voice croaking, chanting, and praying.

Everything about the shaman was weathered and old. He had proven himself a powerful healer and had an uncanny ability as a seer to his people. He drummed the goatskin spirit drum and used a spear called a sulde[21] to draw in the spirit of the wind and sun to revive the wind horse of Chilger. His scepter, acting as a drumstick, rattled and pounded, sending messages and vibrations through the clan, through their bodies into the soil and heavens. He called to the living Universe for healing. He prayed to Tengri and to Mother Earth. The steady thump of the drums called to the Great Spirit.

The old shaman wore the long feathers of the golden eagle on his head, and his face was obscured by a protruding, painted ornamental beak. His armor was heavy with leather-strip bands that dangled from his arms and hems like feathers, swinging and swaying dramatically as he moved ceaselessly around his patient. The metal panels on his apron and kaftan rattled and clanged as he moved, a cacophony of voice, drum, bell, and brass. He summoned the spirits to join them and made offerings. He burned juniper branches and berries, always beseeching the fire mother. He called on the Great Bear and nursed the claw wounds with a herbal salve while he did. His low, guttural monotone droned on and on. He listened intently to Chilger's rants and joined him, trembling and wailing. The shaman's eyes rolled back white in his head, the sound of the Great Bear growled forth, and the ger shook with the explosive energy raging within. Mirrors were laid all around the boy and placed on his chest to frighten away the evil spirits that might choose his time of weakened state to possess him.

Chilger had called out about Atitala, the deluge, the earthquakes. He had called to Theron; he saw giants, flying machines, oceans, pyramids; he watched a son die before him, murdered by a spear, and he watched another have revenge. He walked up white steps in white robes, he visited the land above and the land below, and he understood that he was a dot, made of billions of smaller dots, and that the trees, the birds, the people, the mountains, his thoughts, were all the same. Everything came from the first dot. All were connected.

And he saw Borte. Over and over, the little girl from the market returned to him in his fevered state, always when he was closest to Tengri. Always when he thought he might give in and move into the brilliant welcoming glow ahead of him, he would see her face, and she would smile and tell him to come back. "Not yet," she whispered. "Come back."

Chilger did come back. His fever broke on the third day, and the exhausted shaman made arrangements with his relieved and fearful parents for him to be trained. His fevered ravings had left them frightened and unnerved, and they were happy to know that he would soon be under the full-time care and guidance of the wise shaman.

"His wind horse is ancient and powerful. Though your family has no history of the gift, he is meant to be a shaman. The Great Bear chose him on this hunt to become a part of the world above and below. I listened, and he told many tales. He has traveled and lived among the spirits. He has lived many lives and it is certainly his destiny."

Chilger heard the shaman's words, and in his sleepy haze he heard his superstitious, simple father grunt his assent; it would not have occurred to him to do otherwise.

Chilger trained with the old master through his teen years and proved to be a profoundly gifted spiritualist. His Marcus-brain generated wisdom and understanding of heaven and earth. That history, combined with this lifetime, belonging to a people united with the soil and sky all at once, helped him to tap into a profound and powerful psychic energy. He shared that energy and connection with his village. Soon his wise mentor realized that his prodigy would soar beyond him, willing and able to connect with Mother Earth and Father Sky in every possible way.

Chilger constantly heard the whispers of the world around him. He understood and anticipated the animals, the weather, the vegetation, and he helped his people succeed in honoring and reaping their fruits. He would silently lower the bow of a fellow tribe member with a calm gesture, leaving a fat marmot to eat in peace as her young emerged from the brush, joining her. He would understand when the milk of a mare soured, and he would comfort her and sing to her and feed her the grasses to make it right. The birds were drawn to him and he used them as guides and tools.

In his fifteenth year, he rescued a large golden eagle with a wingspan beyond eight feet. Her left wing had been damaged in a particularly difficult battle with a wolf. Chilger had watched the duel and approached the injured bird cautiously, humming, droning. His own eagle feathers not yet earned, he had looked more like the wolf in his bear-fur coat and cap than the bird he would later embody as a full shaman. The eagle struggled and thrashed, her talons and beak like razors, viciously defending herself, grounded and vulnerable.

Chilger called for wisdom, for comfort. He slipped a new, young rabbit from his cache, an intended ritual offering, and he sang his prayer, offering help and healing to the bird in a language known only to the pair. The eagle calmed and hooked the rabbit in her beak, allowing Chilger to help her. He found that her wing was broken, and against all reason and nature, she allowed him to maneuver her.

Chilger tenderly folded her muscular wings into her strong body and she screeched, dropping her meal and pecking his arm, a reminder to be gentle. She had torn through his thick fur jacket and opened a bloody gash. She was not angry but in pain, and she cocked her head at him, confused. Their black eyes met and the great bird understood that he was a friend, and she allowed him to continue, no longer afraid. He stroked the healthy wing and continued to hum and vibrate, unaware of his own injury, undaunted and ecstatic. He wrapped a long silk strip, pulled from his waistband, around both folded wings, preventing attempts at flight and further damage. He then carried the massive bird back to camp. Later, he would not remember much of the experience, but he was used to that. He often lost track of time and place when overcome by the rapture and wisdom of the spirits.

Chilger was a miraculous sight entering the camp. Man and beast trusted one another in complete cooperation and harmony. The giant eagle rested in his thick arms, proud and erect, eyeing the terrified clan members and the recoiling animals as they passed. The eagle slowly rotated her regal head, taking it all in, one with her host.

Generations of Merkits would have spoken of this amazing scene in fire-dances and tales. They would have sung of this young shaman-to-be, this gifted boy who had walked into camp with a golden eagle for a friend, if they had had the chance. Had the tale not died with them.

Soon after that day, Chilger was preparing to dress in the accessories and kaftan inherited on completing the journey to becoming a shaman. The ancient clothing and trims were all passed down from elder holy men. The first costume layer was symbolic and infused with old power and ancestral energy, and his mentor explained the significance of the passing down of the wardrobe and the importance of each piece as he helped him dress. For the first time, Chilger donned the leather belt hung with mirrors that he would wear daily for the rest of his life. The mirrors would reflect his inner and outer selves and ward off evil spirits.

The sacred ceremony was long and the entire clan attended, bringing gifts and offering sacrifices and gratitude to the gods. Chilger was honored with a headdress, like his teacher's, of three long, thick eagle feathers and a painted beak that hung over his forehead and camouflaged his face, giving him the advantage of observing others unseen.

The wounded eagle had survived her injury. Once healed, Chilger had released her silk bonds, and she had soared joyfully free into the vast open sky. He watched in amazement as she returned to him, seeking his company. She refused to leave him for long and stood like a sentry next to him, pecking and nudging the fabric of his clothing.

She now accompanied him through the village, a thick leather saddle blanket strapped to his left forearm for their mutual comfort. She was a fantastic hunter, and she brought him trophies and gifts as if to say thank you. Though no one else dared touch her, she was no threat in the village. When she was not hunting, she remained a constant companion to Chilger, who treated her with sustained respect and reverence. He never presumed to give her a name.

Marcus was fascinated and awed by his natural instincts and experiences in this lifetime. He enjoyed a profound connection to the Earth that he had never known before, an ability to interact with the natural world around him that happened spontaneously, without thought. It was innate and unteachable, and Marcus was humble and grateful to be so honored.

Chilger had been earmarked by the spirits before birth, and his psychic wind horse was so strong that he frequently had visions and dreams, not only of his Marcus-past but also of the future. He wasn't always sure which was which, and he often did not understand his dreams, but as he grew older and spent more time in contemplation and meditation, his understanding grew.

Lately a dream had been coming to him both night and day. Vivid and gory, he saw and felt thousands dead. Humans slaughtered, dismembered, and left to die on the steppe, plains, and hills of northern Asia. Chilger shared his visions with the old shaman and together they sought clarity, for if the gods were sending the images there must be a reason.

After many days of prayer, song, and meditation, surrounded by pungent aromas and deprived of sleep, an image was conjured in the thick smoke before them. Chilger saw the face of the man who would bring the bloodshed upon the people. He saw a leader with hair like fire and eyes like emeralds, who would wreak havoc and be both celebrated and hated.

Chilger did not know the man whose face appeared before him, nor did his old companion, but the wind horse was familiar. He was clearly a chief, but he was no one that they had encountered in this life. Marcus instantly recognized Helghul's energy. He was not surprised that once again their paths would cross.

But where is Theron? Marcus wondered, not for the first time, and as always the answer came when the right question was asked.

The face of the little girl from the market immediately popped into his mind—Borte. "Not yet . . . come back," she had whispered in his haze when he was near death, fallen off his horse and left to the bear. He had already met her in this lifetime. He had known her, played with her, and watched her be carried away by her stern father. Chilger was overcome with emotion, and the smoky, unfamiliar face of Temujin dispersed into the fire-lit air, returning to darkness and shadows.

Chilger fell to his knees, feeling physically ill and overcome with sadness. Borte was Theron. He knew it now. How would he ever find her? His visions clearly told him that his purpose in this lifetime was to counter the red-haired menace, but he was distracted and torn. He must find Borte. He convinced himself that together they would know what to do; they would be a more powerful force. He did not know that Borte had already met the figure in the smoke, and to her he was much more than simply a red-haired stranger.

CHAPTER 22

A PROMISE HONORED

Temujin had not come for Borte on his twelfth birthday as was agreed. Nor had he come in years following. Borte's father became concerned that his beautiful, sweet daughter would be left to wilt like a field flower. He had learned that Temujin's family had been cast out after Yesugei Khan's death, but he had heard no more. The agreement was still in place, despite the fact that the suitor was no longer the strategic and valuable alliance he had once seemed; it would be dishonorable to act otherwise. Borte's father could only hope and pray for news that Temujin had been killed. Then he would be free to make a better match for her. They waited, year after year, they waited, but no word came.

It was an evening in midautumn. Borte was in her seventeenth year and had grown muscular and strong, but she maintained the outward appearance of fragile loveliness. Her soft brown skin was red and toughened where it had been exposed to the elements. She had worked ceaselessly all day, using a thick bone needle to stitch seams through dense skins that would aid in the winter comfort and survival of her family. Her father, the chief, was alerted that a rider approached. As the unexpected stranger grew nearer, his red hair and green eyes were unmistakable. Like a spirit from another time, Temujin returned unannounced to claim his bride.

"It is Temujin, daughter, make haste to be ready," the chief ordered. Borte was stunned and overcome with uncertainty and fear. She grew frantic as she realized the significance of the rider. She clutched her father's arm like a small child.

"Tell him to go away!" she begged, her eyes wide and imploring, her belly churning. Her father's heart raced at the vision of Temujin rising like sacred fire, red and blazing across the landscape. He snapped at his daughter, consumed by his own anxiety.

"Hush, daughter. You know nothing of the world!" he scolded, uncharacteristically harsh. He was unnerved by the image of Temujin rising on the plain, looking more spirit than man.

The chief returned to the calm, controlled voice to which she was accustomed. "He comes to us like a raven on the wind, daughter. Settle yourself; soon he will be here and we will see he is just a man. We must welcome him into our family as we have promised. We will hear his tale and pledge nothing else until he has had his say."

He placed his hand on his opposite elbow where Borte gripped him uncertainly. Borte's mother and grandmother had joined them outside and he steered his daughter toward them. "Take her inside and make ready, for tonight we share our home."

Borte was led inside, her pulse and mind racing. Though she had waited many years for Temujin to come, she could not help but wish him away. He was a stranger, after all, and he was coming to them so suddenly. Borte felt a great charge in the air, and she knew that change was certainly upon them.

Once inside she collected herself nervously, and she helped to organize an honorable seat for their guest near the corner that housed their ancient ancestors. Borte said a prayer, requesting guidance and blessing in the night ahead. She was attended by the other women, and they all flitted about their home.

"At last he's come. Our prayers have been answered," her mother said respectfully, nodding in almost a full bow toward the fire in the center of the room and to the sacred vessel on the northern side of the shelter.

"It is all so sudden, I can barely breathe to be useful. Like smoke this stranger appears and I am to marry him? A boy I met when he was half this age? To see him riding solo toward us is to feel invaded . . . under siege . . . but he is to be my husband, not my conqueror," Borte said aloud, all the while busily placing carpets and furs, and then rebinding her waist-length black hair with laces of well-softened leather.

"It is one and the same," her mother chimed in, and the older women laughed knowingly.

"Would you wish instead to grow old and sour, forever in your father's care? Do you not want children?" her grandmother admonished, with a wrinkled, gap-toothed smile. Her skin was so aged from the sun, wind, and brutality of life on the plain that she looked well past her fifty years.

I would hope to know love, Borte thought to herself, but she kept quiet for the remainder of their preparation. Those were thoughts that she would never share with anyone. Silly and impractical, there was no time for such frivolity.

Borte had known since childhood that her duty as a daughter was to become a good wife and the mother of a strong hearty brood to make her parents and husband proud. She would know love through her children, and she would grow to respect her husband if he was gentle and kind. She hoped that he would have smiling eyes like her father that twinkled and spoke to her, and a quick wit like her brothers. She hoped that he would not be severe like some of the men of her clan.

Borte loved to laugh and tease, but as she peeked slyly through the slim opening where the door flap fell closed, she could not imagine the stern, red-faced Temujin doing either one. She saw no smile, no soft kindness in his face. He looked all business. Her father gesticulated, spreading his arms wide to the heavens and then to the earth as they spoke. Borte guessed that their guest was explaining his long absence, and her father was suggesting that it must be the will of the Universe that things be as they were.

Temujin and the chief soon entered the ger, and the curious clan members, who had been feigning disinterest, adjourned to their own chores and homes to speculate in private. Borte confidently came forward to greet Temujin. No longer a skinny child, she had become a sturdy, beautiful woman. She found it hard to suppress a nervous smile and Temujin nodded in return.

Once again Helghul was overwhelmed by Theron's energy. The thick bands of color and the life force that surrounded and flowed from her accosted him at once, dipping in and out of him, dancing with his life soul and sending him spinning. He saw her emanations woven intricately through the ger, flowing in and out of her parents and family. They all looked upon her adoringly, deeply affected by her but oblivious to the corporeal radiant force enveloping them like a cosmic embrace.

Temujin remembered her powerful wind horse from their first meeting, her psychic pull, and as she had aged it had obviously grown exponentially. She had overwhelmed and filled him in every way, and she continued to do so. He knew that she was special, and over the years, with the help of his ancient ancestors—his Helghul-brain—whispering to him constantly, he had come to understand that she was Theron. He sent his energy out to greet her and, like a desperate thirst finally quenched, he drank her in and realized that he had missed her and that he longed for her. Somehow, in her presence he felt whole and balanced.

"I hope your eyes are bright and clear, and your songs are strong and true." Temujin said respectfully, presenting her with the thick sable fur that he had been holding.

Borte was startled, having assumed that the gift was for her father, and she took the luxurious prize gratefully in her hands. It was the loveliest thing that she had ever felt or seen, and she wrapped it around herself, expressing her simple gratitude as she held it out to her family so that they could feel its softness. It was an extravagant and valuable token, and she was honored.

"You will have many beautiful things when I am a great khan," Temujin said matter-of-factly, immensely pleased by her obvious pleasure at his offering.

"I am grateful," she said, searching his face and meeting his eyes. "I need only to live a simple life and to be of use to others, if it pleases the gods," she added.

Temujin's chemistry exploded as their eyes met, and his entire body boiled under her gaze. Every hair follicle and cell was electrified and tingling. Borte also stirred; she felt the air of something she didn't understand swirling like wind around them.

"I have asked great Tengri and Mother Earth for many years to bring me back here," Temujin explained, as he was ushered in to sit. He took his place of honor on the floor, surrounded by warm furs and carefully woven carpets and blankets.

He reluctantly shared the story of his family's downfall, starting with the assassination of his father Yesugei Khan but leaving out the most gruesome and murderous details of their life abandoned on the plains. He explained that he now led a tribe of his own, comprising his siblings and their families and others from the old clan that had been glad to join him. He said he had come to honor his promise to Borte and to the gods, if she would still have him. He intentionally mentioned the spirits with a reverent nod to heaven and earth and to the ancestral vessel that sat before him, subtly manipulating her to accept him.

His Helghul-brain was in full motion; it whirred and ticked calculatingly. She belonged with him. He would harness her energy and use it to his benefit. He would use it to lure and control others. She would bear him sons who would become great warriors and generals, and together they would rise up and, as intended, they would unfold the map of their destinies together.

Upon listening to his tale, and surrounded by the expectation of her family, Borte felt absolutely bound to honor her accord with Temujin. It never occurred to her to do otherwise. She was profoundly spiritual and had been brought up to respect commitments and family. She had grown up praying many times a day over her work, her home, and her food. She followed their customs carefully to ensure the best of luck. She thanked Mother Earth for the berries that she collected, she thanked the great birch spirits for the branches she would burn, she sent blessings to the animals that gave their lives to feed and clothe them. She felt absolutely certain that it would please the gods to accept Temujin. She was drawn to him and, in his presence, felt a familiarity and connection that was well beyond their affiliation.

There was no reason to wait. They had waited long enough. The lush oranges and reds of autumn would soon be replaced by the frigid whites and grays of winter. Though Temujin was nearly a stranger to her, Borte prepared to leave her family and join his clan.

Within days the couple were married with ritual offerings. Borte heard the bells, smelled the smoke, and saw the glowing fire that sealed their sacred path onward as one. Still, a nagging, unexplained feeling of angst took seed inside her and tugged at her heart.

Borte took her place as Temujin's wife, and the couple set off to join his tribe. After three days of being jostled on horseback and diverted by tales of his grand plans for the future, they arrived in his camp.

Temujin's mother, Hoelun, was the first to greet her, and Borte was quiet and composed, as a daughter-in-law should be. She graciously accepted her gifts and well wishes, and Temujin watched proudly as her glow washed over his people. He was certain they all felt the mysterious attraction and euphoria that sprang from her, and he was aware that his once notoriously beautiful mother was resentful. He would have to watch her carefully. He knew that, if permitted, she would make life difficult for his new wife.

The settlement was larger than Borte had anticipated. There were ten gers in all and a good assortment of sheep, goats, and yaks, all herded in for the night to protect them from wolves and other predators. She remained quiet, however, unable to shake the sadness that she felt at leaving her family. Despite her melancholy, her beauty was unparalleled, and curious clan members offered gifts and congratulations to please their chief and to get a glimpse of her.

Temujin's ger was near the outer, northern tip of the nomad camp. He had welcomed Borte to her new home, and she settled into the eastern quarter, making it her own.

On the first morning, Borte took her place among the other village women. Her duties included: collecting berries, roots, and fuel; curing and drying skins; and preparing the daily meal. The terracotta grasses blew in waves as a warmly bundled Borte helped to tend the sheep that were being led out to graze. They had been gated tightly together in their pen of birch branches to preserve their body heat through the cold night, and they sang to her a myriad of pleased and annoyed bleats as they enjoyed the thawed water she offered them.

Borte scanned the horizon and took in the beauty of the snowcapped mountains, purple and blue around her and farther in the distance. There were stories about the great mountains, legends of a magical mythical place hidden within and the extraordinary people who resided there.

Temujin had not touched her since their marriage, but he spoke clearly of his plans to build their family and extend his clan. She knew that it was only a matter of time until he would come to her in the night as a husband, and she was both nervous and curious. She had heard whispers of what it meant, old ladies crudely poking and pinching, but she didn't know what to expect. She knew that sometimes her father had joined with her mother, and that it seemed to make them both happy and sleep well. She knew that it was the way that babies were implanted if the gods wished it, and she longed for a child of her own to adore. Her mother had briefly warned her that it might hurt and that there might be blood as there was on her moon cycle, but she had smiled and soothed her when Borte had become concerned.

On their fourth night in the ger, Temujin announced that the first snowfall would soon come and before then he would leave on a hunt. It was on that night that he first took his husband-place beside Borte. She heard him moving and breathing in the dim light, and he silently lay down next to her. He was not rough—he moved carefully and said nothing as he slowly peeled away the layers of her clothing and exposed her naked body.

She was soft and round and more enticing than he had imagined. He studied the curves of her breasts in the firelight and her cold, erect nipples fascinated him. His rough, calloused hands explored her, and she sucked in her breath as he moved his hand from one hip bone to the other. Gooseflesh erupted over her body.

At the sound of her gasp, his arousal heightened and his breath quickened in response. He ran his hand from her hips to between her thighs, and he felt a warm place there—a soft, wooly patch that guided his way.

Borte realized how rigidly she was holding herself and she tried to relax under his hand, swallowing the lump that had formed in her throat. Her thighs opened slightly and he sought the deeper, warmer place within her. Her eyes remained tightly closed. He was not harsh or rushed, but after a few minutes of discovery and temptation he shed his lower coverings and moved overtop of her. She didn't see his naked flesh but she felt it, hard and urgent, pushing against her. She felt confused and slightly nauseated.

Temujin, now on top of her, breathed loudly in her ear, flesh to flesh. She let herself be maneuvered as he opened her legs to him. He entered her, more urgently now, and she let out an involuntary cry of pain. She felt a warm trickle as her hymen was ruptured, and she was uncertain what to do and was afraid to move. The pain did not last long, and Temujin quickly became more rigid between her thighs and then, grunting, he arched and rolled away. He was done and Borte had a new understanding of the business of men and women.

Borte covered herself and rolled over to sleep, crying silently in the darkness, though she was not sure why. She felt embarrassed by the wet stickiness between her legs and, for the first time in her life, felt disconnected from her own body. Temujin was unable to sleep and, having heard her weeping, he restlessly resisted the desire to mount her again for the remainder of the night.

Temujin, armored with a thick leather vest, sword, and bow, departed the next day, assuring Borte that he would soon return. He looked at his beautiful wife, her eyes now following him curiously, studying his rugged young face more openly as he prepared to leave. He felt a twinge of pride that she belonged to him, and his manhood stirred in response. He adjusted himself, mounted his horse, and was gone, leading the hunters already gathered on the plain. Borte watched him go and then returned to the ongon[22] at the north side of the ger. She asked the spirits to bless her with a child and, wrapping herself against the cold, she began her daily chores.

Hoelun watched them from the ger she shared with her daughter, having been displaced by the arrival of her son's new bride. She saw how Temujin looked lustily at Borte, and she recognized the blush of a new wife. She had no generous thoughts and whispered no blessings for her son's wife's fertility.

Temujin had been gone two days, and Borte was busy collecting late blueberries to dry for winter. She had followed the other clanswomen on the long walk from the sheltered mountain location of the winter camp to an abundant field. The temperature and winds were still fair, and Borte was happy to be free of the mountain's shadowy protection and enjoying the warm sun of the open plains. The women whispered all around her, and the young children approached her shyly, giggling and retreating as she playfully smiled and waved to them.

Despite the fact that Borte and Hoelun were originally from the same small tribe, the envious older woman did not draw her in as she should have done, and the others hesitated to act. They were afraid to raise the infamous ire of their matriarch. Borte was patient with them and worked stoically, though she felt sad and alone. She found herself looking forward to Temujin's imminent return.

The blueberry field was abundant and worth the walk, and the women filled sack after sack with the sweet fruit. They ate while they happily worked, rushing to get back before twilight descended. The horizon was violet blue, and for every inch the sun lowered in the sky the temperature dropped significantly. The few remaining summer birds feasted on the bountiful fields as they prepared to migrate, far from the cold and hunger of the punishing northern winter. Borte drank in their song and likened their chirps to the laughter and peals of the purple berry–smudged children around her. Hunched down in front of an abundant bush, expertly plucking and storing without damaging the tender fruit, Borte did not notice the multiple dots on the landscape as they approached.

The other women began to call out and gather together, herding their children, as a horde of more than fifty unknown riders neared. Borte rose, scanning the fields in alarm.

"Merkits," Hoelun announced fearfully, as the men made their final approach.

The Mongols and the Merkits were not allies, but they were not at war. Borte fell in line behind Hoelun and the others. Though the visitors were unexpected, the women only watched, more curious than afraid. The riders came to a stop at the edge of the blueberry patch.

"Which of you is the wife of Chief Temujin?" the lead rider questioned roughly, his leather face scowling involuntarily as he spoke. He was a stern, weathered man of vaguely familiar dress and colors.

The Mongol mothers drew their children in closer to them and the smallest cried out to run free, too young to know fear. Borte was distressed and did not answer the armed warrior. The heads of the other women immediately turned toward her, and they eyed the recent arrival suspiciously.

"She is," Hoelun said haughtily, stepping aside and gesturing her left arm toward her new daughter-in-law.

Borte was stung by the woman's indifference. Her black hair whipped against her face as the sun continued to make its descent in the sky and the winds picked up once more. She adjusted her fur cap more snuggly around her cheeks and silently waited for an explanation.

The village women decided it was wise to put as much distance between themselves and Borte as possible and they backed away, abandoning her completely. There was nothing they could do and besides, she was a newcomer, not one of their own, and she would not be missed.

Borte didn't have time to shift before the lead Merkit made his move. Without a word the center rider reached out and, with a broad and easy sweep, lifted her by her coat. She screamed and hung like a sack of rice in the air, her legs dangling uselessly, and he slung her across his horse. The blueberry sack that she had carefully filled flew from her grasp and broke open, spilling its contents carelessly onto the grass. She struggled to right herself, but he used his elbows in the back of her neck and lower spine to push her snug against his mount. Even through her heavy clothing she felt the bruise of his touch immediately, but she continued to resist. She had heard stories like this—kidnappings, war tactics—but she could not believe she was being used so. Her mind raced. She would be given away, a prize to be won or rewarded or used up.

Hoelun watched as her son's wife was scooped onto the lead horse and carried away. She listened to her terrified cries of protest without sympathy. She had been carried away from her Merkit husband by Temujin's Mongol father in much the same way. She knew the alarm and confusion that the girl must be feeling, but she had no empathy. She was incapable of it. She hid her glee behind a phony veil of concern and outrage, which she wore back to camp.

The next day, when Temujin returned, Hoelun informed him that his new bride had been kidnapped by the Merkits, no doubt in retribution for her own kidnapping by Yesugei Khan[23] so many years before.

The husband raged out of control at learning that his wife had been taken. He looked at his bitter, gloating mother with hatred, easily seeing through her phony facade, wishing the bandits had freed him of her instead. Helghul seethed, and the violent flame within Temujin was fanned. That night he began to plan Borte's rescue.

CHAPTER 23

A GIFT

Chilger's Marcus-brain had become desperate once he realized that Borte, the girl from his childhood, the girl he had been unable to forget, was his Theron. Immediately he had begun a desperate search. He knew only her first name, and it was not a particularly unusual one, so more than once he was directed to an encampment only to have his hopes dashed. He questioned the people of his clan, riding unaccompanied to the neighboring camps, often traveling for days without seeing another human. The nomadic people could be anywhere, and hundreds of miles separated them from one another. He knew that she would be at or near her nineteenth year by now, and the chances of finding her alive, unmarried, and able to join him were slim.

Chilger would not give up; his heightened instincts and his recurring visions indicated that he would find her. She might deny him and send him away, but he must persist. The shaman constantly meditated, seeking signs from the land, from the heavens, from the animals and trees themselves. His companion eagle soared above him, a second pair of eyes, searching for any spiritual indication to help them along, and hunting for both of them when his human-friend was too preoccupied to care about eating at all.

In the evenings, while huddled next to his sacred fire, Chilger sought direction through medicine-altered states and chanting. The visions came and shook him with powerful vibrations and images. Always they were clear: there would be bloodshed, an unprecedented age of bloodshed. Borte and the red conqueror both figured powerfully in his future, but there was someone else—a surreal, majestic, godlike figure that appeared like fog at the edges of the visions and floated, seated, into the forefront. Legs crossed, yogi style, the plump colorful character revealed that he was a king. He reached out to Chilger, urging and beckoning. Chilger felt his face embraced by the bejeweled, fat fingers of the magical father, and then he was gone. Left behind were only whispers. "Seek Shambhala, the land of the reborn."

At first Chilger's thoughts had been only of Borte, but as he traveled alone, at one with the land around him, he meditated, and he was inundated by visions of war and peril with Temujin at the helm. Always the little girl in the market raced ahead of him, and he chased her frantically, certain that he must find her. His Marcus-brain took a second seat to the animal spirits and symbols overwhelming him. Helghul was to yield a particularly brutal impact in this lifetime. He had seen visions of the life tree, running through the center of the Earth, and it reached to him, calling. "Shambhala" it whispered, over and over. In the air the birds cried out, "Shambhala." The fire crackled and rose up as visions of the sacred land—shaped like a giant, eight-petal lotus—unfolded like a map before him. Chilger resolved that he and Borte must somehow reach the fabled Shambhala, but first he must find her.

The visions continued to come but there was no sign of Borte, and Chilger knew that he must return to his clan soon before winter set in or he would surely die. He would have to endure the next nine months and search for her when the harsh winter retreated in the spring. He would use the time to contemplate, meditate, and understand and seek the wisdom of the spirit world. Chilger returned sadly to his camp and was greeted by many well wishers and friends. That evening he sought the counsel of his khan.

They sat accompanied by other respected men of the clan as dusk fell, the fire blowing violently side to side in the shifting winds. The hardy men were untroubled by the elements, and they enjoyed their time to laugh, smoke, and sometimes challenge one another physically.

"I trust that your journey brought you the enlightenment that you sought," the chief said in a low mumbling tone.

Chilger looked at him seriously, his warm fur hat flapping loosely around his face. They passed a pipe slowly around the circle, the bowl protected from the battering wind.

"As you know the gods have sent me in search of the girl named Borte, and I have returned unsuccessful and alone. There is more . . . I see great change coming for the people of the plains," Chilger began gravely. "Blood will run like floodwater from the mountains to the steppe and as far as the desert. A red devil seeks to unite the entire world under one tribe, a tribe of his loins, with no room for another's seed," the wise young shaman prophesied.

An elder tribe member responded, his eyes creased and sagged as if being pulled down by hooks. "The young think everything is bigger and harder than it is," he taunted, eliciting chuckles of appreciation for the sexual innuendo. "I have lived many years and have learned that even the harshest winter ends eventually and that enemies come and go like the seasons," he croaked.

Chilger's mentor then spoke up in his defense. "We have never survived a storm like this old father . . . the eagles fly counterclockwise over the plains chasing away the evil spirits . . . the world will be turned upside down. The dark spirits will slaughter anyone who stands against them," the old shaman cautioned. "Chilger speaks the truth. I have seen only a sliver of what this boy knows. We must listen to him. The gods give us the gift of his great insight. Would you choose to ignore it?"

The men around the fire expressed their concern and support for the young spiritualist with grunts and nods.

A returning party of more than fifty approached in the dusk, diverting their attention. The chief stood and made his way toward the nearing riders, and Chilger watched indifferently.

The clansmen dismounted, except for one small man, who remained seated with his head down. The lone figure had displayed the karmic colors of an Emissary, and before Borte raised her head Marcus knew immediately that it was Theron. A knot gripped Chilger's belly, twisting and tightening like a fist.

"Temujin will soon return from his hunt. Will he prepare for war against us?" one of the riders asked.

"He has no army. He has not the impressive clan of his father before him," the khan replied.

"But certainly he has allies?" the lead rider supposed.

"In any case, there is little chance that he will try to rescue the girl before the winter sets in . . . we have used the season to our advantage. We have righted a past wrong. There may be no consequence at all once the months have passed and he has had time to consider our justified retaliation," the chief suggested.

"Temujin will never let me go. He will come for me," Borte interrupted defiantly, surprising the men with her fearlessness.

"You are so special?" the chief grunted doubtingly. He looked her over carefully, aware of her beauty even in her disheveled state.

"She is," Chilger answered as he approached. His robes blew wildly behind him, and his shaman song filled the air as the metal and glass of his costume chimed. "Tell me, is Temujin the dark raven with the red hair that has plagued my dreams?" he asked her, gently taking the head of her mare in his hands. The tired horse nuzzled him affectionately while he waited, dreading the answer that he knew would come.

"I know nothing of your dreams," she snapped proudly. "My husband has the red hair that you speak of. I do not belong here. The gods will be displeased."

"Oh ho, and now she speaks for the spirits! You tell a shaman the will of the gods?" the chief chastised, angered by her insolence. "You are in no position to speak. You have been brought here to right a wrong perpetrated by Yesugei Khan before you were born. My father's sister, Hoelun, was stolen from us, and the rape of a good Merkit wife cannot go unpunished."

"Hoelun?" Borte gulped, thinking of the cold, distant woman she had only just met. "I am here because of Hoelun?"

"You know of her?" the chief asked.

"She is my husband's mother."

"She still lives?"

"She was made the wife of the khan. She was near me when I was taken."

"If this Temujin is the threat that he is told to be, he will come to us, and we will deal with him then," answered the chief.

"Have we started an unprovoked war?" one clansmen, silent until now, spoke up incredulously. "My totems lead me to be more hesitant of such careless disregard for my life and the lives of my kin."

"The great wolf came to me last night; he was armed and ready for battle. This path is true. Temujin's father stole a Merkit wife many moons past. This is merely the gods' way of balancing the Universe," the old shaman added seriously.

"I am tired of this wind and cold for tonight. My prize awaits me," the khan proclaimed, turning his bulky frame toward Borte's horse, a lascivious glint in his eye. She was now his property, stolen or not.

Chilger urgently took his arm and spoke into his ear. "This is Borte. This is the girl that I left in search of," he whispered.

The leader was astonished by the revelation and the synchronicity of it. "Once again, shaman, your visions and callings seem to speak with the voice of Tengri. She is yours," he said respectfully, stepping away.

To everyone's surprise, Chilger took the head of the mare and led the prisoner toward his simple ger near the eastern boundary of the settlement.

"Where are you taking me?" Borte asked, fear vibrating in her voice and stinging him like salt to a wound. He longed to hold her, comfort her, and ease her worried mind. Her aura was thick with doubt and apprehension.

"Borte, you will endure no hardship or ill treatment so long as you are with me," he assured her kindly. His body floated beneath him, barely feeling the ground at his feet. She was so close, her skin, her eyes, her hands. He watched the tendrils of air as she breathed and he longed to take in every particle she exhaled. His Marcus-brain whooped and cheered and scattered his energy as widely as he was able.

Borte's mind eased slightly and she hoped that he spoke the truth. They made their way away from the group, carefully observed.

"Who are you?" she asked skeptically, mirroring his whisper.

The shaman paused and raised his face to meet hers squarely for the first time, hope and love plain in his deep brown eyes. "I am your friend," he replied earnestly. "I am Chilger . . . do you not remember me?"

CHAPTER 24

FORBIDDEN LOVE

Borte did remember Chilger. She had affectionate recollections of her friend from the market. They had played more than once, and he had repeatedly presented her with little gifts and treats. As is often the case with children, his generosity had endeared him to her.

After offering the appropriate blessings and thanks, Chilger made a place for Borte at the north side of his ger, the place for honored guests—though he secretly hoped that she would someday take permanent residence in the east side of the circle.

"You must help me get home to Temujin," Borte said simply, when Chilger had dealt with the horse and finished stoking the fire at the center of the lodging. She was unsure how he would respond to the request, but she did not fear him.

"Never," Chilger said simply, catching her by surprise. "It is not with him that you belong, but with me," he finished, keeping himself busy gathering furs and blankets for her comfort.

Borte had expected that he might say he could not, or even would not, help her, but she had not expected this response. "With you?" she said, shocked.

Once again he felt a literal sting as her fear rose in her, and the colors swirling around her darkened significantly in the dusky evening light. "Please do not fear me. I can see your panic. I feel it as if it was my own, and it weighs on me. There is so much that you do not understand. So much that you do not remember," he said, sighing, his distress and anguish clear on his face.

He lowered a fur to the floor beside her, and as she sat their bodies touched. It was electric, like the sting of a wasp, only somehow pleasant. The energy between them grew exponentially with the touch, and she found herself being inexplicably pulled in, swimming in a familiar warm bath of elation and sorrow all at once. Her intuition hummed and whirred as their karmic energies rejoined and found one another.

"Tell me what I do not understand," Borte entreated.

Chilger began slowly, reminding her of their interactions in the market, the chance meetings, the joy and freedom they had felt running together as children, and the connection they had formed. He brought her to a familiar and comfortable place in their time together, putting her at ease.

"But there is more, so much more . . . our connection is an ancient one," he said, as they finished giving offering and began to eat together. He let the words hang in the air, his Marcus-brain desperately hoping and wishing, as always, that Theron would know him as he knew her.

"Ancient?" she repeated simply, but the words were far from simple. The notion sent shivers through her, and she stared at the shaman incredulously. Though reincarnation was an accepted tenet of their spiritual beliefs, only a rare few ever professed to have recollection. The idea excited and intimidated Borte, and she longed for more information. She waited for Chilger to continue.

"Do you know me?" he asked, willing her to see his Marcus-spirit.

"I know what I see," she said, but then uncertainly she added, "I always remembered our time in the marketplace. I should be afraid. I was afraid . . .

but now the fear has subsided and you feel . . . familiar. It's like a tingle in the Tengri-god center of my head telling me to trust you."

"I am familiar because this is only one of the many lives we have shared," he explained, his Marcus-brain hopeful that somehow Theron recognized him.

The warmth in the ger was growing unbearable, and Borte gulped as her stomach fluttered and lurched. "I am joined with Temujin," she croaked, feeling burdened with the memory of him. He seemed more like a stranger to her than a husband, and Chilger was here filling her with confusing feelings. She remembered him from her childhood, but there was more. She felt a strong pull at her core drawing her to him.

"Forgive me, I forget that we are not at the same place in this and I leap ahead," he said, worried that he had frightened her. He respectfully leaned further away from her.

Marcus was filled with longing. It had been so long since they had been together as man and woman. They sat in silence for a long time. Chilger would wait. Marcus was used to waiting. He would allow her all the time she needed to process what he had told her.

"Will you tell me everything?" she asked. She was filled with uncertainty and felt as though she was dreaming. She was amazed by her easy acceptance of this stranger. She could not deny the sensation of connection, the ease of their conversation, the unexplored passion he awoke in her.

"Eventually, I will tell you everything," he said, reaching out and gently brushing an errant strand of hair from her face.

Something inside her gave in to him then; that familiar motion, the tenderness and beauty of the gesture. She only faintly leaned forward, bending her neck, but it was enough. It was the cue that he had been waiting for, and he took her into his arms and kissed her gently, slowly stroking her face, her neck, her shoulder, and feeling his spirit seeking her desperately. She melted into him willingly, and hundreds of lifetimes of passion and love flowed between them.

The union of their souls was extraordinary, and their kisses became feverish and hungry. Her inexperience was irrelevant as nature and passion took over. They continued to kiss as they peeled off the layers of their clothing until they lay together warm and naked, toe to toe, thigh to thigh, belly to belly.

Her skin felt like soft cashmere beside him and she could feel his excitement. She breathed heavily against his neck and moaned lightly. In that moment, he was overcome and he lost control, his desire suddenly too much for him to manage. His body became rigid in the clutches of his untimely orgasm. He pulled away from her, humiliated and disappointed, but she pulled him back in close to her.

She was now the instigator and she urgently kissed his face and neck, holding him tightly and ignoring the sticky, damp warmth between them. His hands explored her flesh, not shyly but as a practiced lover, his premature excitement quickly forgotten. He slid his hands between her legs, stroking and rubbing, and her hips bucked and responded. He was overcome by her beauty and sensuality as the fire's glow lit her magnificent silhouette. He saw his Theron there among the furs, and her violet light enveloped them both. It didn't take long before his young body complied and was ready again.

Borte and Chilger did not move from the furs until the next morning. She was at peace, and she pushed the uncertainty that threatened her happiness to the back of her mind. They had found one other. Both of them felt the threads linking them like an intricate web. They were at the center, surrounded by the miraculous glimmering strands that gently whispered their story, but where was the spider?

Though she struggled to maintain the glow of the night before, Borte was worried about Temujin, the consequences of her kidnapping, and what he might do. She spoke to Chilger about her fears, and he assured her that only the gods could have planned things as they were. The coincidence of her coming to his camp on the day that he returned from his journey searching for her was too great. They would have to wait and see what was in store for them.

"Be grateful and live in the moment. Accept the gift that we have been given," he told her. "At the first sign of spring, we will make a great pilgrimage and seek the wisdom and glory of Shambhala. Until then, we must trust that we are in the hands of Father Sky and Mother Earth, and we are their servants."

"What if he comes for me? Will you cut him down like a birch in the forest? Would we see him murdered, though he is my rightful husband and he is innocent?" she asked, tears of shame stinging her eyes.

"We are not murderers. We have been sent here for much greater things. We will understand better when we reach Shambhala. Trust, Borte . . . our path will be revealed to us in time."

There was much preparation to be done in the final days before snowfall and it helped to distract her. Chilger stayed with Borte as they worked together, his shaman apron, all mirrors and metal, clanging and singing to them as they moved, his golden eagle soaring overhead protectively.

He told her tales of their history and the lives that had come before. She questioned and listened, enthralled, without reservation or doubt. He watchfully gauged her response, judging how much she would be able to accept, but she was open. He held back the most brutal and upsetting details, not wanting to cause her any unnecessary pain. He was burdened with knowing all of the sad and tragic details; she need not be. Reincarnation was an accepted truth for her, and when he spoke she believed every word and envied his clear recall, though when he spoke of walking in the spirit world she was frightened.

Over the next few weeks, the snow began to fall in flakes of every size, on violent winds and in gentle sheets. The landscape around them was washed clean, and Borte was relieved that there was no sign of Temujin. She settled into Chilger's ger as his wife, accepting his Marcus-memories to be the absolute truth, and her feelings for him intensified. She was cosmically drawn to him and felt as though they were stitched together down the center, from the inside out, each chakra meeting and interlocking so that when he spoke she could easily imagine the images that his words painted.

"Why do you remember and I do not?" she queried one evening, as she lay naked in his arms under layers of fur, their bodies still racing and sparking with recent pleasure.

"My connection to the spirits in this lifetime is great. I am humbly grateful," he said, carefully avoiding her question.

For the first time in many lifetimes, Marcus reaped the benefit of having taken the potion. It had allowed him to find Borte . . . but had he found her? He had looked and had intended to find her, but the gods had delivered her to his door with no input or effort from him. It was as it should be. He was reminded that his having taken the potion did not make finding Theron more likely, it only made him languish for her when he could not. They came together when it was meant to be so and, despite his best efforts, he was never in control.

"If we are meant to be together in all these times, why would the gods first send Temujin to me?" she asked, speaking his very thoughts.

"They did also deliver you to me. I am a prisoner to fate like all men. Our lifetimes will unfold as they are meant to do, and it is not until they are over that we can look back and understand the lessons," he replied, instantly feeling guilty that he had yet to share any knowledge of Helghul with her whatsoever. Chilger had only seen Helghul in his dreams and visions, the red devil of the plains, but he was the very description of Temujin, and Chilger was certain that they were indeed one and the same.

"You have seen the world after . . . after death?" she gasped in amazement. "And you remember?" she marveled, her mouth open in awe. She had been lying with her back to him, cupped by his warm body, and she quickly twisted to face him, her eyes glowing but afraid.

"Do not be alarmed, it is a place where we have all been many times. There is nothing to fear in it. It is the Meadow, a vast landscape more like this place in summer than any other land I have ever known. Like here, the trees and grasses and flowers and animals speak to the souls around them, and they flow together in harmony and are One. We are all One with the Source, and the connection and joy that we feel there is indescribable."

"Why do you come back?" she asked.

"To find you," he replied, and they kissed with the passion of an eternal bond, and she wept knowing that he was telling the truth. He kissed each tear and wiped them away. and they made love again.

Borte did not want to be rescued, and she shuddered to think what chaos and bloodshed would occur if Temujin came. He would not expect to find her in love with her captor, connecting at a level that she could not even begin to comprehend.

Chilger knew that Temujin would come, but he also knew that Temujin would have brought war upon the Merkits and all of the clans of the north in this Iron Age regardless of whether Borte had been taken or not. He had seen it in the fire. It was destined that Helghul's brutal way would be forged. It was the peak of power for the Darkness as the Great Year realized its ultimate descent. Temujin's Helghul-brain would have known Theron, and he would seek Borte until he found her or died searching.

What little sleep Chilger got was riddled with dreams and premonitions. Always bloody, awful battles, and the cherubic king of Shambhala beckoning to him, demanding that he and Borte seek the sacred place. Legend promised that in Shambhala, the land of the reborn, Theron would know him. Borte would have full recall of her past lives and he longed for that possibility. But there was more. There was a duty that they would perform. Would they be able to prevent the mass bloodshed and carnage that filled Chilger's dreams night after night? The fat king called to them; there was no doubt that they must set out. Everything would be revealed to them in time.

Winter had battered the Merkit camp for three long months, when Borte anxiously revealed to Chilger that her moon cycles had stopped and she believed that she was with child. He was initially overjoyed, but the realization of what a profound complication a pregnancy was in their situation worried him. They had a difficult journey ahead.

Borte never voiced her fear that the child might be Temujin's and be born with a head of wild crimson hair. Or worse yet, Temujin might steal her back and murder any child that did not obviously resemble him. She was sick with pregnancy and worry, and she spent the next few months retching and green, sipping bark remedies and praying for her unborn child.

Soon Borte's belly protruded sharply where it had once lain flat and smooth. The clanspeople smiled and nodded, happy for their young shaman and his mate. At first she had been nervous, always scanning the white horizon for riders and staying very close to the ger. But as time passed—weeks, and then months—she began to relax and believe that Temujin might never come.

Chilger was never so naively optimistic. He knew that it was only a matter of time before Temujin sought them out. Helghul would search for Theron, their destinies in this lifetime once more cruelly tied together. He would never rest until he reclaimed Borte and annexed the Merkits completely.

What Chilger didn't know was that Temujin had, months earlier, appealed to his blood brother and childhood friend, the Khan of Jadoran,[24] for assistance.

"Jamuka, we can use this to our advantage. The Merkits have taken Borte—it is a reason to bring war upon them and take them over. Blood brother, I ask for your assistance in retrieving what is rightly mine. There is great benefit in it for both of us," Temujin reasoned, pacing beside the evening fire, his horse tended and settled for the night. It had only been days since Borte's disappearance, and Temujin and his clansmen had ridden hard and long to reach Jamuka as quickly as possible.

"My brother, your father started this when he kidnapped Hoelun, but I agree we can use it to our advantage. It is not only us with an interest here . . . Toghrul Khan of Kerait should be brought in . . . you come with too few warriors . . . he has a vast army of more than twenty thousand men."[25]

"You are right, brother, I will go to my godfather. We will form a great alliance and crush the Merkits," Temujin said.

Jamuka rose from the log on which he was seated, and the blood brothers embraced and smiled widely to one another. Just as it was when they were boys, their clinch became a competition, and soon the men were laughing and grunting as they wrestled. Heads down, shoulder to shoulder, they pushed back and forth, side to side, struggling to unfoot one another.

The spectators cheered and hooted as the men grappled in the frigid dust. Then, in one quick motion, Temujin was down, flat on his back, his chest heaving, with his friend's body pressed hard against him. For the first time ever Jamuka had bested him. After a moment of still triumph, the khan, pleased and beaming, stepped off and held a hand out, helping up a surly, sour-faced Temujin. It was not until later that night that Jamuka found himself wondering if Temujin had let him win to curry favor. The suspicion significantly soured his feelings of victory.

It took eight months to prepare the armies and to wait for the ideal season to arrive. Temujin offered a valuable sable fur as a gift, the same fur he had once given to his bride. Toghrul was a smart khan and he easily understood the strategic and financial benefit of a Merkit defeat, but he wisely insisted that they wait until Tsagaan Sar: the celebration that heralded the coming of spring and meant travel and warfare were possible.[26] Toghrul had no reason to rush. Temujin had to wait, but Helghul was used to waiting, and he used the time to plot his rise to power.

A week before the celebration of Tsagaan Sar, a bedraggled Merkit rider returned to the camp and informed the chief that a vast multitude of warriors was amassing two days' ride away. The men of the tribe immediately mobilized. The arrows and bows they had been crafting were being bundled and readied, and the clan planned to move to a more strategic location in preparation for war.

Borte requested and was granted an audience with the Merkit khan. He greeted her outside his ger, both of them heavily bundled against the burning winds.

"May your wives bear many healthy, fat sons, good khan," she said.

"Kind words. I hope you bear a son with the wind horse and wisdom as great as Tengri himself," he said sincerely. "Now you must be quick. The seasons change and there is much to do, since it appears we will soon be at war."

"Great khan, you must send me back!" she exclaimed, shocking the leader.

"I do not understand. Is Chilger not your mate now?" the Khan asked, confused and surprised.

"I am only one person, a woman, not even Merkit. For me to cause the loss of even one life is too many. I do not wish you to battle on my behalf. Please send me back and let there be peace," she pleaded.

"I do not remember asking your permission when you were taken . . . and what of that Merkit child in your belly? Am I not responsible for the care and safety of all of my tribe? Be sensible, woman, they would cast you out . . . or worse!" he warned, trying to scare her.

"I am not afraid. It is the right thing to do," she retorted bravely, but the chief was unmoved. She appealed to him again, but he shook his head and walked away. Borte desperately dropped to her knees on the icy ground and beseeched him, "You can prevent this bloodshed and death by sending me back. Please, good khan, I beg you," she called after him.

The chief stopped and, feeling both compassion and annoyance, faced her. "Pick yourself up. I will not be commanded by you. You were brought here to right a wrong. Chilger has warned that this war will come regardless. It is a threat that cannot be avoided. If this clash comes, it will be they who provoked it, not us. But worry not, for we can fight if we have to and we will rise victorious."

The khan was finished talking to the emotional woman and he simply walked away, leaving her kneeling, as Chilger ran to her side in concern.

"What is it? What has happened?" he asked.

Borte raised herself up awkwardly, her belly heavy in front of her. Her distress was plain in her mottled face. "I must go tonight. I must go before anything starts. I will find Temujin; he can still stop this," she resolved determinedly, pushing past him toward their ger.

He strode after her. "Temujin will not be thwarted, Borte! You cannot go to him! He will wage war no matter what you do; it is his role in the world!" Chilger said.

She stopped walking and turned on him, her eyes wild with fear and guilt. "And my role, Chilger? Is it to do nothing? I am a part of this, I must at least try!" she growled indomitably. She rushed the rest of the way to their ger, surprisingly agile and swift considering her growing girth.

Chilger followed her inside, grateful for the privacy and warmth. "Your role is to be my mate. To bear my children," he said, pulling her resistant body into his arms, knowing that his words were false. He placed his fur-covered hand on her thickly covered belly. "I have chased your spirit lifetime after lifetime, and always like smoke you slip through my fingers. I have loved you forever and I have finally found you," Chilger said, choking on his words. "We have been called to Shambhala, Borte. We will set out on the long dark night, Bituun, the last night of winter, when there is no moon to betray or mislead us. We will be led only by our spirit guides. We will not be idle and do nothing to help this world, we will go where we have been called and our path will be revealed. It is our only chance to stop this war and save our people."

Borte raised her dark eyes to his, and they were so warm and deep that he was consumed. He swam in the depths of her compassion and self-sacrifice, and he tasted her goodness. He was overwhelmed in every way and he bent to kiss her. She returned his kiss but soon pulled away.

"I will go with you," she said, finally convinced, and together they began to prepare.

Chilger was relieved that she had given up the idea of finding Temujin, but he found it difficult to answer her questions about where they were going. No one knew where Shambhala was located. There were legends, but they were surreal and unclear, and he had only his dreams to direct them.

The Merkits readied themselves. The nomads packed up their gers, their families, and their livestock and made for more strategic positions. Most of the warriors set out toward the amassing enemy horde, while some accompanied the tribe. Families said their goodbys, in most cases, forever.

Chilger and Borte loaded their belongings, their ger, and their supplies onto the backs of two sturdy horses, and each rode as well. The great golden eagle rested on Chilger's arm and he spoke gently to her, respectfully requesting her assistance on their quest. Their journey would be long and arduous, and the shaman was counting on the assistance of the great sky and earth to assist them.

They would have to be wary—the spirits were in balance, good and evil, and there would be trials and obstacles in their way. So few ever reached Shambhala. One must be called and guided and prove oneself worthy.

Bituun had come, and, as darkness fell, Chilger and Borte began their pilgrimage.

"We must travel through the night," he told her. "This long, moonless trail will unfold before us as it should and we must trust our instincts. If we listen to our souls' songs we will come to the right place; it is our eyes that deceive us. This realm that we inhabit is an illusion, Borte, a trick of our senses. We are blind to the truth of the spirit world alive all around us. In the darkness we can listen to the air and take the hands of the animal and nature spirits that reach out to each of us."

"I trust you. There is so much that I do not understand. I will follow where you lead," she replied fearlessly.

"It is I who will follow. My guides tell me that it is you who is called to Shambhala, Borte. My role is to make certain that you get there."

"Me? It is you who hears the call, and have the memory of the spirit side. I feel like I am a child playing along in a time of real peril."

"Our 'play,' as you call it, is our destiny. We must follow the road and see where it leads. I have prayed for a spirit guide to help us on our path," he answered.

"I am afraid," she said.

"We all fear the unknown. Once there was a great king. He ruled his people well and was a merciful master. Many times he was forced to defend his lands against invasion, and always he was successful because he was righteous. He would ask his prisoners, his enemies, to choose their fate. Would it be the first cave that led to certain death by sword, or would it be the second that led to an unknown outcome? Most men chose certain death by sword, more afraid of the unknown than of death," Chilger told her.

"What was in the other cave?" Borte asked.

"Freedom," Chilger answered, and they continued to ride through the frigid, punishing darkness without talking. Borte contemplated the story and was resolved to overcome her fear of the unknown.

It was unusual to travel at night—the evil spirits were so much more likely to interfere—and it was odd and unnerving for Borte. Chilger chanted loudly as they moved, and their horses and garments jingled lyrically with bells and mirrors, scaring away the evil that would do them harm.

The stars were bright in the sky and offered a road map to the young shaman who followed them. Shambhala was real, he was sure of it. They had only to be worthy and seek it. Legend told that one had to be invited to Shambhala—many had perished searching for it, and many had just disappeared.

Though the first day of spring had come and gone, the weather continued to be cold and unkind and brutally battered the pair as they rode. The winds whipped and punished them, blowing the icy snow off the plains all around them and pelting them with the hardened crystals. There was little need or opportunity for conversation, and they rode in the direction of the Great Desert. Chilger chanted and prayed to the spirits of land and sky until he was hoarse. He called to the animal totems for guidance, and he followed his companion eagle as she protectively guided from above. On the second day she was joined by a male golden eagle, more vast and imposing than she, and together they soared majestically overhead.

In the evenings Chilger and Borte would stop and construct their shelter, to protect them from the biting cold that hindered their progress forward. They never failed to honor the gods with offerings of food and incense, and they prayed as they gratefully lit their sacred fire. Borte was in the last months of her pregnancy and dropped, exhausted, into a heavy sleep as soon as she could. The distended girl was finding it more difficult to be comfortable, but she never complained. Chilger noticed that she shifted her body often, and he longed to ease her discomfort. They were indebted to their hearty ponies, for though Borte was used to walking great distances, the journey would have been well beyond her at this stage.

The first week of their quest had ended and they had had almost no human contact, except for one small tribe of Tatars who had passed them, heading north, on the fifth day. Borte was worn out and her lips were cracked from exposure, despite her best efforts to heal them with thick animal fat. At the end of each day she had dropped, exhausted, into her coverings and fallen deep asleep.

Chilger was growing more concerned that, despite the fact that she should still be expanding, Borte had already visibly lost weight. They had not suffered for food as of yet, but the journey was taking an obvious physical toll on her. Chilger left the shelter and went out into the darkness of the evening to study the glowing skies for answers.

Two hours passed, then three, as he struggled pitifully, unable to call upon his totems and enter a trance-like state. The harder he searched for the answers, the more elusive they became, and it had been two days since he had felt connected to the Great Spirit at all. He had observed carefully, watching for a sign—animals, trees, plants, birds, all of the world to which he was so naturally attuned—but for the first time in his life he felt shut out and closed off. The tingling energy of Tengri that had vibrated through his skull and his center, humming in each chakra since his earliest childhood, was distressingly still and silent. The whispers of the wind, the trees, and the birds that had always spoken to him and soothed him were suddenly empty sounds, hollow and dead in his ears. The harder he listened and looked for answers and the more doggedly he sought direction, the less clarity he found.

Chilger's mind was clouded by the added complication of Borte's pregnancy, and he was growing desperate. The dark energy that fed on his desperation and guilt multiplied and wove its way in and out of every thought and instinct, threatening to hinder the shaman completely. His bright energy was diminished, filtered by fear and doubt that billowed like a sinister fog around him. Though he did his utmost to remain outwardly positive, Borte felt the change in him, and his bleak desperation made her shiver.

Chilger's Marcus-brain tried to lead him and soothe him, but he was beginning to panic, wondering if he had taken Borte on an expedition that would never succeed. His faith in himself and his abilities was shaken, and he worried that they would fail and die on their journey. He wondered if he had been deluded, duped by his own dreams and selfish agenda to awaken Theron. Perhaps he was a victim of the tricky evil spirits that so liked to play with mankind and watch them flounder. Borte remained optimistic and hopeful, and Chilger prayed he would not fail her.

Wandering the perimeter of their camp in the frigid starlit night, Chilger lit his pipe and longed for the altered state that it offered. He had taken only two puffs when he heard a deep vibration that originated somewhere close by. The horses whinnied and stamped in fearful response. Immediately his heart leapt and pounded in his chest. His blood raced instinctively in response to the absolute imminent danger that the growl represented. With increased panic, he realized that he had left both his bow and his knife uselessly in the ger. He turned toward the shelter to retrieve them and to place himself between the unknown threat and Borte.

It was then that he saw it: directly between him and the unsecured tent flap paced a fierce snow leopard. Clear in the bright evening moonlight she growled again, and Chilger's blood quivered at the sound. Her white fur bristled like shackles on her neck, and her silver ears jumped and twitched at the myriad sounds unheard by the inferior human. Chilger was close enough to see the blue of her eyes, and his body trembled instinctively.

It is a sign, he told himself. *It is your death!* his mind cried in response. She did not look like an apparition or a dream. She was all heat and fur and breath, and she exposed her teeth and growled once more, deep and threatening.

"I am no enemy to you, beast," Chilger began. "We seek Shambhala and nothing more."

"That is everything!" an unearthly, growling voice replied from deep inside the creature. The cat began to pace, never taking her piercing cobalt eyes from Chilger.

Back and forth, she blocked the opening behind which a vulnerable, unaware Borte peacefully slept. "We come in service. We come to help the world," Chilger said simply. His fear managed now, he knew what he must do, and he was elated that their journey had finally met a fresh turn.

"We see all . . . *she* comes in service . . . with a pure heart," the snow leopard said, nodding deliberately toward the ger. "*Your* intentions are not so clear. There is a selfish air around your journey that holds you back. You seek Shambhala for both selfish and unselfish reasons, and yet you expect to succeed?"

"It is true . . . I do not desire to fool anybody. I bring her here so that she will know me, our ancient souls so long apart. I crave her recognition and recall, but that is not the only reason . . . we have been called by the great King of Shambhala, who has visited me in my dreams. I know I am an imperfect mortal—there is no other kind—but she has a purpose, that I am sure of, though I don't fully understand what it is. We come to Shambhala to learn. To stop the red devil that seeks to bring the Darkness to this land."

"Perhaps *he* is meant to do as he does, just as you are," the feline purred, and fear flowed through Chilger. He could not save them if the leopard chose to attack.

"Perhaps," Chilger agreed diplomatically.

"There is a price to pay if you are to reach your destination. For every action there is an equal and opposite reaction. If you agree to my terms, I will help guide you the rest of the way," the leopard bargained.

Chilger paused, his skin prickling cautiously, suddenly reminded of the stories he had heard: hunters, shaman, being fooled and misled by evil spirits in disguise. There was a low and dark feeling about this creature that Chilger had never known before in nature. He hesitated—he did not know what to think. He had never been on such a profound journey. Perhaps the protectors of Shambhala all had a necessary and frightening energy, to weed out the unworthy. He proceeded cautiously.

"If Father Sky and Mother Earth bless this alliance and show me that you are true, I will agree. I have prayed for a guide and perhaps they have answered my prayers . . . how can I know that you are not a devil sent to lead us astray?"

At that moment the night split open, and the eagles soaring overhead screeched wildly as they attacked the luminescent leopard. As their claws tore into her, she hissed and growled ferociously, but in an instant she faded to black and magically became smoke and shadow, then disappeared as if she had never existed. She was gone, a mirage dispelled, and the eagles probed the dirt searching for further sign of her.

Chilger immediately understood how close he had come to entering into a doomed contract. The eagles would never have attacked a true guide. He felt sure that they had only narrowly escaped being led away from their destination to certain peril. Chilger thanked his friends the eagles, but he still felt lost and disconnected, no further ahead than he had been moments before. He finally took the warm place next to Borte but slept fitfully without helpful dreams.

When Chilger woke in the morning, Borte was already up arranging a simple breakfast for them.

"I had a dream last night," she said hesitantly, as Chilger began to move. He waited for her to continue. "A wild beast came to guide us . . . and we followed it right to the gates of a beautiful crystal city."

Chilger became rigid and she watched him, gauging his response. Immediately he feared that he had made a mistake. Had his doubt and fear chased away their only chance of finding Shambhala?

"I know that my intuition is nothing compared to yours, but it was so real and beautiful," she smiled, remembering.

"Do not underestimate the strength of your wind horse, Borte. You have an incredibly powerful and beautiful spirit. Promise me that you will tell me if you have any other dreams or visions, anything at all. We are on this journey together," Chilger said. Borte nodded and continued with her work.

They would be entering the mountains that day. Chilger had hoped that they would not have to venture into that treacherous terrain. Spring had brought longer days, but the temperatures were still severely cold and, when combined with wind and elevation, threatened to end their journey in tragedy.

The sun had been on the horizon for only half an hour and everything was covered with a thick, glistening, frozen crust as they prepared once again to move on. Chilger exited first, and he stopped so quickly that Borte crashed into the back of him. Fifty paces away, at the edge of their camp, was a large blue wolf.

He did not growl or snarl or even react at the sight of them. His sapphire eyes examined them calmly as he sat at ease at the edge of their camp. It was not the glowing leopard apparition of the night before. This was a full grown, flesh and blood, male wolf, his thick neck and head impressive and beautiful.

"He's come!" Borte marveled, staring at the beast. She trembled slightly but she was not afraid, though all reason would dictate she should be. Chilger was more hesitant, remembering the scene from the previous night.

"Good wolf, we wonder if you are sent by Tengri . . . we seek guidance to our destination," Chilger called out.

The wolf, which had been crouched on his hindquarters, lay down flat and lowered his head as if to bow—a show of respect, peace, and deference.

The horses remained unperturbed, grazing, tethered nearby, paying no attention to the predator in their midst.

Above, the two eagles soared once more and miraculously, as if called by a master, Chilger's companion came down and landed on his outstretched arm. From there she flew across the camp and serenely landed next to the wolf, scratching at the ground before him. Mortal enemies, side by side, staring at the humans, the message was clear: This wolf came with blessings and was a gift.

Borte and Chilger embraced one another, relieved, and prepared to set out for the day. The sun shone warmer, their burden felt lighter, and as they mounted their horses, the wolf took up the lead as they expected he would, and they followed dutifully.

Chilger watched the subtleties of the world around him, searching for signs and direction, and blissfully he found them. Everywhere he looked spring was bursting from the soil, and the naked outstretched branches, speckled with fresh buds, pointed the way.

"It seems as though the whole world is guiding us now!" Borte said, after a few hours of silent reverie.

The wolf stayed well ahead of them but never out of sight, always stopping when he got too far away. Higher and higher their strong horses carried them, their breath heavy and deep.

At every pass and plateau there were stupas—cone-shaped prayer mounds of various heights. As they had done throughout their journey, Chilger and Borte dismounted at each of the sacred shrines and bid their respects. They walked three times clockwise around each man-made tower of stone, and each time they placed a rock on top and gave a small offering.

Chilger wondered if their supplies would run out, but the offerings were made in the belief that the gods would bless them and continue to provide for their needs. Borte took these opportunities to rest and take her fill of water or mare's milk.

As they climbed higher into the mountains, Chilger wrapped Borte in additional furs. She was shifting heavily on her horse; her lower back ached relentlessly, punished from the bouncing and pounding of the trail and the weight of her unborn child. She kept quiet as long as she could; she did not want to be a burden. She finally spoke when she could ride no more. The lack of support often made it preferable for her to walk, which slowed them down dramatically. When her feet and hands swelled like engorged sheep bladders she would once again try to mount, but the travel days were considerably less progressive.

Chilger chided himself for not having thought to procure a cart. He had underestimated the toll the journey would take on her. Would they die on this mountain and return into the Grid, only for Marcus to once again begin his searching? Would Helghul be left to massacre the people of the steppe and plains because Chilger had misunderstood the call of Shambhala?

From the cliffs above them a great black bear stretched and yawned, her hibernation over. With pure hearts they had crossed the Field of Reeds and now, after five days of climbing, they had reached the summit of the fabled Mountain of Ascension. Though they did not know it, Borte would not have to travel much longer. They made their way down the other side of the mountain, faithfully following the great wolf, which still guided them like a shadow in the distance.

"What is it we are looking for exactly? How will we know when we find it?" Borte asked, not for the first time, as they set out into their third week.

"It will find us, Borte."

"I near the time when the baby will come, Chilger. I have not done this before and, though I have seen a woman bring a baby, it only makes me more afraid to do it alone."

"You will not be unassisted, Borte, I am here. I will help you," Chilger promised, but neither of them felt easy. The women traditionally helped bring the babies.

Borte missed her mother and grandmother more than she had in months, and the usual nervousness and fatigue of the last weeks of pregnancy drained her. Chilger offered her herbs and remedies to dampen the discomfort, but she knew that their journey must end soon because, equally soon, she would be unable to go on.

The mountain trail widened up ahead and they saw them: stupas. They were everywhere, speckling the rocky, brown landscape as they descended into the spacious open expanse. It was a sight to behold, as if pilgrims had become stone midquest and stood waiting to be liberated.

The sight caused Chilger deep concern, for if they acted respectfully and walked clockwise three times around each one and made an offering, it would delay them for hours and significantly deplete their stores. The shaman did not delay. There was no choice to be made. He dismissed his urge to forgo the proper ritualism and respect.

With thanks and gratitude in their hearts, Borte and Chilger honored every stone monument, conscious that someone had built each one in great joy, sorrow, celebration, or need. They opened up to the energy, and they shared the overwhelming power of the vast, stippled meadow. Their wolf guide left them, likely to find a meal, but returned later and sat patiently waiting at the outer edge of the field.

"Last one," Borte smiled. There had been one hundred and seven in all, and the sun had moved significantly across the sky.

Chilger came to her and took her arm. "One more," he said, placing a large rock in her hand, and immediately she understood.

Together they bent down and began to build the one hundred and eighth stupa, encasing all of their own dreams, wishes, and fears within. They were grateful during every moment of its creation that they were there together, they were healthy and able to build, and they were able to pray for guidance on their continued journey. When it was completed, they walked clockwise three times around the shoulder-height mound and Chilger emptied the last of their rice onto it. He would have to hunt to provide their night's dinner, but he did not resent the offering.

They mounted their horses to move on, but they did not get far before it was time to set camp for the night. They came upon a beautiful spot that had a sweet freshwater creek running through it, allowing them to drink and bathe themselves, truly clean for the first time in weeks. Though he expected many animals near the water, Chilger saw no trails and not a single beast came. He had watched the landscape carefully but was unable to snare a rabbit or a marmot, and for the first time they went to sleep hungry. Borte held Chilger close and assured him she was all right, but he felt shame that she and his child should sleep unfed.

When Borte and Chilger rose in the morning, they were stunned to find that the creek had disappeared. What they did not understand was that the fabled Stream of Purification[27] had appeared and served its purpose. Not a drop of water remained, no puddle, no evidence it had ever existed.

In its place stood a formidable stupa, twice Chilger's height and twenty paces around. How could it be? They could not have missed it the night before. Its many strips of silk and cloth waved greetings in the wind, and its stones were piled and balanced precariously all around its ancient base, where their wolf companion now sat waiting for them. It was not an illusion. They ran their hands admiringly along its bumpy stone exterior. They began to pray and walked clockwise around the miraculous temple, having only flower buds to lay in offering.

As they completed their third turn, Borte gasped. The southern wall of the sacred monument had transformed into an archway, and standing in the opening, resplendently reflecting the sunlight in multicolored prisms as if he were made of crystal, was a fat, robed man. A glorious crown glowed like a halo on his smooth, dark hair. Beside him stood a tall, willowy male companion. The wolf rose and found a place at the right hand of the cherubic man, who happily placed his multiringed fingers on the animal's head. Particles of light and silver sparkled all around them like tiny swarming lightning bugs.

"Thanks to Father Sky and to our glorious Mother Earth. We give them thanks and hope that they are pleased, for they have brought us here. We humbly request passage to this world's sacred heart, where the truest of truths will be revealed," Chilger said, dropping to his knees and helping Borte to kneel beside him. They raised their arms and hands together and bowed. From a distance many animals watched the magical scene.

"I am the King of Shambhala. You seek the higher dimension, which allows for the soul's full expression. You are a spiritual pair. Shaman, you understand that there is a world above, and in the middle, and below. You seek the realm that allows for the expression of all of these to ascend into higher understanding. This is where spirit and matter are at one," the king said.

Borte huddled next to Chilger and listened in awe. The vibrations of the holy king made her teeth chatter, and she placed her palms flat on the ground to steady her tremors.

"We know why you have come. You have proven yourselves worthy and devout and we have called you. Many are called, but so few are listening. Before you enter, you must be clear that only the will of the Great Spirit exists within. We exist not for ourselves or for mankind. There is no argument or action great enough to alter one's destined path."

"We understand. We are honored," Borte and Chilger chimed, unpracticed but in unison. Chilger's Marcus-brain exploded with joyful anticipation.

"There is a cost to everything . . . for each high an equal low . . . for each blessing a burden," the king warned lastly, his rainbows cast so far and wide now that all manner of bird and beast gathered in abundance nearby, peacefully observing the spectacle and paying their respects. Chilger quickly scanned the sky and, as always, his companion eagle and her mate were within view, playfully soaring in apparent celebration.

The king stepped aside, exposing the dark opening of the stupa, which reasonably should have led nowhere, and motioned for them to enter. Borte and Chilger rose, and he held her hand as she awkwardly climbed the high first step into the doorway. As they passed the king closely, the silver rain that swirled around him enveloped them like a cool mist and smelled of sweet lotus petals. Borte reached out and stroked their wolf guide, projecting her thanks as she passed, and her hand momentarily touched the hand of the king. She felt bliss, pure and loving.

As they moved into the complete darkness of the stupa, expecting to butt against hard stone at any moment, the king and his companion moved in behind them and the archway disappeared like water running into a drain. And then, suddenly, it was gone.

The king continued glowing, without the reflection of the sun. Once the portal was sealed he held up his hand, illuminating a single bright, vibrant crystal that Borte assumed they would use like a torch. She could tell the stupa was obviously much larger than it appeared, but she was unprepared for what would come next. The king placed the crystal in a small notch carefully carved into the solid stone wall. Borte noticed the beautiful flower symbol carved behind it.

As the crystal was placed, a chain reaction occurred. The light from the first crystal traveled like a laser down into a deep chamber and ricocheted magically time after time and from wall to wall, illuminating an enormous curving tunnel at least fifty feet in width and height and of unknown length.

For the first time in months, Borte was light of foot and felt as though air blew up beneath her, helping her to hover, barely touching the earth at all. Chilger held her hand, overwhelmed with the spirit of the place, and they both succumbed to tears of happiness and relief, embracing one another before they moved on.

As they followed the king, all around them balconies, alcoves, and precipices magically appeared in the cavern walls. The people of Shambhala were illuminated, emerging from the surroundings like chameleons changing color. Each one of them was as different and varied as the people of the world can be, but they all raised their right hands to their hearts and bowed, smiling, as the honored guests passed by.

"Surely this display is for the king," Borte whispered to Chilger. But her supposition was rebutted immediately, by way of thought, from every direction.

It is for you, good Emissaries of Atitala, all of the citizens answered, without words. Their multitude of voices were like music, a symphony in the minds of the couple, and again Borte and Chilger were staggered. He had told her that they were Emissaries, but before that moment it was just a word. To witness this reverence and to be so venerated filled Borte and Chilger with a sense of humility and responsibility greater than they had ever known.

The beautiful music that filled them continued, and as they moved on, they, too, placed their right hands on their hearts and nodded respectfully to the thousands who welcomed them.

The grand tunnel opened up into an enormous arching cathedral, and Chilger saw that there were five other caverns that led to this central spot, like the petals of a flower. The flower of life radiated in every direction from this place.

Everything was illuminated and glistened as if liquid, and sunbeams burst from the ceiling high above as if the sun was peeking through and casting spotlights onto its own private menagerie.

All around them the people of Shambhala emerged. Their soul-songs echoed like the deliberate beat of a shaman's sacred drum, and rainbows of energy and auras floated and danced, happily interconnecting the many as One.

A platform materialized at the center of the spectacular room and on each side of it, seven stairs appeared. The King of Shambhala stood on the platform, patiently waiting for his astounded guests to join him. A large green, sparkling tablet floated in front of him, and Borte stared at it like a child as she easily made her way up the left-side stairway unassisted. Chilger was directed to the other side, and the two stood looking anxiously across the glistening stone at one another. The king rested a tender plump hand on the head of each of them, and his touch buzzed like an electric current that was pleasantly ticklish.

"These good Emissaries come from Atitala, and though to them time seems long and arduous, we know that one cycle, ten cycles, a thousand cycles on Earth are but a flash in space and time and are a tiny part of the larger cycle. The

Emissaries are the world's Light in this time of the Great Darkness, and we have called them here to replenish their energy and recharge their souls."

The buzz in the room was electric. The king directed Chilger and Borte to place their right hands on their hearts and their left hands on the slab of green atlantium crystal. All around them, white-robed people of every race prayed, sang, and projected their loving support to them.

Immediately, as their hands touched the blessed stone, a warm current surged through them, through every vein, artery, and cell of their bodies. Brilliant, healing white light of the connecting spirit radiated from their eyes, ears, mouths, and noses. They felt a jolt, and then their bodies moved as if in slow motion, at one-quarter normal speed, as their sleeping shells fell softly like discarded garments and rested gently in a heap. They had been left behind, useless in this moment. The glowing soul of Borte's baby rested, protectively cocooned, within her body below.

Marcus and Theron's spirits had shed their corporeal forms, and in the pure, bright light they floated, emancipated, above their empty vessels, connected only by thin shimmering threads. They felt no concern, no fear, no sense of loss, only joy, love, and glory, as they joined the larger band of light above them.

Theron's spirit took on an ethereal, smoky appearance resembling closely the lanky girl that she had once been. All around her she saw images and energy swirling and telling her stories of what had been so long ago. Her vibrant purple aura hugged her, and she luxuriated in it, letting it rain over her like a warm waterfall.

There was no sense of time, or purpose, or urgency, but she felt a pull to open up, and there in front of her she saw Marcus. Marcus was in the pulsing, rushing band of light with her! Her joy was compounded, and in that moment she knew him! Her love, her Marcus . . . and she remembered being kept from him on the deck of the ship on the night of the exodus, but she felt no pain. She stared at him, glowing purple and silver, his shape dark and muscular and glistening in the light of eternal energy around them. She remembered saying goodbye to her dear friend Plato, her Marcus. He had been her mother, her child, her lover, her friend, and so much more. She remembered that he knew her . . . he always knew her.

Marcus watched Theron and was overcome by the sight of her discovering herself, her energy so pure and strong. He too felt no sadness, no anxiety, and no bitterness at the wasted years they had lost. He felt the same euphoric recollection and connection that she did, and all of the memories that had lain dormant or muted blossomed, vibrant and alive, and they were each surrounded by a garden of their own making.

Only when Marcus sought to join his spirit with Theron's and to flow freely with her, through her, did he realize that they could not cross the stone beneath them. An invisible barrier made it impossible for them to touch, but he knew that she knew him, and they watched each other and they joined the Grid, the band of light which flowed with the healing, loving energy, and they were One with each other and with all creation. There was no illusion of separation and they understood the truth. There was no longing, memory, or sadness. They were renewed.

How much time passed? Perhaps it was seconds or days or years, but the moment came when the King of Shambhala called them back to their bodies, as he was meant to do, and they came immediately, changed but the same.

They entered themselves like a thread through the head of a pin, through the crown chakras in the tops of their skulls. Their spirits traveled down, occupying each subsequent chakra, ballooning and becoming full and upright until their feet puffed and filled. Borte's baby kicked and rolled happily in her belly. Their eyes opened dreamily, they smiled and swayed as if they had ingested a powerfully euphoric drug.

They stood face to face and were led down the left staircase. The people of Shambhala—red, white, black, brown, and yellow, and of all ages—waited to greet them and embrace them. They were human . . . flesh and bone people who had overcome the limitations of the suits of armor that they had inhabited and reached enlightenment.

Chilger and Borte were taken to a sparse white chamber to rest. There was a wide, soft bed on one wall with fluffy pillows and light silk sheets. On the opposite side of the room there was a small fountain that flowed from the outer wall and continually filled a beautiful crystal bowl with clear, jasmine-scented water. There were glass doors that opened to a wild garden, and every plant thrived and burst with fruit and blooms. It was alive with the sounds of a million thriving creatures. There were no fences or gates or pathways; the entire garden looked as though it had been planted a century before and never groomed.

The smell of the paradise was intoxicating, and Chilger looked forward to exploring. He walked to a nearby pear tree and plucked a golden yellow gem and offered it to Borte. She suddenly realized her hunger and enjoyed its juicy, sweet perfection as its liquid ran down her chin. Chilger, biting his own, reached and brushed the errant juice away, and his hand paused on her jaw.

"To have you recognize me, for you to know our history and our lives, is a gift worth anything to me."

"How do you bear it? Always having memory?" she asked sympathetically.

"Because sometimes it brings me to you, and when it does, knowing you is worth all the longing that has come before."

"How is it that you remember everything and I do not?" she asked.

"I took a potion. I didn't want to forget you," he admitted.

"Why didn't I take it?"

"You weren't given the choice. I have regretted my decision a thousand times. But then every time we meet again, I am so grateful to really know you that it makes it all worthwhile," he said.

"Temujin is Helghul," Borte announced suddenly.

"I know," Chilger replied.

"He's not so bad, Marcus," she added.

"He is, and I am here to find out how I can stop him. He will turn the plains red with blood if left unchecked."

"I need sleep. I don't think I can stand up much longer," she said, taking his hand and leading him to bed. They wrapped their bodies around one another and slept easily, exhausted from weeks of punishing travel.

Shambhala was an incredible city, enormous and advanced in every way. It was not only a paradise, it was also a technological marvel. The sky was full of iridescent aircraft that hovered, disappeared, and reappeared as if by magic. It was a place that enjoyed a perpetual Golden Age of great learning, rest, rejuvenation, purpose, and growth. In this sanctuary, Chilger and Borte soaked in as much of the knowledge and wisdom as they possibly could. They were unsure how much time they had.

In the time to come, Borte studied with the citizens and teachers, and they marveled at her natural ability as a healer. She learned how to channel energy and tune in to the chakras of an individual to help them on their path.

Chilger asked the teachers what he could do to stop the coming of war and darkness to their lands, and the wise citizens joined hands and prayed with him but had no answers. They encouraged him to seek the counsel of the king, but three times he searched and was unable to find the elusive king.

Chilger and Borte were inseparable, empowered by the absolute clarity of their Marcus- and Theron-memories. Time held no place in the soul of the Earth, and as they went to sleep for the fifth time, Borte remarked drowsily to Chilger that she missed the cool night sky of home. He leaned in and placed his forehead to hers. They went to sleep imagining the familiar starry skies that they had both known so well.

CHAPTER 25

BORTE'S SACRIFICE

The Merkits had positioned themselves strategically as Temujin's warriors and allies attacked. The battlefields were bloody and cruel week after week. As Chilger had toiled in the mountains, lost and desperate and looking for Shambhala, his countrymen had been under siege.

The plains, hills, and marshlands budded with the first scent of spring and reeked with the stench of death. The frigid winds had become cool breezes, and the sun shone high and long in the sky while blood soaked the ground. Some of the dead were retrieved and laid hundred by hundred in ordered rows for cremation, while many others were left to become the food of scavengers and to rot unceremoniously in the dirt.

Temujin, in full war armor, was ready to lead the final assault. As a military strategist he had proven he had no equal, and Jamuka and Toghrul Khan now listened carefully to his innovative plans. Toghrul had helped to conquer the majority of the Merkit territory and had returned to his lands jubilant and enriched, leaving the last stronghold to be conquered by his worthy allies.

"My brother, I find myself grateful that we do battle on the same side," Jamuka said, lifting his eyes from the map that Temujin had laid out before him. "I have no doubt that you will rise as a great khan someday . . . perhaps almost as great as me!" he chortled, clapping his blood brother on the back.

Temujin smiled wryly. He knew full well that someday he would surpass Jamuka's power as khan; they both did. He liked the idea of having such a close ally, a blood bond for life. There were only two people that Temujin could trust: his blood brother, Jamuka and his mother, Hoelun.

"We will strike when the sun is high in the sky, and ride at them with its glare on our side. They will not see the arrows fly, blinded by the brightness," Temujin declared, and then his voice changed slightly. "Has there been any word of Borte? Is she with any of the women and children that we have taken so far?" he asked.

"No word since the Tatar group two weeks back. We believe she is still traveling with the shaman."

"We'll catch up with them today. This is the last of his clan. They will not be far off. I will have her back by nightfall," Temujin said confidently. If his dreams were correct, which they always were, he expected to rescue Borte in the valley of the giant beasts. He had had the dream repeatedly since she was kidnapped, and when he had interrogated the first group of Merkit captives, they had confirmed the dream's infallible accuracy: Borte was with a shaman who wore the feathers of an eagle, and Helghul recognized him as Marcus even under the mask of his sacred costume. Once again Marcus had interfered in his relationship with Theron, and Helghul plotted severe retribution for his meddling.

Temujin prepared for combat. He mounted his strong horse, which was heavily armored. He adjusted his battle helmet and shifted the thick nose shield that was cutting his vision. Together he and Jamuka rode out to address their troops. They would lead an attack from the east that day.

Temujin's Helghul-brain assured him victory ahead. He imagined Borte in his custody by nightfall, and he was excited by the prospect. Against his will, he had been drawn to her more powerfully than to any other person in any other lifetime.

The sun was rising in the sky and the plains were in motion like an active comb of honey bees. Thousands of hooves gently swished through the budding grass, as row upon row of men on horseback and on foot moved through the fields. Straight-faced and prepared to die, they surged forward at the command of their leaders, looking more beast than human in their war skins and masks. The horde stank of coagulated blood, sweat, and murder. The weeks had been long and difficult. The procession stopped and prepared to be addressed by their khan.

"Your day of triumph is here! You have fought hard and well. Today we will crush our enemy once and for all, and tomorrow we will journey home victorious!" Jamuka shouted. He looked to Temujin, who took his cue to speak.

"You have honored your gods, your chief, and your people. This will be the final victorious battle. At the end of this day, you will share in the celebration *and* the riches that we reap!" Temujin promised, and his words were met with a great cheer. Jamuka looked at him sharply, but he continued undaunted. "Every soldier will return richer. Every man will be rewarded for his loyal service and sacrifice. Now join together, and we will crush our enemy! We will share this victory! Share in the glory!" he roared, full volume, as the air shook with thunderous shouts and the clamor of swords and shields.

In response, Jamuka raised his arm and signaled for the first assault to begin. The warriors bolted and crossed the half-mile distance to the waiting enemy lines.

"Big promises," Jamuka said angrily, steering his horse past Temujin.

"Mine to honor," Temujin replied, unperturbed.

"That they are," Jamuka snapped, whipping his mount and galloping away. With a slash of his arm the Mongol horde surged forward.

The skilled warriors had broken through the last of the Merkit barricades. With a sword in each hand, Temujin was slashing left and right, holding his seat with solid, determined thighs. His leg and arm muscles rippled as his blades tore through flesh and bone. The noise and clatter were deafening. Horses whinnied and warriors attacked: grunting, crying out, and falling to the ground. The stink of sweat, feces, and blood filled the air, carried by a gentle breeze.

Temujin's face was covered in the thick, sticky blood spray, making it difficult to see. Blood soaked his vest and gloves. His arms ached from brandishing the swords and from the weight of the resisting corpses as they crumpled. His throat was raw and burning from his sustained shouting. His eyes gleamed in anticipation of his victory.

The troops pushed forward, scattering their foe, gory and broken, across the landscape. The final battle was won, and the males of the Merkit clan were virtually annihilated.

As was the custom, the cowering women, female children, and property were collected as the spoils of war, and the leaders claimed them. Temujin honored his promise, and the filthy, haggard troops celebrated their increased wealth and the generosity of their leader, Temujin. Jamuka watched his blood brother with wary interest but gave up none of his own spoils to compete for popularity.

The troops tended their injured and set up camp upwind to the grotesque battlefield. They made offerings of thanks to the gods of Earth and Sky for their victory. Tengri was honored with dance and wine, and the exhausted warriors, husbands, and herders enjoyed the celebration.

Temujin, his face cleaned and wearing a fresh vest and gloves, prepared to set off in search of Borte, who had not been among the women and children captured. He tied a thick fur bag to his mount.

"Jamuka, I am riding into the valley to retrieve Borte. I know the shaman is close by. This is his clan, his people, yet this coward hides and keeps what is rightly mine."

"I will ride with you, brother, if you wish. Or better yet, let us send a search party and they can bring her back to you here if she is found," Jamuka offered, without moving from the comfortable spot where he sat cleaning himself over a carved wooden bowl.

"She is there. I will go," Temujin assured him, and wordlessly signaled to a small group of his clansmen nearby to join him. They obeyed and fell in behind their chief.

A mile beyond the camp, the mountains rose and the valley narrowed. It was as Temujin knew it would be. The giant, ancient skulls of monsters long dead were posted to ward off enemies—dinosaur remains pitched high to frighten away the superstitious and skittish. Temujin was neither. He knew the animals that had left the bones were long extinct. He had no fear of the valley.

Helghul had thrilled at the brutality and harshness of the day, feeding greedily off the violent energy. He was further exhilarated by the search ahead. He shifted the weighty fur bag awkwardly on his saddle and continued to ride. The warriors at his flank dared to pause, unnerved by the menacing skulls with their massive teeth and horns.

The nearest monster, a large Tarbosaurus fossil, was propped on a rock the height of two men and shrouded in a patchwork of second-rate animal skins. Temujin's cohorts were visibly troubled; they called under their breath to the great gods and to their personal totems to protect them. Their leader said nothing. He offered them no reassurance or kindness but simply rode on, and they had no choice but to follow.

The sun slipped near the horizon, casting deep reds and oranges across the sky. In the twilight, a single ger and four horses came into view. Two large golden eagles circled clockwise above the dwelling, and Temujin felt a jolt of excitement at the realization of his dream. It was exactly as he had expected. In the sky, the stars opened their blinking eyes. Helghul thrilled with the anticipation of being reunited with Marcus and Theron.

Borte awakened, confused. Though she was safe, comfortable, and warm, she did not know where she was. She had no memory of reaching Shambhala.

"Chilger!" she whispered in the dark, shaking him. "Wake up!"

Chilger opened his eyes dreamily and was met with an overwhelming sense of loss and despair. "It's gone," he said weakly, realizing that they were once again in their travel clothes, rather than the flimsy, silken garments of the tropical Shambhala. Their ger was correctly laid out as it had always been, except that the sacred fire at the center had not been lit. "I never spoke with the king! I didn't find out how to stop Temujin!" he cried.

Borte tried to soothe him, though she was confused and assumed he had had a terrible dream. He jumped up and began pacing noiselessly. His metal shaman apron lay nearby. It was then that he heard the movement outside the ger. One of the horses whinnied and he rushed to the opening.

Temujin had ridden the last of the dusty journey alone, commanding his inferiors to stay behind. As he had expected, Chilger emerged from the dwelling as he approached. He was thrilled when he recognized Borte behind him, despite the darkness of their fireless camp. His heart pounded at the sight of her.

"Temujin!" she cried.

"Get inside!" Chilger demanded, placing himself between Temujin and Borte. But it was futile, and even in the dimness he knew that Temujin must have seen her.

Borte ignored Chilger's command. "Please, husband, do not hurt him, he did not take me," Borte begged, running clumsily past Chilger toward Temujin, with her hand slung low under her bulbous middle.

Chilger cringed at hearing her say "husband" to Temujin, and he reeled with alarm. Temujin smirked and Helghul reveled in her words. He still had a hold on her.

"Go inside or the shaman dies, *wife*," Temujin ordered severely.

Borte stopped short and, glancing at Temujin's hard face, she quickly obeyed. The men were left alone.

"Have you enjoyed *my* wife, Marcus?" Temujin sneered.

"Helghul, we both know that she is my true wife. Your crippled soul doesn't belong near her," Chilger raged, ready to charge, though he was unarmed.

"There are two choices: she will live a good life as my wife, or she and that child will die in pieces, tortured bit by bit this very day. You decide," he hissed, making certain that Borte did not hear.

"We don't fear you. We don't fear death! She'll never go with you, she would rather die!" Chilger challenged, certain that they would die together that night.

"Borte!" Temujin called from his horse.

She immediately appeared, her eyes fearful and wet with tears.

"Decide Borte. Die here today with the shaman, or save him and *my* baby."

She was shocked. She had assumed he would kill them all. "Oh, husband! Oh, generous husband! Spare him!" she begged, falling to her knees. Chilger was horrified and lifted her to her feet, holding her shaking body against him.

"If you come with me, I will care for my child as though you have never been gone, but you must promise never to search for this man. If you agree, I will let the shaman live. If not, all of you will die," Temujin proposed, stoned-faced.

"I'll do it," Borte answered without hesitation, stepping away from Chilger. He pulled her back while Temujin watched their dance gleefully. "Chilger let me go! It is the only way to save you," she squealed, twisting in his arms to free herself. He was forced to release her or risk injuring her.

"You don't understand! He lies! This cannot be your purpose!" Marcus shouted, but as he said it, he knew he was wrong. The truth was flooding over him. In Shambhala, the place where all questions could be answered, he had been unable to ask the question about how to stop Temujin. It was clear: he was not meant to stop Temujin. That is why the question had not been asked and the answer had not come.

Chilger remembered the words of the mysterious snow leopard: "Perhaps he is meant to do as he does, just as you are." He finally understood why Borte had first been promised to Temujin and not to him, and he knew that Theron's destiny *was* to go with Helghul, just as it had been his to ensure that she arrived safely in Shambhala.

Theron's light had been recharged in Shambhala, though she remembered none of it. Her spirit shone brighter by far than it had only days earlier. The Emissary was a teacher and healer, and she would balance the Adversary Helghul.

"This time was a gift for us. It was always stolen time. Our child will be born. You must let me go. Save yourself," Borte whispered, taking Chilger's hands in hers.

The tightly bound fur sack moved slightly as Temujin dismounted. He had cautiously drawn his sword and held it loosely in his left hand. He would never again underestimate his fellow Emissaries. He was untying a horse for Borte. He did not interrupt their brief farewell, but instead fed on the despair, rage, and sadness that hovered around them.

After a moment, Temujin called Borte away from Chilger. The shaman did not release her, he could not, but it was not his decision to make. Temujin called again, this time more severely. Chilger's Marcus-brain resisted, but Borte pulled away. He let her go, knowing that he must.

Borte wrapped herself in her warmest layers, and with much assistance she was lifted onto the horse.

"Journey straight out to the south, *wife*. After a brief ride you will come to my clansmen. Tell them they are to take you back to camp immediately. I do not wish to birth a baby myself on these dark plains," Temujin commanded.

Borte nodded and, realizing that his concern was legitimate, the heartbroken woman obeyed, looking back mournfully as the dark swallowed her up.

Temujin turned on Chilger, his blood-stained weapon in hand. "You will be only one of the many men I will have killed today, but you will be the one I most enjoy."

"She will never love you," Chilger said smugly, and Temujin struck him angrily across the thigh with the sword. The shaman crumpled to the ground, clutching the gaping wound. Instead of fear, he found himself fascinated, as if he were watching a theater event. *So this is how I die this time*, he marveled, ready to be gone, resigned to return to the Grid, to the Meadow. He did not wish to continue in a lifetime with no hope of Theron.

Temujin sank stakes in the ground nearby and tied Marcus to them, his limbs outstretched. Chilger's injury was bleeding heavily, and he was feeling weak and knew that he would soon fade away. Once Chilger was securely tied, Temujin retrieved the fur sack from his horse.

"She will love being my wife. The child will be the image of me as a man. They will be mine . . . body and mind . . . and I will bend them and shape them to my will," Temujin mocked, his eyes glowing in evil pleasure. He kicked the helpless prisoner in the abdomen and Chilger grunted reflexively. "And you . . . you'll be dust . . . nothing! She might remember you for a while . . . but eventually she will forget . . . her tiny slip of time with you will be nothing compared to a lifetime with me," he taunted.

Chilger did not react; he was deep in meditation and was surrounding himself with the spirits of all nature. As blood continued to leak from his leg wound, he saw the bear, like fog floating up above him, and just beyond it the eagles circled ominously counterclockwise, swooping and diving.

As Temujin prepared to enact his final revenge, he was enraged by Chilger's serenity. He opened the fur sack that he had safeguarded for weeks and tipped its lumpy, jumbled contents onto Chilger's chest.

The composed prisoner immediately howled in response, his composure shattered by the electric sting of the hideous Mongolian death worm. The worm was a fabled creature that was rarely ever seen but that all of the nomads knew existed. It resembled a pile of red, lumpy internal organs and was as long and thick as Chilger's leg. It continued to sting him, and the smell of sizzling flesh was unmistakable. The victim writhed in excruciating pain.

Temujin stood nearby, rejoicing in the misery. He narrowly missed being clipped by an angry wing when Chilger's eagle and her mate swooped down to attack the worm and rescue their companion. Temujin, however, was a skilled adversary, and as the birds tried to pluck off the creature, they were thwarted. Temujin had loaded his bow in seconds, and the whistle of two rapidly fired arrows screeched ominously as they tore into the birds. The eagles both dropped near Chilger with a thud.

The worm continued to torture its nearly unconscious prey, moving on to its next sinister phase. Chilger would be eaten, but the worm would first regurgitate a ferocious burning acid onto him, liquefying his flesh on contact so that it could be easily ingested.

Staring at the familiar starry sky that he and Borte had known so well, Chilger understood that suffering was part of life. He welcomed death, ready to transform yet again, and found peace in the final moments before his final breath.

Borte was waiting anxiously for Temujin when he returned to his clan, though he took his time circulating in camp before returning to his ger. "Did you let him go?" she cried as he entered, fresh tears on her face.

"He will live on," Temujin grunted roughly.

Borte was relieved and leaned back in the furs and skins on the ground where she had been lying.

Borte's child, Jochi, was born four days later, with the help of the clanswomen. Hoelun attended her delivery and glared at her through the entire painful ordeal. As was the tradition, Borte was sequestered with her child after the birth because, as a recent portal for new souls, she was believed to be slightly dangerous.

The child Jochi grew and thrived and had the dark hair of his mother, or perhaps of Chilger.

Summer had barely finished, and fall was proving to be bitterly cold. Borte worked tirelessly to prepare their ger for winter. The torn felt needed repair in spots, and she mended it using an ingenious bone needle and fine leather strips.

She crouched in front of the sacred fire at mealtime while her young baby suckled hungrily at her breast. Temujin had been gone a few days, hunting, and she hadn't bothered to eat since he had left. She was surprised by how little appetite she had.

What if I never ate again? she wondered. *What if I let this dry, dusty seed stuck in my throat grow into a bulb and then take root? What if I welcome this despair and let it envelop me? Finish me from the inside out?*

You are stronger than that, she heard in her head. *Your son needs you. Jochi needs you.*

Putting a sleeping Jochi down, she pressed her forehead flat to the ground. She crouched with her knees pulled in underneath her as tightly as her bulky wardrobe allowed, and she prayed. She understood that to exist was to be a part of the gods, but she could not find it in her. She had fallen so far into her desolation in the past months that she worried she could not pull herself out and fulfill the role ahead of her. She must begin to speak out, to heal, to teach, but she was tired and it seemed so hard.

Maybe I don't want to be so strong! her mind cried out, but there was no time for selfishness. She was from a strong, hearty clan. It took determination and grit to survive the winter and it was upon survival that she needed to concentrate. Loneliness, heartbreak, and self-pity had no place in her world.

Borte spent hours reinforcing the protective skin of the ger, reinforcing her own protective skin. Once she was wrung out, empty of tears, empty, empty . . . she knew that it was enough. It was enough, and there was the knowledge that we are all One and, as difficult as it can be, there is meaning to our lives.

She took a bite of bread and a sip of tea. Perhaps she had something to offer the world . . . but not today. Today she would immerse herself in her chores and survive as her people had done for centuries. Today she would be nonphilosophical and unthinking. She would not consider what might have been or should have been. She would think of the work that was yet to be finished—the child to be cared for, the fuel to be collected, the animals to be tended, the furs to be cured, the grains to be packed and dried. She would leave no room for her heartache and for thoughts of Chilger. Was he somewhere in the world thinking of her? Someday she would become a great teacher and healer and empress, today she would simply take a bite of food and choke it down.

CHAPTER 26

THE RISE OF GENGHIS KHAN

Temujin continued to show great skill and ingenuity and was soon khan to a rapidly expanding tribe. His relationship with his blood brother, Jamuka, became strained. Upon defeating and murdering his former ally, Temujin assumed his leadership and his property. Despite his absolute assertions that Jochi was his son, doubt and gossip would batter the boy throughout his life.

Before Jochi's second birthday, his first brother was born. Borte was a good wife and a fertile mother, though she often wondered about Chilger and imagined him happily living as a shaman and healer somewhere on the plains. She never forgot him, and her heart ached for the soul that had reached inside and affected her so deeply.

Borte searched for him in each passing caravan, at each market, in the face of every male stranger or rider who passed her, though she never saw him again. She continued to share the understanding and healing that she had learned in her time with him and, though she loved all of her children, Jochi held a special place in her heart.

Upon hearing Borte's tales of searching for Shambhala, Temujin spent the first ten years of their life together obsessed with the idea of finding the sacred land. Though he searched, he was never able to unlock its secrets. He was never called to enter and the city remained hidden, somewhere on another level or dimension, out of Temujin's grasp.

By Jochi's fifteenth year, there was little in the world that remained out of Temujin's reach. Temujin had become a feared and celebrated leader and was given the honored title of "Genghis," meaning "right or true."[28] Genghis Khan continued to battle ruthlessly for decades to come, and he conquered and decimated a huge territory stretching from China to Persia and Turkey, amassing one of the largest empires ever created.

Borte was honored as the Empress of the Mongolian Empire and was the most respected and valued of Genghis Khan's many wives. Helghul wreaked havoc in the world of man, as was his role, and he basked in his ever-growing power and glory, sowing his seed literally and figuratively across the continent.

As Jochi aged, his striking resemblance to Chilger was obvious, and resentment grew. Genghis and his other sons never accepted the boy, though he remained his mother's favorite. His likeness to Chilger offended the khan, though the Adversary knew that Marcus's soul was elsewhere.

Jochi was poisoned and died in his forty-first year.[29] According to tradition, he was buried in an unmarked grave on the plains under the stars. Borte never suspected that Temujin had murdered him just as he had murdered the boy's look-alike father decades earlier.

CHAPTER 27

ANCIENT KNOWLEDGE

Present Day

Quinn returned from a museum exhibition feeling nostalgic and suffering his loneliness. There was no one to talk to. There was no one who felt how he felt. There was no one who had memory and knew what he knew . . . except perhaps Helghul. Happily Quinn hadn't encountered him in this lifetime.

Quinn had spent too much time alone lately. Nate was busy with his life and Quinn had moved farther from the city, so the few friends he had made there slowly faded away. He wanted more than companionship. He wanted Theron, but waiting for her took its toll. He reminisced alone, remembering the other lifetimes, the many lifetimes, when the museum artifacts he had just viewed had been new and whole.

The Emissary had blogged the day before.

TheEmissary: Art and music are nourishment for the higher self. They have the ability to soothe the soul. This explains why artists and musicians are celebrated in Golden Ages and are vilified and censored in darker times. Recently in Caral, Peru, an ancient city and pyramids were found with scores of musical instruments but "no trace of warfare."[30] What a paradise it must have been.

Quinn dropped into his chair; he had so many ideas bombarding him. He was anarchic with his blog topics, because he was constantly studying and dissecting the vast array of websites, trying to address rumors, conspiracy theories, and incorrect ideas. Most of all, he wanted to choose topics that would make people think. Not just the ramblings of some pot-smoking recluse, but something valuable. He wanted to help pilgrims on the path to enlightenment, he didn't want to just preach or draw too much attention to himself. It was a fine balance. His list of followers was growing weekly, but he had his favorites.

TheEmissary: I am back on the topic of lost knowledge and civilizations. We have so much to learn from the Ancients, but first we must admit that they existed.

Adam's Calendar in South Africa is a seventy-five-thousand-year-old stone astrological calendar, made up of one hundred thousand ancient stone ruins, spreading out over the mountaintops.

A lost city, Gobekli Tepe, has been rediscovered in Turkey. There have been discoveries in the south of Spain, at Lake Titicaca in Peru, and so many more.

The ancient pyramids in China are not documented in any of their records, indicating they were already there, before the time from which records have survived.

So many of the ruins we have already found—the Pyramids at Giza, Teotihuacan in Mexico, and the Anuradhapura stupas in Sri Lanka, to name a few—are aligned with specific constellations at certain times in history. Clearly the builders knew something about the stars and their importance that we do not. Did they have information that we still do not understand?

Dvaraka, the lost city of over a million citizens in the Bay of Cambay, and Rama's Bridge in India were both consigned to myth in ancient Vedic texts. Evidence has now been discovered that they may have indeed existed.[31] Imagine, a man-made stone bridge linking India to Sri Lanka, twenty miles long! This accomplishment is not possible if we cling to antiquated assumptions.

Through the Dark Ages a linear approach to sociology was embraced, denying the idea that our ancient ancestors had more knowledge than we do. Further, with the advent of Darwinism, the popular belief became absolute: mankind must progress in one direction, from primitive to modern.

There is another more accurate truth: civilization is circular. One Great Year of approximately twenty-six thousand years marks the rise and fall of civilizations as they move through one entire precession of the equinox.

The Golden Age is the longest of the Ages and is a time when civilization and humanity are at their height of purity, Oneness, and innovation. This is a peaceful time during which human consciousness is at its peak, manifested through levitation, telepathy, and the complete understanding of God.

Leading in and out of a Golden Age are a Silver Age, a Bronze Age, and then the shortest, the Iron or Dark Age. Based on this notion, I think it is a Dark Age from which we are now emerging. Has the Bronze Age already begun?

In the book *Hamlet's Mill*,[32] the authors identify at least thirty separate civilizations with early references to the Great Year cycle. One example is the ancient Vedic text that described the "yugas": a four-seasoned, twenty-four-thousand-year cycle.

All indications seem to point to a cyclical rise and fall of mankind . . . but why?

If a divine cycle known as the Great Year exists . . . why does it exist?

Is it random? Chaos? Lessons? Choice? Experience? Enlightenment? Through these highs and lows do we become something . . . more?

One must wonder; can the cycle be altered? Can the wheel get stuck in a particular Age?

When we admit ancient civilizations existed, we can learn from them and new questions arise. Without questions there can be no answers.

Wisdom, knowledge, and enlightenment cannot enter a closed mind.

Ping! The blog comments started coming in.

Twenty minutes passed, then an hour. Quinn could have gone out, over to the pub, to a movie, to the gym, he could have hooked up online like others were doing, but he preferred to stay home. He slipped out of his jeans into sweats, rolled a joint, and cracked a beer while he interacted in cyberspace.

He sat at his computer late into the night, blogging and scouring the Internet for evidence of the next great Age. The clues were readily available to anyone. Had the enlightenment begun? Would the lands be tossed and crumpled like too many blankets? Quinn didn't know, but regardless, the Iron Age must be ending. Mankind must have begun the ascension toward a new Bronze Age, on its way to a better time. Was there any other option?

Quinn marveled that he hadn't thought to ask the Elders more about the precession of the Great Year when he had had the chance. He knew that no one could have answered his questions anyway—free will made them impossible to answer. He struggled to remember how the Elders had behaved in the end in Atitala when the Golden Age had crumbled and the descent had begun. *Was a biblical Armageddon imminent? Was the shift out of the Darkness guaranteed? Would devastation be the catalyst, or the awakening that had to occur before humanity ascended to the next Golden Age? Was the upswing certain, or could the Darkness prevent it? Could one side defeat the other in the cosmic tug of war between Dark and Light, or was there always balance?* These were Quinn's unspoken questions.

Quinn didn't have the answers, but he watched diligently. His inner voice told him he needed to be sober and straight to hear more. He ignored the voice, tired and sore from the mountain of memories that he carried. He found relief from loneliness under his foggy mental blanket.

The Emissary kept one eye on his blog responses, but they seemed to argue more about the length of the Great Year than to answer why it happened. The opinion was split exactly fifty-fifty as to whether or not an Age could be forestalled. Finally Anderson88 made a brief appearance and it got more interesting.

> ***Savetibet911***: A cycle has to be able to stall. Free will must allow for anything, and where is the lesson in a cycle if there is no changing it?
>
> ***Anderson88***: Perhaps the cycle continues but our souls proceed differently through them or through higher level dimensions cycles as we ascend. Maybe it's not the same experience for everybody at the same time. Maybe it's like a ladder, or more like a group of interlocking circles . . . we pass from one to the other as we climb up.
>
> ***Hansonrocks***: A combination of string theory, the Great Year, and Buddhism! I love it! What if the cycle can also be reversed . . . turned in the opposite direction?

Across town, things were as they were meant to be. Nate was at the home of a fellow movie buff for the screening of a quirky art film. Nate's passion was filmmaking, and as a director of photography (DOP), jobs were scarce in the current economy.

Nate had met Eden when he first arrived at the screening. She was a vivacious documentary filmmaker who was searching for a DOP for her current project. They had immediate chemistry and made a date to meet the following evening to discuss a possible partnership just before she had to rush away. The fated meeting marked the beginning of an adventure and the end of an Age.

CHAPTER 28

THE CRYSTAL CHILDREN

Quinn had fallen asleep about three a.m. with a comfortable beer–and–BC Bud buzz. When he opened his bleary eyes for the first time at ten o'clock the next morning, a mountain of neglected computer repairs was beckoning. There were customers waiting, and he was anxious to meet his promised delivery dates and get their units back to them.

Quinn rolled out of bed, mindful of last night's blogging and news. He had enjoyed some interesting chats, some great feedback, and some especially sharp reader input, and he was happy. The numbers were growing daily; he was reaching people one keystroke at a time.

Freshly showered, his second cup of coffee in hand, Quinn was ready to do some work that paid. He was dressed in a plain white T-shirt and loose-fitting jeans and was just beginning when there was a knock at the door. He looked through the peephole at Nate, who bounced excitedly from foot to foot. He looked nothing like the guard at Stone-at-Center or like Amnut, but the colorful aura and familiarity around him were undeniable.

"You won't believe what happened to me last night. It was over the top!" Nate began, before Quinn could close the door against the drizzle. Nate stripped off his soaked coat and threw it carelessly over the back of the sofa.

Quinn smiled, moving the garment to an overflowing hook by the door.

"Is that new?" Nate asked, noticing the large, multicolored silk tapestry of a square with a circle inside hanging on Quinn's wall.

"Nope, it's always been there. It's called a mandala."

"Mandela? I love that guy."

"No, not Nelson Mandela, mandala. It's the Sanskrit word for 'circle.' It's my life story," Quinn said.

"Hmm, never noticed it . . . anyway . . . I met the most amazing woman, her name is Eden, like paradise, ya know? And not only is she totally hot but she's a filmmaker! She's a writer and director and she needs me for camera! She wants to collaborate, and . . . get this . . . she's totally into me. We just, like, clicked . . . totally clicked . . . and I know that sounds like a line, but it's . . . well you can see what it's done to me!" Nate couldn't stand still. He strode back and forth in front of the door, oblivious to the wet splatters his black boots sprayed across the floor.

"I'm happy for you man, brilliant," Quinn said sincerely as he took a seat at his desk and had a slurp of hot coffee. He always saw young Amnut so clearly in Nate.

"I'm seeing her tonight. We're going to meet to talk about her project. I need to have a sample of my clips for her, you know, I think it's pretty much a formality, we just ..."

"Clicked," Quinn finished.

"Yeah, I said that. I know I sound like a teenager . . . I feel like a teenager," he said from the kitchen, grinning, where he was helping himself to coffee with plenty of milk and sugar.

"You practically *are* a teenager. I hope you can still get this excited when you're old like me," Quinn teased.

"Naw, man, when I'm your age *I* won't be single," Nate said, not realizing the slight until the words were out. "Um, well no, I mean . . . I hope I won't, umm, that's not ..." the younger man stammered, wishing to ease the offense. Quinn chuckled, and Nate was relieved.

"No worries, I know what you meant. Whaddya know about her?" Quinn asked.

"She's beautiful, thirty-five ..."

"An older woman," Quinn interjected.

"Only six years," Nate said defensively. "The documentary is about special Crystal kids. Have you heard of them?" Nate continued.

"Yeah, some . . . but go on," Quinn said, his interest piqued.

"Well basically there are all these kids being born within the last twenty years or so, and they're, like, touched by *God* or something. She says they are vibrating on a higher frequency, and there's some evidence that they have an evolved genetic makeup or something. They have, like, a higher consciousness, psychic shit like future telling, mind reading, talking about stuff from other countries and other times that a little kid couldn't know about . . . obviously, I don't have all the info."

"Do you think there is some truth to these Crystal Children? It's pretty controversial."

"She does . . . and I dunno . . . it seems pretty farfetched to me, but it's a project ..." Nate paused.

"And you like her."

"Yeah, I really do. Whaddya think about this, you're into all this kinda airy-fairy shit?"

"Thanks," Quinn said, shaking his head with a smirk. "Well, I actually think you might be on the verge of doing something important. I've read quite a lot about these kids. They're called different names, sometimes indigo or rainbow. There are websites and they are all over YouTube. You should check it all out before you see her tonight . . . don't go in cold."

"Yeah, I will, I know, I really want to blow her away. I am so sure this is going to be huge for me."

"How do you know she has what it takes movie-wise? What's she done?" Quinn asked, and for the first time Nate looked uncertain.

"Well, to be honest, up until now she was a special-ed teacher in an elementary school. Before university she worked in the film industry as a production assistant and she just fell in love with the business."

"Well, that's a pretty big leap, isn't it? How do you put that much faith in a totally unproven writer and director? And where does the budget come from? " Quinn asked, sounding like a protective father.

"Not sure, I think she's a single mom, so I don't think there's a whole lot of money actually, but she totally talked about hiring a DOP last night, so I guess I will have to figure out how to ask that without sounding like I am only in it for the bucks . . . but as far as her ability, wait until you meet this girl, she's just . . . got it."

"I can't wait. What are you planning to tell Sarah?" Quinn asked, referring to Nate's girlfriend and housemate.

"I already told her . . . this morning. We're done . . . and that kinda leads me to my next question …" Nate said, pausing.

Quinn raised his eyebrows and waited for what he knew was coming.

"Can I crash here for a while?"

"You left your girlfriend of four years for a girl you met last night?" Quinn said incredulously, though he had suspected for a while that Nate was unhappy in the relationship.

"We've been done for a long time, I just didn't wanna pull the plug," Nate said, hanging his head.

"Yeah . . . of course, you're welcome here, get your stuff . . . and hey," he added as an afterthought, noticing the chaos of his kitchen counter once more. "I'm putting you in charge of recycling 'cause there's not room here for all of us. Either you, me, or that mountain of shit has to go!"

"Small price to pay, man, thanks. It won't be for too long," Nate replied.

"No worries. I can't wait to meet your Eden," Quinn said, as he settled in to the pile of work behind him, happy to have Nate's company to look forward to.

"My Eden, hmm," Nate mused, as he carried boxes of cardboard and beer bottles out to his car and retrieved a duffle bag of clothes.

Seven hours and six phone calls from the crying ex-girlfriend later, most of Quinn's apartment was filled with steam from Nate's shower. Quinn didn't mind—he had significantly reduced his pile of work to be done, and two customers had picked up and paid for their computers that day. He took a self-satisfied puff on a small joint and offered it to Nate, who refused with a frantic wave.

"You might want to have a pull just to calm your nerves a bit, buddy, you're pretty wired," Quinn said.

"I want to be sharp tonight. I don't want to miss half of what she says because I'm stuck in some stoner zone-out."

Ouch. Nate's guileless honesty once again hit a nerve, and Quinn was made conscious of his fuzzy state of mind. Nate was too distracted to notice and smoothed his hands down his shiny black shirt and black pants. He checked his equally shiny, spiked-and-angled hair in the mirror by the door as he left.

"Good luck!" Quinn called out, hoping for his friend's sake that he wouldn't see him again until at least noon the next day.

Quinn was typing frantically an hour later when he heard Nate's key in the door. Not good. This was not good. A one-hour turnaround on the date of a lifetime did not bode well.

"Hey, man, what's up?" Quinn asked, as a surprisingly cheerful Nate rushed in.

"Oh, man, I am so glad you don't have a date tonight," Nate started.

"Nice. Rub it in, why don't ya?" Quinn said, shaking his head. Nate's candor was truly a test of Quinn's ability to shed his ego.

"No, oh sorry. I . . . have kind of a big favor, well, I sorta made a promise actually, but just say no if it's too much."

"What's up?"

"I have Eden's laptop, she's out in the car. She didn't want to put you on the spot, so just say no if you want . . . well she's having trouble with it and it's, like, totally her lifeline. She can't function without it. All her work stuff's on it and everything, and I told her that you're the best at this . . . I said maybe you could look at it tonight and we could pick it up in a few hours?"

"I can't promise, I don't know what's wrong with it, but I'll take a look," Quinn said, inwardly disappointed that the flow he had just found in his writing was going to be lost.

"Thanks, man. You're the best," Nate said, happy to have good news to take back to his date.

"Give me three or four hours—after that I'll be in bed, so I'll leave it on the table by the door. Hey, how's it going?"

"I'm in love, man," Nate grinned, opening the door.

"Cool," Quinn said, and he opened the notebook, wanting to finish as soon as possible and get back to his blog.

CHAPTER 29

EDEN FOUND

Quinn's slight irritation with Nate for hijacking his evening dissipated quickly. Eden's computer was a simple fix: some new security software and cleaning up spyware and a nasty virus. But within minutes of beginning the job, Quinn had begun to feel physically ill. Eden was his notable blog devotee, Anderson88! The coincidence seemed too great. Quinn had a clear profile of who she was. He knew her income, bank, address, and employer. He knew that her son was eleven-year-old Elijah James and that he was a bit of a handful. He knew how she spent her money, who she emailed, and how often.

Quinn couldn't stop reading and snooping, and he felt guilty and exhilarated all at once. He knew he shouldn't read her private messages, her Facebook entries, or even her datebook noting her menstrual cycle. He knew everything about her and his Marcus-brain was vibrating with excitement.

He had assumed Anderson88 was a guy and, though he had begun the blog to reach out to people, connect with other Emissaries, and possibly find Theron, he hadn't given any one contributor much thought. He had intentionally used the name "TheEmissary" to spark a response. He couldn't pretend that he hadn't hoped. And now Eden, the beautiful blue-eyed brunette that smiled at him from the photos stored on her hard drive and from her Facebook page, was on a date with Nate.

"We clicked," he had said.

"Like old friends," Quinn guessed, and his stomach flipped with the possibility that she might be his Theron. Her responses to his blog hinted that she was. Her passion and topic as a filmmaker and her chance meeting with Nate all indicated she could be a part of Marcus's soul group, the key to his soul. Theron! She could be Theron! Though he searched desperately to confirm it, he knew he had to see her in person to verify his suspicion. His intuition was hammering at him. He could hardly wait to meet her face to face and know for certain.

It had been just under three hours, and Quinn was startled by the sound of Nate's easy laughter as he jingled his key in the door. Quinn exited the photo gallery he had been scrutinizing and clicked off Eden's laptop.

"Hey, just finished, good ..." Quinn began, but he was struck silent by Theron's powerful karmic energy as it flowed into the room.

The petite beauty stepped out from behind Nate, and she was almost completely obscured by the light and color that Quinn saw surrounding her. Eden's purple aura glowed, and Marcus was ecstatic as it reached out to him. Their energies intermingled like grains of sand in a powerful tide, and Quinn was overwhelmed and unable to speak.

Eden smiled broadly at Quinn, oblivious to what he was experiencing, and reached out a hand that jingled with her many bracelets as she moved. Somehow Quinn found the ability to use his legs, though he didn't remember walking across the room, and he held her hand in his.

"Eden, Max Quinn . . . hey . . . are you crying, dude?" Nate asked incredulously.

Until that moment, Quinn hadn't realized he was. "No, no, it's just my eyes from working all night," he explained, reluctantly releasing her fingers and wiping away a tear. He had been electrified by Eden's touch and its warm, familiar vibration. He turned his back to her, momentarily overcome, and struggled to pull himself together.

Eden had also experienced something powerful and compelling, and she was unsettled. "So sorry to make you work tonight! Thank you, I hope it wasn't too much trouble," she said, misinterpreting his emotion as fatigue and his turning away as a dismissal.

"No, no, simple fix up," Quinn said emphatically.

Nate noticed a strange tremor in his friend's voice. "You sure you're okay?" he asked with concern. He had never known Max Quinn to be less than totally cool and composed.

"We should go. I don't want to intrude. What do I owe you?" Eden asked.

Quinn's brown eyes flashed up to meet hers.

Pow! There was a jolt to her solar plexus as the intensity of his gaze ignited her chakras and tingled up and down her spine.

"No, nothing . . . no worries. Just stay. I've been cooped up here all night. Let's all have a drink and hear about your project," Quinn said, maintaining eye contact with her and quickly regaining his poise.

Quinn's Marcus-brain was frantic. Theron must not leave. He had missed her so terribly. He had craved her spirit the way an addict craves a hit—his blood, his soul, and every breath was ignited by her.

Nate, however, was not enthusiastic. He wanted Eden to himself, and he was puzzled by Quinn's behavior. A buddy should know better. Guys understood one another, and Quinn was playing dumb and doing it all wrong.

Nate and Eden were both intuitive and, though they could not see the auras mingling magically around them, they could feel the heightened energy. It moved through them like wind through leaves, and Nate sensed that he was a bystander, an obstacle between his date and his best friend.

"No, no, we can't stay . . . we're going to go for a drink down at Charlie's. We just wanted to pick up the notebook before you were asleep," Nate answered, regretting the decision to show her off. He was anxious to leave and break the spell that had been conjured.

Quinn decided that he must breach sacred guy-code and invite himself along to Charlie's, but he didn't get the chance.

"Let's stay," Eden piped up, surprising them all. She didn't want to leave. She hadn't had time to think why, but she knew she wanted to stay longer in the messy little apartment with the books, diagrams, and sketches pinned and spread about. She was aware of the attraction she was feeling for Quinn, and it surprised her. The computer wiz was at least ten years older than she, and though he was undeniably handsome, he was Nate's buddy. If she and Nate were going to work together on the Crystal Project, she couldn't have any romantic complications. It would be unprofessional and it could jeopardize the venture.

Eden hadn't had any inclination of a romantic relationship with Nate. She could tell he was interested, but she was accustomed to dealing with crushes, and she hated to admit that sometimes it helped to have a slight edge. She was certain she could keep the relationship with Nate strictly professional. Quinn, however, was another story. Eden was surprised how far she had already taken her thoughts about the stranger.

Nate began to protest, but Quinn quickly led Eden toward the sofa, where he cleared a spot for her among his array of pictures, books, and dog-eared magazines. He chatted about her computer while he searched for a corkscrew, and Nate reluctantly took a seat next to her. He tried to catch Quinn's eye, but the Emissary intentionally avoided looking at him.

"All fixed now though," Quinn chirped uncharacteristically, as he poured three glasses of cheap Merlot. "I've been reading about Crystal Children for a while. They're remarkable when they are authentic, which I think some of them are. What made you interested enough to want to make a film about them?" Quinn asked, now staring directly into Eden's clear blue eyes, his self-possession restored.

She was once again aware of how attractive he was—the cleft in his chin, the emotion in his eyes—and she struggled to focus. "My son Elijah's the only reason I know anything about the Crystal Children. He's always been so unusual and unexplainable. It started as soon as he could talk and that was really early . . . full sentences at about fourteen months. He told me about all these dreams and bizarre stories about places and people and inventions. He started drawing crazy, detailed pictures, some quite disturbing. I was a mental health worker and special-ed teacher, so my first instinct was to take him to a child psychologist, or three actually, but they wanted to 'fix' him and drug him when I thought he was gifted, so I looked elsewhere."

"Like where?" Nate asked, and Quinn wondered why he hadn't already heard this story. How could it not have been his first question?

"Everywhere: the Internet, other moms, then the shaman of a local Native band who's a friend of a friend. Eventually, as he got a little bit older, I just asked Elijah what was up with him."

"Wise," Quinn said, smiling. He wanted to reach out and touch her. It was painful to sit so close and not feel her skin and complete their connection. "What did he say?"

"He said he's a traveler, an advanced soul with a special mission," she said, smiling, "I know it sounds crazy," she added, taking a sip of her wine and sensing the skepticism Nate was trying to conceal.

"Cheers," Quinn said, tipping his glass. "But you believe it," he added.

"I do. I've just seen too much. There are three-year-olds painting like Monet, playing piano without a single lesson, speaking foreign languages, and telling stories of ancient times that they can't possibly know. Yes, I believe it."

"There are lots of things that sound crazy but are true . . . they require a leap of faith. I think you are definitely on to something," Quinn added.

"You do? Wow, I wish everyone was that easily convinced!" Eden laughed.

"I've had some background; you didn't hit me cold," Quinn smiled.

Nate watched the bonding pair in distress, anxious to jump in, to be a part of the exchange.

"How old was Elijah?" Quinn asked, intrigued. He stared at her perfect little nose, her sparkling blue eyes, and he basked in the tingle of her.

"He was three and a half then. He still couldn't say his L's and R's, he sounded like Barbara Walters, all W's instead. 'Messenjow.' But the stuff that kid knew blew my mind."

"How old is he now?" Quinn asked, certain that the boy must be an Emissary. Quinn had wondered many times if the Crystal Children he had read about were Emissaries, but the way they spoke and communicated on the Internet implied some past-life memory. They had an advanced connection to their higher consciousness that he had not seen in Emissaries in prior ages, but they were moving into a Bronze Age, so changes were bound to happen. Would all of the Emissaries have memory soon? Would Theron? There was no way to know, but meeting Elijah would get Quinn one step closer to an answer. Was Theron's Crystal Child one of *them*?

"Eleven. He just had his birthday, he's an Aquarius," she said, taking a gulp of wine.

"I'd love to meet him," Quinn said.

Nate was dumbfounded, aware that he was outside what was happening between them, and he grew more annoyed by the minute. "Hey, uh . . . Eden, you said something about an early night 'cause of your sitter?" he reminded. Maybe she would invite him in if he could just get her out of there.

"Yeah, oh, it's getting late . . . yeah, we should go," she stammered, looking at her watch and draining her glass.

Nate was relieved, and he jumped up quickly.

"You sure I can't pay you something? I really appreciate you fixing me up," Eden said.

Quinn shook his head without a word, his eyes locked with hers once again. Eden stood and, as she walked toward the door, realized her wine glass was still in her hand. She reached to place it on a stack of books on a side table and noticed the title of the top volume: *Hamlet's Mill*. She gasped. She had just read about that text in her favorite blog and there it was.

"We'll let you get back to your blog," Nate said, as he opened the door.

"What's your blog called?" Eden asked, looking from the book to Quinn, certain she already knew.

"The Emissary," Nate and Quinn both answered at once, and Eden's mouth dropped open.

"I read you all the time!" she said excitedly. "Holy shit! What are the chances?" she squealed.

"Chance or synchronicity?" Quinn said calmly.

Eden spontaneously hugged him like an old friend, and Quinn's entire body was on fire at her touch.

"I can't believe it's you! Nate, you never said! Oh my God, it's unbelievable! I'm Anderson88! I have so much I want to talk to you about! I've thought more than once how fun it'd be to have dinner with you and talk!"

Nate mumbled sullenly. He was completely obscured by their connection now, and he resented his pal's intrusion into his plans, no matter how unintentionally it had begun.

Quinn ignored the emotions emanating from Nate and swirling miserably around him. He didn't want to injure his friend, but he wouldn't let anything come between him and Theron.

"I thought Anderson88 was a guy," Quinn said, thrilled by her response.

"Nope, not a guy," Eden said, smiling, her eyelids lowered seductively, her enthusiasm obvious.

"Lucky for me," Quinn flirted. "I'm so glad you enjoy my ranting."

Eden opened her mouth to reply, but Nate cut in. "You must have known," he realized out loud. Suddenly it made sense. "When we got here, you must have known. You had just worked on her computer for three hours. Did you know when we got here?" he asked, his tone accusing and disappointed.

Quinn swallowed; he wished he could say no. "I knew," he confessed.

Eden put her hand to her mouth. "But you didn't say anything? Oh, I mean . . . you know everything that's on there, don't you?" she said. "You should have said, but . . . I guess you have a ton of readers, don't you? Silly me to think I would matter to you! Oh, I must sound like a total egomaniac!"

"You stand out," Quinn said, his voice full of emotion, wishing he could pull her back into his arms.

Nate's face was flushed with anger. "Let's go. Thanks a lot, Max, for fixing her computer. I . . . okay, let's go," Nate said, taking hold of Eden's elbow and steering her out the door. He had used Quinn's first name, something he never did.

Eden waved as the door closed behind her.

Amazing! The whole thing had been so extraordinary, and Quinn sympathized with how confused the others must be feeling. He was overwhelmed with emotion and *he* understood why. He pitied them their disadvantage.

Nate didn't come home to Quinn's apartment that night. The Emissary blogged and waited. He stayed online, desperate to reconnect with Eden. It grew late and then early. Nate didn't return and Eden didn't write. Quinn felt a lump from stomach to throat burning inside him. Had she invited Nate in? Were they together now? Finally at dawn Quinn collapsed onto his rumpled bed. His sleep was restless and riddled with lucid dreams of sacrificial caverns, searching, and loss.

The next morning at eight Quinn was at his computer, coffee in hand, when he heard Nate's key in the door.

"I was hoping you'd still be sleeping," Nate said, without looking at his friend. He walked across the room and began picking up his belongings from among the disorder.

"Listen Nate, I know I have some explaining to do," Quinn began, and Nate rounded on him, his eyes flashing furiously.

"Seriously? Dude, *seriously*? You tried to back door me! I *told* you how much I like this girl and you just . . . you tried to sweep her up into your charisma or whatever! You blow off *everyone*! All the women I've seen hit on you, and you move in on *her*? Why?"

"What's happening here is bigger than you know. I think you were meant to guide her to me, Nate," Quinn said simply, still seated.

Nate fumbled with his sneakers and a pair of sweatpants. "Fuck you, you condescending prick!" he said, his face dark with anger.

"Nate, listen to me, please," Quinn said, getting up and walking toward him. "There's something I have to tell you . . . I . . . you've always said you felt like we've known each other before . . . we have. Many times, but she and I have too. This is how it's supposed to be."

"Nice for you! And who are you to say how it's *meant* to be? And suddenly this talk of *knowing* each other before . . . that's convenient! Bullshit!" Nate snapped, like a wounded animal.

"The truth is in you, you've just forgotten."

"Save it. Save your shit, man. I told you I loved her," Nate countered.

"You just met her."

"Not according to *you*! I'm outta here, man."

"Did you spend the night with her?" Quinn couldn't help but ask.

"Yeah, I fucked her brains out," Nate said venomously. He stuffed a few more items into a bag, and he grabbed the cord of his phone charger with an angry tug, breaking it as it ripped from the wall, sending pieces flying in different directions. He threw the shrapnel down at his feet and quickly left, slamming the apartment door.

Ping! There was an incoming blog comment.

Anderson88: How about getting together?

Quinn had planned for this.

TheEmissary: I added myself to your contacts. Call me.

Moments later Quinn's phone rang, and he was full of anticipation as he answered.

"Hey."

"Hey, it's me, Eden."

"Yeah, I'm glad you finally logged on. Thanks for calling."

"You put your number on my computer?"

"In case you needed more repairs," he lied.

"Really?" she asked doubtfully.

"No."

"That was pretty wild last night . . . meeting you like that after all that blogging. I felt pretty bad for Nate when we left your place, he seemed so pissed. He didn't say much, but I hope I didn't give him the wrong impression."

"He's a big boy," Quinn said, uncharacteristically coldly, relieved that Nate had obviously *not* fucked her brains out.

"Well, I hope it won't mess up me and him working together. He seems like a really good guy and I felt a real connection there."

"He is a good guy, it'll work out," Quinn said coolly. He didn't want to talk about Nate. He didn't want her to feel guilty or conflicted about him. He knew her heart and her empathy, and he knew it had derailed them more than once. "Can I take you to dinner tonight?"

"How about lunch, while Elijah's at school?" she replied.

"Better. Can I pick you up?" he offered.

"Sure. I'll give you my address."

"Got it," he said. "Don't worry, I'm not a stalker," he added, though he knew that for her, he could be.

"I'm not worried," she half-whispered, her throat choked by the energy that flowed between them, even over the phone. "See you at noon."

Quinn hung up and, beaming with satisfaction, looked at the ceiling and silently said his thanks with a deep celebratory breath. Only three more hours. He had waited so long already, what was three more hours?

CHAPTER 30

TRUE, MAD LOVE

Quinn picked up Eden at her tidy-looking, one-story bungalow in Seattle's Capitol Hill neighborhood. He had chosen a restaurant close by with old-fashioned booths that were cozy and private, and from the moment they came together the conversation flowed easily. Eden knew so much! She understood the Universe. She meditated daily, she did yoga, and she volunteered at the rape relief shelter down the road. She had read everything that Quinn had ever deemed worthy of reading, including Plato.

Marcus was amazed by her insight, though he knew he shouldn't be. Theron had always astounded him. In each lifetime, she had not required past-life memory or kinky potions to keep her on track. She was truly a worthy Emissary. He maintained his belief that he had become an Emissary only because of her.

Quinn sat across the table from her determined to suppress his eagerness lest he frighten her away. He encouraged her to speak, listening blissfully while her voice vibrated through him.

"There are so many people asking how to become enlightened . . . wanting to embrace spirituality and not knowing where to start. Your blog is such an inspiration. Would you consider being a part of the Crystal Project? There's no money in it, but if this documentary goes big enough, we could really help in this shift of consciousness that's going on," Eden said. Her chestnut bangs fell over her forehead as she took a sip of her green tea.

"I'd love to work with you. I agree people *are* looking for answers, I see it in my blog all the time. Do you think you can show people how simple it is? It's just a matter of plugging themselves in to the humanity around them, looking around and asking questions, and not droning after the material bullshit we're constantly told is so important."

"I think that anyone who is ready and willing will pick up on the simplicity of the connected Universe. We are all wicks lit from one eternal flame, we only need to join together to increase the light and understanding," Eden declared.

"I'm no filmmaker, but I think those are the kinds of whimsical statements that tend to lose the skeptics," Quinn said, laughing.

"Shit! I know! You're totally right. I have to work on that! That's why I need you. Your blog is so no-nonsense. You just say it and make it seem so normal."

"And rambling and crazy! Like I said, I want to help. I'll do everything I can. I'll be at your disposal for whatever you need."

"I need you for the way you think, for what you know . . . don't forget I'm an Emissary blog devotee! Plus, if you help with the website, social media, downloads, connections, all the technical stuff I just don't do, you can help take this thing big . . . viral, I hope!"

"You overestimate me," Quinn said, reminded that she always had. Quinn wondered, as he had many times before, what he was supposed to be doing in this lifetime. He was certain that the coming together of Eden, Nate, and himself must be significant. Events would unfold and become clear, but he still cared first and foremost about pursuing his great love.

"I don't think so. I'm a very good judge of people. It's a lot to ask, I know, you barely know me and I'm making demands . . . I understand if you don't want to do it, but of course I'll pay you!" she said.

"I told you, money's not my big objective, *and* I don't feel like I barely know you," he said, reaching across the low table and taking her hand in his. He had wanted to do it from the moment he had seen her. Their connection sent shivers up both their arms, visibly raising the hairs.

"I know what you mean," she said, giving his hand a squeeze but pulling away. "We have to go," she said suddenly.

Quinn withdrew his empty hand. "Oh, yeah, okay," he said, conscious of the awkwardness of the moment.

"No, it's not that . . . the restaurant's been closed for half an hour, and if we don't leave soon he'll lock us in!" she laughed, gesturing toward the kitchen behind him.

They had been there for three and a half hours, too wrapped up in one another and their rapid-fire conversation to notice the tired owner, anxious to close until the dinner rush. Quinn apologized as they left, and he threw an extra tip on the pile.

"Where to now? Do I have to take you home, or can we take a walk and continue our date right through dinner tonight?" Quinn suggested hopefully, as they neared his car.

"Date?" she repeated, with a question in her voice. "I'm sorry, but . . . everything's just …" she began, and Quinn felt as though he had been kicked in the gut.

She was pulling away. He had pushed too hard. She had already said that she hadn't been interested in Nate, that it was only business. Why hadn't he asked her about Elijah's father? He hadn't wanted to know. He hadn't asked because he hadn't wanted to entertain the possibility of anything keeping them apart.

"No, I'm sorry. I should have read you better," he interrupted.

"You read me exactly right, Max, but we can't . . . if we're going to do this project together, and I think we are *meant* to do this project together. What with the blog and then Nate . . . it's too much 'synchronicity' as you'd say. It must be destiny. I just don't want to screw it up. I feel it, right down to the roots of my hair—it is so important that we do this."

"Okay, I get it . . . I'm on board. I wanna do it. It might be exactly what we are meant to do together . . . but I don't think that it's *all* we are meant to do together," Quinn added, with a wink. He was flirtatious and casual on the outside, but inside he was churning with alarm that his longing for her would go unanswered.

"Friends . . . professional. We need to keep focused," she said. "You okay with that?"

"Do I have a choice?" he said, forcing a smile.

"Oh, Max, there's always a choice," she said.

As they got in his car, Eden wondered if she could work with Quinn and ignore her growing attraction to him. The thought made her feel both guilty and excited all at once.

They drove the short distance to her home, enjoying the warm spring sunshine through the windshield, and finally Quinn spoke.

"Tell me about Elijah's dad," he said, and Eden took a deep breath.

"He was killed in Afghanistan just over a year ago. I'm still in shock most of the time. I'm so used to him being away, sometimes I just forget he's . . . *gone*. Gone . . . I expect him to show up, you know?"

She absentmindedly played with the ring dangling around her neck while she spoke. She hadn't said dead, she had said "gone." He was still alive for her, and Quinn understood how hard it must be. If there was one thing he had learned in his many years, it was empathy for loss and grief.

"I'm so sorry. Was he a soldier?"

"No. Jamie and I were both aid workers when we met. After I had Elijah, I got a more family-friendly job and settled down here near his parents. Jamie was an engineer and stayed with the relief agency, traveling back and forth."

"Sounds like a good guy."

"He is . . . was. It's been really hard on Elijah. We were supposed to meet Jamie in Egypt this June. It was going to be the summer that we got back on the aid trail . . . this time as a family. Elijah's home-schooled anyway, so I guess I was just waiting until I thought he was old enough before we became full-fledged gypsies again."

She had planned to return to Egypt—the land of the Great Pyramid, Alexander, and the Emerald Tablet. Did it mean something?

"And now? What'll you do when you finish the project?" Quinn asked.

"It's going to take a long time, and I don't plan anymore, Max. I knew better even back then. Life always throws curves, and plans fall away. Now I try to live in the moment, and I know life will unfold as it is meant to as long as I stay open and watchful."

I was watching for you, Quinn thought, but instead he said: "Absolutely right," and they drove in silence for a moment.

"You need a kickass website that can handle as many millions of hits as could happen. It has to have easy YouTube links, Twitter, Facebook, all the social media that will attract viewers. It has to be able to run the entire documentary . . . that is what you want right?" Quinn said, changing the subject. Enough sadness, enough grief, he wanted her to look forward, not backward.

"Yes!" she said, her excitement renewed. "We want to make it free for the world, so anyone can see it and be a part of the movement forward. I don't want anything for sale on the site. Only links to some of the other great inspirational and informative sites I've found."

"I hate this part Eden, but I gotta ask . . . how are you funding this? Filming costs money if it's done right. You said you're not working now that you've started this full time."

"Life insurance. Jamie had a policy. I have about three hundred thousand before I am totally broke. I thought that would last us a few years, but then the idea for the project hit me and I knew I had to give it everything . . . even if it is risky. I feel like that's what the money was for. Of course we still have to live and pay all our monthly expenses. I figure we have a year to get it done, and since the kids we interview don't charge, it's really just me, Elijah . . . now you and Nate, and equipment and lighting and travel and, oh shit . . ." she said, obviously overwhelmed.

"I can take care of me, don't worry about that. As for Nate, his trust fund has more money than he could ever spend. That's why he can fool around doing the creative scene and choosing his projects, instead of shooting crap commercials."

"He was upset the other night. I hope I didn't lead him on," she said kindly.

Theron was shining through, and Quinn felt the thickest sense of déjà-vu, except he understood why.

"Well, when he finds out you shut me down too, he'll be fine," Quinn laughed, though it hurt him deeply to say it.

"Oh God, you do say what you think, don't you?"

"Always. And Eden, after the bulk of the work is finished, I want you to promise you'll see me then . . . if you want to."

"I can't promise. You could very well meet someone in the meantime, you could change your mind. We never know where we'll be, I've learned that," she insisted.

"I can guarantee *that* will not happen," Quinn said, smiling and resisting the urge to kiss her. *Oh God! The next few months are going to be hell*, he thought, and he was right, but things would be far worse than he imagined.

CHAPTER 31

EDEN'S QUEST

As Quinn had predicted, Nate was happy to commit to the project with only the slightest urging from Eden. It had not, however, been only her persuasion at work on him. The Universe was in league with the idea. Everywhere Nate went he saw articles about the new consciousness and the countdown to a better world, and even as he walked the block from his place to the shop up the street, he marveled at a name on the corner. "Cosmic Crystal's Coffee Cafe," the sign said, and Nate took note.

He was opening up, slowly, but Nate remained skeptical about all of the New Age spiritual crap he was being exposed to. He wished he could be as convinced and full of faith as some of the others around him. He just didn't know how. How did one become like them? They seemed so compassionate, peaceful, and Zen all the time. They didn't seem to have the same worries as the rest of the world, as if they had found the key to happiness. Were they naïve? Deluded? It didn't matter. Nate knew he wanted to work on the Crystal Project. He wanted to be as close to Eden as he could.

Nate had not forgiven Quinn, but when he was assured that there was no romance going on between his friend and Eden, he had gone to retrieve the last of his belongings.

Quinn was happy to see him and greeted him warmly. After some brief and slightly awkward banter, Quinn dared to ask the question foremost on his mind. "Have you met Elijah yet?" He was hoping Nate would have some insight or feeling of familiarity to share.

"No . . . tonight. Man, this is so exciting. I got the best new camera for this gig. It shoots video that looks like film."

"That must've cost you a bit," Quinn said absently.

"She's worth it," Nate said simply, eyeing his companion carefully, and once again Quinn felt a knot forming in the center of his chest.

"Yes, she is," Quinn replied.

"I'm still pissed at you," Nate said, though it was obvious.

"Nothing happened."

"It's not like you didn't try," Nate said bitterly.

"Right, but it is what it is, buddy. There are things going on here you just don't understand."

"Ugh . . . the condescension. You don't even know you do it! Why do I put up with you?" Nate said, shaking his head, immediately inflamed.

"You and I are part of the same soul group, man, we've been doing this together for a long time."

"Yeah, you said that. I'm starting to worry about your mental health," Nate scowled.

"We've talked about a lot of spiritual stuff. I know it sounds crazy to just say it, but I've known you *and* Eden . . . many times."

"So what? So you think you got dibs? Seriously?"

"Don't do that. Don't turn it into something as weak as that," Quinn said, suddenly irritated.

"Weak? I'm here making an effort, even though you tried to steal her away right in front of me, and you call me weak? Listen . . . as you always say, 'it is what it is.' So, may the best man win," Nate said coldly.

Nate had reason to be smug, knowing that the next day he would embark on three months of uninterrupted traveling time with Eden, as they ventured to the other side of the planet to interview the Crystal Children. Quinn, wishing he could accompany them on their coming journey, had had little more than one afternoon with Eden. But he said nothing more, so Nate left without looking back.

Quinn was determined to help Eden's project succeed. The Crystal Children were the future. Soon everyone would be able to do what these children could—it was the evolution of the human consciousness, a result of the ascending Age. As people saw what was possible, the frequency would heighten. He was determined that when they finished the project, he and Theron would finally be together again.

The blogger worked tirelessly on the website: colors, links, downloads, every bell and whistle. All along he kept up his blog, and Anderson88 continued to comment from afar, though far less frequently. She had a busy schedule, a new blog, and a Twitter account of her own to maintain.

Due to rising fuel costs, travel was more expensive than Eden had first anticipated. However, Brisbane and Sydney had been successful and she was excited about their progress. She chattered in a jerky video conference across Quinn's computer screen, announcing that she had amazing footage she couldn't wait to share with him.

"You should be here, Max! Oh my God, these kids just *get* it. We've only found one poor little victim so far . . . uuchh . . . hideous parents. This poor little girl was barely five and her parents were parading her like a freak in a circus . . . so obviously faking stories and drilling her for memorized information. She was a sweet kid, but not . . . gifted. In the end I just told them they wouldn't be getting famous or rich by exploiting her with *our* help."

"Do you worry that the documentary might cause more of that? More victimization, circus mentality?" Quinn asked, his forehead creased with concern.

"I do. But what's the alternative? To let the world ignore their amazing potential for contribution? They have a message to bring, and maybe it'll help some people nurture their kids instead of thinking they have mental problems!"

"Hopefully."

"I'd love to get all of these kids together in one place someday. It'd be amazing!"

"A school," Quinn said, thinking of the Mystery School and knowing what a fertile ground it had laid. He had begun dreaming about the Mystery School often and had many flash backs to his life as Plato. He imagined himself and Eden gathering the Emissaries from around the globe and working toward a peaceful, loving vision for the world. His dreams were speaking to him as they often had, and Quinn was wise enough to listen.

"Exactly! But there have already been 'special' schools, and some have been a bit of a scam and a mess . . . and really, what do we know about running a school?" Eden said apprehensively.

"We could do better. I know something about teaching and you were a teacher, how hard can it be? Anyway, they just need a place to gather and teach one another, don't they?" Quinn asked.

"I like it. I like it a lot! But one step at a time. We can't think about that now. First we have to finish the film. We have months of editing to do once the footage is shot, and then there's all the marketing and promotion. How's the website coming?" she asked excitedly, though wanting not to be demanding, since he had yet to accept any payment from her.

"Ready when you are, all we need is your footage."

"I wish you'd let me pay you something," she said, smiling, and the screen froze, her grin perfectly captured for a moment, her dark hair loose and flowing over her shoulders.

"Why, so you can boss me around?" Quinn said, laughing, and she laughed too, enjoying his smile. "You're going to have to deal with a lot of skepticism . . . you ready for that?"

"I'm ready. There's nothing wrong with good opposition, it can make us stronger . . . you know, ramp up our game. It's not the criticism or the questioning I mind, it's the bold-faced lying and abusive garbage," Eden admitted.

"Aw, people are pretty smart, at least the ones you have any hope of reaching," Quinn assured.

"We're trying to reach everybody, and unfortunately the naysayers and rumor mongers are pros, and they come across as trustworthy and concerned about child exploitation. Maybe they are. Maybe they just don't understand what we're doing. They're just not open to it . . . I can't fault them for being on their own path."

"You can never fault anybody. Have you blocked that guy who was swearing and abusing you on your blog yet?" Quinn asked protectively.

"If I block him, I look like I have something to hide. I'd rather show both sides, the duality, so everyone knows what we're up against."

"Yeah, that's actually a good argument, but don't let it go too far," Quinn conceded.

"Are we ever really gonna get this done, Max? I seriously feel like I'm running out of time . . . that's why I am bugging you so much," she lied. They both eagerly looked forward to their blog and video conferencing time together.

"Patience. It'll happen. As long as you're working toward it and envisioning where you want to go, you'll get there."

"*We'll* get there," she corrected. "We're partners in this, aren't we?"

"Partners. Yeah, we are," Quinn said. They had been so much—so many combinations and complications—and he wanted to be more than her partner in this life.

"It takes so much money to accomplish anything these days. What if we do all this work and no one sees it?" Eden said.

"I wish I could help you there, but I pretty much always worked just enough to live, travel, and take care of myself. Money's never been a focus for me."

"I didn't mean ..." she began, the odd delay in the video conferencing chopping and overlapping their thoughts.

"No, I know. We're doing it for the right reason. The Universe takes care of those working in service to it. Ugh, I sound like a flake. Let's just say: Have faith, it'll all work out."

"I know, you're right," she said, smiling.

"Where are you headed now?" Quinn asked, aware that she was Skyping him from the Sydney airport lounge.

"Christchurch, New Zealand, got added to our schedule unexpectedly. This keeps happening—everyone knows someone else amazing. It's quite a connected little grid. We find five kids when we expect to meet only one."

Quinn smiled at Eden's use of the word "grid." It was all the Grid, the great pattern, visible and invisible, weaving in every direction, shape, and speed, connecting everything.

"Are things okay there, they had that earthquake a while back?"

"Yep, things are okay . . . aftershocks, but nothing I am too worried about. Hey, I gotta go now. I have so many notes to finish up and we fly out in an hour. Elijah's itching to get on here and talk to some friends," she said.

"Have fun in New Zealand, it's gorgeous. Be safe," Quinn added as her image waved, blinked, and disappeared from his monitor.

Excruciating. Was it more painful not knowing where, when, or how Theron would appear, or knowing exactly where she was and being unable to have her? Quinn contemplated the question as he smoked a joint and threw himself into a particularly brooding blog entry.

When Quinn woke late the next morning, the news channels were transmitting tsunami warnings for New Zealand, the west coast of North America, and all of the smaller lands in between. Another in a string of devastating, high-magnitude earthquakes had hit Japan overnight. The television and Internet were full of video and panic but little detail.

When he heard the tsunami warning for Christchurch, Quinn tried unsuccessfully to reach Eden and Nate. There was nothing, no email from them, no message, and Quinn felt ill. He didn't leave his computer for hours, and he was relieved when he finally read a general Facebook entry from Eden, assuring all of her friends and family that she and Elijah were safe.

Relieved, Quinn jumped in the shower. He was interrupted mid-suds by a slow rumble and sway. At first he was disoriented, thinking he was off balance and too consumed with earthquake images from the net. As the motion intensified, the bottles and shelves began to crash around him. There was no time to think, but there was no need. Marcus had lived through many times and tragedies. Quinn was incapable of panic, though adrenaline flowed through his body as it would for anyone.

A terrifying sound reverberated through the air and, as the earth violently bucked, it reawakened a host of ancient memories in him. Quinn stumbled out of the shower and steadied himself under the doorway, while the ground continued to shake violently. He felt as though he were a young child, lifted and shaken by strong adult arms.

Naked and cold, Quinn was growing more alarmed; the trembling was extreme and was lasting too long. He was certain it was causing devastation and death. His was an old building and low, not a skyscraper. Downtown buildings would be swaying, crumbling, and dropping tons of glass and brick to the sidewalks below. Quinn said a prayer for the victims and the loved ones they would leave behind.

Finally the shaking subsided and Quinn sidestepped the broken glass at his feet; his cologne lay shattered. He pulled on his jeans and was awed by the destruction in his apartment. The large gilt mirror once secured behind his bed had ripped away from its anchors, dropping onto his headboard and shattering where he had lain sleeping only hours before. He shuddered to think that his new beginning with Theron might have ended that abruptly.

Books were in heaps on the floor, emptied from shelves and tables, joining the many that had been there in piles before the quake. The kitchen was a mess. Most of the cupboards had fallen open and spilled their contents onto the floor.

Quinn flicked the lights. No power. He thought of his battery-powered radio . . . somewhere. As he began to search for it, the ground once again began to shake. He heard an ominous ripping sound as an opening to the outdoors was cleaved into the plaster of the apartment's southern wall. The building was collapsing. Quinn knew he had to get the hell out. There was no time. He found shoes and moved stealthily into the outside corridor, shirtless and stumbling under the power of a second tremor.

The earth continued shaking, more violently than the first time, and Quinn rushed to the aid of his neighbor, who was also trying to escape. The young mother had two crying babies in tow, and they were being thrown mercilessly about as she struggled to regain her footing. Her knees were bloody and scraped, and a third child, of about six years, was fighting to stay in the crumbling apartment, too terrified to leave. He was planted firmly on his bottom, his cheek pressed to the doorjamb, his eyes squeezed shut. The desperate woman's arms were loaded with the two wailing siblings, and the boy was immovable as she begged him to release his hold. Quinn swooped in and picked up the older child, easily loosening his grip.

"I gotcha, buddy. I gotcha, hang on to me," Quinn said calmly, over the screech of fire alarms and wailing babies. The boy attached to him like a monkey to a branch and buried his face in Quinn's neck. "This way, this way!" Quinn commanded, supporting the young mother with his free hand and guiding her to the distant stairwell. He had seen the south side of the building listing and crumbling; he hoped the stairs on the north were still passable.

Once safely clear of the wreckage, Quinn left the traumatized young family lying in the grass a hundred yards from the building, grateful that the May weather was warm and dry. He rushed back to see what further help he could offer.

Neighbors were clamoring about, though many were away at work, which sadly may have proven fatal for them. The second tremor had ended, and the sobs and calls continued as Quinn cautiously re-entered the building, knocking on doors and making certain there were no unattended victims.

The building was ruined, completely unsafe, but thankfully there had been no deaths in his small patch. Sirens, smoke, and alarms were ominous in the distance, and no one expected medical attention any time soon. Keys, coat, laptop, and wallet in hand, Quinn sat in his car and listened to the alarming satellite reports of the damage to the Pacific Northwest.

The entire west coast from San Diego to Alaska had felt the quake. Seattle was in discord, even though the epicenter of the 8.0-magnitude quake had struck hundreds of miles north, hitting Vancouver Island, Canada, directly. The large Canadian island and the smaller surrounding islands had been completely devastated, and tsunami tides threatened inhabitants on both sides of the Pacific Ocean.

It was Eden and Nate's turn to worry. They didn't eat or sleep as they watched reports coming out of North America with horror. Finally, seven hours later, they learned via email that Max Quinn had survived.

Sadly, more than six thousand had died when office buildings, hospitals, shopping malls, and schools had been damaged. There had been looting in places, especially the big cities, but in many instances people had acted with surprising generosity and brotherhood.

For some, the tragedy had reawakened them to what was truly important. Obsessions with video games, handbags, and bigger and better cars were replaced by the appreciation for friends and family, charity, compassion, and the love of their fellow human beings.

Suddenly there was more to life . . . and less. Simplicity: an epiphany. A light went on and people wondered how they could have missed what it was all about. How could they have lived so robotically, in a fog, unconscious? The spiritual world is necessarily separate from the material world.

The bigger question was, would they remain conscious or would they slip back to their old patterns?

Over the next two months, the aftershocks continued and rebuilding commenced. Quinn couldn't help but think the Earth was voicing its displeasure. Plato had discussed the idea of anima mundi, the world soul. Would things get worse before they finally got better?

Eden's initial instinct had been to return to the Pacific Northwest immediately and assist with the cleanup. Quinn had spent hours debating and counseling her in her helplessness, but he had ultimately convinced her that the Crystal Project was now more important for the unification of people than ever. The citizens of the world needed to see the human potential that the children would exhibit. They needed to know what was possible and that there was a brighter future ahead.

Finally, Eden resumed interviewing the Crystal Children, meeting more wherever she went. Across the oceans people were detached from the turmoil in North America, and though they felt sympathy for the misfortunes of their distant neighbors, they had their own hardships to contend with. The headlines changed and the "Great American Quake" was quickly old news.

Life continued, as it always had, only harder and more uncertain by the day. Man-made disasters like civil wars and riots were becoming the norm, and countries that had been living in Mafia states for a long time were getting worse. In places like Mexico, Ukraine, Russia, and Serbia people trusted no one. Only money and power had a voice. Governments and police were corrupt. Students had to pay under the table for the opportunity to take their exams, and babies in daycare only had their diapers changed if their parents paid extra. People were miserable and enslaved, and charity and compassion were uncommon or hidden from view.

Quinn wished that the ascent through the Bronze Age could be sped up; sometimes it felt as though the Dark Age had somehow been extended.

It was an important time for Eden and Elijah. For the first time, the boy didn't feel isolated and abnormal. Instead, he felt that he had been chosen to do something important in the world. Eden quelled his natural tendency to grow proud and self-important by reminding him to stay humble and compassionate. It was a struggle.

Nate and Elijah grew to be friends, and Nate continued to pursue and flirt with Eden. More than once, across a dinner table, she had considered him romantically. He was kind, funny, and eager to please, but her heart belonged to another.

Eden kept in daily contact with Quinn, who had found a temporary place to live and was spending most days toiling with disaster cleanup. Rebuilding had begun, and as he worked, he spoke in his calm, hopeful way and inspired those around him. His life suddenly seemed to have direction and, unbeknownst to him, his soul purpose was soon to be realized.

Quinn was grateful that Eden was safe. She was scheduled to proceed to Morocco and then home. He was anxious to see her again, but he knew that Washington State was not the best place for them to be. The relief and cleanup had been bungled, reminiscent of the Hurricane Katrina debacle in Louisiana, and many of the citizens of Washington, Oregon, and California were angry and suffering shortages. Alaska, always hearty and independent, had fared much better, but summer was passing quickly and there was much left to do.

"I'm thinking I should come meet you in Marrakech and we can work from there. Things are still a mess here, and I don't know when they'll be back on track . . . hopefully before the snow comes. It's already brutal with all this unseasonable rain," Quinn said, from his recently purchased cellphone. He was a traveler again; he had no choice but to give in and get one, just to stay connected.

"It's still *that* bad? Oh shit! Honestly, I haven't wanted to worry you, but its bad here too. Pretty chaotic in the streets. I don't even know how you can get here! It's so bloody expensive. I was going to tell you—we've decided to postpone our return another month, because I've been searching for flights and couldn't manage anything."

"All the more reason I should come to you," Quinn said. He wouldn't be swayed. Theron had been separated from him too long, and he didn't know what the Universe might throw at them next. He did know that he certainly wanted to be with her no matter what was to come.

"That sounds great, and Max, I can't wait for you to see the footage we got. There are no phonies here; these kids are the real deal. We met one girl yesterday,

Anjolie, she's fourteen. She's been keeping a journal since she was four! She has fifty-one completed notebooks, about fifty pages each. No one taught her to write, she just writes . . . but that's not the amazing part. She writes in perfect Greek and Russian and English, and other languages I can't even recognize!"

"Fantastic! What does she write about?"

"Everything. Sometimes it's terrifying, about floods and ancient ceremonies. She can't even read the stuff in the other languages, she only speaks French. She says her 'inside-brain' writes it all for her and tells her in French what it's about."

"Fascinating. I'd love to meet her," Quinn said honestly, wondering who she was, certain she must be an Emissary. Quinn was thrilled that so many of the Crystal Children seemed to have ancient knowledge. It had to mean that the darkest part of the cycle was nearing an end. Could Theron soon have memory too?

"Do you ever feel like you're one of them?" he asked hopefully.

"Me? No! Well, not exactly, though I have to admit, sometimes lately I am having the strangest feelings of déjà-vu. Like they're rubbing off on me. I'm dreaming like crazy too, and my dreams are so lucid, of places I've never been but I can recall in fine detail."

"Such as?" Quinn asked.

"I dreamed we had a school, you and I. We didn't look like ourselves but I knew it was us anyway. I was standing with you on a high set of white steps, and we were surrounded by students. We all had white toga-style clothes on, and I could see every face and eye color and cloud in the sky. You had a craggy old-man face but a gentle smile . . . I woke up deliriously happy from that one."

"Maybe the school is in our past?" Quinn said hoarsely, filled with emotion by her remembrance of them in Ancient Greece.

"I didn't think of that . . . I was thinking it's about our future. I think it was a confirmation that we're supposed to go ahead and create a school when we're done this."

"Mmmm," Quinn said, happy that she was thinking about a future with him. "I like hearing your dreams . . . any more?" he asked.

"No, it's silly. Anyway, when are you coming?"

"As soon as possible. I'll let you know as soon as I'm booked," he said.

"Great! Umm, Max, do you really think we knew each other in a past life?" she said sheepishly, and he knew she was embarrassed even though he couldn't see her blushing.

"I am certain of it," he said, his voice full of longing for her. He heard a quick intake of breath.

"You'll have to explain that certainty to me one of these days," she said demurely. "We're leaving Lyon tonight for Marseilles, and then we should be in Marrakech in three days. Keep me posted," she added.

"See you soon," Quinn said, and for the first time he hung up before she did.

CHAPTER 32

THE SEDUCER-PRODUCER

Quinn had little time to savor his conversation with Eden; he had to arrange a flight to Africa. The earthquake and continuing wars and volatility in the Middle East had sent fuel prices soaring, and shortages had driven them further upward. Quinn used his laptop to secure himself a hideously overpriced flight through London to Morocco, nearly eight thousand US dollars. His credit was maxed out. Finished.

August first, Quinn's plane set down at Heathrow airport. The customs lineup was ridiculously long, seven hours at least. Quinn knew that he would certainly miss his connection to Marrakech and, though flights from Europe were not as outrageously priced as out of the US, his credit cards were useless and his cash was severely depleted.

"Max Quinn? Max Quinn?" An airport security member was calling out his name. Quinn raised his hand and worked his way to the edge of the snaking, endless lineup. "Follow me, sir," the guard said politely.

"Where? I'm already gonna miss my flight."

"You'll make your flight. Follow me," the man commanded.

Quinn was relieved by the promise and complied willingly, while the bedraggled travelers around him looked on with envy.

"Hey, I have a flight to catch too," a pissed-off Swiss banker called after them.

"Where are we going?" Max asked, intrigued. He soon realized that no explanation was forthcoming, so he stopped asking and followed the tightly stuffed uniform in silence.

Inside a lavish private room nestled in a secret corner of the Heathrow terminal, Quinn was left alone to ponder his circumstances. His instincts were prickling and unsettled. Would it be Helghul? Had Marcus been discovered somehow? A thousand possibilities could have been entertained, but instead Quinn kept his mind clear. He had lived too many lives to fear the unknown or to waste time with useless worry and speculation. He would deal with reality when it arrived. He waited patiently.

The door finally opened and Quinn was startled to see a handsome, familiar face. He had seen the features many times staring back at him from magazine covers, newspapers, and television interviews. "Seducer-Producer" the tabloids called the man, alluding to his irresistible charisma and monopolization of the mass media industry.

The celebrity strongly resembled a forty-something Paul Newman; his salt-and-pepper hair was cropped short, and his blue eyes glowed in his darkly tanned face. He was a striking physical specimen—muscular, trim, and beyond six feet tall.

Quinn was difficult to impress, but the man before him awed him on two counts. Oswald Zahn was a renowned philanthropist, movie producer, and mogul, but more importantly he bloomed with the light and violet aura of Grey Elder. Quinn was jolted by the recognition.

"You're a difficult man to find, Marcus," Zahn said, smiling. Quinn was startled by the use of his true name.

"Grey Elder! You remember?" Quinn almost shouted, and the two men merrily embraced.

Marcus was elated to be in the presence of someone other than Helghul who had memory. Only Red Elder had also had memory, and the last time they had met was in Heliopolis more than two thousand years earlier.

"You remember back in Stone-at-Center, Marcus?" Zahn asked.

"Of course," Quinn nodded, urging him on, absently running his hands through his thick hair and holding them there, pressing, as if trying to contain the myriad of thoughts hammering against his skull.

"I talked to you then about the burden of having taken the potion . . ." Zahn's voice trailed off.

"I remember . . . I was so young, so stubborn and self absorbed . . . I should have known that all the Elders would have memory," he said, shaking his head.

"We all have choice, don't we?" Zahn said smoothly, a rebellious glint in his sparkling eyes.

"It's been so many lifetimes since then. I've often wondered why we haven't met again," Quinn said.

"We've been close many times. I listened to you speak in Ancient Greece, but the crowd was large and you were well out of my reach . . . Another time in Jakarta, I was born to you and died . . . it was your lesson, not mine," he said sorrowfully.

"Ohhh," Marcus breathed, immediately remembering that difficult lifetime and, for an instant, filling with the grief of that mother love. That had been such a hard and short life, during which Marcus had met Siddhartha Gautama, the man who had gone on to be called simply "Buddha." Like Socrates, he had not displayed the karmic colors of an Emissary, but his energy and charisma were unmistakably pure and powerful. Of course, Marcus hadn't known then how profoundly important that individual would become. "How did you find me?" he asked curiously, his mind filled with questions.

"The Emissary," Zahn said simply. "Interesting blog. It was easy to find out who registered the name. I went in person to see if it was you, but I was too late. Your apartment building was in ruins. It wasn't until you booked this flight that you showed up in the system again."

Quinn was unnerved at having been hunted but was pleased to be reunited with one of the wise Elders of old. He had so much he wanted to know. "I guess fame and fortune have some perks," he smiled. "But why look for me?"

"Because we have work to do. I need your help."

"*You* need *my* help? I was just thinking the same thing!"

"Do you know where Theron is?" Grey Elder asked, and Marcus hesitated protectively. "I see little has changed, Marcus!" Grey Elder laughed.

"Yes, I know where she is," he answered.

"Is her name Eden Anderson?" Zahn asked hopefully, and Quinn nodded, raising his eyebrows in surprise. "Excellent! I haven't met her yet, but I understand that she is working on a project with many of the young Emissaries."

"I knew it! The Crystal Children *are* Emissaries," Quinn exclaimed.

"Yes, as are many others. Does she have memory yet?"

"Yet? No, well, not really. Why? Should she?" Quinn said hopefully.

"It may come. The cycle has turned, ascending into a lighter Age."

"I'm on my way to meet her now. I don't know what else we are supposed to be doing. Why didn't the Elders prepare us better?"

"You're more prepared than you know. Everything you've learned up until now will guide you. Just trust me."

"I do, but I need to know what to do, what to expect."

"The Crystal Children have been born with special intuitions, memories, and psychic skills that will help the world pass through the shadow and into the Light. You and Theron need to gather them, and I am going to help you. All of my wealth, prestige, and resources are at your disposal." Zahn said, and Quinn was stunned.

"This is unbelievable . . . we talked about recreating the Mystery School, but we didn't know how we could do it! And now here you are with a blank check and all the influence we could hope for."

"The Universe provides, but we have to move quickly," Grey Elder warned.

"It's hard to do anything quickly these days. I hate to rush you, but I gotta go *now* or I'm going to miss my flight." Quinn said, distractedly.

"I'll take you from here, Marcus. My fleet of jets will be at your and Theron's disposal. There is more . . . I have already built the school, with everything the Emissaries could possibly need," Grey Elder informed, and Quinn was dumbfounded.

"Built and ready?"

"You forget, Marcus, I've always known what my role would be. I have been preparing for nearly thirteen thousand years."

"Right. Shit . . . I . . . Where is it? Egypt?" Marcus asked, thinking that *he* should have been doing more . . . preparing *somehow*, but he didn't know what he would have done differently.

"Torres del Paine, the cradle of the living Earth's chi."

"South America?"

"Chile. The children are being targeted by dark forces as we speak. I have a secured location. They're vulnerable, and Theron's filming and blogging has made it worse. Those children are in serious danger, and we have to get them to safety as soon as possible. We'll reintegrate them into the world exactly at the right time."

"Danger?"

"There is evil at work that would hope to hold the world in a Dark Age forever."

"Is that possible?" Quinn asked in alarm.

"Anything is possible," Zahn replied.

"We have to get to her! We have to tell her what's going on!" Quinn said, panic rising in him.

"We can go now," Zahn said, opening the door.

As the men exited, an entourage of bodyguards and assistants closed in around them, creating a barrier.

"What if we can't convince the parents of the children that they need to come with us?" Quinn asked, as they walked toward a private hangar.

"I can be pretty persuasive, and parents will almost always do the right thing when they fear for the safety of their children. Look at all of the parents in World War II who put their children on trains to England unaccompanied. Anyway, we can take the parents along, because there's plenty of space and provisions."

"South America?"

"South America. Wait till you see the set-up down there—luxury. It's going to blow your skull. Spared no expense. Everything's under control."

"So tell me again why you need me?" Marcus said, shaking his head in awe.

"You're an Emissary. Having memory makes you even more . . . useful. And let's not forget, you have a lot of influence with Theron."

Quinn snorted doubtfully. "I can't believe her stupid blog put them all in danger. Shit! It was my bloody idea too. Who would hurt a bunch of innocent kids?" he said angrily.

Just as the words were spoken, his mind flashed to the brutal dark rite in the cavern so long ago. He remembered clearly the night when Helghul had been entered by the dark entity. He had often had vivid dreams of the screaming younglings as they were smashed and beaten against the walls of the cave. For nearly thirteen thousand years, the memory had haunted and tortured Marcus. He had relived it countless times. He knew he must get to Theron and gather the children immediately. None of them were safe.

"Wait until Eden finds out that the famous 'Seducer-Producer' has stepped up to fund her movie project and a school," Grey Elder said, smiling and speaking of himself in the third person.

"Unbelievable," Quinn said, as they finally entered the private hangar, where he could see no less than six jets with Zahn's company logo emblazoned on the side. "Thank you," he said, making eye contact and stretching out a hand to shake as they stopped.

"Il destino, Marcus," Zahn said, accepting the hand and clapping him familiarly on the back.

CHAPTER 33

THE NEW MYSTERY SCHOOL

"Can I get you anything, sir?" the blonde flight attendant asked Quinn, her buttons straining against her tight-fitting uniform, her cleavage spilling out the top. He ordered a martini, shaken not stirred, and chuckled to himself while he watched her walk the length of the private jet with a sexy sway.

Quinn's rumpled shirt and scruffy jeans were out of place in the sleek surroundings, but he didn't notice. He was just glad to be in the air, one step closer to Theron and to gathering the Emissaries to safety. He had sent only one cryptic email telling her he was on his way and to stay inside her hotel and off of the Internet until he arrived.

He turned to Zahn. "Nate's a buddy of mine. We've run into each other more than once over these centuries, though of course he doesn't have a clue. He's a huge fan of yours," Quinn said.

"An Emissary?" Grey Elder asked hopefully.

"No, just a very good soul."

"That's all right, we need all the help we can get," Grey Elder said seriously.

Quinn was excited that his lengthy journey was finally coming to an end. "I can't believe you've done all this. It's too good to be true."

Clunk. Quinn regretted saying the words. He didn't want to hear them. Old proverbs were full of true wisdom, and Marcus had learned lifetimes before that when something seemed too good to be true, it always was.

"I saw you together," Zahn said, smiling a flawless, white grin and distracting Quinn from the paranoia that prickled deep in his brain. "You and Aristotle . . . I saw you. I was happy to see you'd found Theron."

"I'm never complete without her," Quinn replied. And his internal voice reminded him that he never *was* without her—that all are One—but he brushed the reminder aside. He wanted Eden both spiritually and physically.

While they traveled, Zahn explained the coming expedition. "There are other Emissaries already in South America, but so far they don't understand their full purpose in this lifetime. They've all been led there under the guise of research and preservation. Only I know their true mission."

All Quinn could think about was his approaching reunion with Theron. He worried that something would prevent them from being together and caught himself. The world was in such a difficult time, and the Crystal Children were in danger. Could he really be thinking about himself at a time like this? He chastised himself for his inadequacy.

Marcus wondered again if he was ever meant to be an Emissary at all. Perhaps he should have been weeded out. If not for Theron urging him to make haste for the boats, he would likely have died in Atitala like so many others. It occurred to him that he was no better, no more worthy than the dark, self-serving, self-centered people he was supposed to be leading to the Light, and he shook his head.

Zahn watched Quinn as he silently squirmed, bearing the weight of his self-recrimination. Quinn's aura was dark violet and brooding, and he was forgetting his divinity and his connection to the Source. Grey Elder had found Quinn in a worse state than he had expected. He was truly an example of the human condition. Despite his absolute certain knowledge that he was spirit and was One with the Universe, he doubted himself and felt a sense of guilty responsibility. He felt a need to be the perfect Emissary and to do . . . more.

Zahn flipped open his cellphone and made calls to proceed with the next steps of their mission as planned. The wheels were in motion.

"You're early," Nate said, as Quinn called up to Eden's room from the hotel lobby.

Not the warm welcome Quinn had hoped for. Nate had held tightly onto his grudge. "Lucky to be here at all," Quinn replied, hoping for more.

"Three-three-three," Nate said, clicking off without another word. He was not happy Quinn was joining them. The cameraman hadn't made the progress with Eden that he had hoped to. At times she had seemed receptive, but then she would retreat from him. He couldn't be sure, but he suspected that if it weren't for Quinn, she would have been his.

The door was cracked when Quinn and Zahn arrived.

"Hello?" Quinn called out, pushing it wider.

"Hey," Nate said from the sofa where he sat typing, his laptop on his knee.

Zahn was surprised to see that Nate hadn't even raised his head.

"Is that all the welcome I get?" Quinn asked, stung by his buddy's coldness. Nate had only perfunctorily responded to Quinn's many emails, but Max hadn't expected this. "I . . . wanna introduce our new benefactor," Quinn said.

Nate looked up in confusion. "Holy shit! The Seducer-Producer!" Nate said, jumping up and dropping his computer to the carpet with a crunch.

"I prefer Zahn, or Ozzie, thanks," Zahn said, shaking Nate's hand and genially bending to pick up Nate's notebook from the floor.

"Holy shit!" Nate repeated, looking at Quinn.

"Yeah, you said that, close your mouth, man," Quinn said, embracing him and giving him a strong clap on the back, trying to infuse Nate with the camaraderie and closeness that he felt for him.

"Where's Eden?" Quinn asked, looking around the room eagerly.

"Market," Nate said smugly, aware that Quinn had, without explanation, instructed her not to leave the hotel. Eden was not good at taking orders, and she had stalked about the small room, thoroughly annoyed, before marching to the market as she had planned before receiving the puzzling email. Nate was happy she hadn't returned yet.

"I got good news, buddy. Zahn's on board for the whole package: distribution, marketing, everything. We have to get the message of the Crystal Children out to the world," said Quinn.

"Why? What do you get out of it?" Nate asked shrewdly, turning to Zahn.

Quinn was surprised by his friend's rudeness, but Zahn answered, unperturbed. "Fair question. The answer is . . . nothing. There's not a thing in it for me."

"Publicity," Nate guessed, his head tilted suspiciously.

"I've got enough of that, thanks," Zahn said, winking and chuckling as he walked toward the window and looked out at the honking traffic madness below.

"Too good to be true," Nate whispered to Quinn, not wanting Zahn to hear. He was wary of the patron's motives, but he didn't want to piss him off either.

"Trust me, Nate, he's one of the good guys. There's more . . . he's made it possible to have a school, to gather the Crystal Children together."

"What? Like summer camp for super-kids or something?" Nate clarified.

"Yeah, something like that," Zahn said, joining the conversation. "Listen, I'm going to give you guys some privacy and time to . . . reconnect. We can meet up later. Nice meeting you, Nate."

"Yeah, cool," Nate said, clearly awestruck, shaking the handsome mogul's hand. "Oh, man, I can't wait to tell Eden, she is going to be blown away!" Nate exclaimed, as the door closed.

"Yeah, I can't wait to see her face. Why isn't she here?" Quinn asked.

"How did this happen?" Nate asked, ignoring the question.

"He's an old friend, and he found me right when we need him most," Quinn said, twisting the truth.

"I can't believe you never mentioned him. Anyone else would have mentioned being friends with Oswald Zahn, at least once in three years!"

"It didn't matter until now," Quinn said simply. *I didn't know until now!* he thought, more accurately.

"I'm a DOP, man! My life is film. It never occurred to you that the Seducer-Producer would be a good contact for me?"

"Well, I haven't seen him in a very long time . . . it's a long story."

"Hey, forget it, dude. No worries. Eden'll be back soon, so why don't you head to *your* room and clean up, and I'll tell her you're here," Nate said bitterly.

"Sorry, Nate," Quinn said sincerely, but his friend did not respond. He simply turned his attention back to the screen once again perched on his knee. Perhaps he hadn't heard. "Zahn's rented us a room up the street at the Empire," Quinn tried.

"I prefer the sofa here. I've gotten used to Eden and Elijah's company."

"They should come too. It's not just for me. Zahn wants us all there."

"Well, I'm sure he's used to getting what he wants."

"Nate. You're going to have to drop this bitter, competitive thing. We're lucky to have him. He's bigger than friggin' Oprah."

"I know perfectly well how big Zahn is, thanks," Nate snapped.

For the first time in many years, Quinn felt a bubbling anger inside himself. He wanted to smack the sarcastic guide across the back of the head. "Smarten up!" Quinn's own father would have quipped irritably in the same circumstances. What had happened to his pal, Amnut? To easygoing Nate? Quinn wanted to mend the gap between them but was unsure how to pacify his friend without promising to deny his love for Theron. That was something he would never do.

"Can we go find Eden?" Quinn said, choosing to ignore his friend's dismissive attitude.

"Naw, no point, we'd never find her in the total chaos of the marketplace. She'd end up back here waiting for us, while we wander around like a couple of tourists."

"We are a couple of tourists," Quinn replied and, as he hoped, Nate cracked a smile. *It might be okay after all*, Quinn thought.

Quinn's cellphone rang. It was Zahn.

"I've got bad news. An Emissary in Lyon was killed last night. She was one of the Crystal Children," Zahn informed.

"In Lyon? How?" Quinn said, his stomach clenching.

"They know it wasn't an accident, that's all they're saying."

"Was it the girl who wrote in different languages? Anjolie?" Quinn asked.

"That's the one," Zahn confirmed.

"Shit, Eden just interviewed her. I'll let her know," Quinn said sadly.

"My planes are waiting. We have to move those kids," Zahn said urgently. "You and Eden have to convince their parents before there are any more victims."

"We can do it. It's 'summer camp for super-kids' hosted by Oswald Zahn. No one will pass that up," Quinn said, using Nate's words, and the younger man winced behind him.

"You get Eden and the kids organized, and I'll have the transports waiting where we need them. Oh, and Quinn! You can't tell them where they're going! It has to be a secret. If that information gets out, they won't be safe anywhere."

"I may need you, I mean, your face, your influence, to get everyone on board," Quinn said.

"Way ahead of you. Our website explains everything and touts the school as the ultimate learning experience. It shows the luxury, the comfort. It doesn't divulge the location, but they'll understand the need for secrecy when *you* explain the threat. You have to tell them they're in danger. Their fear will move them. We'll board my plane in two days and head to South America. We have to get Theron and the other Emissaries to safety."

"She should be back any minute," Quinn said.

"Good. Keep me posted," Zahn said, and they hung up.

Quinn told Nate about the murder of Anjolie the night before. Nate was horrified. He couldn't believe it. Distracted from worrying about what might develop between Eden and Quinn, his jealousy was forgotten.

When Eden finally returned to the hotel, she rushed into Quinn's arms. Theron's energy staggered him, as it always had. He stumbled backward, gripping her tightly.

"Thank God you're finally here in person. We're all together, no more worries!" she exclaimed.

Quinn hated that he would have to worry her again so soon. "I'm so happy to see you. You're beautiful," Quinn complimented, holding her longer than was necessary. His hands were buried in her thick, loose curls, and his skin tingled at her touch. Eden was flooded by the energy that flowed from him.

"There's so much to tell you, I don't know where to start," Quinn began.

"Oswald Zahn brought him in his private plane! He wants to fund our project!" Nate interjected excitedly.

"Is he kidding? Zahn? Holy shit!" she said, looking from one man to the other in disbelief.

"That's just what I said!" Nate said, as she squealed and jumped happily into his waiting embrace.

"There's more," Quinn said, interrupting their reverie.

"More? More than the richest media mogul in the world?" Eden said incredulously.

"He's built a school. A luxury haven for the Crystal Children," Quinn said cautiously, not wanting to be too joyful, knowing the dark news he had yet to impart.

"Oh, Max! Oh my God, it's all too much! Are you serious? Holy shit!" she said, letting go of Nate and hugging Quinn again. "What's wrong? There's something more . . . I can tell there's something you're not telling me. What is it?" she asked, now only inches from his face and staring directly into his eyes.

"The kids are in danger. Serious danger. There has already been a . . . victim. There are people, dark people, who realize the importance of the Crystal Children in the coming days, and they have begun targeting them."

"What? Why? I don't understand," she said, her happiness supplanted by confusion.

Quinn led her to the couch. "The girl in Lyon, Anjolie," he began.

"Is she okay?" Eden interrupted desperately.

Quinn shook his head. "She was murdered, last night. Zahn thinks the Crystal Children are being targeted," he explained.

"Oh my God! Why?"

"Because of their gifts. They have the potential to change the world, and there are people that don't want it to change."

"Who?" Eden and Nate both asked.

"I'm not sure," Quinn replied.

"We have to protect them!" Eden exclaimed. "I have to get Elijah! He's down at the pool. We have to contact the rest of the parents and tell them to keep their kids close and be careful until we figure out what to do!"

"I'll come with you," Quinn said.

Nate scowled, wishing he had spoken first. Eden rushed to leave the room, Quinn right behind her.

"This is a nightmare. It's all been for nothing," Eden said to Quinn as they walked. "We can't release this film. We can't publicize who and where these kids are if it'll put them in danger!"

Quinn placed his arm around her shoulder to comfort her, and their energies soothed one another. "You were meant to do the film. The world will be given hope and direction by these bright lights," he reassured.

"I can't even think about that now . . . poor Anjolie! Her poor parents! We can't endanger anyone else, Max!"

"They're already in danger, that's obvious. Zahn has planes and a secure school prepared. We have to contact all of the Emmis… Crystal Children that we can and convince them, convince their parents, to get to safety."

"They knew it was coming …" Eden said numbly as they opened the doors leading to the hotel pool. "More than one of the kids asked me if I had come to take them away. I thought it was such a strange question, but now I understand . . . they knew this was coming."

"We have to leave as soon as possible. It's a good idea for you, Elijah, and Nate to come back to Zahn's hotel with me. It'll be safer, and he's rented us a beautiful suite with staff, guards, everything."

"We're still packed, it won't take long. I'm going to need more details, Max, this is all so overwhelming. Start again at the beginning and tell me everything," she said.

Just then, Elijah saw her and gave a shout.

CHAPTER 34

HELGHUL RETURNS

Eden interrupted her conversation with Quinn and embraced her soaking wet son.

"What's going on, Mom?" Elijah said in surprise, scrunching his shoulders and patiently waited for her fawning to stop.

Quinn stared at the eleven-year-old boy, unable to move.

"We're going to a new hotel for a couple of days," Eden said, without explaining.

"Why?" the youngster asked, but Eden didn't want to remain poolside. She wanted to get her son to safety.

"Elijah, this is Max Quinn. Max, this is my Elijah," Eden said, standing behind her boy with her hands on his shoulders.

Quinn feigned a friendly smile, desperately trying to hide his horror. Nausea rocked him and bile rose in his throat as he reached out and shook the hand of Helghul.

The skinny eleven-year-old contemplated Quinn carefully and cocked his head to one side. "Do you know me?" the boy asked oddly.

Eden gasped, accustomed to Elijah's strange declarations but surprised all the same.

"Do you know *me*?" Quinn countered.

"I've dreamed you . . . or remembered you . . . I recognize your aura . . . your energy makes me . . . no offense . . . I feel like barfing."

"Elijah! Oh, Max, he just says whatever. Sometimes he doesn't think how it will make other people feel," Eden apologized.

"What? I'm just being honest," Elijah said.

"It's okay . . . no offense taken. I feel a bit like barfing myself," Quinn answered truthfully, and Elijah smiled and snorted in appreciation.

Together they made their way upstairs. Outwardly Quinn maintained his composure, but privately his mind was in utter chaos. His Marcus-brain was spinning with the predicament. Helghul was Theron's son! She would be his unyielding protector in this life, the mother bear! And what would they do now? How could he take Helghul to South America and put him in the center of all of the Emissaries, all of their hope? He had to be eliminated, contained, something! But Quinn had no idea what to do. Grey Elder! Grey Elder would know what to do!

Back in the room, Nate was happy to hear Elijah's opinion of his mom's "creepy" friend, Quinn. Ignoring this, Quinn got the group organized and delivered them to their suite in Zahn's hotel, then left them to go find the Elder.

"Helghul? Here in the hotel, now? Imagine that," Zahn said calmly.

"It's terrible! How can you be so calm?" Quinn said in astonishment.

"Keep your enemies close, Marcus. He is less of a threat if we know who and where he is. I am thrilled we have him in our power."

"You think we can influence him? Turn him?" Quinn asked doubtfully.

"Yin-yang, Marcus. Good is evil, dark is light. They are one and the same. I am sure I can influence him, if I can get close enough. Did he know you?"

"No, not completely, but he knew something. He might remember everything by now."

"We are no longer in the darkest of the Ages, Marcus. It will be getting harder for him to remember and easier for the Light. We may have some time. You'll have to deal with his mother."

"Whaddya mean?"

"Theron doesn't know what he's capable of. Even if she begins to have some memory and recognizes Helghul, she'll never turn on her child. You may need to keep her away from him, neutralize her a bit, so that I can do what needs to be done."

"You wouldn't hurt him?" Quinn said, envisioning Elijah's innocent face.

"He's Helghul, Genghis, Alexander. He's a boy now, Marcus, but as his memory returns he will continue on his path."

"Unless we can turn him . . . there is always choice," Quinn interjected hopefully.

"Leave him to me. I will do everything I can," Grey Elder promised.

Quinn left Grey Elder, more distraught than before.

By the time Quinn returned to her suite, Theron had already made two dozen phone calls. "So far I've contacted fifteen families. They're all on board! They were so easy to convince, even before I told them about Anjolie. It was like they were just waiting for the call."

"They probably were," Quinn said absently, unable to fully enjoy the feel of Theron with the threat of Helghul so close, and worrying how Grey Elder would handle their problem.

"I told them I would call with the details of when and where to meet their flights by tomorrow. Are we really doing this, Max, or is this just another one of my crazy dreams?"

"It's real . . . where's Elijah?" Quinn asked, aware that the suite was free of Helghul's prickly vibrations.

"Gym has a basketball court. He's there with Nate and some of Zahn's bodyguards," she answered distractedly, her ear still to the phone. "I told him and Nate to get out so I could have . . . Hello?" she broke in.

Quinn left her to her phone calls. He departed to his room to gather his thoughts and seek counsel through meditation. Within moments, he had become deathly still and his heart rate dropped to less than fifty beats per minute.

Thirty minutes later Quinn opened his eyes rejuvenated and serene but without further insight. He would have to wait and see what was to come. He would have to trust. Quinn knew better than to fear the unknown. He trusted that things would unfold as they were meant to, but he knew he must be vigilant and connected. He surrounded himself and the hotel room in white light and sent loving energy to the world. He had entered a time of change, and he hoped that the new consciousness would be strong enough to tip the balance.

CHAPTER 35

THE DEAL BREAKER

Zahn expressed his regrets at not being able to travel with the rest of the group to the secret base. Eden and Elijah were disappointed at having missed the opportunity to meet him, but they were assured that he would be waiting at their final destination. Grey Elder and Quinn had agreed that it was better not to alert Helghul to the Elder's presence, unsure what level of recollection the boy had achieved. He hadn't admitted to recognizing Marcus, but Helghul was shrewd. There was no telling what he did or did not recall.

Eden had been stunned by Zahn's influence, affluence, and power as his employees had arranged no less than fifty separate flights to collect groups of Crystal Children and their families. Some of them Eden had only met via email and blog, but all of them were anxious to be a part of Seducer-Producer's gathering. As Zahn had predicted, fear had been a powerful tool of persuasion, though Eden hated having to utilize it.

Only three families that were contacted had refused the offer of protection. They were willing to take their chances. They didn't trust the Hollywood-type at the helm, certain there must be a catch and, of course, there was. Those parents would later regret their choices when, within a week, as had been forewarned, their gifted children disappeared. They were gone from their swimming lessons, driveways, and backyards, all without a trace. The police were unable to find any clues whatsoever. The parents tried to contact Eden for assistance but were unable; she was thousands of miles away by then.

The first flights united a huge group of travelers for a night in Atlanta, Georgia. The Crystal Children and their families were thrilled to meet each other and interacted excitedly, coping with language differences admirably as they enjoyed nachos, pizza, sodas, and beer in the hotel lounge.

Quinn watched Eden and Elijah as they hugged and laughed with almost everyone. It was startling how the pair moved together through the crowd like drapes in a breeze, feeling the energy pushing and pulling them, in unison, from one table to the next.

"They have an amazing connection," Nate said from beside Quinn.

Quinn didn't answer. He didn't trust what he might say. How could he admit his resentment and animosity for the child? He would not be understood. Elijah had likewise begun to avoid him, near but ever separate, like water and oil. It was obvious, as it had been when Eden first introduced them, that their energies repelled one another.

"It's a bit eerie, isn't it? The way they sometimes make exactly the same gesture at the same time," Nate continued, his third beer loosening his tongue.

"What do you think of him, Nate?"

"He's just a kid. He's an unusual kid, smart as hell, you know . . . but I still don't fully *get* it. I haven't really seen him *do* anything *miraculous*. We filmed some pretty great shit for the documentary. He sorta just pales in comparison to some of those other kids."

"Don't underestimate him. There's more to that kid than meets the eye," Quinn said cryptically.

"Whaddya mean?" Nate said, draining his beer and holding up the bottle as a cute, young waitress passed by with a nod.

"I dunno. Just a feeling."

"Sure you're not just jealous?" Nate said, the bitterness returning to his voice.

"Maybe I am," Quinn said disarmingly.

"He just seems . . . a bit too old for his body, to me," Nate replied more kindly.

The waitress delivered another beer for both men. "Where y'all going?" she asked, looking at Nate's funky hair and vest with interest.

"No idea," Nate replied with a grin.

The next day at five a.m. they boarded a Boeing 747, accompanied by an understated squad of private soldiers. The protectors wore simple tan uniforms and, though they were physically intimidating, they were adept at fading into the background when they wished to do so.

Three other similar flights had departed almost simultaneously from other locations. It wasn't until after final takeoff that the passengers were informed that their destination was Torres del Paine, Patagonia, Chile. The students had cheered, but many of the adults remained tentative. Zahn had arranged for comforting video footage of the luxurious accommodations and grounds to be shown during the flight. Along with happy, reassuring music pumping through their headsets, it had worked well to put the passengers at ease.

The groups arrived in waves over several days at a private airstrip in southern Chile. Armed escorts continued to guard the passengers, protecting them from an unspecified outside threat. Upon landing, the passengers were loaded onto air-conditioned buses and shuttled to their final destination.

When their turn came, Elijah sat with Eden, and Nate and Quinn sat directly behind them. Quinn stared at the back of the boy's head, knowing that inside, alive somewhere in that shell, was Helghul *and* the *thing* that had become part of him. In that child lived Helghul's memories, his intentions, and his cruelty.

"Mr. Quinn, don't you have a book?" Elijah said coolly without turning around, obviously aware of Max's eyes on him.

Eden looked up from her own book and glanced back at Quinn apologetically. She nudged Elijah with her arm.

Quinn didn't answer, but he was more uncomfortable than ever. Helghul's energy was heavy and it pressed on him, and he speculated how much Elijah actually remembered.

Out the window there was nothing but nature. Hours of bumpy travel with only vast open skies and bright peaks in the distance. They passed no cities, only one small village, and that had been hours ago. Finally the dusty ride came to a halt as the sun dropped below the deep-red horizon. In the distance, the craggy, pink-tinted mountains of Torres del Paine towered.

"In the twilight, they look like the Eagle Nebula," Eden remarked to Elijah, pointing at the jagged peaks.

"From the Hubble telescope," Quinn interjected from behind.

Eden smiled, looking back at him. "You know the Eagle Nebula?" she said.

Quinn was very familiar with the image—the noticeable "beak" and the black and white duality of a bald eagle. "It's my screensaver. They call it the birthplace of stars," Quinn said. It had reminded him of his faithful golden eagle companion from centuries before when he had been Chilger.

Eden nodded, and a thick ball of loving energy gathered in her throat. Quinn was always surprising her. It was as though he could read her mind.

Nate looked out the window, annoyed that he had no idea what they were talking about.

"Smooth, but I bet your screensaver's really a picture of yourself planting a flag on some mountain somewhere," Elijah scoffed cynically.

Quinn wasn't surprised by the boy's sudden outburst; he had been waiting for Helghul to reveal himself.

"Elijah!" Eden exclaimed. The happy lump in her throat was replaced by embarrassment, just as Elijah had intended.

Elijah didn't know what bothered him about Quinn, but he felt horribly uneasy whenever the man was nearby. Quinn waved off the slight; he understood Helghul's motivation, even if the boy did not.

The multitude of buses stopped in a line and their doors opened. Sleeping passengers woke, and casual conversations were replaced by confused chatter. The passengers were unloaded at the edge of a fire-lit field speckled with a few tan-colored, army-style tents. Even in the evening light it was obvious that this was not the sanctuary that they had been expecting, though they were greeted by four musicians playing happy music next to tables filled with fresh fruit, delicious snacks, and jugs of icy fruit punch. The dusty place looked nothing like the pictures they had been shown.

The Emissaries began to speak loudly.

"We must not be there yet. Is this a stop in between?"

"This isn't what we were shown? What is this?"

"Mama, where's the pool?"

"Where're we supposed to sleep?"

"I thought there were gardens . . . there's nothing here!"

"Is there even electricity?"

"There are not even enough tents."

The multitude of voices whispered over one another while the people helped themselves to the abundant refreshments. The security forces that had accompanied the groups reassuringly ushered people toward one central tent.

Quinn was uneasy. *Why would Grey Elder lie to me?*

The wind chose no direction and whipped at them from every side. Eden removed her sweater from around her hips and put it on, buttoning it closed. The other travelers donned their jackets and shawls. There were torches stuck at angles in the dry soil; their blowing flames flickered across the low scrub brush. The heat had disappeared with the sun and the night had become cold. Stars dotted the sky as the last glow of pink faded in the west.

"This way, line up here," a guard called, competing to be heard over the Latin quartet. The assembly moved toward a plain fifteen-by-fifteen-foot canvas tent. One after another the confused visitors entered, and the line shrank quickly. Impossible. People continued to cross the threshold of the tent, but no one exited, and miraculously the small shelter did not grow full and burst at the seams. One hundred, two hundred—they all filed in, amazed by what they found inside.

Inside the mysterious tent was a large, perfectly square hole in the ground with an open trap door of thick steel. Within the hole was a steep metal stairway with fifteen steps. It was well lit and the walls were dark and earthy. It smelled of soil and moisture, and the Emissaries entered hesitantly, some needing more reassurance and encouragement from the guards.

"It's amazing down there. It's a secure underground facility with everything you could possibly want and more," they promised. "Zahn spared no expense."

The foursome was in the middle of the pack. Nate descended first, followed by Eden, Elijah, and then Quinn. They were anxious to see what awaited them below. *What did I get us into?* Quinn thought, anxious to speak with Zahn.

The tent was certainly more than a tent, that much had already been proved. At the bottom of the steps there was a long, smoothly cut tunnel about seven feet high, lit brightly with electric bulbs. There was a "welcome" sign running six feet in length, and the younger children were excited by the streamers and balloons along the path. The tunnel was at a decline and took the travelers deeper into the cool earth.

At the end of the corridor there was a massive copper door that shone brilliantly, reflecting the light. The guests were stunned as they passed the threshold and it opened into an enormous room. It was modern and glowing, with pale marble floors and walls and a ceiling of the same polished copper. There were so many people—not only the Crystal Children but hundreds of other Emissaries that Grey Elder had brought to Patagonia with his unlimited resources.

Quinn's head was reeling and he watched Elijah suspiciously for any sign of Helghul. The boy stood innocently at Eden's side, wondering aloud with the others. People all around remarked in astonishment and proceeded deeper into the expansive structure, pleased with what they found. It wasn't what they had expected, but it was modern and comfortable all the same.

They were all relieved when they saw Zahn appear through the door with the last of the straggling passengers. The Seducer-Producer, flanked by his massive bodyguards, strolled casually toward the waiting crowd, which was gently moved back by his security barrier. Zahn's tan linen pants and white shirt hung casual and loose. He still wore his Serengeti shades.

Quinn tried to move around the guards toward Zahn but was prevented. "I just need to talk to him," he said in surprise, but the sentries remained silent and impregnable.

"Zahn! Over here," Quinn called through the unyielding flesh barricade.

Zahn's eyes scanned to the left in response. "Ahhh, Quinn!" he purred, as if surprised to see him. At the flick of his perfectly manicured hand, the guards stepped aside.

Quinn looked back at them smugly as he passed. "What is this? Where are we?" he asked. They stood in front of the copper door, separated from the rest of the group by five yards and at least twenty stern-faced men. He wanted a simple, reasonable explanation. He wanted to hear that they were heading somewhere different tomorrow. He wanted to hear absolutely anything except the horrible truth that he had only just realized.

"Haven't you figured it out yet, Marcus?" Grey Elder sneered, and Quinn's stomach constricted. The intuition that he had been struggling to ignore let loose, and he felt a bitter sting as his Marcus-memory fully recognized the familiar feeling of captivity. He felt nauseated and briefly missed the sanctuary of his apartment. His Marcus-brain was feeding him information and explanations that he was loath to accept: he had been deceived. He had led them all into a trap. He had willingly walked down the stairs into his own prison.

"Helghul is *my* creature, Marcus. *I* was in the cavern the night you saw him sacrificed to the Darkness. *I* was the hooded mentor," the Elder hissed menacingly, pausing to allow the monumental declaration to set in.

Quinn pounced—fast, but not fast enough. The veins at his neck were bulging as he strained against the thugs, who easily restrained him on either side.

"You bastard!" he snarled through gritted teeth.

The crowd became agitated as they watched in confusion. Zahn appeared composed and had not even flinched. He neared, within a breath of Quinn's face, and removed his sunglasses. His hollow blue eyes had lost their phony sparkle, and the aura that surrounded him had turned an ominous dark purple as he revealed himself.

"You killed those children? Anjolie?" Quinn accused, referring to the Crystal Child from Lyon who had been murdered. He heard Eden gasp at the accusation, and she tried to break free of the crowd, but the mercenaries barred her way.

The weight of his error was crushing him. Quinn had brought all of these children and Eden and had delivered them to the Darkness! How could they light the world now? Would the Dark Age continue because of his failure?

"What's he saying, what's happening?" Eden and others around her demanded, but Zahn continued to speak only to Quinn.

"I, like you, have lived many lives, and in each I have conspired and manipulated to arrive at this very place. I have carefully planned for this day. In this life I was born to a useless pair of simple people but, as you can see, I rose to power as I always have. Memory and money are wonderful tools. I am proof of the greatness *you* could have aspired to if you had used the power you were given," Grey Elder said in a low voice.

Though Quinn had stopped struggling, the guards continued to dig steely fingers into his flesh. "There's nothing great about you! You're a murderer and you'll be stopped," he said smoothly, determined to keep his emotions hidden. He wouldn't give in to any more outbursts. He didn't want to give Grey Elder the satisfaction nor add to the apprehensive energy growing behind him.

"Stopped by whom? You? A pot-smoking blogger hiding in a dumpy hovel instead of living life? When did you get so *weak*? At what point did the Darkness win and break you down so completely? You were Plato and you have fallen just like Greece, from greatness into ruin. You've had the advantage of memory and have done *nothing* with it. You were so easy to manipulate, Marcus. What a disappointment," Grey Elder taunted, pacing back and forth in front of him.

Marcus refused to be provoked and the Elder continued: "With your and Theron's help, I've found almost every Emissary. You'd like to go back, wouldn't you? Run away with your dear Theron . . . shirk your responsibilities . . . give up on mankind just like I knew you would. She has *always* been your weakness, Marcus."

"What do you want from us?" Quinn demanded.

Eden was afraid, not having understood the bits of the disturbing conversation she had overheard. She wondered who Theron was. Who had always been Quinn's weakness? What lifetimes? The crowd was growing more anxious, and she pulled Elijah closer to her.

"If the Emissaries are here, they can't hinder my progress. You'll be contained and I will have my way in the world."

"The people will surprise you!" Quinn warned. "There are many good, enlightened people and they don't need the Emissaries like they used to. We've done our job. They're learning to connect with spirit and be conscious. You can't stop it."

Zahn laughed and his guards chimed in, though they were ignorant to the meaning of the conversation. "What? Like Nate there? The good soul you told me about who tossed you aside for the slightest bruise to his ego? For jealousy?"

Nate was surprised to hear his name, and he colored, shamefaced, as the truth was spoken. The guards drew their weapons protectively as Zahn's revelations raised panic in the multitude.

"You underestimate people. There *is* unity and compassion," Eden chimed in.

Zahn turned with a sudden jerk and indicated the unsettled crowd. "And they look to *me*! *I* am their idol, the great humanitarian, the Seducer-Producer, the great Oswald Zahn. *I* am their god. Celebrity and money is all they value. You say 'God' and most of the world tunes out. They shut off, or they divide into their religious trenches and prepare for battle! They think God is some imaginary old being sitting on a throne in the clouds, not something inside *them*! It's too late.'

He turned back to Quinn. "You think they've come so far? Look at how broken down *you* were, and you're supposed to be one of the *chosen* ones! Do you really think the rest of them have a chance?" he snapped, flipping his hand toward Quinn in disgust.

"You're wrong," Quinn challenged.

"You know better than anyone about the wonderful drugs . . . legal and illegal . . . the anti-depressants . . . letting them all tune out and feel numb . . . grey . . . no light or dark, just indifferent and apathetic. It makes them ripe for the picking."

"This *is* a time of awakening. There is a collective consciousness emerging. You're afraid or you wouldn't have us here," Eden rebutted.

"The hardship's just begun. I'll fan the flames of their innermost fears. They *will* shed their false cloaks of goodness and light, and scatter like cockroaches to hide themselves in the darkest corners. I will crush every Light-sentient being that walks this Earth, and the Darkness will reign forever," the leader hissed, enunciating every syllable.

Elijah whispered to his mom, and she hugged him tightly.

"Why?" Nate asked simply. Nate, a man without memory or understanding of the higher consciousness, had asked the most important question of all.

"It is my destiny. It is . . . my *role*," Grey Elder answered simply.

"But why?" Nate asked again.

When it was obvious that Grey Elder did not intend to answer, Quinn piped up.

"Because without choice, there is no true goodness. If there is no evil, and therefore no opportunity to choose *between* good and evil, then there is no real good at all. It is the original intention that we all develop and grow *into* the Light by choice, denying the Darkness," Quinn said.

"The strife, the darkest times . . . they wake the soul and can lead to the greatest light," Elijah interjected from where he stood with Eden's arms wrapped around him. His childish voice was high like a lizard's chirp in the night.

Zahn looked at him disapprovingly. It was important that he separate the boy from his mother as soon as possible. "The Emissaries have failed. The Bronze Age will not rise. The Great Darkness will remain," he announced proudly.

"You can't keep us here!" the father of one of the Crystal Children protested, and more joined in.

"This fortress is impregnable. I suggest you prepare for a long stay," Zahn shouted for all to hear.

The frightened group erupted in dissent and tears, but resistance was useless. The intimidating guards shifted their weapons, at attention.

"Bring the boy to me," Zahn ordered, pointing at Elijah.

As a guard took hold of him, Eden punched and howled, all the while clinging to her son. Quinn was still restrained, but Nate and others near them joined the fight.

"Gently now!" Zahn shouted at the guards. He did not wish to injure or offend Helghul.

The melee ended quickly as a gunshot echoed through the air. Soldiers descended upon the unarmed group, pushing people roughly to the hard floor and easily scooping Elijah up.

"NO!" Eden screamed, as they held her back.

Quinn and Nate were unable to intervene. Eden did not relent and continued struggling and shouting.

"MOM!" Elijah wailed hysterically as he was carried like a sack over a beefy shoulder.

Elijah was maneuvered into Seducer-Producer's Range Rover and sandwiched in by guards on either side. Zahn climbed into the front passenger seat and did not look back at the crying boy as they departed.

Quinn was released by his subjugators, and the copper door was slammed and locked. Copper ceiling, solid stone floors and walls—Quinn was powerless to stop Grey Elder. He went to Eden, who was sobbing in Nate's arms. Quinn and Nate held Eden on either side as she continued to sob for her abducted child.

"I'm sorry I got you into this. I trusted him. It's so fucking obvious now. I can't believe I trusted him!" Quinn said, hanging his head.

Eden couldn't register his apology. It didn't make sense. There was nothing anyone could say to console her, but she had so many questions.

"He fooled everyone. The whole world thinks he's a saint or guru or something. He's on the board of half the world's biggest charities," Nate comforted, his injured ego forgotten. "Max, who is he, *really*?" he asked from Eden's other side.

"I should have known better. I should have seen through him. How could I be so naïve after all these lifetimes?" Quinn said miserably, flashing back to the night in the cave, the many dreams about it. It had been there in his memory. Grey Elder had been the cloaked grand master to Helghul on the night of the exodus from Atitala. It had been Grey Elder who had first separated Marcus from Theron, with what Quinn now suspected had been a phony leg injury. How could he have missed it? He had gone back to the dream so many times; was he meant to have seen it? Had he failed? Could he have figured it out? Could he have paid closer attention and prevented this nightmare?

Seducer-Producer had been too good to be true, and Marcus had delivered to him all of the Emissaries. They were innocents, now trapped in some isolated outpost, useless and doomed.

CHAPTER 36

A TRUTH TOLD

Quinn could see the amethyst karmic code surrounding the crowd, and he noticed that their auras joined together and grew thicker and stronger when their energies combined. He hadn't been in the presence of more than two or three Emissaries at one time since leaving Atitala thousands of years earlier. Despite the anger and confusion that the prisoners felt, Marcus sensed that their spirits remained optimistic.

"It will be okay, things aren't so bad here," one kind-faced girl had said brightly, putting her hand on Quinn's shoulder as she passed.

You don't understand, Quinn thought, his cool demeanor strained by the gravity of their predicament. He looked desperately from face to face, searching for understanding and recognition, but there was none.

They were doomed and only he knew it. None of them knew the truth of why they were there or understood how they were alike. They saw the polished marble floors, miles of immaculate hospital-bright hallways, and stainless steel dorm beds and kitchens around them and they remained hopeful. Only Quinn knew for certain that Zahn had collected them like butterflies pinned under glass. They were neutralized and trapped beneath the beautiful remote wilderness.

There were Emissaries from every continent, of every age and color. Zahn had lured them with as many false pretenses as there were people. He had sent out pleas, calls for help, donations, and volunteers. In response, from around the globe doctors, teachers, environmentalists, and artists had flocked to him. The Elder had appealed to their sense of duty and service. He was the Seducer-Producer after all, his persona carried influence, especially among the philanthropic.

Zahn had identified and collected the Emissaries easily, like shiny rocks on a beach. Certainly he may have missed a few, or there were others yet to be reborn, but he was ever vigilant. He was determined to silence them and to withhold their energy from the world.

People sat on modular benches and cubes instead of traditional tables and chairs. It reminded Quinn of a modern university campus. It was amazing that a subterranean world like this could exist, but it did. It must have cost a fortune. Despite having Nate and Eden beside him, Quinn felt desperately alone.

Eden's head was pounding. She was terrified for her son, and in her head she replayed the conversation between Quinn and Zahn. *Murder? Theron? Plots? Ghouls? What had they been saying?* Eden's heart was heavy, and she felt responsible for having led so many of the people around her into danger. What the hell was going on?

"Where's he taken my son?" she demanded, rounding on Quinn. The tiny woman shook. Her throat constricted with emotion.

Quinn hesitated. He didn't know what to say. A few fellow newcomers hovered close by, anxious to hear anything they could, and those who had already been imprisoned there observed the exchange curiously.

"I don't know," Quinn admitted. He watched helplessly as Eden was once again overwhelmed, turning to Nate for support. Quinn ached to console her, but it was not him she had reached for.

After a few minutes Eden's sobs subsided, and Quinn placed a gentle hand on her back. They each felt the powerful tug in the solar plexus, as though the very cores of them were connected. His energy affected her unlike any other. She did not blame Quinn for their predicament.

"What was all that crazy talk? What the fuck is going on?" Nate asked, bewildered, and Eden shuddered, her misery catching in her throat.

"I trusted him. I had no reason to doubt him," Quinn said, but as he spoke the words they felt like a lie. Once again he flashed to the images of the cloaked figure in Atitala, and he wondered if he had always known that it was Grey Elder. Perhaps he had chosen not to see.

"We were all fooled," Eden said with a gulp. She took another deep breath, summoning her inner strength and regaining her composure. Her chestnut hair was wild around her face, and strands were pasted by tears to her cheeks. Her eyes were bloodshot and glowing bright green, and Quinn thought she looked magical. "I'm no good to Elijah crying on the floor. We have to figure out what's happening and find him. Tell us everything you know that we don't."

"I don't know where to begin," Quinn said.

"Start anywhere! Just gimme some answers," she demanded, a leftover sob catching as a hiccup as she spoke. She was standing on her own now, and Nate stood beside her, anxious for Quinn to explain.

Quinn was tired before even beginning. He spoke in low tones, not wanting those eavesdropping nearby to hear. "Eden, this is not the first time that we've met . . . nor is this the first time I have explained this to you. We come from a place long ago where we were chosen. We are Emissaries . . . many of the others here and all of the Crystal Children are Emissaries as well. We are envoys, chosen to bring goodness and hope to the world, to deliver the secret of creation and guide the world back into enlightenment. Like you . . . the rest of these people don't know it."

Eden, and especially Nate, stared at him skeptically, but he had anticipated their disbelief and apprehension.

"Emissaries?" Eden said, repeating the word and remembering Quinn's blog name.

"There are a lot of us," Quinn explained.

"This is impossible . . . I mean, it's too unreal . . . I don't *know* the secret of creation. How can I teach it, if I don't even know it?" she asked doubtfully.

"I've wondered that myself, but you always seem to find a way . . . all of you do . . . you just seem to . . . know."

"Who is Theron?" Eden asked.

Quinn gulped. To hear her say the name was overwhelming. "You . . . it's you. Your name was Theron," he said, and Eden gasped in surprise.

Nate listened carefully, the hair of his neck standing on end. Quinn could see and feel the karmic energy around Eden billowing and exploring as it joined with the many auras united in the room.

"Me? What do you mean?"

"It starts with the soul."

"Oh, here we go," Nate moaned.

"Shhh! Go on, Max, I need to know what all this means if I'm going to find my son," Eden said, frowning at Nate briefly. The tears in her eyes had been replaced by determination. She was collecting information now, building a plan to rescue Elijah. She needed to understand everything that Zahn had said.

"There is an intrinsic essence in each of us that survives our bodies and connects us to one another . . . if you don't believe that, then there is no point telling you anything else," Quinn said, exhausted both from eons of enduring his predicament and by the hopelessness of their situation.

"You know I believe it," she said.

Nate did not claim to accept the idea of a soul, but he listened with new consideration. He wanted to believe.

"Go ahead," Eden urged, gesturing impatiently.

Quinn began to explain. "Our home was called Atitala. There have been many civilizations before ours. They come and go with the cycle of the Great Year. A Golden Age ended about thirteen thousand years ago. We were chosen as Emissaries and given the responsibility of maintaining the Great Light and leaving clues of the ancient knowledge for those who would seek it. Our world shifted dramatically and we were scattered like seeds to the wind. We have been reincarnated many lifetimes, driven by our purpose. There is much Darkness in the world, our Adversaries. I thought Zahn was with the Light—he was an Elder, one of our leaders—but I was wrong. Now the Great Year is due to once more begin its ascent and eventually take us into a Golden Age. Zahn is trying to prevent that."

Eden contemplated him intently. She had read the theories about the twenty-six-thousand-year cycle. It was everywhere: the notion that human history dated back much farther than historians and theologians believed, the belief that the placement of the stars mattered, and that civilizations came and went in cycles. There was even a yearly Conference on Precession and Ancient Knowledge[33] that she had hoped to attend someday.

She looked into Quinn's eyes. There was no guile there, no urgency, no pleading or need to convince her. She saw only patience, weariness, honesty, and longing. With her gaze fixed on him so intently, the ache within him grew like grass being touched by sunlight.

"And who are *we* to each other?" she asked intuitively.

Quinn's eyes changed and became smoky and his lids lowered slightly. Nate grew rigid next to her—the talk about the Light and the Darkness had been confusing, but *this* he understood. The undeniable bond between Quinn and Eden was about to be explained.

"We . . . are *everything*," Quinn rasped, and his aura was deep purple and green, radiating in beats around him. He dared to sweep the hair from her face, and he placed his hand on her cheek. Would she push him away? Would she reject his touch? He couldn't stop himself. To be so near, so close to her, and yet apart was agonizing.

Eden raised her hand, but she did not deny his touch. She placed her fingers over his and shocked both him and Nate by reaching her other hand behind his neck and kissing him. Quinn swept her up into his arms, and they kissed with the passion of centuries of longing. Nate wanted to stop her, but she was Quinn's, and it had been obvious since the beginning. Quinn was euphoric; Eden was overwhelmed. The power of their ancient energies binding together filled them both. Hesitantly, Eden pulled away.

"Why is Elijah separated? Why isn't he here with the rest of us?" she asked.

"Elijah's . . . special," Quinn answered diplomatically, though even in his joy his jaw clenched at the thought of Helghul.

"Special *how*?" Eden asked. Their forearms were locked together, holding one another at the elbow.

"He's powerful, more powerful than most. So are you," Quinn explained.

"Is he in danger?" the mother asked, desperate for reassurance.

"I don't think so. I think Grey Elder will try to use him again," Quinn answered.

"Again?" Nate and Eden echoed simultaneously.

"There've been many lifetimes," Quinn said cryptically.

"I dreamt he was an emperor?" she said.

"He was. They weren't dreams, they were memories. Zahn said your memory could start returning. It's another sign of the Dark Age ending. You probably know more than you think; you've just classified your memories incorrectly. They were past *realities*."

"I've had a recurring dream about the Mongolian plains ever since I met you four months ago," she admitted.

"We were there," Quinn confirmed.

"Egypt?" Nate gasped.

"We knew each other there, but the first time I saw you was in a place called Stone-at-Center," Quinn said.

"So I'm a ..." Nate said, struggling to say the right word.

"Emissary?" Quinn finished for him. "No. All living beings are reincarnated. Most people will sometimes have flashes of memory and recognition, they just don't understand them." Quinn could see Nate's disappointment, so he added, "That doesn't mean you're not important. We *must* be a part of the same soul group," Quinn explained, but Nate was obviously unsatisfied.

Eden jumped in: "So we're . . . soulmates, and my son is some sort of leader, but what now? We're prisoners here? What do we do *now*?" she asked.

"We pray, we meditate, and we wait. The answers will come," Quinn replied.

"Oh, for fuck's sake, really? That is all the wisdom we get . . . just sit and wait?" Nate said in frustration.

"With spiritualism comes trust and acceptance, Nate. Anyway, have you got a better idea?" Quinn said calmly.

"Hard to have a worse one," Nate snorted.

Eden looked at him with compassion and placed her hand on his arm. "He's right, Nate. We just have to wait and ask for guidance. Do you think they know?" she asked, gesturing to the others.

"No."

"Why? Why are *you* the only one who knows?" Nate asked curiously.

"We weren't meant to remember. I took a memory potion and chose a torturous road."

"Why didn't I?" Eden asked.

"You didn't have the opportunity," Marcus said, too simply. "I've searched for you in every lifetime," he told her, stroking her wrist as he spoke.

"Did you find me?"

"Too often, I did not."

"It must be lonely being the only one to remember," she sympathized. "Was it difficult?"

"I traveled my path . . . and I learned that there is no shortcut to enlightenment, even for an Emissary. Separation and loneliness are illusions. We are all One and are therefore all connected . . . always. I just need to remind myself of that when I get lonely."

"Like bubbles in the same glass of champagne?" she suggested.

"Exactly. It is only on this plane that we experience the isolation associated with the false belief that we are independent beings. *That* misapprehension does not exist elsewhere in the Universe. We come into our bodies to feel this, yet many of us spend our entire lives trying to get back to unity and connection," Marcus said.

"You have to tell *them*," Eden said, gesturing to the diverse, multicolored crowd.

"They won't believe me," he answered.

"They need to know. I think this is *why* you took the memory potion. This moment, this time right now is why *you* have memory. It is so you can help us *all* understand."

"Once again you imagine me nobler than I am. I stumbled my way into becoming an Emissary, and I may have doomed all of us with my blindness," Quinn confessed miserably.

"You have to tell them," Nate said sternly.

Quinn and Eden looked at him in surprise.

"Well, they have a right to know . . . to make up their own minds. At least you owe them that. I'm trying, you know. I wanna believe this Oneness thing. I want to think I've been here before and I'll be here again, and that life has some meaning. But it's easy to say, I just wish I *knew* it, *really* felt it, like you two seem to . . . like the monks and nuns and whoever. There's so much faith and I just don't . . . *feel* it."

"You will, eventually," Quinn answered. "It's like building a pyramid—keystones, base, and then one layer at a time until your reach the top. The light is much brighter closer to the top, so it's easier to see it."

"So you're closer to the top than me?" Nate tried to clarify.

"No. You can't compare people like that . . . but I am currently more conscious than you. I'm an Emissary and I have memory . . . there just aren't as many mysteries for me. There are truths that I know absolutely."

"Such as?" Nate asked, intrigued and wanting to be convinced.

"It is not my place to convince you . . . you will come to it on your own, when you're ready."

"Maybe you're supposed to teach me . . . so I can get there quicker. Maybe that's why *I'm* in *your* soul gang."

"Soul group," Quinn corrected.

"Whatever," Nate said impatiently. "Tell me something you know, tell me the mysteries."

"Okay. But you could have found this information anywhere. That's the thing about the mysteries. They are all around us. People just *don't* see or *choose* not to see." Quinn paused, and Nate rolled his hands over one another, gesturing impatiently for him to continue. "When we die our souls recycle back into the Grid . . . think of it like a web of superhighways, but electric current and light, not matter. We are whole and connected, and we know and see totally differently. We see and taste and hear and experience with every part of our spirit, not through limited senses, and it's . . . heaven. Perfection. Words are inadequate."

"I knew it!" Eden said excitedly. "You have to tell *them*."

"What am I going to say? God help me! What should I say?" Quinn said desperately, and instantly an answer came before anyone could say a word. It was a whisper, a silent instinct inside his head. *The truth. Tell them the truth.* "The truth," Quinn whispered.

They stood together, and Quinn called out to the crowd around him.

"People, everyone, I need your attention, please!" he exclaimed, unsure how to proceed. Would they believe him? Would they think he was insane?

The crowd came closer and grew quiet, except for the younger children zooming about. As people grew nearer to one another, their karmic energies grew more brilliant. Quinn waited.

"My name is Maxwell Quinn," he began, "and I have a message for you, a story to share." He paused. There were others echoing his words in whispers to one another, translating from English and trying to make sure everyone understood.

"It's about time!" someone grumbled.

"I suspect that for many of you, in your lives you have felt a sense of urgency, a purpose, a need to do good and to heal others in the world." The crowd around him looked on in anticipation. "This might sound crazy . . . but I'm here to tell you that you are chosen people. Most of you are Emissaries reincarnated into this world as teachers, healers, and messengers. I have just learned . . . too late . . .

that Zahn is a fallen Elder, a dark soul, and he has gathered us here to control and neutralize us . . . to extinguish our Light and to cast the world into Darkness."

The crowd listened intently, stirring with skepticism and emotion. The room was electrified, and Quinn felt the hum of the bonding collective energies as they warmed the air. It was reminiscent of the connections Marcus had experienced in Atitala. He knew that Eden had been correct. Having taken the memory potion was allowing him to play this role. Marcus knew that if he had it to do over again, he would make the same choice.

"But what can we do? How do we get these kids outta here?" a male voice called.

"I'm afraid," a female voice said.

"No way, you're nuts," someone else said.

"How can we make a difference stuck here?" a deep voice intoned.

Quinn had the answers they sought. "We have to try. One thing that I do know is that fear and doubt keep the soul from moving forward and growing and advancing. By being conscious of that, by choosing to face our fears, we can overpower them. We are connected *and* we are spirit. We never stop being spirit. If you believe you have a soul, then you must know that your divinity never leaves you. When we join together with others like us, others who understand the power of Oneness and connection, then we can illuminate the darkness around us. We can affect the vibration of the collective world consciousness."

"But we are here, we're trapped God-knows-where. How can we illuminate anything from here?" a woman asked.

"God-knows-where . . . you said it yourself. It is not on a human, physical level that we must battle . . . we can't beat Zahn that way. Those soldiers and their guns are real. Ours must be a spiritual resistance. Spirit cannot be contained by walls or chains. It crosses an ocean or a continent without a moment's passing. If we recognize that we are One and join in spirit, we may be able to send hope to the world outside these walls, enough positive energy and connection to link with others and make a difference," Quinn answered optimistically.

"The power of prayer," someone added with a smile.

"Yes . . . and unity," Quinn said. "There will be millions of people reaching out spiritually; good people. They, too, will be struggling to abate their fears. As Emissaries we each chose this mission and purpose. We can merge our positive energies with theirs. We can fight against the Great Darkness. Our skin and bones come and go, but we are so much more than that," he finished, with his adrenaline flowing, feeling slightly like a crazy evangelist. He was reminded of his lifetime as Plato and his connection to spirit as Chilger all at once. He looked out at the many faces, and he prepared himself for the arguments and doubts that he knew would certainly come.

"I have to get out of here! I have children, a family! You don't understand, they'll be sick with worry!" one Russian woman near the back called out in despair.

Others chimed in, their concern and fear understandable and essentially human.

"Americans did this!" a Punjabi man near the front said in broken English. "You are one of them. Why should we believe you?" he asked suspiciously.

"We cannot be divided. I know it's shocking, I know it's difficult, but we must trust one another," Quinn answered.

"We can't help anyway!" another exasperated voice intoned.

An African woman near the front spoke up: "It looks like we are here indefinitely, so shouldn't we at least try? Are we better to retreat into despair? Or should we channel our energy and our hope?"

"I prayed for the monks and they were killed just the same. It's a waste of time," a Tibetan woman said softly.

"Many died, but many more *lived*," Quinn answered.

"I don't belong here," an elderly, thickly accented Frenchman spoke up. "I am not one of those . . . those things you talk of. I am a surgeon, I have a practice. There are people who will die, who likely already have. I must get back to Paris. I don't even believe in this soul business . . . when we die, we just die," he said, arching a bushy silver eyebrow.

"Why should we believe you? A strung-out hippy?" an unkind voice called out.

"What could I possibly want from you? I can't make you believe me . . . I can only tell you what I know is true," Quinn answered, more tired than defensive, and buoyed by the tight grip that Eden had on his arm.

"So, Monsieur, tell us . . . why do *you* know? What makes *you* so special?" the old surgeon queried with less sarcasm than Quinn would have expected.

"I am not special, *you* are. I don't think that I am nearly as special as any one of you. I am along for the ride, a hitchhiker you might say. Believe me or don't, I've done what I can. All I ask is that you sit *still*. *Listen* to your own thoughts; they will take you where you need to go if you let them."

" 'And he shall magnify himself in his heart and by peace shall destroy many. He shall stand up against the Prince of Princes, but he shall be broken without hand.' Daniel 8:25![34] The Bible forewarns of this time in the End of Days when God's people will resist without violence and overcome the Great Darkness!" a man wearing the robes of a minister exclaimed.

The crowd was buzzing, mostly with positive energy and hopefulness. There was doubt and fear, but many believed. The karmic energy was building and Quinn could see it all around them. People pondered and contemplated and discussed, and, despite their personal losses and misgivings, a fiery current pulsed through the congregation. It had grown with every word, as Quinn had confirmed for them what many had already known deep inside.

"How do we start?" Eden asked, with a fresh strength in her determined jaw.

Quinn met her direct gaze and was once more electrified by her indigo aura, thick and compelling, mixing with those near her. She looked much younger than her thirty-six years.

Before he could answer, a very young child spoke out from near the front, her aura glowing indigo and tipped with golden light. "We need to come together," the girl said, her innocent voice heard clearly across the large gathering.

"Exactly," replied Marcus, placing a gentle hand on her head.

One by one, some more hesitantly than others, the Emissaries began linking arms.

CHAPTER 37

THE REVELATION

Quinn embraced Eden, and Nate placed his hand on her shoulder. They were soon joined by others, hand to shoulder from the center out in concentric rings, which from above would have resembled a web. The energy surrounding them grew exponentially as more joined them, one hand to one shoulder at a time.

"I hope it helps," the tear-choked voice of the Tibetan woman said softly.

"It won't hurt," someone near her said kindly, placing a reassuring hand on her shoulder.

Quinn placed his forehead to Eden's and was shocked by what happened next.

Zip! At that point in time, facilitated by the powerful energy of the fellow Emissaries, Theron was catapulted into her memories. It was like being sucked skyward in the vortex of a tornado. She gasped at the vivid, colorful show. Her lives became known to her, and the couple rested their heads together with a filmstrip of many lifetimes rolling between them. Theron saw her heart's true love and she spoke his name.

"Marcus," she breathed as they entwined their hands, their foreheads touching, their eyes closed, sharing visions that both could see. Everything around them was forgotten as they came together once more.

You remember? Quinn asked telepathically, in mind pictures. It was his very greatest wish. Not since the brief time in Shambhala had she remembered, and even then it had been fleeting and he had been unable to touch her.

I do! Ohhh, I remember . . . everything, she answered, without speaking, as the stories unfolded without any sense of time passing. All of her memories came alive inside her simultaneously, singing like the multitude of angels in heaven. Many tunes played at once but remained clear, beautiful and distinct from one another, and she knew them intimately.

Quinn knew that it was a gift, and he was overcome with gratitude. In an instant she remembered and felt everything that they had ever been.

She saw that Marcus had located her in Prague just before she was shipped to Theresienstadt. She'd been an elderly grandfather, a Jewish doctor, Ivan Petracov. Of course she hadn't recognized Marcus then. He had been unable to save her. It was only after the war that Marcus had found the record of her murder. There was no gravesite; there was only Ivan Petracov's name on a list.

The vortex spun: another life, making love in a ger. Then Inti, the son of a great woman, and Aristotle, and so many more, with and without Marcus. Nate was there too, and Elijah, always swirling and popping in and out. She saw her soul group and understood it as she had never been able to do before. There were others, some of them huddled in the group around her right now.

Lifetime after lifetime, Theron and Marcus were connected. Sadly, they saw their near misses; when they had been close but unaware of each other. There had been hospital beds in the same building but on different floors, and passing on opposite sides of a marketplace on the same day. Their destinies were beautifully bound together, like a tapestry carefully woven with the finest thread, but they had only found one another when it was intended to be.

Eden was filled with love and gratitude. The vortex slowed and, like a plume of ash settling to the ground after a volcanic eruption, Quinn and Eden returned to themselves. Their recollections no longer forgotten, the couple became once again present. Neither spoke, they just held one another, connecting with all of those around them. They had joined and were sending the world compassion.

Everyone present had had the same experience. The gathering of the Emissaries had produced an unexpected result. Zahn hadn't anticipated this. They had awakened to their souls' past lives. As they had joined hands to shoulders and connected together, they were immersed in memory and knowledge.

The cynical French surgeon had seen himself as Joan of Arc and was privy to her every memory and thought. The young girl who had suggested that they pray had seen her lifetime as Mother Teresa. The other Emissaries: Sir Isaac Newton, Louis Pasteur, Charles Dickens, Mirabai, Pythagoras, Sri Yukteswar, Copernicus, Marie Curie, Leonardo da Vinci, Helen Keller, Edgar Cayce, and so many more, famous and not. They were all there, remembered—swirling magically in the energy and communion of the gathering, and joining in the work yet to be done.

The Emissaries could see their auras and recognize one another. Having come together, they understood completely who and what they were. Even the family members of the Crystal Children felt empowered and more than a little overwhelmed.

Grey Elder was unaware of the vibration rising in the prison bunker and was ignorant to their recollections. He had immediately departed with Helghul to the airport, pleased by how easily Marcus and Theron had been manipulated. The most powerful part of the Emissaries still slept, like a bear hibernating for the winter. He would make certain that spring did not come. His plan was unfolding just as intended.

CHAPTER 38

THE KING OF THE ADVERSARIES

The private jet had been in the air for two hours. Zahn occupied a roomy leather seat across from Elijah, who had not spoken since leaving Torres del Paine.

"You'll have to talk to me eventually. It would be better just to accept that this lifetime is more complicated, so we can move on."

"Where's my mom?" Elijah snapped, folding his arms across his puny chest. Though the boy was angry and afraid, he was drawn to the Seducer-Producer and had remembered glimpses of past lives with him.

"She's safely contained so we can do what needs to be done," Zahn replied, popping an olive into his mouth from the decadent platter in front of them. "Help yourself. They're Niçoise, the very best," he added, chewing while he spoke. Elijah glared at him and looked out the window.

"I'll kill you if you hurt her," he said, and he meant it. Helghul had begun to emerge in flashes, but the boy remained powerless and intimidated by his captor.

"I don't suggest you try that. I have no intention of hurting her. You and I have so much yet to accomplish."

"What am I doing here? Why me?" Elijah asked.

"I think you have some idea, but it doesn't matter. You'll remember soon enough."

"Remember what?"

"That you are special, Helghul. You are the yin to the yang, the King of the Adversaries. With my assistance you will rise up and claim this time for the Great Darkness. Your many lives have led you to this end."

"I am not what you say," Elijah countered, but Zahn smiled and munched a thick slice of bread and Brie.

"Have you ever seen yourself . . . as someone else? Do you have memories that you couldn't have . . . know things you couldn't know?"

"You know I'm a Crystal Child. My skills are no secret," Elijah answered.

"You are far more, Helghul," Zahn assured, and Elijah couldn't help but feel a twinge of self-importance at the comment.

"Why do you call me 'Helghul'?" he asked.

"It was your name, a very long time ago."

"So who were *you*?"

Zahn moved from where he was sitting and took the seat next to Elijah. The boy shifted away, but inwardly he was conflicted. His instincts drew him to the man next to him, despite his having been the reason he had been separated from his mother.

"I was called Grey Elder. You and I have always been allies. When you search your memories you will know the truth of our connection. You have had many lifetimes. You can access them if you try, if you haven't already. It will come easier as you get older, but there is no time to waste anymore. You may remember that your mother is Theron—she's safe. I don't want to pit you against your mother, her destiny is her own. You are meant to lead again, as you have always done. There is more going on inside you than you know."

Elijah suddenly knew that it was all true. He was looking through the eyes of a child but thinking with the mind of a man. His daydreams and his random, strange memories had new meaning for him. "I was happy where I was," he retorted, renouncing the emergent thoughts.

"But there is a far greater destiny awaiting you. As the Great Year turns, the Bronze Age will ascend. You will lose knowledge, power . . . we must not let that happen. We can keep the Darkness alive in the world."

"How?" Elijah asked curiously, his body responding in excitement.

"Chaos, discord, terror—we'll pull the wings off this insect one torturous tug at a time. They'll stare and squirm, wondering who's next, and beg for protection. Watch tomorrow's headlines and you'll see just what *we* are capable of."

Elijah said nothing but nodded. He had been having so many strange dreams in the past few months. They were full of shameful thoughts that he had been unwilling to share with anyone. Zahn seemed to understand. Were they allies after all? The memories bubbled up, and the dreams and daydreams began to make sense. Elijah reached out to the platter, satisfying his empty belly with a large slice of bread and cheese.

The youngster's mind was a pendulum—one moment he was Elijah, and the next he was Helghul, filled with a thirst for power, and aware of centuries of foggy memories and ambitions.

CHAPTER 39

THE NOBU VIRUS

The project did not officially exist. No information about Nobu could be found in any official document, and, until now, no president had ever needed briefing on the program. Only a small handful of high-ranking uniforms, suits, and lab coats had heard of the Nobu Virus, but when they watched it decimate an entire continent, they recognized it immediately.

The airborne contagion had been accidentally discovered by NASA scientists in the late twentieth century under the frozen wasteland of Antarctica. It had lain dormant, isolated beneath the ice, where it should have remained, ever harmless. Video footage had captured the scientists' jubilation at having found live bacteria under such conditions and later had recorded their horrific fate.

Vastly underestimated, the microorganism's ferocity had not been fully appreciated until two full teams had died. Upon contact, the airborne virus tore through the body like fire upon brittle branches. Despite their masks, gloves, and suits, precautions had not been adequate and the scientists had become infected. The symptoms had begun with excruciating internal pain and ended with vomiting blood. Like acid, the virus attacked the linings of the stomach, throat, and nose, as well as fingernail beds and all soft tissue, rapidly eating its way out of its host.

The loss of the first team was officially blamed on a gas leak, and the second team's loved ones were told their plane had crashed into the ocean. No one could know about Nobu; it was too valuable. Scientists had learned from the losses, and with extreme caution they were able to contain the deadly virus and move it to a top-secret location for further study.

Suddenly, the virus surfaced in Australia. The world observed in horror as the gruesome images were scattered across the Internet and television. Within a few short hours of exposure, the victims' tissue and skin boiled and blistered, liquefied from within by the pitiless germ. As the devastation unfolded, the Internet was flooded with footage as terrified Aussies captured images of the shocking scenes, transmitting to the world and begging for help. The virus spread and the reports slowed. There was no one left to tell the tale. More than one amateur correspondent left his or her video rolling as they were devoured and became bloody, unrecognizable corpses. The audience watched as the victims rotted in eerie silence until their batteries ran out.

A Sydney traffic camera captured the image of a toddler in only a diaper, faltering blindly through the streets, trails of blood from his eyes where tears would have been. No parent nearby, the child stumbled into traffic while cars honked and swerved, their panic-stricken drivers also suffering and afraid. The boy was crushed under a tire as the helpless audience looked on.

The infected prayed for death, and it came quickly. The virus progressed at an unprecedented rate; a large adult was dead in less than six hours from start to finish. The suffering was not prolonged. The disease was absolutely fatal. No human or animal had yet survived exposure.

"That cannot happen here! My God, that poor child! What is it? I'd kill myself before I'd die like that!" people across the globe exclaimed from their offices, living rooms, and shacks.

The Emissaries were unaware in their isolation beneath the soil of Chile.

With Elijah at his side, Zahn watched triumphantly from his opulent Egyptian apartment as millions were wiped out in a single day.

"Oh, this footage! We couldn't have hoped for better footage. I love the technology. It makes it all so much easier! Fear and panic will smother the world and maintain the Great Darkness. They'll come eagerly now, seeking protection and promises," Zahn gloated.

"You did this?" Elijah asked, both shocked and impressed.

Grey Elder blinked a slight nod.

"Won't it make them all sympathetic and mournful? Pull together, send aid, and all that?" the boy asked. He looked back at the television as though he were watching a movie rather than gruesome reality. Helghul had filled Elijah so completely that he had little time to feel eleven, little time to *feel* at all. He rarely thought about his mother, Eden, the way he once had. However, his mind often wandered to memories of Theron.

"We will easily sweep away the shattered bits of charity left behind. People are compassionate only until they are threatened, when *their* lives, *their* family, and *their* skin are set to be burned, their sympathy and selflessness leaves them."

Zahn had chosen Australia because it had allowed for containment. He had considered other locations—Hawaii, Hong Kong, New Zealand, Malaysia—but they were all too risky or too small. He wanted to make a big impact, but it was imperative that he maintain control of the volatile bug. He didn't want to wipe out the planet . . . not yet.

Some flights had departed Australia before the threat was known, the people on them unaware of what was happening until they arrived at their destinations, where they were aggressively quarantined for days. Others, who had taken off only shortly after them but had been infected, had crashed mid-ocean when their crews swiftly succumbed to the illness.

Leaders around the globe scrambled to reassure their citizens, with only empty guarantees to offer. None of them knew what had happened or why, but the Americans and British had quickly commanded a quarantine and containment of the infected continent. After that, no planes had left Australian airspace and no boats had left her harbors, though many, large and small, had tried. They had been turned around or blown apart. Either way, the result had been certain death.

The American president had watched in real time like everyone else. He had been moved to a well-guarded, undisclosed location and was preparing to address the American people. Just before he was due to go on air, he received a call from the chairman of the Joint Chiefs of Staff.

"I am going on shortly. I hope you have something to tell me that I can use," the president said, while his hair and make-up people fussed over him. They removed the protective paper that had been guarding his collar from thick face powder as he carefully checked his profile. It was more important than ever that he looked calm and reassured; the dark circles under his eyes must be well camouflaged for the taping.

"I have information Mr. President, but I'm not sure how much you can use on air," the general replied.

The president was intrigued, and he irritably waved away the people buzzing around him. "Go," he commanded, and the room immediately emptied. When the door finally closed, he urged the general to continue.

"The situation in Australia was caused by an ancient virus called Nobu, unknown to the modern world. I don't know how it was released." The general paused, giving the leader a brief moment to comprehend what he was hearing.

"How do you know this? Why haven't I heard of this 'Nooboo' virus?"

"It was accidentally discovered by NASA over a decade ago during a mission to Lake Untersee, Antarctica. It's untraceable. I'm sure I don't have to explain."

"NASA? Then how the hell did it get into the hands of people who would do *this*?"

"No one has taken responsibility for it yet," the general replied.

"Don't give me useless fucking answers I already have!" the president barked angrily.

"There's been a pharmaceutical company working with the virus—top secret—that's all we know."

"Which one, God damn it! Find out who fucked up!" the president shouted.

"We know which one. It's owned by a corporation linked to a friend of yours, Oswald Zahn."

"Ozzie? Good, now we're getting somewhere! Get Oswald Zahn on the other line right away!" the president shouted to his assistant, who heard him through the door. She knew better than to ever venture beyond shouting distance. There were no secrets from Shirley.

"Find out who fucked up, whose plan it was to annihilate half the globe, and why. And don't call me again until you do!" The president clicked off, and threw the cellphone onto the sofa beside him. It bounced and hit the floor with a clunk.

The president made a reassuring address to the American public and the waiting world, imparting no new information. He apologized to the grieving families of the US soldiers who had been stationed, and died, in Australia. He assured public safety. He promised to share information as he received it. He promised to do everything he could for those tourists and others still alive, trapped, in the small scattered towns of the outback. In other words, he lied. The president had no intention of telling anyone what the virus might be until he had a plan to combat it, and he sure as hell wasn't sending any more Americans to Australia without an antidote.

When the lights and the cameras switched off, Shirley was standing in the wings. She rushed to her boss, a phone outstretched. "Zahn," was all she said.

"Ozzie!" the president said jovially, with his best politician smile habitually pasted to his face, despite the caller's inability to see him.

"Mr. President," Zahn said. Helghul listened from beside him, impressed.

"I'm calling about one of your companies . . . they've done some work with a particularly vicious strain of virus."

"I keep my distance from the day to day of my investments. Not my area of expertise. I prefer the starlets and casting couches," he said, chuckling.

"We both know there isn't anything you don't know about your business, Ozzie. I don't care who dropped the ball, which families or influences are behind this. I just need you to look into it and help *my* people out."

"From what I understand, Mr. President, *your* people have already taken over the files . . . the labs and everything else. I got a call an hour ago. I told them to cooperate in every way. I'm just as bewildered and concerned about this as you are."

"We don't want to be next. No doubt the perpetrators are poised to release the virus again. I don't want people out there panicking. It brings out the worst."

"They already are sir, but I'll do everything I can," Zahn declared before he hung up.

"Are you going to help him?" Elijah asked.

"Better," Grey Elder responded, and he began to eagerly dial his phone, setting the next stage of his plan in motion.

Two days later, Zahn's call to the president's private line was immediately answered.

"We have a vaccine. We can prevent what happened in Australia from happening again," Zahn declared.

"Thank God! How soon, how many people? What kind of timeline are we looking at?" the president asked, releasing a breath that felt like it had been held for a week. The deep creases in his forehead eased slightly.

"We can start immediately and keep up production of the vaccine while we expand to less populated areas. I've put all my resources into getting this done as soon as possible."

"How much? What's this going to cost us, Ozzie?"

"Nothing. I'm willing to provide the serum at no expense," Zahn replied.

"To whom? You can't mean to all of America, that would cost . . . millions," the president exclaimed.

"No, sir," Zahn said. "To the entire world, and it'll cost billions."

"It's too good to be true," the president said.

And it was.

CHAPTER 40

HAIL THE SAVIOR

Television and Internet focused on every possible aspect of the chaos surrounding the events in Australia. The topic hijacked regular broadcasts, cycling the devastating home-shot images over and over. People were riveted to the gruesome show, and Grey Elder was elated by the swell in dark, loathsome energy around the globe. The world had tuned in, blogged, and Tweeted, theorizing about the vile pictures coming from down under. Confusion and terror monopolized all modes of communication, and still no one had heard of the Nobu virus or its vaccine.

There were little pockets of Australia's outback that had managed to avoid infection, but the Nobu would eventually find them unless they stayed far from the infected zones. There was no hope of rescue; not even the leaders of the World Health Organization would risk contamination to visit the continent. There were no attempts to enter the region, which was completely cordoned off—the airspace and seaports were guarded by allied air and naval forces. Experts on biological warfare gathered at the nearly empty United Nations building in New

York to confer, but they dared not enter the infected area either. They remained completely stymied by what they had seen from a distance. All around the world fear bubbled and swelled, and Grey Elder let the pot stew.

The name "Nobu" started to emerge, first on the Internet and then eventually on mainstream news channels, intentionally leaked by Zahn. Still, little was known about what Nobu was or how the outbreak had occurred. People speculated and cried out for an explanation. Zahn understood that the unknown caused more chaos and fear than even the nastiest reality, so he offered no more information. He delayed the announcement and onset of vaccination intentionally, reveling in the panic that gripped the world. Everywhere there were rushes to hoard water, supplies, and any variety of flu drug available..

Riots had broken out in many places. At a big-box store in Kentucky, a pharmacist had refused to sell unprescribed malaria antibiotics to frantic customers and three people had died, including a seven-year-old girl who was crushed by a toppled display shelf.

Theories about terrorism abounded but became confused when people wondered why the easygoing Aussies had been attacked, not a more likely target.

"They are all disposable. I have faith in the selfish, fear-driven nature of humankind. They will come like rodents to a feast," Zahn explained to Elijah from their safe haven on the outskirts of Giza. It was dangerous in the ancient city now; violence and unrest had become the norm. The hotels had been ransacked and abandoned.

The American president once again appeared on television, this time to confirm the rumors about the Nobu virus and to announce the offer of humanitarian aid by Oswald Zahn.

"You have to tell the world that it was terrorism and we don't know the perpetrator, Mr. President. They have to know how grave it truly is; no sugar-coating it. People have to fear that it could happen anywhere or they won't agree to be vaccinated. All of the countries, even our enemies, have to be on board. There has to be urgency and full proliferation. We don't want that virus taking hold and mutating on us," Zahn coached over the telephone.

"I can handle it," the president assured. He hung up and cleared his throat, preparing his most convincing Churchill voice.

The countdown began. "Three, two, . . . "

"My fellow Americans and our friends around the world, this is indeed a dark time in history and for humankind. I am here to tell you that what occurred in Australia was not an accident. The innocent people of that unfortunate land were deliberately murdered without provocation, without warning, by the intentional release of the Nobu virus. The United States and our allies are outraged at this horrific and blatant disregard for life," he said predictably, failing to mention NASA's link to the bacteria.

"We still do not know who is responsible for this heinous crime, but we will find them and hold them accountable. I guarantee it. It is imperative that we pull together now. Do not panic.

"An antidote to this syndrome has been produced. American humanitarian Oswald Zahn has rallied his considerable resources in the interest of helping the world. In conjunction with his many charitable organizations and the government of the United States, the vaccine will be made available to everyone, free of charge. No one who chooses to be vaccinated will be denied. This man," he said, pointing to the still picture behind him, "this savior, has come to the aid of his country and the world, and offers the only known protection from this cruel virus."

The feed snapped off and flickered, and suddenly a prerecorded clipping of a composed Zahn took over the world screens. His chiseled, handsome face and voice were blasted in every language across the globe simultaneously. The world watched skeptically, desperate for answers and reassurance.

"I am not a savior," Zahn began pragmatically. "I come in this uncertain time to lead the way *out* of confusion and fear. I am a citizen of the *world*, not of one country. White, black, brown, yellow—it doesn't matter to me. We are all the same underneath our skin and in our hearts. We are all in this together.

"I have made arrangements to make the antidote available in most major cities immediately. We will expand out from there as we are able. It is my hope that each and every one of you will be vaccinated within a month," he said emphatically. "You must each think of yourself and your family now, and do what *you* need to do to survive.

"We don't know who is responsible for this act against humanity, but we can protect ourselves, though it must be done quickly—we have no idea when and where the terrorists could strike again.

"Vaccination will be your choice. The vaccine has no side effects and will only leave a small crescent-shaped scar on the inner wrist. Protected, we can all move forward, unified in this terrifying time of chaos."

The Emissaries, and the other prisoners being held in South America, had no idea what was happening in the world outside their walls. Eden was oblivious that she had inadvertently saved the lives of the Crystal Children she had led to Chile from Brisbane and Sydney. The captives were in awe of their collective energy and memories, and they remained deeply affected as they interacted with one another, now as old friends.

Quinn and Eden had hardly left one another's side since her memory had been restored. Marcus and Theron were reunited, and her love for him was no longer restrained. She couldn't take her eyes off him. How had she not seen it before?

Strangely, Nate had spent a great amount of time running his hands along the smooth walls and floor of the bunker. Finally Quinn questioned him about it.

"There are tunnels under here, I'm sure of it. I remember them. I've been here before," Nate said, pulling Quinn and Eden aside so no one else would hear.

"Why haven't you said anything?" Eden asked.

"Shame, I suppose. I was a German soldier, a Nazi under General Hans Kammler. He brought us here." Nate's memory had been growing stronger every day.

"There is nothing to be ashamed of, Nate. There's no group that is entirely bad or good. You must have had a role to play somehow . . . maybe to have this knowledge to help us now," Quinn suggested.

"What about the tunnels? Where do they lead?" Eden asked.

"Did you ever read *A Journey to the Centre of the Earth*? I think the tunnels are ancient, like Atlantis kind of ancient," Nate said.

"It would make sense if Grey Elder was Kammler. Maybe he started this place way back then and he always planned to come back," Eden offered.

It sounded likely, but Quinn knew the truth. He didn't tell Eden that he had seen for himself that Helghul, not Grey Elder, had been Kammler. In 1939, then a young Czech scientist, Marcus had been forcibly recruited to work on the secret Nazi Bell project by Kammler. The project had used ancient knowledge of gravity-free flight and had depended on Marcus's memory to succeed. Helghul had used Theron's imprisonment in Theresienstadt, a Jewish ghetto, to blackmail him. Even still, when the Nazis had somehow unearthed the necessary atlantium crystal, Marcus had intentionally blown up the Prague installation, thus destroying the Nazi's best chance of winning the war.

"What if it's Shambhala?" Eden suggested, remembering her time as Borte.

"The Nazis searched for Shambhala relentlessly, all based on Nicholas Roerich's book!" Nate exclaimed.

"That's it!" Quinn said. "The underworld of Mother Earth is linked by scores of caverns and tunnels."

"But how do we get to them?" Eden asked.

"I'll guide you," Nate said simply.

Quinn smiled at his old friend. "Of course you will," he said, clapping the guide on the back.

The American president was harshly criticized for supporting Zahn.

"You can't give him so much power and influence! We're American, dammit, the world expects us to lead!" bellowed a heavy-set senator in frustration.

"He has the antidote! I have no doubt that without him we'll be the next continent of corpses!" the president countered.

"Did you ever think that maybe *he* was responsible for the outbreak?" the politician boomed.

"Why? To what end? He isn't even charging for the vaccine! If he was benefiting somehow, making billions, I might think you're onto something," the president argued.

"They're touting him as some kind of savior! Did you read the *Washington Post* and the *New York Times* today? 'A saint,' they said. They'd crown him fucking king of the world if they could!"

"We need him," the president argued.

"We have access to the best scientists and doctors in the world. We can find our own antidote," the senator continued to rage.

"How long will that take? How much money will it cost? Are you willing to risk lives? Your wife and daughter's? I'm not. My ego can stand down and let him pay the bill. If you haven't noticed, our economy is already on the brink of collapse. Popsicle sticks hold the fucker together. We couldn't afford to vaccinate Oregon, let alone the planet!"

"How can *he*?"

"That's his problem," the president retorted.

"So if he didn't unleash this virus, who did, and why?" the senator asked for the thousandth time.

"I've thought of nothing else since it happened. I've been hoping for a note, a sign, someone taking credit. Nothing! Did you ever wonder . . . maybe the nut jobs are right? Is it fucking Revelations? You go to church on Sunday. You've read the Bible. My wife read me a quote last night, from the book of Zechariah. It says something about 'flesh consuming away while we stand on our feet, eyes and tongues consumed in their holes.'"[35]

"Armageddon? Are you serious? You think it's the end of the world?" the man asked, stunned.

"All I know is our people are running scared and they *need* a savior right now. Zahn fits the bill! The economy is in total collapse. We cannot fight a war against an invisible enemy! He's offered his help and I'm happy to take it!" the president shouted, grateful for the outlet of emotion.

"At what cost?" his cohort asked simply.

"I don't know," the president breathed, resigned to their helplessness. "Time will tell."

"If it is Revelations, we're in bed with the Devil."

"If I had a nickel for every time I've been called the Antichrist, I could afford to vaccinate the goddamn planet myself," the president said. "And remember this. If Zahn *is* responsible for Australia, then he *has* the virus and he's prepared to *use* it. *That* is not an enemy I want to make."

Across the Atlantic, half a day away, the British prime minister was involved in a strikingly similar conference call with the leaders of Germany, France, and Belgium. They had agreed to the vaccinations but felt less than grateful.

"It's goddamn Revelations, for Christ's sake! What're we supposed to do?" the British leader moaned, exhausted.

"If you truly believe that, I suggest you rethink your expletives," the leader of Belgium advised wryly over the speakerphone.

"Bloody hell!" the Brit said, running his hands through his thinning hair and gulping his Scotch.

"That's better," the German chancellor interjected. "Now what are we going to do about this mess?"

CHAPTER 41

FREE WILL

After Zahn's broadcast, people around the world responded with desperation and panic. They had naively hoped that Australia was an anomaly. They had hoped that they were safe in their distant lands. Many were anxious to get vaccinated as soon as possible, while others were unconvinced.

Grey Elder's campaign for mass vaccination had been prepared well in advance, and he was busy putting the plan into motion. He was interfacing with both the cooperative and uncooperative leaders of the world.

The Chinese head of state had refused Zahn's offer of protection. Before his refusal became public, he died of what was officially recorded as a heart attack. He was actually poisoned by his second in command, who then assumed the leadership and willingly agreed to allow the vaccinations to begin. His life was spared and his bank account was buoyed. More than a billion Chinese would be given the option of survival through inoculation. Like people across the entire planet, each individual would have to choose for themselves.

There were other leaders who resisted, and Zahn surreptitiously bought his way into many unwilling countries: North Korea, Iran, Pakistan, and more. His wealth and power seemed endless, and the leaders were bribed and threatened as necessary. No one wanted their country to be the next Nobu graveyard.

Clinics were set up in hospitals, schools, churches, synagogues, mosques, and town halls. Immunizations were quick and virtually painless. The individual's identity was recorded, the left hand was placed face up, there was a quick pinch-click to the inner wrist, the serum was injected, and vaccination was complete. Only a crescent-shaped mark remained. The individual was now free from fear of the virus.

Millions lined up to be marked, some tentative and some relieved. By car, train, donkey, camel, and foot people came and waited, sometimes for hours or days. They had come willingly to receive the vaccination. They had made their choice. Some felt no difference, but others wandered away staring at the scar on their skin, feeling that something profound had occurred. In some cases, a heaviness descended over those who had complied. Could there have been something more to the vaccine, an undeclared side effect? Sometimes they regretted their decision, but it was not a choice that could be undone.

"I take it back!" one wild-eyed mother exclaimed outside a clinic in the streets of São Paulo, Brazil. In the air, she held up her hand and the wrist of her crying infant. The child bobbled at her fleshy hip, jostled by her dismay. "I should not have done it! I marked my child! I sold our souls to the Devil! Walk away, mothers. Walk away, people. I feel my blood polluted and changed! It is our power that we hand over!" she shouted and wailed in rapid Portuguese, begging others to resist and rubbing at the immoveable mark until it bled.

Some did walk away, but most stayed and averted their eyes. Even the majority of those who had left returned later and were likewise marked. They felt the snap-click of the vaccination, and for a few that was all—the simple prick and blemish. However, for the majority, stating their name and choosing to be stamped disturbed them beyond their expectations. The finality and permanence of the imprint was troubling. The alternative was much worse, wasn't it? What else could they do? Parents, caregivers, breadwinners—how could they stand against this disease unprotected?

It didn't make any sense, yet people refused. En masse, publicly, and privately, millions of individuals and groups made solemn oaths denouncing the inoculation and refusing to be marked, prepared to live or die with the consequences.

Over the next few weeks Zahn's immunization initiative monopolized world news. Families were torn apart by the dilemma of whether or not to proceed with the vaccinations. The whole world was dividing into friend and family groups.

"How do we know they're not going to poison us with the injections?" people wondered fearfully. "Maybe it's a plot, population control …"

"He's American. The Americans are behind it all; we can't trust him. They are trying to control the world," a million voices cried, in dozens of languages.

"He's a saint."

"It will turn us into zombies or robots!"

"It's just like in the Bible! The mark of the beast!" others cried, terrified.

"I'd rather die," some exclaimed bravely.

"I must be first in line!" others schemed.

The pope, who had gone into hiding, broadcast via the Internet from a secret location. He called upon people of all races and religions to unite. "We are all One. Christian, Muslim, Jew. There is no separation. In this time of darkness, renounce the false prophet and do not be marked! It has been foretold that a beast will come with falseness, cloaked in charm and guile. Do not be fooled! God will protect and reward the brave. Heaven awaits. There is a far better place than this," he promised.

Holy leaders from around the world continued to argue both for and against vaccination. The pope was called both a saint and the Antichrist by different sides, and the debate raged on the Internet, in the streets, in bars, and in private homes.

Whatever the response, there was panic and discord that fed the dark souls of the world, strengthening their energy and pleasing Grey Elder. Crime was at an all-time high, especially violent crime. There was a noticeable undercurrent everywhere, like the energy of a packed house on fight night after the main event. The crowds were keyed up, their adrenaline and testosterone pumping. Gangs roamed neighborhoods looking for trouble. The innocent and weak were afraid to leave their homes except to work, and most avoided the streets, especially after nightfall. Neighbors didn't nod and smile at strangers, afraid of who might take exception. Riots and uprising around the globe continued to escalate.

Merchants preyed on the fears of the people, selling weapons and pepper spray by the boatload. Advertisements for alarms, armaments, and self-defense products screamed from the televisions and radios with dire warnings and prophecies. Fear-mongering drug companies infiltrated the collective psyche of the population with rumors, comprehensive advertising campaigns, and Internet blitzes. They recommended bogus antidotes and prescriptions and warned of inevitable shortages. They claimed that children would be the first victims, and terrified, vulnerable parents hoarded supplies, turning their homes into bunkers. All for money, money, money.

Headlines and rumors warned the population to comply and be vaccinated.

"The Unvaccinated May Be Carriers!"

"Non-Compliance Leads Virus To Mutate!"

"Absolute Compliance Is the Only Protection"

"Failure To Vaccinate Endangers All"

"Earthquakes Caused Nobu Outbreak"

No one was safe, but despite the fear-mongering and regardless of the threat, many continued to refuse the injection. They congregated anywhere, despite the risk of repercussions and exposure. Where they gathered there was hope and resistance. It ballooned exponentially around them, and the positive energy was delivered to the chakras of the world like a salve. The resistance was peaceful, but it helped. They joined hands and prayed or wished for or imagined better days, and that positive energy mushroomed.

"Imagine our prayer is a living, breathing entity," one of the many wise spiritualists preached from a dim basement. "Millions of particles like clouds are channeled by your thoughts and can heal this broken planet. That is the power of prayer. Together we can neutralize the growing shadows around us. One point of light can illuminate vast pockets of darkness."

"Join together, send forth your love and hope to the world, and in doing so, we can rise up," an evangelist called to his congregation.

The Internet was like a vein of power and defiance. It offered the isolated and afraid an outlet and a community. Knowledge was shared, and the conspiracy theorists gained influence, identifying Zahn as a corrupt megalomaniac and naming his conspirators and cronies.

People dared to hope. They couldn't have known how much it helped, how their optimism and hopefulness cut ribbons through the inky darkness.

It had been six weeks since the destruction of Australia, and the vaccinations had been extensive. Zahn and Elijah remained in Egypt near the Great Pyramid, observing the chaos that had enveloped the world and constantly fueling it.

"Will we get vaccinated?" Elijah asked.

"There's no need. There *is* no vaccine. It's a placebo. If the virus is uncontained we're all dead," Zahn replied.

"What? I don't understand. Why bother with it all? You've spent so much money!"

"The vaccine has fueled people's fear and divided them. If they had been given an absolute death sentence, people would have found camaraderie. When there is no hope there is peace and resignation. We gave them something to cling to and the uncertainty of what may come. In doing so, we have caused absolute chaos. We have torn apart families, communities, and countries and filled them all with fear and doubt."

"*And* they call you the savior," Elijah added shrewdly.

The Emissaries remained securely detained within the solid walls of the bunker.

Populations in the sacred sites of the world swelled as people left their homes and jobs on pilgrimages. Rome, Mecca, and Jerusalem had all become dangerously unstable. Yet people continued to gather in prayer. There was a movement of humans throughout the globe as they joined, hopeful and determined. Families were torn apart as travelers began to make their way to Mount Sinai, Giza, Chichen Itza, Stonehenge, Delos, Croagh Patrick, Emei Shan, Song Shan, Tikal, Borobudur, the Temple Mount, Teotihuacan, Angkor, and on and on. In America they congregated on the mountains, in the forests, in deserts, in the cornfields, near streams, or anywhere spirit was felt. The energy of the Earth—what Plato had referred to as anima mundi—vibrated, and the collective consciousness heard and responded.

Zahn regarded the pilgrims with disdain. If he had his way, they would suffer extended torment beyond the brief agony that Nobu would have brought them. Grey Elder's thoughts were interrupted.

"Where is Theron now?" Elijah asked. It had been weeks since he had mentioned his mother at all. In the presence of Grey Elder, and with his constant urgings, Helghul's memory had grown clearer by the day.

Zahn had shared most of his plans with the boy, though he had saved the finale for himself. "They remain in South America, neutralized," he said.

"Unharmed?" Elijah asked.

"Is it possible you still care for Theron above others, even when she has consistently chosen Marcus over you?" Grey Elder goaded.

"She has been both a thorn and an aid to me. I have used her like a useful tool."

"It would be better not to think of her at all. Think of Marcus instead. Think of Quinn once again supplanting *you* as the love of her life, and let that anger stir and fortify you. He is her soulmate, the masculine to her feminine. You are the yin to his yang. It is as it should be."

"And you. What am I to you? I have done nothing since you brought me here except eat like a dog at your table. What purpose does it serve to have me listening to your sermons day and night if you do not let me *do* anything?"

"It will soon be clear. I do not take you for granted. You are a powerful ally, and when the time is right, it is *you* who will stand on the slab and pronounce our victory," Zahn promised, appealing to the boy's ego.

Elijah was placated . . . for now. He longed to join the noise and bedlam of the Egyptian streets. He wished to be amid the chaos and feel the hot wind of the garbage fires on his face. He craved excitement and was tired of living in his memories. Helghul was anxious to realize his purpose and role in this lifetime.

"Tomorrow we will reclaim your treasure," Grey Elder said cryptically.

"Treasure?"

"We will retrieve the Emerald Tablet," the mentor replied.

"How? It is lost to me. I have sought it in many lifetimes since last I laid it in hiding, but others have moved it."

"It was I who last found it. All is as it should be."

"You know where it is?" Elijah asked eagerly.

"Tomorrow," Grey Elder replied, and he left the room for the night.

Elijah was alone and, as he thought about the Emerald Tablet, he once again become engrossed in the film strip of his past lives.

CHAPTER 42

THE RETURN OF THE EMERALD TABLET

Zahn's plane touched down in Alexandria one hour before sunset. Elijah was thrilled to return to the city that he had built and that had been named for him so many centuries before. Helghul felt the power of his life as Alexander the Great surging through him. He filled with recollections, though the city little resembled the perfect specimen he had once designed.

"The site of the old library? Is that where you've hidden it?" Elijah guessed.

Zahn smiled mysteriously but chose not to answer. The men were dressed in the robes of the local lower class in an attempt to avoid attention. They did not want to stand out. Zahn easily managed the black sports bag he had been toting since their flight as they hailed a public taxi to the harbor. The sky was fading into evening when they found the fishing boat that had been tied to the pier, waiting for them. It was nothing special, a filthy little skiff. As Zahn dismissed the driver, Elijah was concerned.

"Why this one? It looks like it's about to sink," Elijah said, scanning the docks, his nose wrinkled, disgusted by the sour smell. He saw no less than ten better-looking options in the immediate vicinity.

"We want to blend in," Grey Elder responded, dropping his baggage aboard.

The boat was adequate for their needs, and Grey Elder untied and cast off. Elijah steadied himself on a bare wooden seat, avoiding a dive tank and a tangle of smelly, worn nets at his feet. He prepared for a long, bumpy ride. He was startled when the choppy engine cut after only a few minutes, still well within the harbor.

"I don't understand? It's *here*?" Elijah said incredulously, as Zahn dropped the anchor. He knew that in his life as Alexander, where they floated now had not even been covered by the sea.

Zahn removed his robe and shoes and revealed a thin wetsuit underneath. He pulled a mask, flippers, mouthpiece, and headlamp from his bag.

"Why here, with so many people around?" Elijah asked, as Zahn quickly attached his mouthpiece to the regulator and adjusted the tank at Elijah's feet.

"It's murky and there's a strong current. Directly below us is the original lighthouse of Alexandria. It's well hidden, but if anyone were to get close to the Emerald Tablet the water's natural phosphorescence would mask the glow. Here," he said, handing the boy a nine-millimeter handgun. "It's loaded. If anyone comes near, shoot. No hesitation, no questions. Dead."

"Dead," Helghul repeated, turning the heavy pistol over in his hands.

Zahn dropped backwards into the cloudy water, and his light disappeared below the chop. Elijah had plenty of time for contemplation. Five minutes passed, ten, fifteen—the sun set, red and orange fire on the horizon, and darkness descended. Elijah began to panic, relying on his Helghul-brain to remain calm. Boaters passed closely by, too self-absorbed and rushed to bother with the straggling skiff. Helghul cradled the gun in his lap.

If Zahn drowned he didn't know what he would do, where he would go, or how. He was on his own in a foreign city, and though he was Helghul on the inside, he was a skinny, penniless American boy on the outside. *At least I have a gun*, he thought. Then he began to wonder if he could find Theron. Could he trust her now? Could she be manipulated to help him rise to power once again?

After twenty minutes the boy wondered if the harsh current had taken Grey Elder. He searched for bubbles on the dark surface but saw none. Elijah's alarm had peaked just as he noticed a green glow rising from deep below. He helped Zahn with the load on his shoulder.

On first contact, the charge of the stone surged through him with a million vibrations. The Emerald Tablet was wide and flat with smooth, polished edges and raised, bas-relief lettering on one side. It weighed about twenty-two pounds and glowed a brilliant luminescent green. Elijah's heart was thumping, and he felt the energy emanating from the atlantium crystal. It had been so long, but the magic of the object had not waned. Helghul saw himself in Atitala, then as Katari, Genghis, Alexander, and so many other brick-and-mortar lives.

Elijah rested the edge of the tablet on the hull to manage the weight, tipping the boat slightly. The boy held on to it tightly, feeling his bones vibrating against his skin. Once the tablet was safely on board, Zahn passed up his dive tank and climbed out of the water. He placed the precious tablet in a thin, solid gold box that had been hidden in his bag.

Ninety minutes later, Zahn reclined comfortably with Elijah on his jet, heading back to Giza, enjoying snacks and sodas. The gold box was on the floor at their feet. Even though it was concealed in the sports bag, the tablet electrified the air around them.

"What now?" Elijah asked, when the flight attendant had been sent away.

"Soon we will use the Emerald Tablet to ensure the extension of the Dark Age."

"Use it? How?"

"The pyramids serve many purposes. They are much more than just symbols. Remember how they glowed in Atitala? They read and transmitted energy. At the end of the last Golden Age, the Emerald Tablet was removed from its place in the Grand Pyramid of Atitala. The tablet reads the collective consciousness of the world and magnifies it.

"The Great Pyramid of Giza is a resonator. When the tablet is placed in the Great Pyramid, consciousness will be converted into energy. The despair and panic that we have so carefully orchestrated will be amplified and sent into the Universe. We will stop the ascension to a higher Age and strengthen this time of the Great Darkness. The pyramid was not meant to be restarted until the dawn of the Golden Age. But we have memory. We took the potion. We have the knowledge to make it happen now and to amplify the Darkness instead of the Light," Grey Elder explained.

"What about the Emissaries?" Elijah asked.

Zahn searched the boy's face watchfully. "Are you Helghul, asking about your enemies, or a boy, asking about his *mommy*?" Zahn sniped. He didn't wait for an answer. He raised his cellphone and began making a call. Elijah had been dismissed.

For a moment Helghul's thirst for power wavered. He felt a desire to see his mother and to protect her. He remembered a simple day in his life as Elijah, at her side, interviewing Crystal Children and being one of them, feeling love and connection. He thought of his hand safely in hers as they laughed at Nate singing from the vehicle's driver seat . . . but that was before . . . before he knew what he really was. The innocent, childish part of him had been overcome, and the inky darkness that warped his soul flooded him once more and overwhelmed the child he might have been.

CHAPTER 43

THE EMISSARIES UNITE

"Sir, it's the prisoners," the guard said, in Spanish.

"What is it?" the stout man said. The creamy sauce from his dinner had gotten stuck in his moustache, and at any other time his cohort would have laughed.

"The prisoners haven't been eating or drinking and . . ."

"A protest?"

"No sir, there's more. We wouldn't have noticed, but when Eduardo put his guitar down next to the fire . . . well . . . it kept playing. The ground was vibrating so much that the strings . . . sang," he said, searching for words.

Full from his meal, the stocky boss heaved himself out of his comfortable chair. "I didn't feel anything. It's not vibrating now," the captain reassured. He was not the superstitious type. Ghost stories would not get the best of *him*.

"But it is. Listen," the nervous guard said, and sure enough the twang of the open notes could be heard. The guitar lay on the ground, abandoned, and five armed killers stood staring fearfully from a distance.

"Maybe a small avalanche? Prepare to go below!" the leader ordered.

It had been Zahn's directive that none of the captives be harmed unless it was absolutely necessary. The prisoners had been no threat, no problem, and the guards had paid little attention to them.

They hadn't counted on what they would see when they entered the bunker.

Seven hours earlier, Eden, Quinn, Nate, and six of the other Emissaries had slipped the bonds of their captives unnoticed. The runaways had no idea that as they contended with their own troubles beyond the bunker, the guards were raiding the prison they had left behind.

As promised, Nate had somehow found the location of the gateway. He had been certain he was standing at the place where it once had been, though the ground and walls on the southern corner of the holding area had shown no sign of ingress. The foundation was solid. There was no hollow reverberation, no loose stone, no hint of a possible exit.

One of the Crystal Children, a four-year-old girl with blonde curls and a yellow T-shirt, had moved toward the confounded threesome and begun singing. It was then that their eyes had perceived a slight change in the wall.

The child hadn't learned the strange hum, she had simply known it. In her crib as a baby it had first come to her, and year by year it came more clearly.

The girl had been drawn to the corner, and as she had sung—without words, only clear, melodious notes—something amazing had happened. She was joined by five other Crystal Children of varying ages, and they had united in her unusual song. As they had sung, the wall before them had begun to move. The smooth, polished stone of the barrier had divided and shifted, like a bird rustling its feathers and opening to take flight. The partition had shaken and, as the dust settled, an archway and tunnel had become visible—but not to everyone.

"I knew it was here!" Nate had hooted happily.

"It's miraculous," Eden had marveled.

"It must have been here all along, we just couldn't see," Quinn had answered.

The six young Crystal Children had continued their song, and before anyone could stop them, the fearless little ones had entered the darkness. Eden had hesitated to follow and had looked to Quinn for counsel.

Meanwhile, life in the large room had continued unchanged. The Emissaries and other captives had remained completely oblivious, grouped in various stages of meditation, prayer, conversation, and rest.

Eden was shocked that other people did not seen the gaping portal. "But they're all Emissaries, why don't they see? Surely we're all meant to escape from here," she had proclaimed, staring at the archway and worried for the young ones who had already entered.

"It is not their course, and it is not for us to decide. There must be a reason so few are at a frequency to see this gateway," Quinn had surmised. "Who opened this portal when you were last here, Nate? Do you remember?"

"I don't know. I recall a tangle of paths, like the roots of an ancient tree. I think we have a long journey ahead of us."

"We can't just leave the others behind. We can't just disappear! What if Elijah's brought here?" Eden had said, horrified at the prospect of abandoning the Crystal Children she had innocently helped to lure there.

"Elijah won't be coming here, Eden, *that* I can guarantee. Helghul is far too important to Grey Eld..."

"Don't call him that! I know what you think, I know who he's been . . . but he's my son! He's my *baby* and I won't give up on him as long as I have breath left in *this* body! Not as long as *I am his mother!*"

"Of course you won't and I won't either," Quinn had promised, taking her shaking body into his arms. "I *do* understand the love of a mother for her child. As you've told me many times, there is always choice . . . we can hope . . . we can help Elijah choose the Light," Quinn soothed. "But first, we have to find him."

"You think this leads to my son?" Eden had asked, her eyes flashing toward the wall.

"I think it opened to us for a reason, and Hel . . . your son is as good a reason as any."

Nate, who had been silently listening to the pair, had interjected urgently, "We need to go quickly. The children are gone and this passage could disappear any second."

"Not yet. Come help me," Quinn had said.

For weeks he had been teaching the secrets of the Unity Grid to the captives, just as he had once taught the children in Atitala. When the portal had opened, he had immediately recognized that the time for the joining had come.

Once gathered, the group had built their human web, conjuring the kaleidoscope of colors and energy in the air above them, just below the copper ceiling. It hadn't taken long. The Emissaries' powers had grown intense. By the time Eden, Nate, and Quinn passed through the portal, the Unity Grid had been in youthful bloom in the air above the peaceful Emissaries. The Emissaries were doing their part.

Once Quinn, Nate, and Eden had passed through the portal, the stone wall had sealed itself behind them. Turning back was not an option. The six Crystal Children had disappeared deep within, but there was nothing to fear in the tunnels of Shambhala; or was there?

CHAPTER 44

A DIFFICULT PATH

Once the gateway disappeared, they saw that the walls of the tunnels were lit by glowing crystals.

Nate directed them forward. "This way, I think," he said uncertainly, as the paths split from two into three, then five, then eight.

"Where will we come out?" Eden asked, feeling simultaneously hesitant and exhilarated.

"I'm as lost as you are, but I keep thinking of Egypt . . . I know how crazy that sounds," Nate replied.

"More crazy than doors appearing and disappearing? I think these tunnels lead everywhere. You were right, Nate. They're like the roots of the world. We need to use our intuition and believe we will end up where we are meant to," Quinn said.

"We don't know where we're meant to be!" Nate protested. "I'm not sure what I got us into."

The threesome didn't speak again for a few minutes as they proceeded through the passage. Eden screamed just as Nate turned to speak again. Before anyone knew what was happening, she fell. A gap had suddenly opened up in the floor between them and, with a gust of wind, she dropped into it. The tips of Eden's hair brushed through Quinn's outstretched fingers as she disappeared. He tried to follow her, but the floor closed up as magically as it had opened, and his knees and elbows slammed violently against solid stone as he dove after her.

"Theron!" he cried in anguish, his legs smarting from the impact.

Nate stared in disbelief. "Oh my God! What's going on? What's happening?"

"Theron," Quinn whimpered, his forehead pressed against the solid ground.

Nate paced back and forth around his splayed companion. "There must be a trigger," he supposed, doubling back, over and over.

Desperately searching, Quinn ran his hands frantically along the smooth floor.

After about ten minutes of panic and pacing, Nate finally spoke again. "We have to keep moving," he nervously counseled.

"I promised I'd never leave her," Quinn said miserably. "Why does this always happen?"

"I don't know, man, but she's not coming back the way she left. We can't just sit here, we have to go on."

"You're right. I know you're right," Quinn said desolately, getting to his feet.

"Do you hear that?" Nate asked nervously. A low grumble had become audible. "Earthquake?" he guessed.

Quinn knew better. "We gotta move! We could be in trouble," he said.

The path continued to wind and twist, and Nate led the way.

"Just follow your gut. There's a reason you're here, Nate, a reason you are always there to guide me. I need you to believe in yourself," Quinn assured. The grumbling had grown significantly louder, and it was clear now that it was a growl. It was the deep, resonating snarl of a large creature. "We need to get as far away from here as possible."

"Or as close," Nate countered bravely. "Maybe they're trying to scare us away from something, a passage that we need to take. As much as I hate to admit it, my instincts are telling me to go directly toward it."

"Oh shit, you're kidding me," Quinn said heavily.

"I wish," Nate said, shaking his head and heading toward the sound.

The tunnels were chiseled into solid, multi-veined stone. Crystals lit the way as the path ahead of them branched in eight different directions.

"This one," Nate stammered nervously, pointing at a darkened path that was narrower and lower than the others. Sinister cries echoed from within it, growing in number and volume. The reverberation ignited their biological responses as their adrenaline surged. They descended deeper into the damp earth.

As his blood pounded in his ears, Marcus thought only about Theron. Where was she now? Lost? In danger? What if he died? How would he help her then?

"Here it comes!" Nate shouted. "Holy shit!"

An enormous beast, resembling a male lion but twice its thickness and muscle mass, was upon them. Its giant head swung side to side as its loud, hollow breathing echoed menacingly through the tunnel. *Huff . . . Huff . . . Huff*, the men heard, and felt. The sound, so near, so calm and so deliberate, was far more frightening than the howls had been. The beast aggressively tossed its mane, which was twisted in tight loops and knots, rattling the studded, armored cuff around its neck and chest. It snarled, bearing its lethal fangs. The fur on its neck bristled and spiked like barbs.

"I've heard of these things, Nate. They're the Guardians of the outer Grid," Quinn shouted.

The Guardian looked more horrible than he had ever imagined, and its glowing eyes flared like hellfire in the dim light. Nate backed directly against Quinn, and the wicked creature crept closer. The rancid odor of decay that clung to it choked them. Its shoulders were almost the height of the low ceiling, and its massive head was extended forward on its outstretched neck.

Nate was reminded of the shishi lions he had seen so many times in his travels through Asia, their giant stone paws resting possessively on the sphere representing the world and the Grid. He knew there was no time to waste; the lions were almost always depicted in pairs.

As the monster approached, there was a *click, click, click* of extended claws on the stone floor, each nail as thick as an ivory tusk. They could not flee. The Guardian would surely be on them, ripping out their insides in an instant. And in the distance, another deep grumble resonated.

Suddenly, Nate knew what he must do. He saw an opening. Without another thought the guide shouted, "You must get through!"

"No!" Quinn bellowed, but it was too late.

Nate sprinted directly past the front of the Guardian down one of the branching tunnels. With a fierce pounce, it took the bait. "Run!" Nate screamed.

Quinn paused, not wanting to leave his friend, but he knew it was a lost cause. The beast was on Nate easily. He had ducked under its chin and wrapped his arms around its banded throat. It was too strong. It shook him free and was on him, razor sharp claws pinning him beneath its weight. It was certain death. Without weapons, Quinn and Nate had been completely defenseless.

It could not be for nothing! Nate's sacrifice must not be for nothing! Quinn bolted through the gap that had opened as the Guardian had been distracted. He must escape. Nate's valor could not be in vain.

Quinn ran until his lungs burned and his sides ached in sharp knots. The beast's hideous roars echoed in his ears. Turn, turn, branch off, and turn. Nate had been only a brief distraction. Quinn could hear the beast close behind him, or perhaps it was another. How many more would there be? He hadn't considered this when they had chosen to leave the safety of their prison bunker.

Nate had been tested and had bravely sacrificed himself. For what? What could Quinn possibly do to make the sacrifice worthwhile? Should he have stayed and fought? Now he would surely die anyway! Should he have died with Nate?

Huff, huff, huff, click, click, click. The Guardian panted as it ran, still growling its deep guttural warnings.

Quinn knew he couldn't run much longer; his thighs and lungs burned as he sprinted. Would he die here? Would this useless end complete this useless life? An Emissary by mistake, there was no doubt left in him now. He was a miserable failure; thirteen thousand years and all the wisdom of the Universe could not help him be a better man. The human condition was difficult for everyone, and once again he was failing to fulfill his purpose.

Shameful . . . shameful. You've done nothing with your knowledge, he admonished himself inwardly as his pace slowed.

"Stop!" Quinn commanded aloud. The sound of his voice echoed through the passages. "No more despair! I am a tool of the Light, and I am not responsible for Nate or for the beast! I will succeed! I will not add to the darkness of this world with unconscious thinking!" he panted.

He was now barely a hundred steps ahead of the charging Guardian, though he dared not look back. He need not look back, for a second Guardian had appeared in the corridor directly ahead of him. Trapped! He was now most certainly doomed, and he could see the bulging eyes of his attackers as they narrowed. He could almost feel the heat of their breath on his neck, and he prepared to be devoured.

"God help me!" he cried, just as the snarling creatures pounced.

A door, just to his right! In the split second it took the hideous sentinels to crash into one another, their prey disappeared. Quinn slipped through the fleeting opening, and when the door had closed behind him it immediately disappeared into the craggy stone wall. It was enough. The Guardians had not passed through.

Quinn found himself in a familiar place. It was the cenote of Atitala. The beautiful place where Marcus and Theron had spent so many joyous hours, and where he and Helghul had battled for her honor. It was exactly the same—the enticing blue water, the hanging roots and vines stippling the sunlight that peeked through the skylight above.

Tunnels shot off in different directions, and as Quinn wondered which one he should take he saw someone emerging directly opposite him. His heart leapt as he thought of Theron, but it was not Eden who emerged through the archway. It was Helghul! Helghul as he had been in Atitala—a man in his early twenties, blonde and smug, his usual sneer directed at Quinn. Quinn soon realized that he too was changed. His body was young and muscular; the skin of his arms was deep caramel brown. He was as he had been as well. Marcus had returned.

"You!" Helghul snarled. "It's time to do what I should have done in the beginning," he said.

The two men ran at one another, determined to battle, determined to end one another at last. As they collided, something extraordinary happened. Instead of meeting flesh to flesh and grappling, they each hit an invisible barrier and rebounded with a jolt. They sat, mirror images of one another, in exactly the same position, stunned, on the stone floor. Marcus stood up and, still in perfect reflection, Helghul did the same. The light and the dark, they stared at one another. Marcus reached out to feel for the barrier between them. As he did so, Helghul's corresponding arm was pressed back in equal extension. But there was no tangible separation, he felt no screen or wall, yet the two men were unable to touch.

"What is this between us? Why do you back away so strangely?" Marcus asked angrily. He had no time for these games. He must find Theron and he must do so before Helghul intervened.

Helghul punched toward Marcus, who retreated in exact response. The men looked at one another in confusion. Helghul nodded his head forward three times and Marcus's head simultaneously bobbed backward three times.

"Stop that!" Marcus shouted, once again lunging toward Helghul. Helghul's body responded in exact reversal and therefore could not be touched. For every movement, there was an equal and opposite counter-movement. For every intention, there was an equal and opposite intention. Marcus turned to leave; he would find Theron and be done with this nonsense, but as he did so, Helghul also turned.

Marcus marched out of the cave, and twenty yards ahead he saw an archway. He entered and, to his bewilderment, he was back in the same cenote and Helghul was entering from the opposite side. Step by step they were in perfect, but opposite, sync.

"What is this? What have you done to me?" Marcus shouted.

"It is you who has done it," Helghul snapped angrily.

"Is there something you are not telling me?"

"We will stay here like this indefinitely. Time is irrelevant in this place. Until we understand it, we are stuck here, together," Helghul said irritably.

"What are we to understand? Tell me so we can be done with it."

"I wish nothing more than to be done with *it*, but the solution to this riddle eludes me just as it does you. Do not tire me with your demands anymore. It is bad enough I have to endure your face, your stench, and your energy. Let me think."

Marcus made some more movements, complex and strange, and in every instance Helghul did the equal and opposite in perfect sync, without effort, each time growing more annoyed. Marcus sat down to think and as expected Helghul did the same. They could not leave the cenote and they could not touch one another, though everything that one of them did undeniably affected the other. Each man thought and struggled.

"What are we missing? I have to get out of here. What are we missing?" Marcus said, wracking his brain.

Suddenly Marcus grew very still. He slowed his breathing, closed his eyes, and instead of trying to think, he tried *not* to think. He emptied his mind and breathed.

Marcus meditated for just less than eight minutes, while Helghul sat nearby in exactly the same pose facing the glistening blue cenote. *Why the cenote? Was it because of Theron? Atitala? The fight so long ago? No!* Marcus jumped to his feet, and Helghul stood beside him.

"It's the water! Water is the most ancient of ancients! Everybody who's come before us is alive in the water. Every birth sac and withered corpse returns to the water cycle like a puddle drying in the sun. The water holds knowledge!" Marcus proclaimed.

It took him a moment to contemplate further. He ran forward to jump in the water but, as he did so, Helghul stepped equally away. As if a rope held them core to core in a tug of war, Marcus could not enter. He had been so sure! What could he be missing?

Marcus bent down and picked up a small pebble. He threw it into the pool, and beside him Helghul mirrored the equal and opposite motions, though he tossed no stone. The single stone dropped in with a plop. In response, a ring rippled out, and then a second. From that zero point were born two rings, and they split one from another, which is not the way of water. Instead of living within one another, the rings split into the vesica piscis, like the splitting of a cell in the creation of life. The rings rippled side by side, and between them, where they touched, was their point of origin, like an eye. Together they were duality—the yin and the yang, balance—and they made the eternity figure eight, which began to spin. Larger and more quickly a great whirlpool was created in the center of the cenote, and the sound of its rushing water filled the space.

"We must go together, side by side," Marcus said to Helghul over the rushing water.

"It appears it can be no other way," Helghul agreed. They both stepped simultaneously toward the edge. "You are still no friend to me, Marcus."

"Nor am I your enemy," Marcus said benevolently, and together, in agreement, they jumped into the magical eddy and were gone.

Whoosh! The ground fell away like a trapdoor, and Eden cried out in alarm. She heard Quinn shouting as his fingers grazed her hair, and then she was gone. Down, down, farther and farther, she continued to fall, slip, and turn across smooth stone. It reminded her of a slide at the water park back home. Back home, she knew where it would come out. Back home, she knew she was safe. Her heart was racing and she wondered if she should hold her breath. Was she about to burst through and be drowned, burned, eaten? Where would she come out?

Theron landed lightly, sliding like a feather into place. It was a strange seat, unlike anything she had ever seen, with carvings and artwork on every possible surface. She had dropped into an ornate golden throne.

It took her a moment to get her bearings and register her surroundings. There was an elaborate gold scaffolding in front of her. The white limestone room had high ceilings and intricately carved cornices and porticos all around its walls. There was a whimper, like the mew of a kitten, that called her attention back to the gold structure before her.

"Children!" she shouted joyfully as she saw the six young Crystal Children several yards above her looking down. They sat on two separate gold platforms with low edges around them, three to the right and three to the left. Eden tried to stand but could not. She was not bound, she felt no weight or pressure on her, but though she struggled, she was unable to lift her stuck body from the seat.

"Please, please, help us! Get us down!" six small voices called.

Eden looked up at the pink, chubby faces beseeching her. The children were between the ages of three and seven. Eden could see the fat, fleshy dimples in their elbows and fingers as they wriggled around, obviously trapped just as she was. The girl with the golden ringlets, who had sung so sweetly, now cried softly.

Eden contemplated how she would get them down once she was able to get unstuck. *It's a scale*, she realized with confusion. "How did you get up there?" she called to them.

"I don't know. We just landed here," the little girl cried.

"I can't move, I can't get to you, there's something holding me in place," Eden said. "I need help. I don't know what to do, I need some help," she added under her breath.

Beginning as smoke and becoming solid as Eden's eyes struggled to focus, the King of Shambhala, in white, gold, and jewels, appeared in front of the enormous scale, almost equal its size. His black hair was smooth and shiny beneath his glittering crown.

The children marveled in awe from either side as he reached out his giant hands to soothe them. They were not afraid; the energy that surrounded the good king was pure and light, and he shimmered like gossamer inlaid with fine crystals.

"Welcome, Theron. What is it that you wish to know?"

"What is this place?"

"You have returned to Shambhala, to the inner world. Before you stand the Scales of Justice. Weighing upon the scale is a sacrifice in equal balance to the gains ahead. There is a door beyond and it leads to that which you seek. To pass you must first retrieve the key. You cannot go back. You must choose," he answered.

Eden noticed for the first time that on either side of the scale, dangling from the bottom of each bowl, was a large gold key on a chain. Behind the contraption was a huge gold door.

"That door will lead to my son?"

"Yes."

"But I cannot move from this seat, it holds me," Eden said.

"You are limited only by your beliefs. Reach deep inside yourself and you will move freely through this chamber and beyond it," the king assured.

Eden trusted. She pulled her feet up onto the seat and crossed her legs. She straightened her back, lifted her chin, and closed her eyes, breathing deeply. Free. Release me. Free, she thought, concentrating her energy on her forehead and on the pineal gland inside her skull.

Eden didn't know how long she sat like that, but finally the lines of her face blurred as she began to take on the appearance of another. Her arms, her legs, her torso began to vibrate and shudder gently. The children watched silently from above as she, like the Shambhala king, became something more like smoke and cloud than solid. A filmy, ethereal spirit stood and stepped out of Eden. The children exclaimed in wonder.

There stood Theron, as she had appeared in Atitala. Her hair glimmered like garnets, and the fine point of her nose made her resemble a bird, perhaps a phoenix. She was completely separate from the uninhabited, resting shell of Eden on the throne behind her—only a thin umbilical cord linked them. It looked like the strand of a spiderweb and maintained their connection regardless of where she moved.

"Miraculous!" she beamed, marveling at her hazy hands and legs and regarding her inert shell.

"To pass, you must make your choice. When you take a key, the balance will falter and the sacrifice will be determined. The side you choose will rise up safely, the opposite will crash to the ground. What will you choose?"

"I have decided," she said, too quickly.

"There is no undoing what will be done. You understand that one side of the scale will be released?" the king cautioned.

The children stirred anxiously. They were young but they understood, and the protests and pleas that rose from the baskets filled the room.

"I know my choice," Theron said loudly, and the children cried in anticipation. "Neither . . . I choose neither. You said I could not go back. You did not say I could not stay here. I choose not to pass. There is another choice. I will remain here. None will be sacrificed by my hand," she said simply, and loud cheers erupted from the children above.

The Shambhala king lowered his head respectfully, and the glittering jewels in his crown flashed throughout the room. "You have chosen well," he said.

Instantly the scale and the children disappeared, and Theron was sucked back into her body, filling it like air into a balloon. Eden became animate and was no longer stuck. She slipped easily from the golden throne, and she followed the giant king through the door opposite her without the aid of any key.

"Through that door," he said, pointing, "you will enter into the sacred Hall of Records. You are one of three from the west who will enter today," the king announced.

"The Hall of Records? It truly exists?" Eden said in amazement.

The Hall of Records, also called the Halls of Amenti, was legendary and was said to contain a complete collection of knowledge from every Age. It held the secrets of the Universe, and only the most worthy could enter.

"It is all there. Blessings, good Emissary," the king said.

Eden passed through the door and he was left behind. She walked up a long, dimly lit corridor, which opened into a vast library.

"What would you most like to know?" a voice from far back in Theron's memory echoed to her from behind a bookcase.

"Where can I find my son?" Eden demanded. With all knowledge and possibility at her fingertips, she was still a mother first, her child's welfare utmost on her mind. Eden's head rotated as if it were on a swivel, noting all of the nine passageways and doors jutting out from the circular room.

"You will find your son in the King's Chamber of the Great Pyramid," the man said. He stepped out from behind some shelves and tables, which were filled with scrolls, tablets, and books. He was a stocky man in white robes with a trimmed salt-and-pepper beard, a round nose, and smiling cobalt eyes. Red Elder, the Keeper of Records, drank in the effervescent karmic colors of Theron.

"Red Elder!" Eden exclaimed happily.

"Yes, Theron, you have known me many times, even in this lifetime before I passed."

"Many times . . . I don't . . . Jamie!" Eden gasped. "Red Elder! It can't be! You were Jamie? My husband?" she said, bursting into tears.

The Keeper of Records embraced her warmly.

"Our son . . . Elijah . . ." she began, her voice muffled by his robes.

"Calm, there is much yet to be accomplished. Your path to the child will be clear."

"Did you know? When we were . . . together . . . did you know about . . . all this? Who we were?"

"Who we are," he corrected gently. "I knew."

"You didn't tell me . . . why didn't you tell me?"

"Your inability to remember was a gift of mercy. It was not my place to take it from you."

"But I remember now."

"That too is a gift, but given well-timed."

"How are you here? Are you real?"

"This place is not wholly of your world. I remain energy and light and flow within the Grid. I am of a parallel universe to yours."

"But I can touch you . . . you're right here," she stammered, tapping his chest.

"Your eyes have been opened. You have come to my dimension, not I to yours. The Hall of Records is Shambhala, Theron. What is solid one moment may disappear the next. I exist in a place of ebb and flow and endless possibility. It is time to deposit your knowledge; the Darkness looms."

"What? I don't under…"

"What have you learned . . . your lesson?" he explained kindly.

"How do I decide? There are too many lessons. How do I choose what to say and not?"

"What do you feel most deeply?" he asked.

Theron thought for a few minutes. "Gratitude," she finally said. "I am grateful that the Great Source has allowed me to experience creation. The birth of a child, my life as a mother, has let me experience the love of the creator for her creation. It is a tiny glimmer of the great love that our creator feels for us."

"It is recorded. Proceed quickly and with blessings."

"Can't you come? Help me find Elijah; he's your son too," she said, taking the Elder's hand as if she would pull him along with her.

"I have played my role in your current life. My place is here. We will meet again."

Eden shivered as an ominous energy coursed through her, prompting her every hair and cell to quiver at attention. She embraced Red Elder, and to her left a corridor glowed.

CHAPTER 45

THE HALLS OF AMENTI

Elijah woke with a start. He expected to be soaked, wet from head to toe, after diving into the cenote vortex with Marcus. His sheets were dry and luxurious.

"Wake up, it's time to go," Grey Elder said, prodding the boy gently.

Had he been dreaming? Helghul knew better. There were certain dreams that were more.

It was ten p.m. A strong wind had blown the clouds and smog away, and the night skies over Giza were clear and bright. Grey Elder carried the black sports bag over one shoulder. His forearm rippled with the muscles that he had maintained diligently, knowing that his duties might someday challenge his aging body. He was dressed in western clothing and had ensured that Elijah did the same. They entered a taxi, and Elijah was grateful for the occasional gust of air through its open windows. The night remained warm, and traffic was noisy and slow.

"I hate baseball," Elijah had complained, when Grey Elder had tossed him a hat.

"We need to look like tourists. That's how we're getting into the Pyramid."

"Can't you just pay our way in?" the boy had asked, turning over the Yankee cap in his hand.

"Of course, I've done that too. Egyptian politicians are easily bribed. However, they don't have the same control of their military as they like to pretend. I have papers allowing us access to the pyramids and surroundings, but we must be prepared to deal with potential problems. We cannot be perceived as any kind of threat. As much as the soldiers are happy to take bribes, they're truly protective of the Great Pyramid and they don't want any trouble. They understand how dangerous times have become."

"Isn't it dangerous to advertise that we're Americans?" Elijah had said, waving the cap in the air.

"It's necessary. When I get close, the guards will know me anyway. This is the body I have to work with. I mustn't look like I am trying to hide it or they'll be more suspicious."

"What if they don't let us in?"

"*You* will get in. Everybody has a price . . . anyway, if I have any difficulty I have my ways," Grey Elder had answered darkly.

They exited the cab and walked toward the Great Pyramid, leaving the streets of chaotic traffic and honking behind.

"Move quickly and don't speak to anyone. The crowds are large and prone to violence," Grey Elder said, as they approached the largest pyramid. It was lit around its perimeter, but the evening light shows that had once entertained tourists had ceased months before when Giza had become too dangerous.

The Egyptian army had been staunch, not allowing anyone entrance, but as time passed the higher-ups had made exceptions in order to reap the financial benefits. Pilgrims and tourists were willing and able to pay for access to the site, and life in Egypt was a struggle for its people, both military and civilian, so they took what they could on the side.

To Grey Elder's displeasure, despite the warnings of danger and the legitimate threat of harm, the area outside the metal barricade fences was surrounded by pilgrims. There were thousands of people from all over the world, who had been arriving for months. There had been a great deal of animosity and violence directed at the peaceful pilgrims, much of it directly engineered by Zahn himself. Despite the danger, they continued to come. From outside the army barriers, they paced, prayed, sang, and just stared at the monuments as though waiting for something miraculous to happen. Very soon it would.

"Open the bag," the soldier at the barricade orderded, but Zahn was prepared.

"It's nothing, just snacks and water," he answered, but as he opened the pack toward the man he held a huge wad of money as a bribe in his hand.

The soldier didn't want to be seen taking the money; he might get in trouble, or worse, have to share it. He pocketed it quickly and waved them through. He had earned more in that brief moment than he would make in five years.

Grey Elder and Helghul had passed the first barrier easily, with the Emerald Tablet safely concealed. Now they had only to make their way to the Pyramid's tourist entrance and into the King's Chamber.

Quinn woke as if from a deep sleep and was back in his forty-something body. He rubbed his aching neck as he tried to make sense of his unfamiliar surroundings. He had escaped from a bunker in Torres del Paine, he had lost Theron, Nate was dead, and he had jumped into a cenote with Helghul. Now he found himself on the floor of an enormous round room.

There were scrolls and books and tablets and shelves that seemed to go on for miles. The white marble walls were steep and polished to a brilliant shine. The room had corridors jutting off in many directions, and Quinn couldn't guess which pointed north or south. There was no wind, no cool, no heat—just stillness and the sound of his breathing.

Suddenly, Quinn heard a small sigh behind him. He whirled. "Red Elder!" he gasped. "Where am I?"

"All tunnels lead back to the Source, some just take longer to arrive," the Elder said cryptically. His robe shimmered as he moved.

"Is this Amenti? Am I in the Hall of Records?" Quinn guessed, looking at the overflowing shelves, and the Elder nodded.

"You are beneath the Sphinx next to the Great Pyramid of Giza. You are the second of three prophesied to come from the west at the end of the Age."[36]

Quinn knew that any answer he could ever seek could be found in that room, if only he knew where to look and what to ask.

"Where is Theron? Did she come before me?" Quinn asked hopefully.

"As always, Marcus, I see little has changed for you . . . or has it? She has come and gone. You are one of three in a destiny. Your fates are woven together like the strands of a whip," the Elder declared, repeating the familiar phrase that Plato had first been told by the Oracle of Amun in Siwa.

"Where did she go? Which way?" Quinn asked triumphantly. Eden had made it safely!

"As it is for her, *your* path is laid for you, Marcus. The outcome is far from certain and the Darkness approaches. You must make haste to the Great Pyramid, but first you must impart what *you* have learned, to be recorded in the Hall of Records."

"There isn't time . . ." Quinn began.

"It is the only way," Red Elder insisted.

"Okay . . . ummm . . . I've learned . . . that memory is a curse and a blessing. I have learned that our path is unclear to us as we travel, but upon looking back the lessons become obvious."

Red Elder did not speak, but cocked his short neck slightly to the right . . . waiting.

"I've learned that loneliness is an illusion . . . that isolation and individuality are . . . well, I can only describe them as holographic projections. In our hearts and souls we are unified at all times as One."

"And what *about* love, Marcus? What about Theron?" Red Elder probed, pushing Quinn to consider himself, pushing him to consider more than thirteen thousand years of searching and struggling.

Quinn paused thoughtfully before answering. He had been rocking back and forth slowly on the balls of his feet, anxious to move on, but he stopped and said, "Love takes many forms, and . . . and they are all valuable. When we know love for everyone and everything, none above the other, then we truly understand Oneness."

"Your deposit has been recorded."

"Thank you, blessings," Quinn said, bowing respectfully as he ran toward the distant passageway that had lit up for him.

"Where are we going? I thought you said we were going to go through the tourist entrance," Elijah said, as Zahn turned toward the Sphinx.

Even though it was nearing midnight, there were many people milling around the area, pointing at the stars and remarking at their brightness.

"I've arranged passage for myself through the tourist entrance. If that is hindered, I will enter by cash or by force. You must enter through the Hall of Records. Your passage is through the Sphinx. We will reunite in the King's Chamber."

"Why?"

"There is a question that can only be answered in the Halls of Amenti. You are one of three who have been prophesied to come from the west. I have prevented Marcus and Theron from fulfilling their destinies. They remain confined in Torres del Paine."

Helghul thought of his dream of Marcus in the cenote. *Was Marcus still captive in Chile?* he wondered.

"Without them there will be no balance. The Pyramid will be activated long before the Golden Age, and without goodness and balance the Darkness will be perpetuated," Grey Elder continued. "There is a phrase that must be spoken to initiate the process when we place the Emerald Tablet in the King's Chamber. I am not privy to this detail; only White Elder knows. But all knowledge is available in the Hall of Records, and all questions can be answered. You must ask for the words to initiate the process."

"Why don't you come with me and ask yourself?"

"I cannot pass. You alone will be granted entry."

"How will I enter? In my life as pharaoh, there were legends of the Hall of Records and the concourses between the Sphinx and the pyramids. I searched, but they do not exist," Helghul said, as they stepped down into the trench surrounding the giant stone lion with its human head. A pair of soldiers passed close by, watching Zahn and Elijah curiously. The boy dropped his head, and they became silent.

"The tunnels exist. It is all in the timing. Pass the right front paw three times, just as you would have done at a stupa when you were Genghis Khan. The entrance will open for you," Grey Elder instructed.

As Temujin would have done, Helghul thought to himself as he began to pace.

Zahn stepped about ten feet away, farther from the lights at the base of the monolith, and blended into the shadows. The Emerald Tablet was tucked closely in its bag under his arm. As instructed, Elijah walked clockwise three times around the Sphinx, beginning at the right front paw. Zahn waited, listening to those passing by, watching for approaching soldiers, prepared to intervene if anyone came near.

On the third and final turn, the boy was confident . . . but the entrance did not appear. Nothing happened, and he looked to Zahn for an explanation. Together they stared at the solid statue with surprise.

Helghul had held some doubt that the entrance would open to him, a remnant of his disappointing days searching for the doorway as Alexander. Once again, he stood perplexed and shut out. Could Grey Elder have been mistaken? What would they do if the door did not appear? *Think!* he railed at himself. *Feel! Listen to your intuition! Why isn't it working?*

"It's vibration. You must chant," Zahn whispered cautiously.

"Yes." Elijah answered. The eerie notes were indelibly etched into his deepest memory, and their recollection was always accompanied by images of the dark ceremony. He was reminded of the carnage and the vision of the parasitic

Darkness as it had entered him and attached to his soul. The harrowing intensity of the energy swelled within him; his attention was a flame to its fire.

Elijah began again, this time droning the low, inharmonious chant. Once, twice, three times he walked clockwise the nearly one hundred and sixty yards around the Sphinx, humming. He returned to the right paw yet again and . . . nothing! *Was the entrance elsewhere? Did it exist at all? Was there a secret word or deed, or was the vibration inadequate?* Elijah looked to Grey Elder, but saw with alarm that his mentor was in an animated conversation with two suspicious army sentries.

"How would Temujin get in?" he mumbled, but he had tried that, and nothing new came to mind. Pace, pace, pace; he walked back and forth. Grey Elder was distracting the guards, but for how long? *How would Marcus get in?* he wondered, just as the guards turned to walk away, and Grey Elder simultaneously turned back toward the Sphinx in the *opposite* direction.

At that instant the answer came to him. His recent dream of Marcus had been a clue! The face of his counterbalance flashed through his mind, and he thought of them jumping, strangely united, into the cenote. Marcus would walk around the Sphinx clockwise three times, humming, just as he had already done. But he was not Marcus. Helghul knew what he must do. *Balance!*

"I have it!" the boy hissed jubilantly to the Elder, who was scanning the sky and looking at his watch.

Instead of walking clockwise, Elijah proceeded *counter*clockwise, once again intoning the ancient mantra.

"Boy! Boy! What are you doing there?" a nearing soldier called out from the opposite side of the Sphinx.

Elijah began running, and just before the outsider reached him, he made his third and final turn. The Sphinx opened, as if it had lifted its paw, and he ducked quickly inside the narrow rabbit hole that had appeared. He slid in, knocking his hat off in his haste.

Elijah didn't hear the astonished exclamations of the soldier, who had been only steps behind and now held Elijah's fallen ball cap. The boy had si disappeared. He was now a world away. Jubilantly, Zahn made his way toward the main entrance of the Great Pyramid, the Emerald Tablet protectively in tow.

The small Adversary stood easily inside the narrow tunnel that stretched out ahead of him. He dusted off the scraped, bloody flesh of his right elbow, flinching. His light jacket had torn through. He celebrated inwardly at having finally mastered the portal that he had sought so fervently in the past.

The corridor was lit, but Elijah could not understand by what source. There were no torches, no bulbs or crystals. There was no window or crack to the outside world, yet the passageway glowed dimly as he advanced.

Elijah came to a spiral staircase and proceeded downward. At the bottom he found another and another, until he had descended nine steep staircases in all and had walked for nearly thirty minutes. He worried that he was taking too long. He needed to reach the King's Chamber quickly. Grey Elder would be waiting.

The base of the ninth staircase rested in the center of a large stone room that was filled with shelves and tables bursting with scrolls, books, maps—every manner of preserving knowledge. Jutting out from the room there were nine long passageways.

As he paused, Elijah noticed that his injured elbow was still bleeding heavily. He thought of the cartoon bandages that his mother always carried in her purse, even once he had grown too old for them. The insignificant recollection instantly took him back to a time, less than a year earlier, when his ancient memory had been foggy and dull. A time when he was more Elijah and less Helghul. He had had a home, a bedroom with posters, and a quilt with a ratty corner that he had often chewed. Back then he had simply been a son to a loving mother. Mom . . . Eden . . . *Where was she now?* he wondered.

Movement to his left pulled him out of his reverie. Near the base of the staircase, waiting to greet Elijah, stood Red Elder. His long robe glowed and swished against the tile at his feet. His eyes were bright white and blue and ...lged slightly. Helghul recognized the Elder instantly . . . but there was more. ... he was missing.

"Welcome, Initiate. I am the Keeper of Records . . . Red Elder . . . Hermes . . . also known by many other names before and after. Will you not greet me, Helghul?"

"You left us," Elijah whispered, recognizing Jamie's spirit. The boy's grief bubbled up and overflowed. "You could have stayed with us," he said sorrowfully, as a son to his father. For an instant he was simply an eleven-year-old boy grieving the loss of his dad. Elijah remembered their last trip together, snorkeling and surfing in the waves off the coast of Hawaii. Jamie had promised that Afghanistan would be brief, no big deal, and they would meet up again in Egypt. This time they would travel as a family for good.

"It was the way it was meant to be. It was not my choice to leave when I did, though I do not question it. You understand that lifetimes come and go," Red Elder soothed.

Elijah stared at the record keeper. "You knew this would happen. You said we would meet in Egypt. You're *nothing* to me now," he said bitterly, his Helghul-brain successfully squashing the sentimental boyhood pain that had spontaneously emerged.

"What is it that you seek?" Red Elder asked.

"I wish to know the phrase that will activate the great resonator."

"As it is below, so it shall be above," Red Elder answered automatically.

Elijah smirked at the simplicity of it and turned to leave. The mysterious light that had led him through the tunnels up until now was no longer visible. The nine hallways leading from the Hall of Records were dark. He didn't know where to go.

"There are many passages that one can take, Helghul," Red Elder said.

"I must get to the King's Chamber," the boy replied.

"You *choose* your destiny."

"I have already chosen, just as *you* have," Elijah said coolly, rejecting Red Elder's familiar karmic energy.

"Your destiny is uncertain. Find the space in your heart where the spirit of the Source resides. There is always choice," Red Elder counseled.

"I wish to go to the King's Chamber of the Great Pyramid," Elijah declared, certain that his choice was decided.

"Like everyone who passes through these halls, you must first make a deposit before leaving. What knowledge have *you* to leave for the Keeper of Records?" Red Elder asked.

"There *is* no new knowledge. Since the First Tribe it has all been done before. The cycle repeats, a balance of all things light and dark, male and female. How am *I* to add anything new? Are these shelves not bursting with that same message, patterns and symbols written in a million ways and languages?" Elijah said, exasperated. He had to hurry.

"Your deposit has been recorded. Follow the path that lights unto you. Follow the Light."

"I don't answer to *you*, I answer to a higher power," Elijah replied. His vulnerable emotions had been smothered and denied existence. One of the corridors to his right began to glow.

CHAPTER 46

THE KING'S CHAMBER

After the first twenty yards, the tunnel leading from the Hall of Records was irregular. Piles of rock and debris littered the corridor, and Elijah had to climb and step carefully to make his way. It was taking so long: up, down, over, and under.

Eden's tunnel was quite a different experience. The floor and walls were smooth and honed. The strange light glowed up ahead and dimmed behind as she ran and jogged up a totally straight, subtle incline. She imagined she felt Elijah somewhere close by, and it spurred her forward. Would she meet Quinn and Nate? They had been separated, but would Marcus be waiting ahead when she found her son?

Quinn had stopped running. He slowed to a jog and then a walk, his chest heaving from exertion. How long would the tunnel be? How much farther would he have to go before he reached the Great Pyramid and hopefully found Theron?

While he walked, he tried not to think about Nate. Instead he contemplated the significance of returning to Egypt. Why the Great Pyramid? He had his theories. He knew that the Pyramid was not only an important symbol of ascension, but it was also the greatest of all resonators. The energy that it was capable of projecting was immense . . . but how? It hadn't functioned in millennia. It had been defaced and altered, and the Nile had dropped so significantly that the river no longer flowed near the base of the structure.

Despite its spiritual significance and intention, the Pyramid was an instrument, and it required certain conditions to function. Quinn wondered if somehow the marvel would again become operational.

Grey Elder had timed everything perfectly. There were many in league with the Darkness. Explosives just south of Aswan had succeeded in collapsing the nearly two-and-a-half-mile-long dam, which had been holding back the Nile in the Nasser reservoir since 1964. Insurgents, terrorists, it didn't matter who would be blamed; the political discord in the country and in those surrounding it made it easy for Zahn to have his way.

The Elder had ensured the dam was built decades before with a financial agreement struck in 1958.[37] Grey Elder had then been chief aide to the premier of the Soviet government, Nikita Khrushchev. The influential mentor had stayed in the wings, pulling strings and making plans, while yet another of the Adversaries shouldered the notoriety and fame.

Though the Aswan Dam was a significant collaboration, Khrushchev was better remembered for his infamous role in the Cold War. Khrushchev had brought the world to the brink of nuclear war during the Cuban missile crisis in 1962. Later that same year Khrushchev's esteemed aide and puppet master died, and Grey Elder was reborn as Oswald Zachariah Zahn in a tiny town in southern Texas.

The torrent from the destroyed dam was flooding the Nile basin and overtaking precious ruins, boats, and villages. Thousands of unsuspecting people drowned in their beds. The swell swept up everything in its path as it headed toward Giza. It was naturally drawn to Port Said, where it would dump into the Mediterranean Sea—but not before flooding the site of the Great Pyramid.

Quinn thought he was hearing things—he heard rushing wind just as something wet and cold scurried across his foot. He jumped in alarm, but it was only water—not a rat, as he had first suspected. Quinn had finally reached the Subterranean Chamber of the Pyramid, and it was filling with water. He didn't know how it had come to be, but he knew he must get to higher ground as quickly as possible.

Quinn could not have imagined the scene unfolding outside the Pyramid. The Nile had risen suddenly, and palm trees and wreckage were moving across the Giza compound.

In an effort to escape the surging river, the guards and tourists were clambering up the two-and-a-half-ton limestone blocks. There was room for everyone who was nearby and had the opportunity and ability to climb. Side by side, helping one another, people scrambled up . . . up . . . up. Everyone at his or her own pace. Everyone facing different obstacles and inconsistent stone heights. When would it be high enough? Would there be room at the top?

"Remarkably like our life paths," one pilgrim noted to another, once safely above the waterline.

Eden was oblivious to the overflowing water that was rushing into the lower levels of the Pyramid. Relieved to be out of the cramped Ascending Passage, she had reached the Grand Gallery—a steep, narrow hallway that led to the King's Chamber. There was no sign of Elijah. The Queen's Chamber had been empty when she passed it, but a strange hum had since filled the air. Up ahead she saw a bright glow near the King's Chamber, and as she climbed the hum grew louder. Her only concern was getting Elijah to safety. Would she find her child? Surely the King of Shambhala and Red Elder had been correct.

As Eden neared the luminous room, she contemplated what she would do if Zahn was with Elijah. He had proven himself to be ruthless. She shuddered to think how ill-prepared she was. She had no weapon, no plan. At no time did she consider that Elijah might refuse her help or might be a danger to her.

As Eden climbed higher, she felt the music move over her like water across rocks, washing her clean, smoothing the jagged edges of uncertainty within her. Theron was awake, empowered and conscious, and she steeled herself to face the unknown.

A large granite box stood in the King's Chamber directly between two vents on either wall. Grey Elder had used the anti-gravitational powers of the atlantium crystal Emerald Tablet to easily move it back to its rightful location, after thousands of years of having been displaced and misunderstood.

The coffer had been the subject of extensive lore and conjecture, even compared to the Ark of the Covenant. Eden had once read to Elijah that it had been intended as a casket for the pharaoh, Khufu. Incorrect. She had also read that the students of the Mystery School had reached enlightenment by lying for a night within the six-and-a-half-foot-long, three-foot-wide structure. Correct. But never had any scholar correctly discerned the purpose of the box.

Both Elijah and Eden now knew the truth; their memories were full and clear. She had lain in the casket herself in her lifetime as Pythagoras but had forgotten. The power of the energy had been inspirational, and Pythagoras had gone on to do great work. Imagine what he might have done if Theron had had memory.

Zahn placed the trembling Emerald Tablet on Elijah's chest and the resonating "A" note grew louder. The note was haunting, and every hair on the boy's body stood up with an electric charge. The boy couldn't see much of the room. He could see the flat rose granite ceiling and the upper walls from where he lay on his back inside the coffer. It was longer and wider than his slight young frame and he fit easily inside, hidden from view. Would Eden know where to look?

Elijah's hands and feet were bound by rope. Helghul boiled inside of him, full of rage at having been duped. When he had arrived in the King's Chamber, Grey Elder had asked him the secret phrase from the Halls of Amenti. "As it is below, so it shall be above," he had answered. Moments later Zahn had easily subdued and restrained him, a confused boy, and had placed him in the coffer.

Helghul remembered the night that he had opened his veins and the dark spirit had attached to him. He had trusted Grey Elder, and he had been intoxicated and thrilled by the idea of power and glory.

"You're going to kill me and release the beast, aren't you?" Elijah said bravely, though the child trembled at the idea of his murder.

"You've lived and died many times, Helghul. Surely you realize that the dark spirit is bound to your *soul*. It doesn't leave you when you die. You are a feed sack . . . an incubator. It feeds on you as you feed on it. The beast requires your human soul to exist in this world. You have had your time as host. The beast will further the Darkness with me, and you shall reside within it. Your bond eternal," Grey Elder said coarsely.

"Liar!" Eden yelled, entering the chamber and running to the serapeum where her son lay bound. "The *Source* is eternal, our choices are not! Forgiveness and repentance are *real*. It's a Grid and *all* roads lead back to the Light," she said, leaning her body into the granite box, pushing the Emerald Tablet off Elijah's chest and hugging her child.

"And all roads lead *away* from the Light," Grey Elder added slyly. Ignoring the interruption, he continued speaking to Elijah. "Helghul, your soul is unified with the beast and always will be. You would not have had the lives you've had if not for the Darkness! Your cycle would have been *nothing*."

"I played my role! I played a role I didn't know *how* to deny. Where there is evil, there is goodness; inside *me* there must be goodness," Elijah yelled, struggling to help his mother untie him while Grey Elder watched unperturbed. It was too late, everything had gone as planned. The vibration shook their bones and the ominous "A" note grew louder.

"I will open your veins and your body will be consumed by the beast. Your soul, which was promised to the dark energy and allowed it to breach the chasm and enter this world, will stay bound to it. Together we will reign over the Earth," Zahn rejoiced. He walked toward Eden and Elijah, his handsome face calm and serene as if he were taking an afternoon stroll. A curved blade glinted in his hand.

"No!" Eden shouted, stepping between Elijah and the Elder.

"The time has come!" Grey Elder shouted, barely audible over the music. The room had grown bright with starlight, brought in through celestial vents and ricocheted by crystals that had been placed deep inside the walls of the Pyramid when it was built. The Emerald Tablet, despite having been pushed aside, was still in the center of the vents inside the coffer and was drawing the starlight into the Pyramid.

Soon the Tablet would measure the unseen fabric of the world's collective consciousness and would expand it. Grey Elder intended that the darkness of the world's despair would prevail and, through the tablet, would resonate into the Universe. The Dark Age would go on. There would be no ascending Bronze Age.

The light landed where Elijah lay struggling. The chamber shuddered and shook as the ground quaked violently, and the energy was sent down the passageways into the surging waters of the Nile. The waters, which held memory, were read by the machine.

Outside, people clung to the trembling Pyramid. The river continued to flow perilously through Cairo to the sea. The stars illuminated the sky, revealing the destruction unfolding. The debris and bodies of the unfortunate floated in the moat that had formed around the Pyramid.

There were all kinds of prayers, in many languages, and they were not only from the people clinging to the pyramids. All around the globe, despite Grey Elder's best efforts, despite the Nobu virus and the riots and the wars, despite all the fear that had been carefully orchestrated, people were hopeful. Prayer groups gathered and people meditated. Leaders of all religions, mediums, psychics, people on the corner . . . they all prophesied a better world. Scientists considered intelligent design. All over the world people embraced love and virtue and their energy mattered.

CHAPTER 47

THE EMISSARIES' LAST STAND

The commander in Torres del Paine felt the threat before he saw it. Facing the tent from five yards away, the soldiers could now feel the strong tremor shaking the ground and air around them. The other guards stood back, waiting for their orders before proceeding. The energy was intense. Had Grey Elder neglected to consider this? How had he allowed *this*?

The mystified commander ordered the heavy trap door unlocked. As it was opened, light and energy billowed from the passageway, and soldiers were thrown back by the force of it.

Just as White Elder had led the other Elders and the people of Atitala on the night of the exodus, someone had led the Emissaries. Had Grey Elder misjudged his former students and underestimated their understanding of the Grid, or had he known it would happen? Had he known that putting the Emissaries together would have such a powerful effect on them and would allow them to remember? Marcus had put it all together. Marcus, with his ancient memory, had reminded them of their purpose and had helped them to unite.

The commander shouted and the guards began frantically descending the steps into the bunker. Their weapons were drawn; they had no idea what to expect.

The Emissaries were joined arm in arm, chanting deep intonations of "om." Their auras had swelled and grown dramatically so that each one was like a thousand more, and they were no longer separate and distinct from one another. Their ethereal spirits hovered side by side, levitating well above their motionless, barely breathing bodies. The magical shapes of the Unity Grid flowered above them in the air, changing like sand patterns on a drum as the frequency heightened.

"Open fire! Open fire!" the commander shouted in fear and confusion. "Take them down!" he howled from his place on the stone floor, his arms shielding his eyes and mind from the brilliance around him.

Across the globe Giza glowed brightly with a phenomenal charge of energy as the Great Pyramid revved to life. Quinn had barely exited the Descending Passage before it completely filled with water. Hunched over, he was growing frantic as he clambered up the squat Ascending Passage. Ahead there remained a faint glow, lighting his path. When he finally reached the Grand Gallery he was able to stand, but only for a moment, before entering the passage to the Queen's Chamber. The Pyramid was vibrating noticeably, and he knew that if he found the source of the haunting notes that were sending shivers through him, he would likely find Theron.

Quinn scrambled, unable to stand upright and dripping wet, into the arched room of the Queen's Chamber. *Nothing. No one.* Quinn knew he had to get to the King's Chamber before it was too late. He must not lose Theron again. If they were going to die tonight, he was determined they would do so together.

Eden stood protectively between Elijah and Zahn and, despite his inclination to do so, the constrained boy was helpless to protect her. Zahn was bigger, stronger, and armed with a dangerous curved dagger. Eden had no weapon and no magical powers to stop him, but she would not stand by and watch as her child was sacrificed. Elijah, still bound, wriggled violently. Against him the Emerald Tablet shook, and it rattled his bones inside his skin.

Eden lunged at Zahn, attempting to knock the knife away. The Elder anticipated her easily and countered, roughly pushing her backward. She stumbled against the coffer where Elijah lay helpless and struggling. As the Elder lunged again, the mother threw herself protectively across her child.

Quinn burst into the tiny room just as Zahn struck, avoiding Eden and slicing brutally into Elijah's forearm.

"As it is below, so it shall be above!" the Elder shouted. The boy screamed in agony, but it was inaudible over the roar of the resurrected Pyramid. Orion and Draconis illuminated the chamber, drawn in through the celestial vents, their concentrated energy directed into the coffer where Elijah and the Emerald Tablet lay.

Quinn bodychecked the Elder harshly away from the coffer, who was jolted against the nearby wall as the dagger flew out of his hand. A fierce howl was coming from Elijah, adding to the pandemonium. Eden's hands were covered in Elijah's blood, as she wrapped her desperate fingers around her child's gaping injury. The gash drained into the stone coffer. A dark soup, something more than blood and less than human, stirred within the wound.

Zahn watched triumphantly as a ghostly serpent with ten heads and the body of a dragon rose like toxic black smoke from the boy's torn flesh. It slipped through Eden's hands, expanding and becoming material and solid in the emerald glow. It represented a departure from humanity; the evil that lay within every person if they opened themselves to it. It was a horrible reminder of what the soul could become.

The horrific beast filled the air above them. The young boy watched in terror as the creature screeched from ten fanged mouths, swooping and hovering, its barbed tail and vicious talons whipping the air barely above their heads.

Quinn repositioned the trembling Emerald Tablet protectively on Elijah's heaving chest and threw himself across both Eden and Elijah.

Take hold of the Emerald Tablet! Quinn commanded telepathically to Eden, his voice useless in the noise.

It's too late. The world is dark and humanity is doomed. Helghul, from within the beast you will reign powerfully. You are the King of the Adversaries. You have helped make possible the continuation of this Dark Age, Grey Elder promised with mind pictures. The beast prepared to devour Helghul's current body and claim his pledged soul.

Elijah's lips moved, but his words could not be heard. He had grown too weak from his injury and the room too loud.

"I choose the Light," he had said.

With Quinn protectively overtop of her, Eden shifted one of her bloody hands from the wound of her son and placed it on the Tablet, which was pressed to his chest. The beast struck, using its razor-sharp tail like a spear, and pierced Quinn's back, pushing easily through him and then through Eden and Elijah. Still sandwiched against the Emerald Tablet, the three became One. One energy. One destiny. And like the strands of a whip, their impact was more formidable and fierce when combined. The trinity of their souls joined and exploded, splintered by the powerful resonation into the Universe.

Marcus and Theron's spirits lifted through the layers of the King's Chamber, their bodies left behind, and they soared freely. Blinding green light burst from the coffer. Zahn was thrown back as the Pyramid was finally fully ignited by the Emerald Tablet, magnifying the consciousness of all of the world's people into the Universe beyond.

A shift in the world's consciousness had occurred—as it had many times before and as it would many times to come. Around the world it was felt, seen, and heard.

Back at the bunker in Chile, at that very same moment, with his arms shielding his eyes from the brilliance around him, the commander had shouted, "Open fire! Open fire! Take them down!"

The shouts had not affected the circle of Emissaries in the bunker. The fear and panic of their captors had done nothing to dispel their unified hope and compassion.

The guards had rushed in as ordered. Some had simply dropped their guns and fallen to their knees—they had been helpless, mesmerized by the sparkling orbs of light that were reflected around the space. Those who had been unmoved and unable to see the orbs had blasted round after round of bone-splitting ammunition.

Ravaged by gunfire, one by one the Emissaries' souls had been released and the last ties to their bodies had been severed. The Emissaries had felt no pain as their human shells collapsed, useless and abandoned, in bloody ruin, to the floor.

The bodies were now obscured by the brilliant celestial bloom that filled the room. Their Oneness, now untethered, resembled a starburst. It was like a newborn child pushing forth in a fit of blinding, glorious color and emotion. The beauty, the vision, was nothing compared to the *feeling*! Every molecule resonated with overwhelming, perfect, and unconditional love.

Their Oneness, the Unity Grid, lifted out of the bunker, passing through the copper ceiling. The Emissaries were free of their prison. Floating and bursting into the sky, their bubble expanded and grew enormous. It lifted into the heavens. Their rainbow bridge became visible around the world, connecting with similar blooms that had been simultaneously unleashed in the moment that the Emerald Tablet had revived the Great Pyramid of Giza.

The Emerald Tablet connected the energy of the world's people and echoed their compassion and love. The miracle that was occurring was obvious, and around the planet people watched in awe. The waters, the mountains, the stones, and the sacred Earth glowed, trembled, and vibrated. The Grid appeared in the sky like an office tower, with multicolored lights turning on—three, five, eight, thirteen windows at a time—as the web became visible and dazzling in the sky.

The loving and compassionate people cried out with joy and answered, raising their hands and their hearts to the sky. It mattered not whether they had or had not been marked. The vaccinations had been no more than a scheme by Grey Elder to divide people and to incite fear among them. It mattered only what was in their hearts. All fear, doubt, and human need were forgotten. The Source was revealed to all, if they would only choose to see it. Many gave themselves up to the Oneness and felt their human bonds release. Winds howled and trumpeted in celebration. Millions of souls traveled upward, regardless of their religion or color. They were sucked like jewels through the hose of a vacuum.

To those left behind, staring in awe and terror, it looked like a million lightning strikes punishing the Earth, and fire erupted where each strike had hit. They were stunned and blinded by the brilliance and implication of it. Innumerable electric branches touched the planet and were gone, sweeping up the people who had renounced the Darkness and who had sought virtue, leaving fire in their stead. There were blank spaces and burning earth where people had stood seconds before.

Those who remained on the Earth didn't understand. Their consciousness was not able to comprehend anything but the destruction and the lightning that continued to pummel the planet. Across the globe, those lingering gawked in disbelief and fear. They did not recognize the all consuming *feeling* of love that was pouring forth, so they were frightened. They understood only the destruction and chaos around them. It was what they had expected. It was what their consciousness was ready to accept.

This was the moment, the last possibility of redemption. The people left behind had one last chance to accept the Universal Truth of the Grid—to choose to see, or to turn away and deny it. Those who were not ready, and the dark souls, did not see.

The Emerald Tablet had read the collective consciousness of humanity—despite Grey Elder's best efforts, there was enough goodness, and the Great Pyramid had exploded with light and color. The prism had projected a brilliant rainbow far into the Universe. A higher dimension had opened up as the spiritual world above had become connected by a rainbow bridge to the material world below.

Marcus and Theron had left their ruined bodies and had come together in a burst of blinding light and color as they ascended to the new world above the old. Free of their human shells, they flew, twisting and blending with one another, their energies uniting in their new form. The love! The love that had never left them, even as they were separated and torn apart, was realized once more. It was powerful and exhilarating, and their energies connected in rapture.

She looked like a shimmering ghost of herself as she had been in Atitala, the same tiny green eyes and freckled nose, with translucent auburn hair flowing behind her. Marcus shimmered, muscular and brown, his dark curls shining. The soulmates embraced in a cosmic kiss surrounded by shimmering flecks of light and shining orbs, as the stars around them joined in celebration. At last reunited, their joy was immeasurable.

They joined the Grid above and were deposited in the higher world. The dimension hovered magically above the lower and was lush and full of life. The glorious population vibrated with song as they greeted one another.

"I promised I'd never leave you," Marcus said to Theron.

"Nor I you," Theron replied lovingly.

Nearby the energy of Amnut pulsed familiarly through the assemblage. Amnut had ascended, and Marcus and Theron felt him and were glad. *But where is Helghul?* Marcus and Theron wondered. *Where is Helghul? Where is Grey Elder?*

The dark beast had been banished back to the dimension below, rejected by its host. It was resealed into a dark chasm until a time when it would be called upon again by those wishing to harness its power.

On Earth, there were so many people missing. The world continued on without them. For those left behind, there was no explanation or rationalization. Those remaining mourned and struggled to go on as normal, but so much of the goodness was gone. It was what their collective consciousness had manifested for them, and they suffered and learned from it.

In the heavens above hovered the Higher Earth, the home to those who had ascended. It was an elevated, parallel dimension. The Great Year continued its eternal cycle, above as it was below, and they were now free to learn greater lessons.

White Elder made her way through the Emissaries, and Theron rushed into her waiting embrace. Her hands, the hands Theron had known so well as a child, lovingly stroked her hair.

"I have been waiting for you. I am so pleased," her mother whispered in her ear. Theron was happy to once again be in her arms.

"I am so grateful that I didn't always have the memory to miss you as I know I would have!" Theron said.

Marcus reflected on his own years of longing.

"I am always with you," White Elder assured and, still holding her daughter, she turned to Marcus. "Even through the harshest circumstances, you have endured and have continued learning. We were right to choose you."

An Emissary by mistake? No, an Emissary by choice, Marcus thought.

"I never doubted you. If only you could see yourself through my eyes," Theron added, smiling, and reaching out to him.

"An interesting prospect Theron, and now a choice must again be made. This Great Year continues. Will you return as Emissaries to the world below and continue to guide humanity to a new Golden Age?" White Elder asked.

All around them Emissaries were being reunited with their loved ones, their soul groups reconnecting. Marcus and Theron looked into one another's eyes and saw love and understanding. They both knew what they would do, and together, they made their choice.

BIBLIOGRAPHY

Bauval, Robert and Adrian Gilbert, *The Orion Mystery* (New York, Three Rivers Press, 1994)

Carlson. Randolph, *Randall Carlson presents: The Great Year*, http://www.youtube.com

Charles, R.H., *The Book of Enoch*, http://www.sacredtexts.com

Cruttenden, Walter, *Cosmic Influence*, podcast http://www.binaryinstitute.org

Cruttenden, Walter, *The Great Year, narrated by James Earl Jones*, http://www.youtube.com

Dalai Lama XIV, His Holiness the, *How to Practice: The Way to a Meaningful Life* (Simon and Schuster, 2003)

De Santillana, Giorgio and Hertha Von Dechend, *Hamlet's Mill* (David R. Godine Publisher, 1977)

Dona, Klaus, *The Hidden History of the Human Race*, Project Camelot, http://www.youtube.com

Dunn, Chris, *The Giza Power Plant*, http://www.youtube.com

Emoto, Masaru, *The Hidden Messages in Water*, http://www.masaru-emoto.net

Encyclopedia Britannica, http://www.britannica.com

Grimes, Pierre, *The Myth of Er*, http://www.youtube.com

Hancock, Graham, *Fingerprints of the Gods* (New York, Three Rivers Press, 1995)

Hauck, Dennis William, *The Emerald Tablet: Alchemy of Personal Transformation* (New York, Penguin, 1999)

The Holy Bible (Nashville, USA Regal Publishers, 1975)

Jung, Carl Gustav and Roderick Main, *Jung on Synchronicity and the Paranormal* (London, Routledge, 1997)

Khan, Paul and Francis Woodman Cleaves, *The Secret History of the Mongols: trans* (Cheng & Tsui, 2001)

Leonard, R. Cedric, *Quest for Atlantis*, http://www.atlantisquest.com

Marrs, Jim, *The Rise of the Fourth Reich*, Project Camelot, http://www.youtube.com

Melchizedek, Drunvalo, *The Ancient Secret of the Flower of Life Vol. I, II* (Light Technology Publishing, 2000)

Roerich, Nicholas, *Shambhala*, reprint (India, Vendam Books, 2003)

Schoch, Robert M. PhD. and Robert Aquinas McNally, *Pyramid Quest: Secrets of the Great Pyramid and the Dawn of Civilization* (New York, Penguin, 2005)

Szczepanski, Kallie, *Genghis Khan Biography*, http://asianhistory.about.com

Tarnas, Richard, *Cosmos and Psych: Intimations of a New World View* (New York, Viking Penguin, 2007)

Tolle, Eckhart, *The Power of Now* (Vancouver, Namaste Publishing, 1999)

van der Sluijs, Marinus Anthony, *Phaethon and the Great Year*, http://www.mythopedia.info/.thegreatyear

Yukteswar, Sri Swami, *Holy Science* (University of Michigan, Self-realization Fellowship, 1990)

http://www.absoluteastronomy.com

http://www.atlantisquest.com

http://www.atlantisrising.com

http://www.crystalinks.com

http://www.face-music.ch/bi_bid/historyoftengerism.html

http://www.gizapower.com

http://www.mongolempire.4t.com/hs_risegenghis

http://www.mythopedia.info/.thegreatyear

http://www.newworldencyclopedia.org

http://www.religionfacts.com

http://www sacredsites.com

http://www.sofiatopia.org

http://www.stanfordencyclopedia.com

http://www.thehistoryguide.com

http://www.theinternetencyclopedia

ENDNOTES

1 Gilbert Fowler White, *The Journal of France and Germany, 1942–1944*

2 Also called the "Platonic Year," http://www.dictionary.com

3 Klaus Heinemann, PhD. (Interview on podcast, Cosmic Influence, with Walter Cruttenden), December 18, 2007, http://www.binaryresearchinstitute.org/bri/radio, accessed June 2011

4 R. Cedric Leonard, *Quest for Atlantis*, http://www.atlantisquest.com, accessed July 2011

5 R.H. Charles, *The Book of Enoch*, http://www.sacredtexts.com, accessed July 2010

6 Benoit B. Mandelbrot, *The Fractal Geometry of Nature* (W.H. Freeman and Company, New York, 1982)

7 http://www.merriam-webster.com/dictionary/om

8 http://www.en.wikipedia.org/wki/synchronicity, accessed August 2010

9 His Holiness the Dalai Lama XIV, *How to Practice: The Way to a Meaningful Life* (Simon and Schuster, 2003)

10 Chris Dunn, *The Giza Power Plant*, http://www.gizapower.com, accessed February 2011

11 http://www.wikipedia.org/wiki/aristocles, accessed July 2010

12 http://www.greekmythology.com/books/bulfinch/bulfinch.html, accessed May 2010

13 Ion Saliu, *Daemonion, Daimonion and Socrates: Philosophy of the Inner Voice*, http://www.saliu.com/philosophy/daemonion, accessed July 2010

14 http://www.wikipedia.org/wiki/aristocles, accessed July 2010

15 Impiety, definition: "lack of reverence or proper respect for a god," http://britannica.com

16 Plato, *Republic*, 354b, http://en.wikiquote.org

17 http://en.wikipedia.org/wiki/Rationalism, accessed July 2010

18 http://en.wikiquote.org/wiki/Aristotle, accessed July 2010

19 Plato, *Apology*, 41c-e, Wikiquotes

20 Paul Khan and Francis Woodman Cleaves, *The Secret History of the Mongols*, trans (Cheng & Tsui, 2001)

21 www.macalester.edu/anthropology/mongolia

22 "A dwelling place for the spirits," http://www.tengerism.org/when_worlds_touch.html

23 http://www.chemistrydaily.com/chemistry/The_Secret_Book_of_the_Mongols, accessed August 2010

24 http://www.chemistrydaily.com/chemistry/The_Secret_Book_of_the_Mongols

25 http://www.newworldencycolopedia.org/khan, genghis

26 http://en.wikipedia.org/wiki/Tsagaan_Sar, accessed July 2010

27 Nicholas Roerich: *Shambhala*, reprint (India, Vendam Books, 2003)

28 http://www.names-meanings.net-genghis

29 http://en.wikipedia.org/wiki/Genghis_Khan, accessed July 2010

30 www.labyrinthina.com/caral, accessed September 2011

31 http://www.liveindia.com/bridge/index.html, accessed December 2011

32 Giorgio De Santillana and Hertha VonDechend, *Hamlet's Mill* (David R. Godine Publisher, 1977)

33 CPAK (Conference on Precession and Ancient Knowledge) is a real conference held yearly and sponsored by the Binary Institute

34 Daniel 8:25, *The Holy Bible*, King James Version (Nashville, Regal Publishers, 1975)

35 Zechariah 14:12, *The Holy Bible*, King James Version (Nashville, Regal Publishers, 1975)

36 http://www.crystalinks/amenti.html, accessed June 2010

37 http://www.wikipedia.org/wiki/gamal/Nasser, accessed January 2010

ABOUT THE AUTHORS

Rene DeFazio was born and raised in Canada and currently resides in the Vancouver area with his fiancée and writing partner Tamara Veitch. Rene is an actor and producer with more than eleven film and television roles to his credit, as well as countless commercials and print ads. A world traveler and lifelong adventurer, Rene has called upon his unusual and exciting experiences in creating *One Great Year*. His tireless research and firsthand knowledge of exotic locations, customs, sights, and smells helps to bring this epic story to life.

Tamara Veitch is a writer, mural artist, and mother. She grew up in Canada and attended Simon Fraser University, studying English and psychology.

Tamara and Rene are currently working on books II and III in this series, while they travel the world documenting the ancient secrets that continue to inspire them in their writing, and are determined to live an uncommon life.